Ne

"Kendra Broekhuis delivers a compelling story with quick, precise chapters that had me enthralled and ready to flip to the next page. James, aka Captain Jim, said it best when he posed this question: 'Is family the people who know and love you or people who cause a lot of chaos and pain? Or maybe a complicated mix of both?' I felt drawn to Dylan Turner as she tried untangling this question while on a self-discovery journey, making one realize that DNA, someone else's mistake, or your own mistakes do not have to define who you are."

—T. I. LOWE, award-winning author of *Indigo Isle*

"*Nearly Beloved* is a moving exploration of how family—the truth, the lies, and the perceptions that fill the spaces in between—shapes who we are. With raw honesty and emotional nuance, the story captures the disorientation of grief and the ache of unanswered questions. A plot full of artfully employed twists makes this character-driven novel impossible to put down. It is a beautifully told journey of unraveling and rebuilding that will linger long after the final page."

—AMANDA COX, award-winning author of
*The Bitter End Birding Society*

"Not every writer can explore a painful topic like adoption-related nonpaternity events (NPEs) with the perfect balance of clever wit and sensitivity. But in *Nearly Beloved*, Kendra Broekhuis succeeds. Opening with a gripping funeral scene, Broekhuis keeps the bombshells coming in this story chock-full of surprises and twisty turns, until you arrive at the unexpected conclusion. If you've ever wondered why taking a genealogy test comes with a warning, reading this book will inform you!"

—LINDA MACKILLOP, Christy Award–winning author of
*The Forgotten Life of Eva Gordon*

# NEARLY BELOVED

# NEARLY BELOVED

A NOVEL

## KENDRA BROEKHUIS

WATERBROOK

WaterBrook
An imprint of the Penguin Random House Christian Publishing Group,
a division of Penguin Random House LLC
1745 Broadway, New York, NY 10019

waterbrookmultnomah.com
penguinrandomhouse.com

A WaterBrook Trade Paperback Original

Copyright © 2025 by Kendra Broekhuis

Penguin Random House values and supports copyright. Copyright fuels creativity, encourages diverse voices, promotes free speech, and creates a vibrant culture. Thank you for buying an authorized edition of this book and for complying with copyright laws by not reproducing, scanning, or distributing any part of it in any form without permission. You are supporting writers and allowing Penguin Random House to continue to publish books for every reader. Please note that no part of this book may be used or reproduced in any manner for the purpose of training artificial intelligence technologies or systems.

WATERBROOK and colophon are registered trademarks of Penguin Random House LLC.

Library of Congress Cataloging-in-Publication Data
Names: Broekhuis, Kendra, author.
Title: Nearly beloved : a novel / Kendra Broekhuis.
Description: New York, NY : WaterBrook, 2025. | "A WaterBrook trade paperback original."
Identifiers: LCCN 2025008140 | ISBN 9780593600771 (trade paperback ; acid-free paper) | ISBN 9780593600788 (ebook)
Subjects: LCGFT: Novels.
Classification: LCC PS3602.R6364 N43 2025 | DDC 813/.6—dc23/eng/20250320
LC record available at https://lccn.loc.gov/2025008140

Printed in the United States of America on acid-free paper

1st Printing

The authorized representative in the EU for product safety and compliance is Penguin Random House Ireland, Morrison Chambers, 32 Nassau Street, Dublin D02 YH68, Ireland. https://eu-contact.penguin.ie

BOOK TEAM: Production editor: Laura K. Wright • Managing editor: Julia Wallace • Production manager: Sarah Feightner • Copy editors: Rose Decaen, Kayla Fenstermaker • Proofreaders: JoLeigh Buchanan, Rachel Kirsch

*Book design by Ralph Fowler*

"Put *me* in your novel." —Jocelyn

"Can *I* be in your novel?" —Cecily

"What's a novel?" —Levi

"..." —Marre


This one is for my kids.

# NEARLY BELOVED

# 1

# Four Questions and a Funeral

Monday, September 22

Forcing consumers to go paperless wasn't a victimless crime. Dylan Turner knew this because of the email splayed across her phone. There they were—her DNA test results—set against a backdrop of blue light, committing manslaughter.

The victim? Everything she'd thought was true about herself for the past thirty years.

And her family.

She'd waited weeks for these results, but now that she had them, they'd arrived a century too early and with the gentleness of a meat grinder. She dreamed of a historical era when someone might sit her down face-to-face with a cup of tea before ruining her life with information. Or, at the very least, handwrite her a letter and mail it through the postal service, giving her a three-second buffer of ignorance while she opened the envelope. A buffer that might make living with the threat of cholera worth it.

Her screen went dark, and cold sweat prickled the back of her neck. She was at her parents' house, standing at the bottom of the stairs that emptied into a gracious foyer. She squinted—would that make the room stop spinning?—but the rust-colored velvet armchairs, ivory rug, and seafoam walls swirled like a kaleidoscope.

If the Bluetooth speaker were playing Tina Guo and fragrant notes of merlot were hanging from the breath of the middle-aged adults piled into the room, she'd feel right back at one of the housewarming parties her dad had thrown each time they moved to a new city. Buzzing, humid, and full of faces so unfamiliar they might as well have been pixelated.

Her knees buckled, and she grabbed on to the banister with both hands, dropping her phone in the process. She wasn't even supposed to be looking at her phone, not on the day of her dad's funeral anyway. Her mom would throw a fit if she saw her staring at it now. Then again, Candis Turner was caffeinated by criticism—giving it, that is. But Dylan hadn't checked her phone as part of some scheme to exasperate her mom. She'd checked it out of habit, like one of Pavlov's dogs conditioned to respond to every ding inside her coat pocket.

Her coat.

That was what her mom had ordered her to do when she got caught staring out of the living room's large bay windows—not at the raspberry mums on the porch steps or the black-throated green warbler perched at the birdfeeder, but at nothing in particular. She was supposed to put on her coat and shoes and move toward the exit so they could leave for the funeral.

She picked up her phone and somehow managed to wrestle each of her arms into a sleeve. Putting her feet into boots proved harder, but that was because her gut decided to float outside her body and hover above, laughing at her because deep down it had always known something was off.

These test results, delivered digitally to the device that was her constant companion, meant her life would never be the same. Not in a way that was like "You just won the lottery! Congrats!" It was more like a fog rising inside her body, wrapping itself around her brain until she no longer knew how to move or think.

"Please buckle." The clipped words dragged Dylan back to reality, where she was now sitting in the back seat of her mom's car. When had she climbed into the car? Let alone walked from the front door, down the porch steps, and to the narrow driveway next to the house where the car was parked?

Maybe she'd been teleported by the sheer force of her confusion.

A sigh as strong as last night's September storm gusted from the front passenger seat. It came from her mom, who checked herself in the mirror, then flipped the sun visor back into place. "Look, I know this isn't easy, but let's just try to get through the rest of today without being at each other's throats."

Dylan wanted to scream her first question at her mom: *Why didn't you tell me?*

"It's okay to be nervous about giving the eulogy," said another voice—far gentler—from the driver's seat. "You're going to do great."

It was "Aunt" Lou, her mom's best friend since college. Aunt Lou had booked a flight from Jacksonville to Milwaukee the moment she learned Dad had passed. She'd also booked a couple of other flights during the past month to give Dylan's mom breaks from caretaking. Now she leaned over and squeezed Candis's hand and glanced back at Dylan with a soft smile. She'd long been their glue.

Did Aunt Lou know already? The thought lit a firework in her chest.

*Does everyone know the truth but me?*

"Yes, thank you again for giving the eulogy." Her mom massaged her temples. "I didn't think I could do it."

It was her mom's only earnest request of her regarding the funeral. She didn't know how she'd get through it now.

Aunt Lou drove the city blocks between the house and Saint

Mark's Presbyterian Church, pulling the car up next to the curb and parking just as a cold rain began to pour.

Dylan heard the drumming on the roof of the car and then felt the drops on her cheeks, where more tears should be by now. Maybe they'd fall once the shock finally wore off, once she told her mom about the email and her mom said it was simply a colossal misunderstanding.

The heavy drops of rain on her skin made her realize her body was moving again—mostly without her help—from the curb to the church's front doors, down the tiled aisle to the front wooden pew.

"Dearly beloved, we are gathered here today to honor the life and memory of Darren Turner . . ."

The rest of Reverend Schwartz's words trailed off into a void, including whatever prayer or reading followed his formal introduction.

"Dylan," Aunt Lou whispered. It was Dylan's turn to walk up to the ornately carved pulpit.

Onstage, she scanned the sanctuary with its vaulted ceiling and long chandeliers. It was small and yet still too spacious for the audience of four that included the minister and a pretty ceramic urn. Her dad would have made friends with everyone in his new city like he always did *and* thrown that party, if only he'd had more time between their move to Milwaukee and his diagnosis.

She put her sweaty hand into her coat pocket. The words she'd composed to try to honor the life of Darren Turner were written in the Notes app on her phone. When she pulled it out and unlocked it, she would be faced with the same bombshell of an email she'd been struck by earlier. Her last ounce of willpower lifted the phone and set it on the podium.

She cleared her throat and looked up at her mom and Aunt Lou, both dressed in black. Candis was wearing a professional bun and pearls, glazed over like a ghost, while Aunt Lou, with her frizzy mane and armful of bangles, kept her warm focus on Dylan.

Aunt Lou nodded, prodding her to begin.

The fog entangling her mind and limbs started to burn off, and she wondered what it would be like to chuck a brick through one of the church's lovely stained-glass windows. She fixed her eyes on the urn sitting on its pedestal a few feet in front of her, full of ashes and memories now tainted.

"He's not my father." The words came out barely a whisper.

Her mom gasped; Aunt Lou's mouth gaped.

*Who is my dad?*

*And who am I?*

## INBOX (1)—DYLANTURNER918@GMAIL.COM

**From:** KindreDNA <testresults@KindreDNA.com>
**Date:** September 22
**To:** Turner, Dylan <dylanturner918@gmail.com>
**Subject:** Your KindreDNA Results Are In!

### GREAT NEWS!

The moment you've been waiting for is here.
The KindreDNA results are ready for: **Dylan Turner.**

### Here is your basic DNA profile:

**Ethnicity Estimate:** 38% German, 23% Dutch, 39% Other regions
**Genetic Matches:**

    **Extended Family:** 1 linked KindreDNA user, 12.2% match
    **Close Family:** 0 linked users
    **Sibling or Parent:** 0 linked users

**Family Tree Name:** Jacksonville
**Family Tree Kindreds*:** 1 user (Darren Turner)

*Family Tree Kindreds are people who follow your profile, not necessarily DNA matches.

**<To view your entire DNA profile, sign up
for our $660 annual membership!>**

# 2

# Like Mother, Like Fodder

Her mom stood up from the pew. "Dylan, what are you—"

"There should be one other user in the KindreDNA database that shows a fifty percent DNA match to me, and his name should be Darren Turner," she explained, though it sounded more like an accusation. "Because I've been told for thirty years that Darren Turner is my dad."

Red splotches covered her mom's neck. "That's what this is about—the genealogy test the two of you did? It's possible your dad's sample hasn't been processed yet. Why are you checking on the day of his funeral anyway?"

Dylan wasn't tuned in to her body at the moment, but she thought she heard herself groan. "We did the DNA test *together* and sent in our vials on the exact same day. We edited our settings so our KindreDNA profiles would be public and automatically linked to our tree when the results came in. When we received our emails, we should have already shown up as matches."

"I'm sure this is all a big mistake." Her mom looked from Dylan and Aunt Lou to the near-empty sanctuary. "Companies like KindreDNA have a margin of error they have to apologize for—switched vials and whatnot. Can we get through the funeral and then try to sort this out?"

She reached for Dylan, who pulled back.

"Is this why you refused to do the test with us, or why you didn't want Dad and me to do it in the first place? Because you knew I'd find out?"

The sanctuary was so quiet it buzzed.

Her mom exhaled. "It's too much to explain."

Dylan's throat filled with bile. "Too much to explain why Dad isn't my biological father?"

"Dylan." Aunt Lou's brow creased with concern.

"Did *you* know, Aunt Lou?"

The woman folded her hands and shrank back into her seat.

"Um . . . ladies?" a trembling masculine voice interrupted. Reverend Schwartz's upper lip was sweating. "It sounds like there might be some family issues to resolve. Can you take it outside the sanctuary?"

Dylan walked out from behind the podium and down the steps, but she stopped at the pedestal holding her dad's ashes. Three people, four orange brick walls, and many more wooden pews watched to see what she'd do next.

She could swipe the urn onto the floor and watch as the plume of gray dust covered her mom and Aunt Lou, but Darren Turner didn't deserve that kind of disrespect. Instead, she picked up the urn and held it tight against her chest. She'd take her "family issue" outside, where, apparently, God couldn't hear them.

Behind her, Mom and Aunt Lou whispered rushed, polite apologies to Reverend Schwartz.

She made it out of the sanctuary, through the narthex, and outside the church before she slowed down. Dark thunderclouds and sheets of pouring rain stopped her from going any farther. Her own car was at her parents' house, and her mom's car was probably locked. She paced under the maroon awning protecting the church's doors. Feeling lost wasn't new to her, but still, where was she supposed to go and what was she supposed to do right now?

"Dylan. Please." Her mom caught up, then finished putting on her coat. "Do you want me to take the urn?"

She squeezed it tighter, like it was her hostage. "No. I want you to answer my questions."

Her mom nodded. "I know you have questions; I do."

"Who is my dad?"

The question, though straightforward, was heavy as a tombstone.

Aunt Lou stepped between the two of them and held out her hands. "How about I take Darren to the car with me?"

Dylan surrendered the urn, then zipped up the coat she'd never taken off. The rain shower was too strong for the church's small awning to keep them dry.

Her mom cleared her throat. "I thought I'd have more time before you got the test results."

"I'm not asking why you didn't tell me before I got the results. I'm asking why you didn't tell me *decades* ago."

Tears spilled onto her mom's cheeks, and Dylan's own eyes welled.

"It's really complicated."

"Then explain it to me, Mom." A realization hit her so hard she blinked. "Unless . . . you're not my mom?"

"Oh, Dylan."

She threw up her hands. "It's not a dumb question."

"None of these questions are dumb, but—you've seen pictures of me pregnant with you."

"AI can do some incredible stuff these days."

Her mom raised an eyebrow.

"If you tell me to calm down, I swear—"

"I'm not trying to tell you to calm down. I just wasn't expecting to have this conversation today. Right now. At your dad's funeral."

Dylan stared at the person whose apple body shape and upturned brown eyes were a mirror image of her own. "That doesn't answer the question."

She gripped Dylan's shoulders. "Yes. I'm your mom."

Why was she so relieved? Her mom's argument about pregnancy

pictures made enough sense. The woman would exist happily in any technology-free time period as long as there were knives and fire. Her mom could barely sign into her email account, let alone make an entire album of doctored photos.

But until today, Dylan had been 100 percent certain she was genetically related to her father too.

"But . . . Dad?"

"Dad *is* your dad, but not biologically."

Dylan turned away just in time for the sobs to grip her body. It wasn't new information, but hearing it from her mom's mouth somehow made it more official. This wasn't some mistake by the lab at KindreDNA.

She thought of her dad—of Darren Turner—and in her effort to make it make sense, she tried to catalog every way they were different from each other. She'd never had his outgoing personality or his tenacity. She wasn't confident like he was, nor a dreamer. Well, she dreamed, tormentedly, but only while she slept. Those were closer to restless nightmares.

She thought of her dad's dark hair and pointed nose, the features he claimed were just like her own. If they didn't come from him, where did they come from?

"Was it an affair?" The words came out before she thought them through.

Her parents' relationship had always seemed subdued. Her dad was happy, gregarious at times. And her mom, well, sometimes down, sometimes an emotional plateau.

Her mom's jaw clenched. "It's not what you think it is."

"That's not an answer. I want the truth."

"No, you don't," her mom yelled, then scanned the parking lot and surrounding sidewalk. "Sometimes the truth is too painful," she whispered, choking back tears.

It was like talking to a wall, a concrete wall barricading her from answers. "This is not some tiny white lie you've told, Mom. It's the story of my entire life. How am I supposed to even know who I am if I don't know who my biological father is?"

"Who you are?" Her mom's tears dried into one of her classic lectures. "You're Dylan Turner, and that's not going to change no matter who your biological father is. Your generation is obsessed with 'knowing who you are.' Do you seriously think knowing will be the magic ingredient to you no longer living your life on autopilot?"

The blow made her gasp. She combed a piece of windblown hair off her shoulder but ran into a snarl near the collar of her coat. This conversation was getting nowhere. If her mom wasn't going to tell her what she wanted to hear, she'd give herself the space she needed.

She walked out from the protection of the awning.

"Dylan," her mom called after her. "Where are you going?"

The question woke a beast. She turned on her heel. "To look for answers somewhere else. Don't call unless you're ready to tell me the truth."

She looked at her mom's car, where Aunt Lou was in the driver's seat, scrolling on her phone, next to Darren Turner's ashes. This day was supposed to offer some closure after months of losing her dad to cancer. It wasn't supposed to be the day she lost him a second time.

She scanned the area for a different ride back to her car and found one on the corner—a public e-scooter. Her parents' house was only eight blocks from the church, and the rain was relenting.

It would have to work.

## 3

# Seek and You Will Be Fined

By the time Dylan walked into her one-bedroom apartment on the second floor of the complex she lived in, the wrath had left her body. She already missed the power it had generated and hated that now there was vacancy for overwhelm.

Typically, when she got back from visiting her parents, her first order of business was to bask in the familiarity of her own apartment. She'd walk the vinyl plank flooring to the kitchen, where a granite countertop separated her white cupboards and stainless-steel appliances from the cream loveseat in the small living room. Then she'd unpack her travel-sized toiletries and crumpled clothes. It was *her* bedroom, *her* walk-in closet, *her* bathroom.

She breathed in the smell of home, a mix of tangerine and vanilla because that was what she put in her two air fresheners month after month. The fact that she didn't own the six hundred and fourteen square feet of her apartment didn't change that, after twelve years, its gray walls were finally starting to feel like hers.

This time, though, she didn't have the energy to do her homecoming ritual. She dropped her duffel bag and marched to her queen bed, where she collapsed face down. Unpacking could wait until she recovered from the past twenty-four hours. Sure, her tube of mascara might dry up and her crumpled clothes go out of style before then, but after the morning she'd had and the nearly two-hour drive, she needed to close her eyes for a minute.

Or many minutes, as it turned out. When she woke, drool was pooling from her lips onto the comforter. She lifted her head and was face-to-face with her laptop, which was in its usual place on the empty side of the bed. Maybe it had answers. She wiped the corners of her mouth and pushed herself up. The tiny clock in the corner of the computer screen said 1:47, which meant she'd slept for over an hour.

She clicked around to load the KindreDNA email, whispering, "Please, oh please, oh please."

But the results were the same.

**Sibling or Parent:** 0 linked users

A shot of adrenaline sent her fingertips to the keyboard. She had no choice but to follow the link in the email to her KindreDNA profile to start looking for clues. Like some twisted Easter egg hunt, except the prize wasn't candy—it was solving the mystery of her own conception.

The link opened to a page full of KindreDNA memberships and their price points. *Discovery, Explorer,* and *All-Access* were just a few of her options, starting with prices that were hundreds of dollars. It turned out if she didn't know who her biological father was, she needed more than a little curiosity and basic computer skills to get the answers she craved. She also needed money. The test alone had been over $100, a price her dad covered, but it only gave her a basic profile with the minimal information in the email.

KindreDNA also had professional genealogists she could hire to dig into her DNA and solve mysteries for her. The base rate was $3,500, which gave her sticker shock but also made $660 for an all-access annual membership—with connections to an entire database of public documents and family trees—seem not so bad. It might lead her to a clue, a name, possibly even a photo.

Still, on her income, $660 was quite the splurge. She'd probably have to cut back in other ways, like her weekly burger at Five Guys, but she didn't ponder for long before typing in her credit card number and pressing Confirm.

When the transaction went through, she felt a spark of optimism for the first time since her dad's diagnosis. According to her confirmation email, she now had twelve months to be an all-access member. She liked the sound of *all-access* and *member*.

Her excitement fizzled when she started clicking around her profile. The KindreDNA website appeared to have been designed by the maker of the Rubik's Cube. All the figures and charts talking about ethnicity percentages and common ancestors and centimorgans were confusing. It wasn't as easy as a box popping up with a picture that said, "Here's your dad's name, address, and medical history. He likes cats."

She opened a third tab on her computer.

> **Google:** how to find bio family on kindredna because your mom refuses to spill the tea

She deleted the last part, a phrase she'd learned from Olivia and Avery at work, then pressed Enter. She could hear her dad teasing her for asking for any sort of instruction manual. He was the type to figure it out by himself, thank you very much. She missed him, even if he could be a bit stubborn at times. At least, unlike her mom, he was stubborn with a smile.

The results page had a long list of YouTube tutorials, as well as a tear-filled testimonial sponsored by KindreDNA:

> Gary's at-home DNA test connected him with a distant relative. Through messages on the KindreDNA Messaging App—yet another perk of the all-access membership— Gary and his distant relative were able to find a common ancestor. After requesting birth and marriage records,

Gary then searched Facebook until he found a promising name. He is now in regular contact with his biological mother.

The next video was from a third-party website that walked test users through the maze of choosing the best genealogy company for them and building their family tree. The smiling woman in the clip explained how DNA matches could be split into different levels of relation based on how much DNA is shared.

> For example, Sam Donovan and Gregory Brown share 12 percent DNA, or roughly 846 centimorgans across 32 segments of DNA. Sam and Gregory are estimated to be a level two match. That means they might be first cousins, a half uncle and half nephew, or a great-grandfather and great-grandson. While DNA testing gives them those relational categories, they will have to work through their DNA matches themselves to determine specifically how they fit into each other's family tree.

It made sense why the help of a genealogist made some people want to cough up $3,500. She had test results but no idea how to sort them into a story that made sense. She read article after article and watched video after video, trying to learn the ropes of genealogy until she could no longer read *centimorgan* or *NPE* without wanting to chuck her computer across the room.

*NPE* was how the internet labeled this phenomenon, she learned in the last video. A situation where someone finds out their father isn't a biological relative is called a "nonpaternity event." Though less common, the term could be broadened to include a person's mother and labeled a "nonparental event." Maybe she'd add that to her email signature like a medical degree: *Dylan Turner, NPE.*

Her phone dinged from her coat with a text message, interrupting her freefall into this rabbit hole. She paused the video on her computer and wiped her eyes, climbing off her bed to grab her coat from her catchall chair in the corner.

Part of her wanted it to be from her mom, whether or not Dylan was ready to talk.

> **Captain Jim:** I hope your extended birthday trip has been fun! Enjoy your time with your parents.

It was her boss. When she'd requested to leave work early last Thursday, she hadn't told him it was because her dad wasn't expected to live through the weekend. She'd said she was celebrating her birthday. The statement was half true—she'd turned thirty last Thursday. It also happened to be the day her dad died.

She then took Friday and Saturday off, plus Monday, for the funeral. Her texts to her manager said she was using her banked days of PTO to extend her birthday trip. It was easier.

> **Me:** Thanks. I'll be back tomorrow.

He reacted with a thumbs-up, a Captain Jim kind of reply.

Was finding out her dad wasn't her biological father a metaphorical second death in the family? And if so, did that merit more time off work? This was already the most days she'd taken off at once maybe ever. Even after she got her wisdom teeth pulled six years ago, she'd only taken two days.

She sent one more text message to her neighbor Tara, letting her know she was back from Milwaukee, then set her phone down and tried narrowing her anxieties into one coherent thought. She was profoundly tired from the past five days, while also feeling like she'd erupted. If she didn't channel her anger into something useful, like scouring the internet for answers, she'd do something less kosher, like commit destruction of property.

The tutorials she'd watched kept saying the best way to start building her family tree to her unknown biological father was with her closest DNA match. Like Sam and Gregory, who ended up being first cousins, there was someone else in the world who'd taken a KindreDNA test that matched 12.2 percent of her DNA. Finding a first cousin seemed like a big step toward finding her biological father, especially when there were so many companies that sold at-home genealogy kits these days. Her blood relatives could have used any one of those.

She clicked on the profile of her closest match, a woman named Kathleen Schulz. Kathleen was sixty-seven years old and lived in Florida. According to her public family tree, many of her closest relatives listed on KindreDNA were in the southeastern United States. Maybe Kathleen was her great-aunt.

Great-Aunt Kathleen Schulz.

Dylan didn't know any of her own extended family. She'd met two of her mom's cousins when she was little but didn't remember her parents ever mentioning them again. Her grandparents had died before she was born.

She zoomed in on Kathleen's photo, looking for any clues that they were related, anything that might hold the key to the other half of her biological identity. Unlike Dylan, who had dark brown hair and brown eyes, Kathleen was blond and blue eyed. Like her, she had a pointed nose. Maybe pointed noses were their family's crest.

She opened another tab and searched for Kathleen Schulz on social media, her secondary source of information. There was a profile for her on Facebook, so she clicked it to see how much of it was public. Enough for Dylan to find out she was married, though it didn't say who she was married to.

Dylan was excited to see Kathleen was tagged in a lot of photos.

There was Kathleen with a group of handsomely dressed people, a bride and groom positioned in the middle. Kathleen with a group of women—all ages—wearing matching silk robes and holding glasses of champagne. The caption for that one read, *Annual Schulz Weekend Getaway.* Another photo of Kathleen with a group in skiing gear, on top of the Alps in Switzerland. Plenty of people shared only their highlight reel online, and Kathleen Schulz's highlight reel screamed money.

Dylan went back to the KindreDNA page and moved the cursor to the button that said Connect with Kathleen. The page loaded an empty box that she stared at for at least two minutes.

She typed, "Dear (maybe) Great-Aunt Kathleen Schulz," then deleted it.

> My name is Dylan Turner, and I'm looking for my biological fa—

Delete.

> My dad died a couple days ago, but he's not my bio dad. Can you please help—

Dylan shoved aside the laptop and covered her face with her hands. There was no easy way to type a basic email when the subject was this complicated.

The scenario reminded her of a different message she'd written years ago when her family moved for the first time—a letter.

Dylan was eight, and she'd struggled after their first move, mostly because she missed Brooke Westmore. The Turners did everything with the Westmores. Her dad and Brooke's dad even worked together.

But then the Turners moved from a suburb of Jacksonville to a suburb of Atlanta.

A few months after, she'd begged her parents to let her call Brooke. She wanted to reassure her friend she didn't like any of the kids at her new school and to see if—hopefully—Brooke missed her too.

At first, Dylan's mom and dad said no, so she taped a sign to her bedroom door: *onlee brooke may entr!!!*

Every time one of her parents tried to come in, she screamed, so at the end of that day, her mom stood outside her closed door and said, "You can mail her a letter."

Two months went by, but Dylan never heard back. She asked her mom if she could write another letter in case the first one got lost in the mail. This time, her mom didn't fight the battle; she just waved her kitchen knife in the air and said, "Fine."

Eight-year-old Dylan didn't know why, but writing the second letter was much harder. If her pencil smudged too much or she hated the sentence she wrote, she ripped the paper in half and started over with a fresh piece.

Her mom made sure to notice the pile of shreds next to the kitchen table. "I hope you plan to plant a few trees when you're done."

She glared at her paper as she tried to write the uppercase *D* in *Dear*.

"It has to be really good so she'll write me back," she whispered, the words catching in her throat. "I have to make it perfect."

"This letter you're writing? Or you?" her mom asked over the rhythmic noise of her knife chopping vegetables on her favorite cutting board.

Her dad came in next, his thick hair combed back and crisp dress shirt still tucked in from work. He squeezed her shoulder so tight it pinched. "If Brooke is going to forget about you, it's best you forget about Brooke."

She didn't want to forget, so she moved on to the letter *e* and eventually put a stamp on the envelope. Her best friend had to answer this time.

One week later, her mom came into her room carrying something covered in gift wrap.

"Is it from Brooke?" she squealed and threw her multiplication worksheet to the side.

Her mom shook her head, then sat on the foot of her bed and patted the space next to her.

Dylan's heart sank, anchoring her body to where she was sitting against the headboard.

Her mom scooted closer. "Dad heard back from Brooke's parents, and . . . I don't think you're going to get a letter from Brooke."

She rubbed her eyes but couldn't erase the way they burned. "But, Brooke is my best friend."

"Sometimes friendships don't get to last forev—"

"What happened?" she interrupted, hugging her knees to her chest. "Did you say something to Mrs. Westmore?"

Her mom's nostrils flared. "I didn't say anything."

"You did *something*. We moved away, and now I can't see Brooke anymore."

Her mom paused and looked up at the ceiling, like she was trying to preserve her last shredded nerve. Then she held out the silvery package. "I got you something."

Dylan turned the other way, resting her cheek on her knees. "I don't want it. I want to talk to Brooke, not be stuck in this stupid room with my stupid mom."

Her mom stood up from the bed and let the package fall to the floor. "I'm sorry for what you're going through, Dylan. You're right—parents can be stupid sometimes, but I promise I'm just trying to take care of you."

She walked out of the room and slammed the door.

Dylan grabbed her favorite plush elephant and rubbed the worn spot on its left ear between her fingers. Soon the smell of her mom's cooking wafted from the kitchen through the crack under her door, which was enough to coax her off the bed to pick up the shiny present. She ripped open the packaging and found a journal. It had a green cover and three blue flowers. Her mom had written in Sharpie, *Dylan's Record of Rage.*

Thirty-year-old Dylan got off her bed and walked to her closet to see if she could find the journal. The most likely place was in her shoebox of keepsakes, which had made every move with her over the years but was more often shoved into random corners than opened. When she'd moved to this apartment, she'd laid it to rest under her jumbled rack of shoes. She dug it out now, admiring the box's decoupaged Lisa Frank puppy stickers and pink glitter glue swirls. The little girl who'd decorated it was naïve, happier, both a stranger and a ghost haunting the person she was today.

She opened the box to find pictures splayed across the top, an entire stack she didn't remember putting there, and flipped through them—slower than the way she scrolled Instagram. Most were of her and her mom. They seemed to be in chronological order, starting with her mom hugging her own swollen pregnant belly. The next one was at the hospital after Dylan was born, swaddled like a burrito in her mom's arms. Her mom was staring down at her, locked in with an awe and wonder that blurred everyone else in the room out of that moment between mother and baby.

If Dylan didn't know the story of what came after, she'd call it love in its purest form.

Many of the photos were candid, including one of baby Dylan

and her mom lying on the floor facing each other, mouths wide open with delight. Another of her sitting in a bucket swing at a playground, giggling while her mom tickled her. The last family photo was of all three of them—her dad included—at her first birthday. Dylan was perched in a high chair, wearing only a diaper and a *1st Birthday* hat, smearing more chocolate cake onto her face than she was eating. Her dad grinned the way he always did, but compared with the rest of the pictures, her mom had changed. Her cheekbones were more pronounced, like she'd lost a lot of weight. She was smiling directly at the camera, but her eyes were empty. It was like Dylan and her dad were making celebratory sunshine and her mom was their detached shadow. Dylan didn't know what to think about seeing such a drastic change in her mom after mere months had passed, especially when the woman in the birthday picture was the mom she knew today.

Where was that other mom, the one in the first photos?

Under the family photos were others Dylan had more memory of collecting, including the last one of her and Brooke. A young hand had scrawled *8 years old* on the back.

She fixed the entire stack of pictures and tucked them to the side of the box. Under a few elementary art projects, she found what she'd come for in the first place. Her journal, appropriately titled *Dylan's Record of Rage.*

Her letters to Brooke may have come up short all those years ago, but the silver lining was that she'd been gifted one of the greatest resources of her childhood. The problem was, it had been so long since she'd read any of the entries, she wasn't sure she wanted to read them now. Some of it had to be cringey. A lot more of it filled with pain.

She took it back to bed with her and sat down.

Inhaling, she opened to the first page.

## DYLAN'S RECORD OF RAGE

### Page 1

*Dear Dylan,*

*Sometimes life will make you angry. The trick is to do something with your anger so it doesn't put you in jail. One idea is to write it down.*

*Love,*
*Mom*

### Page 2

I am 8 and I hate moving away. I mis my frend.

—Dylan Turner

### Page 15

WOULD IT BE SO HARD FOR MOM TO SEND A LUNCHABLE TO SCHOOL?
    She says she loves me too much to poison me but eating poison is better than kids asking if my lunch is made from an endangered species. She never wants to let me eat what I want to eat. She just likes to chop things with her dumb sharp knives I'm NEVER allowed to touch.
    Mom says to be thankful for what I have because there's starving children everywhere but she's not thankful either. Dad just got her a whole bunch of new knives and a fancy

piece of wood and put them in the kitchen with a million flowers and said maybe this would make her happy. And guess what? Mom saw them and started to CRY and ran out of the room! How is THAT being thankful??

This is me screaming into my journal: AHHHHHHHHHH!!!!!!!!

PEANUT BUTTER AND JELLY!!!!

—Dylan Turner, 10

# 4

# A Moment of Cringe

Dylan folded the journal closed and leaned away from it, like the words on the page were a bag of years-old garbage oozing with foul odor. These unfiltered thoughts were the exact kind of cringe she was afraid of.

She paused, allowing her secondhand embarrassment to fade in with the rest of the oxygen in the apartment, and took a moment of silence for her younger self. The stuff she'd written might sound juvenile now, but back then she was just a tired kid who wanted to fit in—which turned out to be a moving target when she switched schools as often as she did. She didn't know what she didn't know, which was that she couldn't copycat her way into Jessica B. wanting to sit by her at lunch, or cute Matt R. thinking she was kind of cute too. Lunchables might've been a total status symbol in elementary school, but no kid could ride their coattails into belonging.

She exhaled and stretched, shifting herself into a more comfortable position on her bed before picking up the journal again.

"I can do this," she lied.

### Page 36

I SAW A COCKROACH FLY!!!!!!!! IT WAS GIANT. Grossy gross gross!

We live in Dallas now. Dad got me a hat and called me Upscale Cowgirl whatever that means. I put on the hat and watched Dad's housewarming party from the stairs. It's all people from his new job. People are good for watching. My dad too. He makes everyone around him laugh.

Mom came out of the kitchen and found me. She told me to go back to bed even though the party is too loud to sleep. Dad saw and said I could come downstairs. He hugged me and said, "Isn't she so pretty? She has me to thank for that."

I liked that he let me stay up. Mom always makes me go to bed at 8 like I'm not actually 10 years old.

—Dylan Turner, 10

### Page 41

Mom made supper with big, disgusting onions in it again. She says I can pick the onions out if I want but they already ruined dinner. Dad knew I didn't like it too. He told Mom maybe next time she should chop the onions smaller than the size of Texas. Better yet, maybe he would make dinner next time.

Mom told Dad he forgot to put the milk on the table but he said Mom never told him to and she was probably imagining things again. I thought Mom was going to cry like she always does, but she said she would be back in a minute and left the table. Dad said Mom is too sensitive and that when I'm someone's wife I shouldn't overreact at everything like her.

I remember Mom asking Dad to go get the milk but I was mad at her about the onions.

—Dylan Turner, 10

## Page 67

Dad came home late again. He works SO MUCH. I hate that I don't get to see him especially because Mom is crabby all the time. He asked me to bring him his plate of dinner and a glass of water and I did.

He said to Mom, "Why can't you be more like Dylan? See how helpful she is when I ask her to do something?"

Mom asked Dad where he was all night and Dad said he was working. She kept asking and asking until Dad got really mad. "After everything I do for you this is how you repay me? If you actually loved me you wouldn't talk to me like this after I got home from a long day at work."

I hate when they fight. I just wish Mom wouldn't freak out all the time. She's probably glad she's going to Maryland with Aunt Lou tomorrow. They go every year. Mom said they started going the year before I was born.

—Dylan Turner, 11

## Page 84

Being the new kid sucks. I keep being the new kid OVER AND OVER AND OVER. The worst part is walking into the giant cafeteria full of a million students. It's like everyone is staring at you AND nobody notices you exist all at the same time.

Everyone here already has friends they've known since kindergarten.

Yesterday there was a nice girl in my math class. Emi. I started school three weeks late because of the move so I didn't have any of the notes and there's a quiz on Thursday. Emi said I can copy her notes. I saw Emi in the cafeteria and she waved me over to sit by her but she only had a few more minutes until her lunch break was over and then I was at the table by myself for the rest of my lunch break. That's how it feels. Even if someone is nice and I try to be nice back, one of us leaves. Usually I'm the one who leaves. Why try to make friends?

I want to live somewhere I can walk into a room and know everyone so well I know who has a pet dog and who has been to Disney World.

Tonight I asked Mom why we have to move all the time and she said she would like to live in one place too. Dad said he's sorry to be such a disappointment to both of us. He doesn't know why he bothers trying to make us happy.

Later my dad came to my room and I tried to tell him I wasn't mad at him and he said he knows. He said it's Mom making me choose sides. Dad said he just wants what's best for me and what's best for me is that he has a really great job so he can give me everything I want.

I didn't say this but: what if for once I just WANT to stay?

—Dylan Turner, 13

## Page 97

We went out to eat with my dad's new boss Mr. Towns tonight. He showed us around Jacksonville first so my dad could think about what kinds of projects he might want to dream up for the city. It's strange driving around a place you grew up nearby for a little bit but still don't really know. We lived in a suburb before, and our new house is in a different suburb on the opposite side of the city.

    Dad kept asking me what I would want to build but I couldn't think of anything. I don't know why but I kept thinking we would turn a corner and see Brooke standing on the sidewalk. I wonder what she's up to. And the rest of the Westmores. I just want Mr. Towns to drive us to Brooke's house one more time with a couple boxes of pizza. That's what I think of when I think of "home." The last place I got to have a real friend. But then I worry she wouldn't want to see me, just like she never wrote back after the letters I sent.

    My dad asked my mom what she would build and she said her dream was torn down a long time ago. Whatever that means.

    When we got to the restaurant my dad kept putting his arm around my mom and kissing her which was kinda weird. They never hug at home. Dad kept talking about how Mom is so intelligent and beautiful with a side of that "strong-willed, Florida spirit," and that everyone was jealous of him when he got her.

    Parents are SO awkward.

    On the way home we drove past a homeless guy on the corner and Mr. Towns asked if I ever took self-defense classes. He said his kid really liked them and I could never be too careful with all the crazies out there these days. Dad said he'd sign me up tomorrow.

    I'm ALMOST 16.

—Dylan Turner, 15

# 5

## Four Questions (Reprise)

What was that Maya Angelou quote again? "People will forget what you said, people will forget what you did, but people will never forget how you made them feel."

That was what reading her own journal was like: a walk through her relationships with her parents. Even more than what they said or did, Dylan remembered how they made her feel. Her dad was the one who tried to make the most of their moves, who brought gifts and made her feel he liked her, at least. And her mom made her feel constant low-level anxiety that whatever she said or did was wrong.

Dylan flipped to the back of the journal and found empty pages. Even though the paper had yellowed with time, they shone like a blank slate. There was more space to breathe.

She grabbed the pen on her nightstand, then walked to her kitchen table and sat down. Maybe making a list would get her spinning thoughts in order. She opened her pen and put the cap in her mouth to gnaw on, deciding she'd start with the questions from her dad's funeral.

1. Who is my biological father?
2. Why didn't my mom tell me?

3. Does everyone know but me?

4. Who am I?

Questions she never imagined would be tucked inside a box a mere six inches wide and four inches tall.

Her dad had presented her with the KindreDNA test kit one of the first weekends after they'd moved to Milwaukee. She was visiting them, and he'd placed it next to her dinner plate before sitting down by her. That was how they always sat—her and her dad on one side of the table, her mom on the other.

"We just have to go thirty minutes without eating, drinking, chewing gum, or smoking. Think you can handle that?" he'd asked with a twinkle in his eye.

"Everything but the smoking," she'd joked.

He'd set another box next to her mom's plate. Her mom looked at him for a long time before she sat down at the table and said, "Supper is seared tuna steaks with relish and herb oil."

Darren rolled his eyes and smiled at Dylan, the look saying, *Your mother's in another one of her moods.* He leaned in and whispered, "We'll do our thirty-minute fast after supper. Just the two of us and my branch of our family tree."

After another supper where the only sound her mom made was the scratching of utensils against her plate, they sat at her dad's laptop for a half hour, punching in the numbers on their test tube labels and setting up their profiles on the KindreDNA website.

The test tube required less than a teaspoon of saliva, which they spit through a funnel. Dylan remembered watching it bubble and slide down the side of the tube, amazed the cloudy substance could give her clues to her ancestral roots as well as other relatives—connections she'd never thought much about. She was more familiar with disconnect: constant relocations, already-deceased grandparents. And there were no cities or small towns either parent shared nostalgic stories about.

The last part of the test was to take the funnels off their test tubes and screw a cap filled with blue solution onto each tube. Once it was tight, the cap released a solution they had to shake together, stabilizing the DNA until the lab could process their samples.

She thought that now, sitting in her apartment, her four questions were bubbling at the bottom of the tube, but without the solution—the answers she wanted. Nothing would stabilize her.

The last question haunted her the most. *Who am I?*

She could dig deeper into the percentages listed in her email. A smattering of European ancestry with roots in Germany and the Netherlands, mixed with her twelve years' experience as a White middle-class Midwesterner.

She could think about the experiences that shaped her into the person she was today. Growing up, she related to the concept of an army brat, minus the "serving her country" part, of course. They'd moved for work that kept them financially comfortable, over and over and over.

She could label herself with her day job—she was an employee with many roles and tasks wrapped into it.

Was she her heritage? Her lived experiences? The output she contributed to the world? Her family—whether or not they were related by blood? Was she the sum of these parts or something entirely new, emerging from where life had taken her over time?

Through all the upheaval she went through as a kid, the one constant was that her parents were her parents. She was Dylan Turner, daughter of Candis and Darren Turner. Now, even that had been taken from her, ripped out of her hands, shoved into a moving box, and shipped across state lines.

*Who am I?*

She wiped her greasy forehead. Nothing had been solved, but at least she had a list propelling her forward. She read it again, and then a third time, when a loud knock on the door startled her.

"It's me and Gale and Peeta," yelled a little voice on the other side. "And Logan," he added with less enthusiasm.

She walked over to open the door for Logan and "me," seven-year-old Tate, her neighbor Tara's kids from the apartment down the hall.

Last week, in her mad dash to get to her dad's deathbed, she'd had a moment of panic when she realized she needed someone to take care of her two guineas. She called five of the nineteen pet boardinghouses in the Naperville area, but not all of them were open twenty-four hours, and the ones that were only boarded cats or dogs. She would've brought them with her, but her mom was allergic to anything that produced pet dander and had also begged her to leave her "lab rats" in Illinois. Her mom had always seemed picky about what she nurtured.

Desperate, Dylan had knocked on Tara's door.

She hated herself for leaving the guineas with someone she didn't know. She'd sprinkled her hatred with more self-loathing when she realized that the first time she was making an effort to talk to her new neighbors was when asking for a huge favor. They'd moved in six months ago, right around the time she adopted Gale and Peeta.

Her only consolation was that the younger of the two kids often waved enthusiastically when they crossed paths in the hall, and their mom always shouted no-nonsense orders when they walked to their car. Her guineas would be in good hands.

She opened the door wide enough for Tate and Logan to carry the large cage into her apartment.

"Hello," she greeted, then pointed to a spot on the floor near where they were standing. "You can set it there—I know it's pretty heavy."

Tate tugged the cage and his sister farther into her apartment.

"Hey," Logan grunted with barely a smile.

Tate, however, stepped from the cage toward Dylan and hugged her waist.

"I didn't want to bring them back yet," he said into her middle, "but when we got off the bus from school, Logan saw your car outside, which was a surprise because it wasn't 3:30, and you always get home at 3:30."

"Thank you so much for watching them, Tate. *And* Logan."

She was about to pat his back, but Tate stepped away and pulled a paper out of his sweatshirt pocket—the instructions she'd scribbled right before she left.

He'd rated his performance on each one.

"I gave them new hay and vegetables every day—five stars. I made sure to hold them with two hands so I wouldn't drop them—five stars. I tried to not freak out when they started eating their own poop, but I don't know, Ms. Dylan. I give myself three stars for that one, because that was kind of disgusting."

He twisted his nose, and she tried not to laugh. Logan, who'd been observing from the wall with slouched shoulders, shivered too.

"It's called coprophagy. I promise it's good for them. And, you can call me Dylan."

He crossed his arms. "No, I can't. My mom would have a coprophagy if I didn't call you Ms. Dylan."

Logan rolled her eyes. "That's not the same word, Tate."

Dylan was only around kids for brief moments at work, so everything about these two fascinated her. The teenager seemed a little scary, but Dylan liked Tate's earnestness.

Bending by the pigs' cage, she held her hands out for Gale and Peeta to smell, knowing they were probably shaken up from their bumpy ride down the hall. Like her, they needed to tour their surroundings when they got home in order to feel safe again.

"Is your mom working right now?"

"Mom works all the time. Every day." Tate squatted next to her and held out his hand, which Peeta scooted closer to sniff. The kid was a natural.

"I'm going to pay you for taking care of them." She dug her wallet out of her purse, then placed a few folded bills in Tate's hand. "Make sure you split that with your sister."

The boy puffed his chest, tucking the cash into his pocket next to the guinea pigs' instructions. "You should know I can watch them anytime because I'm a person who likes to help. Also, my mom said she's worried about you because there's never anybody at your apartment after work and you don't go anywhere except when you run away really fast. She's wondering if that's because you're lonely or just weird."

"Tate! Stop it," Logan hissed.

He rubbed the spot on his shoulder where she'd hit him. "She said we'll have to have you over for dinner sometime to find out. I don't know how you'd ever be lonely with Gale and Peeta living with you, though."

"Interesting." She didn't know how else to respond to his honesty mixed with—unknown to him—a few backhanded compliments.

"Come on. It's time to go." Logan pulled Tate's hoodie toward the door, clearly mortified by her little brother's commentary.

He yanked back against his sister's grip. "Even if you don't need me to watch them again, can I come over and play with Gale and Peeta sometime?"

"Sometime. Yeah."

The boy beamed all the way back into the hall. "Thanks, Ms. Dylan. Bye."

She shook her head and grinned, shutting the door behind them and grabbing the leftover sliced vegetables she'd supplied them with. She took two carrots out of the bag and held them inside the cage.

"Hey, little guy," she said to Gale, who'd scooted toward her and put his twitchy nose millimeters from the snack. "Was your weekend as eventful as mine?"

The orange-and-black-spotted guinea pig moved from the carrot to rub against the side of her hand. She picked him up, holding him close to her middle until he stopped squirming.

"I have a lot to get off my chest, so it's a good thing you're such a great listener. Though I suppose your friendship has limits."

Someday she would need to talk to someone who could talk back, which didn't include the guineas. Even if she got around to messaging Great-Aunt Kathleen Schulz, she couldn't just unload her family's drama on her. It was too much for her own shoulders, so it was too much to put on a stranger.

Who else could she talk to? Aunt Lou was someone she randomly texted throughout the year, but her mom's best friend was right at the heart of one of her core questions: *Does everyone know but me?*

Aunt Lou was currently a suspect, not an ally.

Teresa came to mind; Dylan liked working with her, but so did everyone else. Teresa probably thought of Dylan more like a work friend instead of a *friend* friend.

She set Gale in the cage and held her hand out to Peeta, who ran away from her into his covered bed. Her extensive online research leading up to adopting the guinea pigs had taught her that keeping two together was better for their overall health. Though their instincts as prey made them nervous animals, they were also highly social.

Peeta challenged that information.

"Take all the time you need." She said the words she craved to hear.

Standing up, she looked around her apartment. It was so quiet the walls were starting to yell at her.

*Funeral.*

*Dad.*

*Bio dad.*

*HOW?*

Her heart pounded, like it wanted to scream along with her inner thoughts. She needed to calm down, to get back into her routine before work tomorrow morning.

She looked at the clock in the kitchen. It was 3:24 P.M.

If this were a normal Monday, she'd be getting home from work, gearing up for her run that she always started at 4:00. She decided to skip ahead and changed into a pair of running shorts and a moisture-wicking shirt, tying her shoes in a racer's loop. She put in her earbuds, low volume so she could still be aware of her surroundings.

She'd do what she did every day at 4:00, which was run five miles through the McDowell Grove Forest Preserve, sprinting until she was too tired to scream. Then she'd skip her usual two hours of reality television and give herself a ridiculously early bedtime.

Maybe her questions, grief, and oncoming headache would finally take a rest.

*Yeah, right.*

# 6

# Working Nine to Strive

Tuesday, September 23

3:07 A.M.

Dylan's body jolted, startling her awake.

She was drenched in sweat and breathing like she'd just finished a run, except she was in bed and it was the middle of the night, according to her phone. She wiped her hair away from her forehead and fanned the shirt clinging to her sticky body.

For as long as she could remember, she'd been a vivid dreamer, though she rarely remembered what the dreams were about. What always stuck with her, though, was a low-grade anxiety that lingered all morning. A sense that someone was mad at her for something she'd said sixteen years ago or that she'd forgotten something crucial or that she was being chased by someone—usually the zombie version of *The Bachelorette* winner from her latest TV binge.

When she was little, she'd wake up—her jammies soaking wet—and run crying to find a parent. It was usually her mom, standing in the kitchen near the dim light of the range hood, poring over a recipe book or marinating meat for the next day's dinner. When Dylan finally noticed the pattern, she'd asked why her mom was always awake.

"I don't sleep well either," she'd answered.

Dylan settled back into her bed, wondering if, two hours away, her mom was able to sleep now, and closed her eyes.

6:15 A.M.

Dylan's alarm blared from the nightstand.

"Rude," she groaned.

Her chest fluttered, the morning's way of greeting her. She cracked the kink in her neck, wiped the crusts from her eyes, and remembered. It wasn't something she'd said decades ago or something crucial she'd forgotten. Her nightmares were real and had a name: *Yesterday*.

The email. Her dad's funeral. That had actually happened. And her mom hadn't chased her down after.

She reached for her phone and swiped Snooze.

6:25 A.M.

She still wasn't ready to face the day, but she faced her phone. There weren't any notifications, which meant there weren't any surprises waiting in her inbox. Things were looking up.

She swiped left again and tossed her phone across the bed.

It took a hard bounce and dropped to the floor.

6:35 A.M.

This time, she would have to get herself out of bed in order to stop the sound of synthesized xylophones.

She wished a crane or puppet master would move her body for her, but neither option was available, so she turned to high school physics. If she heaved the mass of her dead weight at a high enough speed, the momentum might roll her off the mattress and into a standing position. Mr. Aguilar would be proud, prouder still if her application of *mass x velocity = momentum* landed her on her feet instead of sending her crashing into the wall.

She regrouped and walked around the bed to pick up her phone, swiping right to stop her alarm. She had only twenty minutes to get to work, and she'd never been late before.

The time crunch pushed her into the bathroom to find her toothbrush. The bristles were frayed, like two sheaves of wheat bending in opposite directions after a storm. She'd only had it for a month. Maybe her dentist was right; instead of brushing her teeth, she punished them. She tried gentler strokes before spitting the foam into the sink and allowing herself thirty precious seconds to stare at her reflection in the mirror.

Her appearance hadn't changed, but the face staring back at her felt like a stranger. Or someone she'd been estranged from since yesterday's unraveling.

KindreDNA estimated her DNA was mostly German and Dutch, a result that had a margin of error, as the testing company explained with painstaking effort. So, maybe she was 38 percent German but with a 38 percent margin of error—who really knew?

Her dad once told her the surname Turner was French, the reason for his attention to detail, his love for a frank debate, and his lust for a good glass of wine. At Christmas, they read books about Père Noël, not Santa Claus, and she set a pair of shoes by the fireplace instead of hanging a stocking. Her mom made bûche de Noël for after Christmas dinner.

Dylan wiped the corners of her mouth with the hand towel.

Could the physical traits staring back at her tell her who she was? Or was their margin of error just as high as a DNA test guessing one's motherland? She'd never had a sense of home, of *where* she came from, but she wanted to look in the mirror and be grounded by her genetics. She wanted her cheekbones, cleft chin, and mole below her left eye to tell her *who* she came from. *Who* she belonged to. She'd thought she was 100 percent Darren's daughter, but her margin of error was 100 percent.

Looking at herself in the mirror every day, twice a day, was going to be harder. Another rejection paired with more internal unraveling. Unraveling was what scared her most. She was used to having a heated relationship with her mom, as well as the lingering anxiety someone might sit her down at any moment to tell her she was moving across state lines. But she had no interest in unraveling any further. The kind that might lead to her losing her job. She had to get through her shift at work, one hour at a time.

She gave the mirror her game face. Her right eye twitched, but it was the best she could do. She grabbed her purse and the sweater she tripped over earlier, then noticed her old journal sitting out. She stared at it for a moment like it was her emotional support animal, then shoved it in her purse before running out the door.

Her red Buick Verano was waiting for her. She climbed in, closed her eyes, and turned the key. If anything should've made her pause before buying something all-access, it was the fact that the car she'd had for twelve years was on her deathbed.

Something underneath the hood sputtered, but after a few seconds, the engine purred.

She patted the dashboard. "Good girl."

Brenda would live to see another commute.

6:59 A.M.

Dylan pulled off her coat as she ran into the building. There was a chill in the air, which made sense for a suburb of Chicago in late September. What didn't make sense was her work uniform, a red T-shirt with a hibiscus on the back, thousands of miles from the tropical, subtropical, or even warm temperate region it was native to.

Putting a hand on her heart, she exhaled.

Getting worked up over a logo wasn't how she wanted to start her first day back. Besides, she'd once read an article saying pent-up anger could reduce a person's life by years. The follow-up article was called "Angry? Spend More Time Thinking About What You're Grateful For." Baited, she'd clicked on that one too. It sounded like unnecessary mental gymnastics, but she'd list everything she was grateful for if it meant not getting fired or dying a young, cynical Scrooge.

In the case of her uniform's hibiscus, she could try being thankful to work in such a come-as-you-are environment.

She took one last deep breath, ready to be Dylan Turner, crew member of Trader Joe's Store 796.

7:06 A.M.

Dylan didn't worry about dying a violent death at the hands of a stranger. She worried about choking on a cashew while watching *The Amazing Race* in her apartment, then lying undiscovered for weeks.

This recurring intrusive thought wasn't completely random. She was cradling three bags of Cashew Butter Cashews with her left arm, using her right hand to line them one by one on a shelf in the snack aisle.

She believed they were as good as everyone said, but she stuck to stocking shelves of them at work, not eating them when she was home alone.

8:00 A.M.

"Morning, Sunshine."

Dylan looked up to see Teresa's head peeking into the aisle, holding on to one of the shelves for support. Even from ten feet away, she could see her co-worker's giant engagement ring sparkling under the store's fluorescent lighting.

She should thank Teresa for not throwing "good" in front of "morning," but she didn't want to explain why. "I don't shine near as bright as that rock of yours."

Teresa fanned her face with her left hand. "This old thing? Recently presented to me by my new *fiancé*?"

"How long do you get to call August 'new'? Hasn't it been almost six months?"

Teresa shrugged. "Might as well ride the bridal high until we're arguing about money and in-laws."

"Good idea."

"I could chat about the love of my life for hours, but Avery is late again, so I'm here to ask if you can do registers for the next hour instead? Dial up the rizz for me?"

Teresa was always educating her on the things today's youths were saying, specifically their co-workers, chronically late Avery and her counterpart, the reliably outspoken Olivia.

"I don't know what that means, but yes, I'll see you there," she replied over her shoulder, heading to the back of the store to return her empty pallet first.

Registers was the only low score she'd ever gotten on a performance review. To her credit, those low scores were from a previous manager who would have earned himself an entry or two in her journal—if she still wrote in it regularly. Sitting in those review meetings with Captain Garrett, being told to open up to customers more and wow them with her interest in their lives always brought back the memory of her first parent-teacher conference after moving to Cleveland in eighth grade, when Ms. Woodward asked her parents if Dylan could see the school counselor.

"Dylan is bright, but she secludes herself most of the time—in class, from extracurriculars, during recess—even when girls make an effort to include her." Ms. Woodward had hesitated. "Dylan mentioned she's moved, uh, quite a few times in the past six years. It's possible that could affect her ability to even *want* to connect with others. There's a new term being used called *social anxiety*—"

"She's just shy," her dad had interrupted. "She'll be fine once she settles in. She always is."

And that had been the end of that.

Dylan still felt shy at times. She was a workhorse in the shelves and a skittish guinea pig behind the register, but it was more than that. She didn't want to act like some court jester, pretending to connect with customers below the surface when it was a business transaction, not a real relationship. Customers went through her line and then left. Even if they were regulars, she spent six minutes with them, tops. Why put in that kind of effort?

She walked to the front of the store and signed into a cash register. Her first customer was a regular named Cindy, who was sporting another new pair of Lululemon joggers.

"I'm just stopping by after spin class to grab a few bottles of Napa for tonight's book club." Cindy smiled, then waited.

The woman's microbladed brows arched, and Dylan could feel the eyes beneath them boring into her, begging for a question about the book she was reading or a little gushing about girls' nights and glasses of wine, but Dylan kept her head down and finished ringing up Cindy's items. Dylan's mom always said if she didn't have anything nice to say, to not say anything at all. She'd never followed the rule well with her mom, but she tried harder at work so she could earn a paycheck.

Besides, the only question that came to mind was, *What secrets are you keeping from your children, Cindy? Isn't this your third "book club" meeting this week?*

Teresa, on the other hand, always lived up to their contract's pledge to "make sure every customer has a fun, friendly, and informative shopping experience." It never seemed forced—she was genuinely curious about people and their lives outside Trader Joe's walls.

No wonder the quiet, handsome president of the local hospital had fallen for her on a random Thursday night snack run a year and a half ago.

She glanced Teresa's way; her first customer appeared to be wearing a burlap sack and Chacos. She overheard the guy saying something like "I'm so hyped to find organic, free-range, grass-fed chicken that's not wrapped in Styrofoam."

"Not as hyped as you'll be to find out we've improved our packaging to be more eco-friendly for nearly one hundred fifty products in the past five years," Teresa replied like some magical cash-register fairy.

Dylan couldn't fake excitement for even that simple of an interaction. She handed Cindy her receipt. "Have a nice . . . book club, Cindy."

Cindy looked longingly at Teresa's line before walking through the exit.

The last customer Dylan rang up during her hour at the register was a frazzled mom with a piece of cereal in her hair. She had an infant wrapped around her body and a toddler who couldn't take two steps in the same direction. At the last second, the mom grabbed a bag of dark chocolates from the display and threw them onto her pile of groceries.

"My daughter knocked over a few boxes of tea in the aisle back there. I'm *really* sorry."

9:00 A.M.

"A few boxes" turned out to be the toddler having swiped her hand along the entire second shelf of the coffee and tea aisle. Dylan didn't mind cleaning up the mess, though. It was another chance to focus on a task, to keep her thoughts busy instead of worrying about the correct answers to existential questions about her own existence.

French Vanilla Ground Coffee. Joe Medium Roast. Organic

Assam Black Tea. She keyed in on getting every box back into its place. The store was hitting its morning rush, and the rule was if a customer came within three feet, she was supposed to ask if they needed help finding anything. This was easier for her than cash-register talk, because it was less about digging into strangers' personal lives and more about product.

The first guy to wander within three feet of her was wearing a dress shirt, boat shoes, and a backward hat. He reeked of booze.

"Hello, gorgeous," he slurred. "Looks like someone spilled the tea."

She clenched her fists at her sides. "Do you need help finding anything?"

He came right up behind her and stood parallel, less than an inch from her body. According to employee math, this guy was close enough for her to ask if he needed help, what his grandmother's maiden name was, and if he wanted to marry her.

*Not today.*

He reached around her hip for a box of tea.

She didn't picture him as the kind of person who drank Organic Ginger Turmeric Herbal tea, but she also knew appearances weren't always what they seemed. Maybe it was what he needed the morning after a wild Monday night.

He leaned in by her ear, his breath hot and sticky against her neck. "Do you need a helping hand?"

She took one large step to the side and turned to face him, refusing to fake smile even if it was what Captain Garrett would have told her to do. "Absolutely not, but let me know if you need help finding anything."

He took the same size step toward her and pointed down at his pants. "I need help finding you in here."

If she were applying the gratitude method to this situation, she'd say she was grateful for the opportunity to employ everything she'd learned in self-defense class. She finally had a righteous reason to give someone a strong knee to the groin, followed immediately by a swift palm upward at the base of the nose.

Thinking about it made her downright giddy.

Until another set of footsteps walked down her aisle. "Sir? You need to step away from her. *Now.*"

Though firm, his voice was what she imagined blue-raspberry cotton candy sounded like.

"And you are?" the man asked.

"I'm Captain Jim, manager of this Trader Joe's." He placed a hand on the guy's elbow to lead him away from Dylan, but he jerked away.

"Excuse me, *Captain,* but I was just talking to this"—he eyed her up and down—"woman right here."

The guy reached out to grab her again, but this time, Captain Jim took his collar and slammed him against the shelves, knocking some of the tea and coffee she'd reshelved back onto the floor. Holding him back with one arm, Captain Jim took the walkie-talkie from his belt. "Security? I need backup by tea and coffee."

The guy flailed, wide eyed and two more degrees sober. "It was just a joke."

Captain Jim tightened his grip on the guy's collar. "I think what you meant to say is that you owe this *very nice* woman an apology."

"Okay, okay." The guy fixed his shirt and turned to Dylan, who tipped her chin upward at him. "I'm sorry," he mumbled.

The security guard arrived in the aisle, and the two men escorted the customer to the exit, leaving her standing among the scattered boxes and canisters. Captain Jim would follow protocol, taking down the guy's name and filing an incident report for the store's records. She rarely had issues with customers, and this was the first time the issue was so seriously disturbing. One person could ruin things for a lot of people.

Ten minutes later, Captain Jim reappeared.

She took in the unsung details that made up Jim Jacobson. His

Hawaiian button-down shirt was tucked in, and his belt matched his casual brown dress shoes. His dark hair was neatly waxed, and even though he didn't appear capable of growing facial hair, he had the best dimple she'd ever seen.

He looked so . . . nice. He'd always acted really nice, too, which made him seem, well, older than his mid-thirties, and was why she was shocked by his response to the boozy customer.

"I'm sorry I knocked over the display you worked so hard on," he apologized, keeping an appropriate distance.

It was the sincerest apology she'd received in the past forty-eight hours, so why was she slamming the boxes of tea back onto the shelf? "I appreciate what you did, but I *can* take care of myself."

His brow furrowed. "Of course."

She finished the row of spiced chai. Her thoughts should be this orderly too. "It's not your job to save me."

"That wasn't my inten—" He stopped, then pointed at her. "Dylan. Your hand is shaking."

She looked down. The box of tea in her left hand *was* shaking, which meant the hand holding it must be too. She willed it to stop, but it didn't, so she set the box down and folded her arms.

"Even if it is, I'm not scared, Jim." Now she'd done it. If this were Captain Garrett and she'd called him "Garrett," not "Captain Garrett," she'd be fired on the spot. "I'm so sorry. I meant Captain—"

"I'm not worried about titles right now," he insisted.

She gritted her teeth. This wasn't his fault, so she didn't know why she was making it sound like it was. "I'm not scared, *Captain* Jim. I'm . . . I'm . . ."

*Enraged.*

Captain Jim clasped his hands. "Dylan, please take a break. Actually, no. Please go home for the rest of the day. I started filing the incident report with HR, and soon they'll need a statement from you too. After that, you should go home and rest. I'm so sorry this happened; it shouldn't have happened."

People didn't usually apologize for what happened to her. Usually, they listed the reasons *why* something happened to her.

For a split second, the knot in her chest was less suffocating.

"You'll be comped a full day's work—I promise."

She wasn't worried about the money, though maybe she should be, thanks to her shiny new all-access KindreDNA membership and Brenda the Verano nearing the end of her life. However, she was done arguing.

She gathered her things, gave her side of the story to HR, and walked out of Trader Joe's Store 796 before her shift ended.

Another first.

9:45 A.M.

Inside her car, the silence settled some of her remaining adrenaline. Her only goal had been to make it through her workday, and she'd somehow come up short. What was she supposed to do with herself? If this was her morning break, she might scroll her co-workers' pictures on Instagram—sometimes the combination of their photos and captions offered context clues to the meaning of the words they used. Like an affordable version of Rosetta Stone for learning to speak Gen Z.

Otherwise, she'd try to better herself by listening to the daily episode of her favorite podcast, *Fencing Your Fury*.

She dug through her purse for her phone but instead found something paper-thin with pointed corners, an envelope held shut with a sticker in the shape of a blue flower.

It was the birthday card from her dad.

He'd given it to her within minutes of her arrival in Milwaukee, but she'd tucked it into her purse for later. She'd needed to be in the room with him, fully present. The time until goodbye had been too short for anything else.

The card had sat forgotten for five days, but not anymore. She hugged the envelope against her heart. These were the last words he'd ever say to her. What had he penned? Words summing up their years as father and daughter? Sentences full of admiration and timeless wisdom that would uplift her in her moment of need?

She clawed open the envelope.

# 7

## Happy Birthday to You!

The greeting on the outside of the card:

*Wishing the Sweetest of Birthdays . . .*

Inside:

*. . . to the Sweetest of Daughters!*

Below the greeting, in his own handwriting:

Happy Birthday, kiddo!
Dad

P.S.: I hurt the most when lost yet also when not had at all. I'm sometimes the hardest to express but the easiest to ignore. I can be given to many or just one. What am I?

P.S.S.: TH3 P3N 1S M16TIER thAN tce SWORD.

# 8

## Riddle Me This

Dylan wiped the greeting card where her tears had fallen, annoyed at herself for wishing there were more.

Her dad had been sick—deathly sick. There hadn't been time or energy for a long-winded goodbye letter. Besides, he'd remembered to include a riddle. He wrote one in her birthday card every year:

*Forward I'm heavy, backward I am not. (Ton.)*

*If you have me, you want to share me. If you share me, you don't have me. (A secret.)*

*I'm where yesterday follows today, and tomorrow is in the middle. (The dictionary.)*

Each year, she would sit down at her parents' table for her birthday dinner and try to guess the answer. She either guessed it wrong or had no guess at all, but she enjoyed the way the small gesture connected her to her dad. It was their thing.

She reread the riddle he'd chosen for this year: *I hurt the most when lost yet also when not had at all. I'm sometimes the hardest to express but the easiest to ignore. I can be given to many or just one. What am I?*

Hugs? Children? Blood? Would she ever find out?

The card in her hands stung with both nostalgia and grief, setting off another wave of tears. She dug through her glove box and grabbed her stack of extra napkins from Five Guys to wipe her sad drip of snot, and it hit her. There was a second postscript.

She picked the card back up.

He'd written a riddle, and then he'd written, *P.S.S.: TH3 P3N 1S M16TIER thAN tce SWORD.* A weird combination of numbers and letters spelling out "The pen is mightier than the sword."

He used to say that all the time when she was a teenager, on the way to her self-defense class. *"Learn to watch your back, Dylan, but remember, the pen is mightier than the sword."*

It would earn him an "Okay, Dad" and a half-hearted smile, but she never understood his deal with the phrase. Why had he written it here, in her birthday card, and now, so close to his death? They hadn't talked about that class in years.

She sifted through her purse to find a pen, praying it would be mighty enough to help her now. Using the envelope she'd ripped in half, she wrote down the numbers and letters he'd changed: *33116thtce*. It looked like DNA centimorgan nonsense, so she unlocked her phone.

**Google:** 33116thtce

After searching the entire World Wide Web, Google came back with a total of eight search results. Eight, and all of them were addresses. None of them were an exact match. She tried splitting the letters and numbers to more closely match how they were separated in the card: *3 31 16 th tce*.

**Google:** tce

TCE is short for trichlorethylene, which is a cancer-causing chemical . . .

Were the letters supposed to be related to her dad's illness? Did he suspect foul play? She read it again: "TCE causes kidney cancer."

Then she exhaled. Her dad had leukemia, not kidney cancer. Her brain could chill on the conspiracies.

Scrolling farther through the results, she learned *tce* was also short for *terrace*, like in an address.

*3311 6th Terrace?*

*331 16th Terrace?*

Neither of those addresses meant anything to her, but she liked that she'd come up with one possible solution for the jumbled cryptogram. A shiver shook her body. It felt like her dad was trying to tell her something. Would it be so hard for someone in her life to just say what they needed to say? Over the past twenty-four hours, both her parents had spoken in riddles. And—with her dad in an urn and her mom not ready to talk—she was going to have a hard time getting answers at the pace she needed.

A loose piece of hair fell over her eye, and she brushed it off her sticky forehead. The air outside her car was still chilly, but the sun streaming through her windshield was creating a greenhouse effect. She unbuttoned her sweater and picked up whatever she could get her hands on from the passenger seat to fan herself and her anxiety.

Looking down, she saw her journal.

She didn't know if she was ready to read more of it. Then again, she hadn't been ready for most of what she'd experienced over the last week. Bad news. A bad funeral. A bad fight. A bad customer. What could one bad trip down memory lane do in the grand scheme of all that bad? Especially if an entry jogged a memory that would help her understand her dad's message.

She flipped past the pages she'd read yesterday covering ages eight through fifteen, then skimmed until she found the entry she was looking for. Each page she turned carefully, as if defusing a bomb.

"Please handle me with care too," she whispered.

Page 100

## 16 Years Anxious
### (16 years old—duh!!!)

Have you ever felt like something is off? What if that something is . . . me?

Our move from Cleveland back to Jacksonville makes for a total of six moves. I know I should be excited to be back here because it's where I lived from when I was born until 8, but nothing's the same. I didn't even unpack. It won't be long before the moving truck is back.

When I turn 18, I'm picking a town to live in and never, ever leaving.

Tomorrow, I have self-defense class again. I like it okay, but if Hendrix would stop being a moron, I would like it even more.

P.S. I started putting titles on my entries because I think it's less boring than page-number blah, blah, blah.

**Page 101**

## The Pen
### (Still 16)

"The pen is mightier than the sword."

This is Dad's speech every time he offers to drop me off at self-defense class. (I could drive myself but he thinks it's in a sketchy part of Jacksonville. Whatever. I told him it was the perfect chance for me to practice self-defense. He didn't think that was funny.)

But he always says this "pen" thing and then goes on a big long lecture about how he's had more power with pen and paper than a gun could ever give him. He talks about how some of the most dangerous criminals in history were taken down by tax laws, not physical force. "That's how you work smart, not hard," he'll say.

If that's the case, I'd ask why he put me in a class all about using physical force, but I already know why. Dad's new boss said his kid liked the class, and Dad likes his new boss. This is one way to befriend his boss right away. I don't mind—it's something different to do with my friendless nights.

The beginning of class was all about situational awareness—keeping one hand empty so it's free to defend yourself, not taking trips from the car with your hands full, and not using a phone while walking.

That's not why I'm enraged, though. I'm enraged because my dad said he thinks Hendrix likes me.

Let me tell you about Hendrix Reed, dear ROR.

He may seem all hot and the other girls in class might be obsessed with him, but in reality, he's full of himself. He always talks about how he wants to become some sort of FBI agent or something. Noble? Sure. But when he says, "Reed sniffs out the weed," I want to barf. I told him that's the DEA not the FBI, and dogs usually do the sniffing, and his stupid little catchphrase sounds like he's the one smoking the weed.

Apparently, his magic works on girls like Stephanie and Tricia and Brit, all at the same time.

Dad saw Hendrix surrounded by a crowd of girls before class and warned me to keep a safe distance from "boys like him who are after one thing." I didn't choose to be paired up with him tonight, though. I think our instructor puts us together on purpose so the rest of the class gets a good show.

We were practicing outside defense against a kick, and every time he kicked at me, I had to practice the motions of moving myself away from the kick, bringing my left hand down in self-defense, and using my right hand at the same time to model a near-punch at his chin while he's still on one foot.

We did this over and over, and every time I did my part, he had something to say about it.

> "That was really good for you, Turner."
>
> "I wish I was as chill as you about learning self-defense."
>
> "I don't care what the other girls say about you. I think you're really nice."

More than anything, I wanted to swipe the smirk off his face.

So what if my hand accidentally slipped and did more than "the motions"?

Who actually cares??

Edited to add: Here is a list of people (in order of appearance) who actually cared:

- Hendrix's bloody nose
- Hendrix
- Our instructor
- Dad, when he got the phone call
- Mom, when Dad told her what happened
- Not me, at first
- Later, me, a little

## 9

## Siren or Sirens?

Dylan scanned the cramped parking lot between her car and Trader Joe's, where customers shuffled into the store with flat canvas bags and out with full arms. Then she shut her journal and opened her phone to The Email again.

Her dad had asked that they both have administrative access to their family tree. It hadn't seemed right to argue with a dying man, so together, they set up their KindreDNA profiles and decided to name it The Turner Tree. Straightforward.

In the results email, however, it said their shared tree was named Jacksonville.

Her dad must have changed it in the time between when they set up their profiles and when they received their test results.

**Google:** 331 16th Terrace

The first city it filled in out of all the cities in the entire country was Jacksonville. When she double-checked the other choices—33 116th Terrace and 3311 6th Terrace—those came up blank.

But 331 16th Terrace, Jacksonville, Florida, was a real address.

She stared at the photos linked to it, which looked like a brand-new development. The description said it was mixed-use commercial and residential. And, again, it was located in Jacksonville. The address, the journal entry, the family tree, even Kathleen Schulz—they were all one big siren call coming from the Southeast, drawing her to Jacksonville to figure out her past.

A surge of excitement roared through her, the same energy she'd felt last night at her computer when she was both exhausted by her sadness and enraged by it having nowhere to go except her typing fingertips.

*Go to Jacksonville!*
*Jacksonville.*
*Jacksonville?*

The pit in her stomach released a haze of fear. How could she even think about traveling outside the state of Illinois again so soon? These clues weren't a siren; they were more likely siren*s*. Warning sirens to stay away because it would be irresponsible to miss more days of work for a wild-goose chase.

She covered her face with her hands and yelled, surprised by how heavy the silence felt when she stopped.

She should go home like Captain Jim said. She loved home, which was why she didn't want to go somewhere a thousand miles away. All the moving she'd done as a kid had sucked the allure out of traveling. She'd lived a childhood where everything was new, all the time, on repeat, and she was over it.

Naperville, Illinois, was her home now. She'd picked it on purpose. At eighteen, she'd googled "best places to live," and Naperville was consistently in the top five. Bloggers described it as charming, one of the safest towns to live in the country. The schools were highly ranked, as well as its library and hospital. It sounded like a place people didn't move away from.

The problem now was she wanted deeper answers to the question *Who am I?* than the suburb she'd picked out. She wanted to pick up the pieces of her story and rearrange them into a more accurate retelling. She wanted to know the truth. And what if that couldn't be found if she wasn't brave enough to go find it?

She had an address, an actual address, and a blood relative. She could start there.

Busying her thumbs, she got to work.

**Google:** flights chicago o'hare to jacksonville

# 10

# Beige Flag

There were multiple glaring holes in her plan to go to Jacksonville on flight UA1106 the next day at 7:10 A.M. The biggest one was she hadn't asked for the time off work. She also didn't know how long she was going to be gone. Her dad's passing was technically a good enough reason for her to ask for extended unpaid leave, but it might be awkward explaining that to Captain Jim now.

September wasn't a blackout month, so that helped. There was more scheduling flexibility compared with holiday seasons when employees could only get time off for grave illnesses.

Either way, making her flight without a debilitating amount of shame the next morning meant talking to Captain Jim. She hoped it wouldn't mean having to quit her job, or him changing his mind about how she'd acted toward him earlier.

She walked back into the store, percolating self-consciousness. Word of what happened had probably traveled the gossip circuit of her co-workers already. She kept her head down and zipped toward the break room, past Olivia and Avery in the bakery zone.

"Are you okay, Dylan?" Teresa popped out of nowhere. "I came back here to check on you earlier but didn't know where you were. Captain Jim Sparrow said something happened and that you went home."

It was one of a few nicknames crew members had come up with over time, along with Captain Vanilla and Jungle Jim.

Dylan tried to smile, but the muscles in her face had dead batteries. Still, she liked that Teresa checked in on her. She liked it so much, she wondered if it would be weird to give Teresa a key to her apartment. For the cashew-choking issue.

"I'm okay," she lied. "Thanks for asking."

Teresa grabbed her shoulders. "Some guy trying to feel you up is not okay, but you don't have to talk about it if you don't want to. I'm here if you need someone to listen, though. Okay?"

She nodded. "Actually, I was wondering—"

A brass bell rang once at the front of the store, to which crew, mates (assistant store leaders in charge of training and development), and captains (store leaders) were expected to respond promptly. The large nautical bells worked like Morse code. One ring summoned crew to help with a surge of customers in the checkout lines, as it meant another register needed to be opened. Two rings, a customer had a question. Three rings, a Karen needed to speak to the manager.

Teresa gave her an apologetic look. "Hold that thought. I'll be back soon," she said and rushed toward the call of duty.

Dylan sighed, trying to hype herself up for a conversation she hoped wouldn't turn awkward. Before she reached the doorway, a phone went off. The ringtone was "He's a Pirate" from *Pirates of the Caribbean*. Captain Jim was the only person she knew who still used ringtones, and this one seemed to be the favorite for many of his contacts.

She didn't want to interrupt his phone call, so she waited in the hallway near the watercooler.

"Hello, this is Captain Jim at Trader—"

"Hello? Is this Gail's Groomerie?" a weathered voice interrupted. "Angel needs to be groomed."

Captain Jim always put his phone on speaker at max volume—a trait that earned him yet another nickname: Geriatric Jim.

"Actually, this is Captain Jim at Trader Joe's."

"A captain? Of a ship? My Harvey used to be in the navy."

"No, ma'am. I'm . . . the manager at Trader Joe's."

His break room chair creaked.

She pictured him leaning back, giving the phone call his full attention while also feeling the ordinary aches of being human.

"This isn't Gail's Groomerie?"

"No, it's my work phone at a grocery store."

"Oh, well, I don't know what I'm going to do." The lady's words didn't sound directed at the phone anymore, more like she was talking to herself or her dog, or maybe to a cloud rolling past her window. "My Angel needs to be groomed."

Where was this going? She watched plenty of reality TV—*Love Is Blind, The Amazing Race, Survivor* season quadrillion—but she couldn't remember the last time any of those shows gripped her like this wholesome reality unfolding in the break room.

"Hold on, ma'am. Maybe I can help you," Captain Jim offered.

"Really?" The voice perked up.

"Of course. Here at Trader Joe's, we're all about producing 'wow' experiences for our customers."

"Oh. I'm not a customer."

The woman didn't get that Captain Jim was being silly, but Dylan did. She thought about the way he'd grinned when he brought her a pallet of eggs in the fridge zone and said, "I brought you something *egg*-stra." She pictured his dimple again, too, but then cold water started spilling onto her hands. The cup she was filling overflowed onto the floor. She jerked it away from the spout, sprinted into the bathroom for a paper towel, then ran back and cleaned up the mess she'd made by the doorway.

"It's called Gail's?" Captain Jim was saying.

"Yes, that's right." The lady's words bobbed up and down like she was nodding her head. "Gail's Groomerie."

"In Naperville?"

"I think so."

Jim shifted in his seat. "If that's the case, then it looks like you were one digit off from their phone number."

"I'm not sure how that happened," the lady muttered. "Sometimes I get confused. I appreciate you helping me, young man."

"It's my pleasure," Captain Jim assured her. "As my grandmother used to say, 'A trouble shared is a trouble halved.'"

"She sounds like a wonderful woman."

"She was. And you know what? She had a dog too—a miniature schnauzer named Dornfelder, after the best glass of wine she ever tasted on the Delights of the Danube river cruise."

There was a pause. The lady might have hung up, which would've been an anticlimactic ending.

"Hello? Are you still there?"

"What? Yes, I'm here." She sounded flustered. "I'm sorry. I set the phone down to turn up my hearing aid because I could barely hear you. What did you say? Something about your skinny trousers? My Harvey was a wiry man too."

"Never mind," Captain Jim said. "Now, I found the number for Gail's Groomerie, but before I tell you, I'd love to hear one thing about Angel. What breed is she?"

"My Angel is a Pekingese," the lady gushed.

"The guard dog of the small breed, but so affectionate too."

Dylan scrunched her face. How did he know all this?

"Yes. Angel really is my guardian angel."

"That's sweet." She could hear the smile in Captain Jim's voice. "Are you ready for the number to Gail's? It's—"

"Hold on. I'm not ready." There was a shuffling of papers and words. "I just moved into this place, and there's stuff all over. Let me get a pencil."

"Take your time."

She couldn't believe it; Captain Jim never stopped working when he was in the store. Even when he had extra time, he filled it by helping crew members stock shelves or ring up customers. Now he was technically taking a break, but it was to metaphorically help someone cross the street so she could get her dog groomed.

"Now I'm ready," the lady said.

"Great. The number is area code 630 . . ."

"You said 630?"

"Yes. Then 5—"

"Hold on," she interrupted.

"Should I start over?"

"I think I got it. Keep going, young man."

Captain Jim spelled out the entire number.

During another long pause, Dylan realized she was holding her breath, hoping to heaven Angel would actually get groomed.

"I think I have it" came the declaration through the speaker phone, but when she repeated the number she'd written down, it was one digit off.

"So close, but that's not it. Let's try again," Captain Jim said in no hurry at all.

"Oh boy, I got it wrong. My Angel needs to be groomed."

"It's okay. Let's start over."

It took three more tries and two more false starts, but Angel's owner finally repeated the number correctly.

"Yes, you got it," Captain Jim said like she'd solved the puzzle.

Dylan felt the urge to clap like an audience member.

"Thank you so much. My Angel needs to be groomed."

"Thank *you* for taking such good care of her. I hope you get connect—"

A dial tone cut him off.

"Goodbye, then," he said to nobody.

*Nobody except me.*

"What are you smiling about?" Teresa said behind her.

She stood up straight and took a sip from her brimming cup of water. "Nothing. Just getting a drink."

Teresa looked back and forth between her and the door, then

walked past her to peek inside the break room. "Oh, I see. You're thinking about how Captain Jim has the hots for you and everyone around here knows it."

Dylan covered her pink cheeks. "Shh. He'll hear you."

Teresa folded her arms. "You mean, he'll hear me say, 'He thinks you're gorgeous and he wants to date you'?"

She fiddled with her cup of water. Nearly every shift, Teresa presented pieces of evidence Captain Jim was into her. Two years ago, when he was first hired, Dylan might've believed her.

He worked evenings then, overlapping with Dylan for only one hour at the end of her shift. They'd acknowledge each other, say polite hellos, but she was even less inclined to talk to people at the end of her day.

Then, on the Thursday two weeks before Thanksgiving, when turkeys arrived in-store, she ran into Jim. Literally ran into him. She'd been tidying the canned vegetable and pasta aisle while answering a rush-hour slew of customers' questions when she glanced backward at the wrong time and plowed into him. He'd been holding an armful of pasta bags until they spilled all over the floor.

"I'm so sorry, Jim," she apologized, horrified that she'd almost knocked him over, too, and bent down to help pick up. "I wasn't looking where I was going."

Captain Garrett was standing at the end of the aisle and saw the whole thing. "We don't have time for this, Turner," he barked. "Pick up your mess. And then check the box before you go."

Captain Jim looked from Captain Garrett back to her, then picked up one of the bags of penne that had fallen to the ground. "You should be sorry, Dylan," he whispered. "That was pre-*pasta*-rous."

She wondered what planet this man making puns about pasta came from.

"Turner?" Captain Garrett yelled again before she could respond.

She gritted her teeth and tossed the bags of pasta onto the shelf. "The box. Got it."

Without glancing back at Jim, she followed orders and left him to finish picking up her mess while she picked up other peoples'. There wasn't much to tidy in "the box," the frigid dairy section of the store that froze her last nerve—a lot of it had been picked over and the next delivery truck wasn't due for another hour, but she pretended to tidy a few gallons of milk and cartons of yogurt anyway.

"*Penne* for your thoughts?"

She turned around to find Jim grinning at her.

Without Captain Garrett breathing down her neck, she had more brain waves to respond. She folded her arms and shook her head. "I hate to say this, but I understand your corny puns better than when Trip called our uniform shirts *cheugy*."

Jim pulled a can of whole kernel corn out from behind his back. "Did someone say corny—"

"Stop it." She pointed at the can and laughed.

He held the can up in surrender. "I agree; that was too far. Also, yes. I love my co-workers, *and* some of them make me feel ancient."

"Like a boomer?"

"*Periodt.*" He looked at his feet, like he was trying to think of what to say next. He took a step closer and lowered his voice. "I came over here because I wanted to say, sorry not sorry for standing in your way back there."

She tilted her head. "Not sorry?"

Jim tossed the can in the air and caught it, coming close to bumping into a customer trying to sneak past him. "It's nice to get more than a hello from you."

Heat flushed her cheeks. "It's not personal. It's . . . well . . . some days I wish working for Captain Garrett was no longer part of my daily *rout-ini*."

Jim stared at her for a moment. Then he laughed, and the sound was like dusk glowing through the hawthorn trees in the forest preserve. Calming. Joyful. Good. She wanted to stay there, soaking up the view.

"R-*amen* to that," he said finally.

And that became their thing.

They crossed paths and said some horrific pun, depending on what product they were holding at the time.

"I walked right *pasta* and didn't even notice."

"You're *bacon* me crazy."

"I *pita* the fool."

What used to be the hardest hour of her shift—the last hour—became her favorite. She started to wonder about him outside work. He was studying for his bachelor's most mornings, which she made sure to check in on. But it didn't matter. Shortly after New Year's, an announcement was tacked onto the wall in the break room: *Reminder: Crew members may date other crew members. Mates/captains may not date crew members.*

Under that announcement was another: *Congratulations to our newest mate: Jim Jacobson!*

Whatever butterflies she'd had in her stomach for the past few months were squashed. She couldn't lose her job or risk Jim losing his either. When she saw him during her shift, she waved but didn't linger in his aisle. She smiled but didn't work as hard to cross paths. He was now doing all his usual work plus training new crew, so she wouldn't make his work harder or busier than it already was. They were adults with rules to follow and jobs to keep and bills to pay.

She had stuff to do anyway, like running and watching reality TV and eventually getting the guinea pigs.

It had been two years since a single food pun passed between them. One year since Captain Garrett's retirement and Jim's second big promotion to take his place. As a sharp reminder to keep things professional, she'd changed his name in her phone to Captain Jim.

They were associates, and always would be, so Dylan didn't know why Teresa thought he might be into her.

"I don't get why you're so hesitant." Her co-worker shrugged.

"Sure, there's rules about dating or whatever, but he's, like, a nice dark-haired Ken doll. Who wouldn't want to date that? Besides all the beige flags, of course."

Dylan rubbed her temples. "Beige flags?"

Teresa lowered her voice. "Let me put it this way. Jimbo doesn't have a bunch of red flags, just a few things about him that are . . . unique. Not deal-breakers, but not necessarily green flags either. For example, the way his phone is on speaker all the time, no matter what—beige flag. He's loud about how much he loves Excel spreadsheets—beige flag."

Teresa wasn't wrong about the phone and spreadsheets thing, but the way Captain Jim had handled that boozy customer earlier didn't seem beige to Dylan, even if he had ruined her chance to drop-kick someone.

Teresa pinched Dylan's cheek like she was her pudgy little baby. "You're kind of a beige flag yourself, though, so maybe that makes the two of you perfect for each other."

"What's that supposed to mean?"

Her co-worker pulled a granola bar out of her pocket and took a bite.

"Whenever I ask if you have any plans after work, you shrug and say you're going for a run," she said mid-chew. "You've either been living the same boring routine for, like, *ever*, or you live a deliciously wild existence you keep secret from the rest of us."

Why did all the Taras and Teresas of the world suddenly have opinions about her life? She wondered if Teresa would think going to Jacksonville on a whim was a beige flag.

"Enjoying my granola bar, by the way?" She eyed the snack she'd packed for herself that Teresa must have snagged from the fridge again. Secretly, she didn't mind. If Teresa kept making work fun, she was happy to provide the granola bars.

"I liked last week's flavor better." Teresa took another bite. "Anyway, back to Happy Cappy Jim. Maybe you two could add a little spice to each other's lives. A safe degree of spiciness, of course. Maybe even a beige spiciness."

She knew Teresa was teasing her, but it pricked at her growing insecurities. She could go on a tangent about how the color beige had weathered hundreds of paint trends, while somehow always making it back onto America's kitchen and bedroom walls. It was reliable. Consistent.

Teresa put her hand on Dylan's shoulder. "Hey, don't worry. Even a habanero pepper needs a glass of milk every once in a while." She squeezed harder, and her face brightened like a lightbulb. "You know what I could do to help? I could invite you both to my wedding, *without* a plus one, and seat you next to each other."

"How big of a wedding is this going to be?" Dylan sidestepped Teresa's comment, hoping to shut down more talk about Captain Jim and pity invites.

"I don't know. Huge?" Teresa grinned. She made it no secret her fiancé and his family were well off. Her first gift from them had been a Mustang Mach-E. "August's family wants a big party, and even though I know it will probably be over the top, I'm okay with that. How often do you put all your *and* your man's favorite people—your 'dearly beloveds' or whatever the ordained guy says—in the same room? Not often. Pretty much just weddings and funerals."

Dylan's mind flashed to her dad's funeral. Reverend Schwartz had begun the service with "Dearly beloved," but he'd said it to an almost-empty sanctuary.

"That does sound . . . nice. And you think that list includes the people you steal snacks from every day?"

Her co-worker finished the granola bar and threw the crumpled wrapper into the garbage inside the break room door. "Of course. I don't know what I'll do without you once I get married and start my bougie life as a stay-at-home wife."

"Maybe your husband will feed you. Or, maybe he'll fill another new car with your favorite flavored granola bars."

"He might. He's the best," she swooned, then turned back toward the store. "Well, I better get back to it. We're almost out of pumpkin spice loaf, so the entire population of Midwestern women are about to riot—"

"Teresa?"

Her co-worker stopped. "What's up?"

This was the part when a *friend* friend—not just a co-worker—would explain she was leaving for a different state tomorrow. Or say that yesterday she'd been at her dad's funeral. Or add a comment that she really appreciated Teresa checking in on her and even thinking about inviting her to one of the most important days of her life.

"Thank you . . ." Her mind went blank and her cheeks burned. "I'll see you soon."

Teresa tilted her head. "Yeah. Sounds good."

She watched her co-worker leave, berating herself for acting so dumb. The worst part was, she couldn't crawl into a hole. She still had to tell Captain Jim about her trip. This time, she wouldn't overthink it, though. She'd put words into sentences that made sense.

Captain Jim was still sitting at a table in the break room, probably working on something related to store operations. She walked up to him, and when he saw her, he straightened in his chair.

"Dylan. Hello." He sounded far less confident than when he was talking on the phone about dog groomers. He folded his hands in his lap, then brought them back up to close the cover of his tablet. "Are you okay?"

"I'm going to Jacksonville tomorrow."

That was way too clear. She braced herself for pushback. A low score on her next review. Maybe even a pink slip.

Captain Jim's eyes widened. "That's funny. So am I."

# 11

## Packs a Punch

Dylan darted around her apartment like her flight was leaving in fifteen minutes, not fifteen hours.

Her scattered brain couldn't focus on one task. First it sent her packing everything she'd need for the trip. Then it distracted her with the worry she'd have to leave Gale and Peeta behind again. She was about to call Tara to beg for Tate's pet-sitting services when she caught sight of her computer. The other thing on her to-do list was to message one Ms. Kathleen Schulz. Long-lost blood relative or kin. Or something.

She glanced at the clock.

Even if she got everything done in the next hour, that didn't leave much time before bed to overthink what Captain Jim had said to her in the break room: "I'm on the same flight tomorrow, but you're going on personal business, so please don't feel like you have to treat me like a boss, if that doesn't sound too creepy. Did that come across super creepy? I'm sorry. I just don't want me being there to make it weird for you."

His bumbling made him less Disney character and more human.

"Yeah, sure," she replied, forgetting to clarify if she meant *yes, that sounds super creepy* or *yes, I'll try not to be 100 percent more nervous about this*.

The good part was that he hadn't made a fuss about her asking for more time off, though he had looked concerned.

Dylan opened the only suitcase she owned—carry-on sized—and folded one outfit into it. It was oddly satisfying to complete a micro assignment on her list, but it immediately triggered another one: laundry. She picked up all the clothes she'd left scattered around her apartment, including the crumpled pile from the duffel bag she'd taken to her parents' house. The beep of the washing machine reminded her of something else she hadn't thought enough about: the weather.

She pinched the bridge of her nose. She'd have to look up the weather in Jacksonville and pack accordingly. Minus her favorite bras and underwear, the clothes swishing around in the washer might not even be useful in the sweltering southern heat.

She ricocheted around her apartment some more.

A bag of toiletries.

Her purse—ID and sunglasses included.

Her *Record of Rage*.

She set it all next to her suitcase so she wouldn't forget anything in the early morning, sent a quick text to Tara apologizing and also begging Tate to watch the guineas again, and then closed her eyes. Everything around her stood still except her thoughts, which were a tornado of dirty laundry, Captain Jim's nice face, and the name K-A-T-H-L-E-E-N.

She pulled a chair from the kitchen table, sat down, and opened her laptop. She wasn't ready to face KindreDNA, so she started with a search.

> **Google:** how to tell someone they're your biological family without giving them a heart attack and furthermore being convicted of involuntary manslaughter

She deleted most of it and instead searched "how to contact bio family after genealogy test."

She clicked on the first video, not only because of the title, "Important Reminders Before Reaching Out to Your Bio Family *TW: NPE/Adoption.*" She was starting to like watching research more than reading it. It was like someone sitting next to her, explaining all the sensitive content, rather than having to figure out all by herself a mess she wasn't responsible for making. With her mind as foggy as it was, even reading was hard.

She pressed Play.

The woman in the video leaned her head to the side and nodded while she talked. Dylan welcomed the patronizing smile like it was a grandmother's warm hug.

> I'm Dr. Juniper Ray from Decoding Your DNA. If you took an at-home DNA test in hopes of connecting with biological family members, there are a few things you may want to consider. First, there is no guarantee that if you send them a message, you'll hear back. It's possible the person you're hoping to connect with did a test just for fun and will never log into the website again. Second—

She hit Pause.

Was the woman implying she should message Kathleen outside the KindreDNA system, or was she saying Dylan should give her time to reply and try other methods later? What was the line between burning curiosity and stalking?

She pressed Play.

> Just because they are your DNA match, they may not know how to help you figure out who your immediate family members are. They might not have fleshed out their family tree or not have interest in doing so—

*Pause.*

She didn't appreciate the way Dr. Ray was saying her fears out loud. She rubbed her forehead and thought back to Kathleen's family tree. It was small—only one generation before and after her. Thirteen people out of the billions currently inhabiting the planet. *Play.*

> This brings me to the most sensitive point I want to share with you today, which is, if you were adopted or are experiencing a nonpaternity event, your DNA matches might not know about your birth. Due to a variety of difficult circumstances, your birth might be a secret or your biological family members may want to remain anonymous. Which means, you may need to prepare yourself for the possibility your DNA matches do not want to connect.

Her heart filled with a dark steam of humiliation.

Her biological family might not want to know she was born. What was she thinking, flying all the way across the country, looking for people who might not be interested in even talking to her?

Tate's comment about his mom raided her thoughts: *"She's wondering if that's because you're lonely or just weird."*

There was Teresa's beige flag comment too. Would her bio family think it beige that, every Thursday, she ordered the same greasy burger and five-pound bag of fries from Five Guys and watched reality TV? She was fine with her modest position in the world. She minded her own business, kept her hands busy, managed to keep most of her anger suppressed. Sure, she was lonely at times, but there was also safety in that loneliness. She knew the sting of letting people in.

She leaned back in her dining room chair. It would really help if her mom would open up. Then she wouldn't have to go all the way to Jacksonville and make a fool of herself. At least, not so quickly after finding out she had a different biological father. Her mom claimed the truth was too painful, but knowing where she came from had to outweigh that pain.

She'd try calling her mom one more time before messaging Kathleen.

The contact card in her phone for *Mom* had a thumbnail image of Candis smiling at baby Dylan, who was wearing a summer bonnet. The photo could fit in with the stack she found in her memory box earlier. She pressed the icon and waited, but it went straight to voicemail. Dylan stared at the screen while her mother's voice came through the internal speaker.

> Hello, this is Candis Turner. I can't come to the phone right now, but if you . . .

Dylan hung up and tried again. It went to voicemail again. Did her mom turn off her phone?

Call. Voicemail.

Call. Voicemail.

The definition of insanity.

She slammed her phone onto the table, then gasped. She had to have shattered it. Flipping it back over, she was relieved to find only one diagonal crack cutting across the otherwise-functioning screen. She could handle this kind of low-stakes damage better than she could take on another errand right now.

Her second question came to mind: *Why didn't my mom tell me?*

On the one hand, it didn't surprise her at all that her mom had kept this private. Her mom was always subdued. She lived inside her own head more than with Dylan. But this information belonged to *her*, not just to her mom.

If her fourth question was *Who am I?* the answer she wanted to scream was *I'm angry.*

She set her phone down again, gentler this time, and folded her arms onto the table so she could lay her head on them. Kathleen Schulz didn't seem as scary anymore. She was a complete stranger who might not want to get to know her, not the mom who did know her and had lied to her. Whatever Kathleen threw at her would be child's play.

She reopened her computer and opened a tab to her KindreDNA profile. The messaging app loaded an empty box for her to fill.

> Hello, Kathleen. My name is Dylan Turner, and it looks like we are a "cousin" DNA match. I would like to learn exactly how we are related and find out if there is a connection between you and my biological father. I'm going to be in downtown Jacksonville for the next few days, staying at the Hyatt Regency. If you're in the area and are willing to talk or meet up, please let me know.

The washing machine beeped, so she switched the damp clothes to the dryer. Feeling wrung out herself, she decided she'd finish packing in the morning and try to get some sleep, no matter how tortured it was.

In bed, her eyelids wavered, and the first picture that came to mind was of her holding her dad's hand, just before the end. He wasn't awake, thanks to the pain medications helping him die in peace. The stillness had allowed her to sit near him, to take in his physical features one last time before they became memory. It was all so different from the dad she knew—the one who was always on the move, craving adventure.

After their particularly hard move to Boston, he'd dragged her out of their house full of packed boxes downtown to the Isabella Stewart Gardner Museum. "Isabella Stewart Gardner was called one of the 'seven wonders of Boston.' A titan of acquiring precious art." He bounded through the museum, from a Rembrandt painting, to a first edition of Kipling's *The Jungle Book,* to an Italian lace border made in 1575. Perhaps the empty frames fascinated him most. "They were left up to honor the thirteen pieces of art stolen in 1990, the single largest property theft in the world. Thirteen, just like you'll be soon." His eyes twinkled so intensely, she wondered if he was soaking up their museum adventure or conquering it.

At his deathbed, his movement finally rolled to a stop. No warm handshakes with a new client or giggly tickle tortures like when she was a little girl. No pacing while he brainstormed his next investment proposal over the phone.

Not even one last charming smile—the cancer took that away too.

Dylan pulled her comforter up to her chin.

*I miss you,* she thought, drifting into a hard sleep.

## 12

# Have a Nice Flight

### Wednesday, September 24

There's a quote that says, "Some nightmares don't end when we open our eyes." The next morning, Brenda the Buick took that to heart.

Dylan turned the key over and over, but the battery only clicked.

"No. Please. Not now."

She turned it one more time, and from somewhere under the hood she heard a long hiss.

"No, no, no."

She dropped her head onto the steering wheel. The horn honked, scaring her upright. She looked around to see if she'd stirred the quiet neighborhood. The coast was clear, so she let herself groan. Paying for needs like a car was so much less fun than paying for wants, like full-access memberships and last-minute flights.

She had to think, had to fix this. Had to get to the airport faster than an Uber could get here.

An idea came to mind, but she hesitated. *Anything but that.*

She was out of options, though, and the clock was ticking, so she searched her contacts.

Captain Jim picked up on the first ring. "Good morning. This is your captain speaking."

*Good morning. This is a mistake.* She wasn't able to match his level of chipper.

"Hey, Captain Jim. It's Dylan. I'm really sorry for asking this, but my car won't start, so I'm wondering if there's any chance you could pick me up and I could ride with you to the airport?"

"Of course." No pause, no hesitation. "Text me your address, and I'll be right over. Sorry about your car, by the way," he said, sounding sincere.

While she waited for him to arrive, she arranged a tow truck to get her car and tucked her keys under the car mat—another reason she liked living in Naperville. She was 85 percent certain she could leave her car unlocked and it wouldn't go anywhere. Not that she ever left it unlocked; she just liked that she could *if* she wanted to.

Soon Captain Jim pulled up in the same Highlander he drove to work every day and parked next to Brenda. He jumped out and grabbed Dylan's suitcase from her hand, then loaded it in the trunk next to his.

"Hey," he said when they were both inside his car.

"Hi." She smiled, hoping it didn't come across nervous or irritated but perfectly within the bounds of their functional relationship as co-workers. She didn't want to start out their thirty-five-minute drive to O'Hare by "making this weird," to steal his phrase from yesterday.

"I almost didn't recognize you." Captain Jim nodded in her direction.

"Because I'm not wearing red? Where's your aloha shirt and set of ship's bells?"

He pointed at the trunk. "Packed in my carry-on, obviously."

She turned to put her purse in the back seat and was surprised to find two car seats littered with crumbs. She had questions, but she clamped her mouth shut. If she didn't want her own private life probed, she shouldn't probe his either.

"Tell me more about your fancy meeting or whatever it's called."

He put a hand to his chest. "The Annual Captains' Meeting. Hasn't everyone heard of this?"

"Not us mere mortals." *Did that sound too comfortable?*

He grinned. "Allow me to educate you, then. Every year, all the Trader Joe's managers gather in one place—corporate chooses a new city each time. We reflect on all the cool stuff that happened in our stores over the past year, and then we get to hear what's coming and how we'll chart our course moving forward. There are usually a few big announcements and celebrations. It's fun being in a room full of people who get excited about the same things."

"Like, for example, the best way to organize the canned vegetables and pasta aisle?" It would be too easy to add, *Nothing's im*-pasta-*ble*.

"Oh, I could ramble for at least twelve minutes about it. And draw a few diagrams."

It was no wonder he set a national record for how quickly he rose through Trader Joe's ranks from crew to mate to captain.

"We have time," she pointed out. "What *is* the correct way to organize the canned vegetable and pasta aisle?"

"At 5:45 A.M.? It's a little early for that. Let's talk about the innovation of our open-door freezer aisle instead."

She was about to say, "A true masterpiece," but was interrupted by a loud, twangy line from Reba McEntire's "My Sister." Another ringtone. He answered his phone like he always did, cheery and on speaker.

"Sister-friend Leslie."

"How are you this awake at such an ungodly hour?" came the groggy reply.

Dylan liked her already.

"Why do you get out of bed before the hour is godly enough for you?"

"Your nephews thought I wanted breakfast in bed. At 5:30 A.M. And, guess what breakfast was? A bowl of Cheerios and milk they spilled on my face."

Nephews. Maybe that was who the car seats were for.

"It's the thought that counts," he answered.

"Hearts of gold, poor timing and execution. Kind of like their Uncle James."

James. His sister just called him James. Dylan hadn't expected her to call him Captain Jim or anything, but James came out of nowhere.

Captain Jim shot her a look, like he'd been caught.

"It took me thirty-five years to learn to not say nice things to you before 8:00 A.M. Your boys will learn eventually."

"Yeah, yeah."

"Hey, Leslie, I wish I could take them for our weekly uncle time, but I have that thing in Jacksonville this weekend. I'm headed to the airport right now."

"I remembered. I just wanted to get in touch before you're all busy and important to say I'm rooting for you. You better call me the second the banquet is done."

He stared straight ahead. "Message received. Thank you, and please say hello to the coolest little boys in the world for me."

"Love you millions."

"Love you gazillions."

Captain Jim tucked his phone away and glanced at Dylan. It was hard not to stare at him after this juicy revelation.

"Can I . . . share something personal with you?" he asked.

She fiddled with an invisible hangnail. "Sure. That sounds great. Yeah."

"My name isn't Jim. It's James."

"What?" As if she hadn't overheard his entire conversation.

"On the day I transferred to Store 796, Captain Garrett introduced me as Jim. Maybe he misread my file or misheard me—I don't know—but I was too nervous to correct him. Around my friends and family, I've always been James. At work, I'm Jim. Captain Jim, I guess. It's kind of embarrassing to admit after all this time."

What was happening?

She sneaked a glance at him, which felt like looking at a whole new person, like Captain Jim had just gotten a "glow-up," as Olivia called it, and transformed into *James*. For one, the name made him seem closer to his age, unlike *Jim,* whose popularity had to have peaked last in the 1950s. And he didn't need it—he already had a nice face—but to her *James* just sounded . . . hotter?

Now she was biting her invisible hangnail. "I admit, this is like meeting you for the first time."

"A little different than Geriatric Jim, I hope. Though I give the crew credit for how clever they are with nicknames. People are so creative."

"Captain James," she marveled, which earned her another sweet smile.

"Just James, please. Outside of work, I like when people know that about me."

By the time they arrived at the airport, went through security, waited in the terminal, and waited again in line with their boarding groups, he'd asked her four times to call him James and not Captain Jim. She was starting to believe him, but it was still a big leap, as her heartbeat tried to remind her by going into overdrive. She was traveling hours and hours from home with *James*. She took deep breaths, deciding she'd compromise with her worry by not calling him by any name for now.

James buckled himself into the seat next to her, and she wondered if it was a beige flag to buckle before the flight attendant gave the safety demonstration. She checked her phone—no new messages from her mom or Kathleen—then put it on airplane mode. Thankfully, the crack on the screen hadn't grown overnight.

"Do you know any of the other captains who will be at the Captains' Meeting?" she asked, tucking her phone away.

James nodded. "My favorites are from Stores 433 and 101."

"Is that how you all talk to each other? 'Hello, my name is Store 796.'"

"The more cultish it sounds, the better."

She shrugged. "At least your cult has good snacks."

"It's what unites us, actually."

"The snacks?"

"And the aloha shirts. See? Now you're getting it. Maybe you should join our secret society, Captain Dylan."

"I'm not nice enough." The words left her mouth before she could stop them.

James seemed surprised too.

"What I mean is, I can't imagine a room full of nicer people than the annual Trader Joe's Captains' Meeting. Minus a few outliers," she added, referring to Captain Garrett.

"Come on. We're the roughest, toughest, baddest crew in town."

She wrinkled her nose. "Teresa heard of a store where the captain declared it 'Life Is a Musical Day.' All the crew were expected to sing their thoughts to each other."

"Like I said. The baddest."

She caught another glimpse of his dimple.

The flight attendant's voice came over the loudspeaker and asked all passengers to stow their trays and computers for takeoff. Soon their flight took off and ascended high above Chicago. From her aisle seat, she tried to catch a glimpse of Lake Michigan and the city's stunning skyline. It was official. She was on an airplane, in the sky, heading one thousand miles toward her past.

Her message to Kathleen came to mind. Was it too much information? Too vague? She would get an email notification if Kathleen messaged her back on KindreDNA, but that wouldn't stop her from checking her phone every quarter hour after the plane landed.

Thankfully, she had a good distraction sitting next to her—the distraction who'd given up his window seat a few rows ahead to sit in the middle seat next to her. Earlier that morning, she'd decided her strategy was to keep James talking so she wouldn't have to. Now that she was sitting on the plane next to him, she was having a pleasant flight, which is exactly what the pilot had told everyone to do earlier.

Two flight attendants pulled a beverage cart into the aisle at the front of the plane. James fiddled with his entertainment screen to access the page tracking their trip's progress, while she tried not to think about how much distance she was putting between herself and her home.

"As much as I love talking about Trader Joe's, my fellow captains, and how to display vegetables, I'd love to learn more about you and your trip."

The air was thicker all of a sudden, and she had a hard time swallowing it. Talking about her reasons for going to Jacksonville might bring up emotions she didn't feel like putting on public display. "I like listening to you talk about how much you love your job. Don't get me wrong—I appreciate getting to work at Store 796, but I wouldn't say I'm passionate about it."

So much for not sharing personal thoughts. About her job. To her boss of all people.

He put a pretend dagger to his heart and twisted it. "Are you telling me working retail isn't your life's passion?"

"I don't think I've ever been excited about something enough to make it my day job. And then to fly across the country to talk about it with other people who love it as their day job."

James seemed unbothered. "Most people don't get to overlap their work with their passions. What do you like? What do you do for the fun of it?"

The beverage cart was inching closer to their seats, but it was still too far away to interrupt them.

Why was stuff like this so hard to answer? She could talk about how she ran at least five miles every day, but running wasn't exactly fun as much as it was a way to blow off steam. There were Gale and Peeta—pets always made for interesting conversation. She could say why she'd picked Naperville to live in, but that might be a weird answer.

"Five Guys?" She thought out loud.

James's face was so blank it looked like he'd glitched. "Excuse me?"

She didn't know how to save herself from her lame answer. "Five Guys," she repeated. "The restaurant."

"Oh. Five Guys, the *restaurant*."

"What did you think?" She grabbed his arm set comfortably on the armrest between them. "You thought I was saying I liked five different men?"

They both looked down at where their bodies were touching.

She pulled her hand away and tried to find something else to look at while her burning cheeks cooled. One glance at James told her he was blushing too.

He cleared his throat. "I realize now how ridiculous it sounds. It took me a second to understand what you were saying."

She had to make this less awkward. "I love their burgers and fries, so I eat there every Thursday. For fun. That's a dumb answer to your question, but it's a happy part of my routine."

"You only get takeout from Five Guys? You never mix it up?"

"I struggle with change." She hoped he would dismiss that as sarcasm rather than an invite to dig deeper.

"Not even other Chicago favorites, like Lou Malnati's or Giordano's?" James's hands were getting animated. "Not even Portillo's?"

"Only Five Guys."

"You're telling me you've never had a classic Italian beef sandwich from Portillo's followed by a chocolate cake shake."

"What's a cake shake?"

He put his palms together like he was saying grace, then pointed them at her. "It is literally a chocolate shake with an entire piece of chocolate cake blended into it. It is a slice of heaven mixed into a colder, creamier dollop of heaven, poured into a cup for people here on earth to enjoy. For the fun of it."

The young man in the window seat wearing headphones glanced over at them. James and his lively description of chocolate and cake and ice cream had become the in-flight entertainment.

"Not gonna lie—that sounds pretty amazing," she admitted, "but no, I've never had one."

James shook his head. "That's it. When we get back to Illinois, we are going to Portillo's and eating chocolate cake shakes together. It *will* change your life, but I promise the change will be for the better."

She warmed at the invitation, kind of like she had at Teresa's wedding invitation. Sort of. That one might still be a pity invite. Either way, invitations were nice. "I'm getting the sense you'd rather manage a Portillo's than Trader Joe's Store 796. Should I be concerned?"

"I'm not abandoning ship." He gave her a second to roll her eyes. "I'm just one of those people who knows art when I see it, and the chocolate cake shake is definitely a work of art."

She almost touched his arm again. "I didn't realize I was in the presence of such a connoisseur."

The flight attendants pulled up with their trolley, reminding her to practice restraint. She pulled her hand away and opened her tray table.

"Would you like a beverage?" the attendant asked. "Water, coffee, juice, or something else?"

They both chose water, which they sipped and set on their trays.

Next to her, James shifted in his seat. "Is it okay if I ask why you're going to Jacksonville? Or is that too personal?"

She tucked a piece of loose hair behind her ear, trying to find a way to keep the story short and vague. "I'm on a bit of a mission. For my dad."

"Interesting."

He didn't pry further, and she didn't know why a spark inside her wanted him to. She hated this tension between wanting to open up and wanting to protect all that was vulnerable.

"I actually lived in Jacksonville before. Twice," she added, liking the way he perked up at her sharing this detail about herself.

"Yeah?"

"The first time was from when I was born until I was eight. Technically, we lived in a suburb about thirty-five minutes outside Jacksonville. It was the longest I lived somewhere before moving around a lot and then settling in Naperville."

"And the second time?"

"A little closer to downtown, but that time it was less than a year. Not enough time to really get to know the area. This trip is kind of a surprise birthday gift to myself to see . . . where my life started. I promise it's the last birthday thing on my schedule."

James eyed her. "Your family sure goes all out for birthdays, even digging into your origin story. Are you sure birthdays aren't your passion?"

She smirked, then leaned over to glance out the window. Whichever state they were currently flying over was mostly sunny—only small puffs of clouds dotting the sky.

James pulled out his phone and searched his apps until he found a drafted email. "This is a little silly now that I know you lived in Jacksonville and that you're here on a mission, but last night I put together a list of places considered Jacksonville highlights. Kind of like a belated birthday gift."

"For me? James, that's—" She stopped, realizing she'd finally called him by his real name and she liked the way it felt on her lips. "That's really sweet, thank you." An understatement in her opinion. "What did the internet recommend?"

"Are you sure? I don't need to mansplain Jacksonville to you."

"I bet it's changed a lot since I lived there. Besides, I want Captain Jim to make sure I have a 'wow' customer experience while I'm there."

He laughed. "First of all, they have an awesome zoo. And, if you're a member of the Brookfield Zoo by us, you get half off admission."

"I do remember going to the zoo a couple times as a kid. But wait. You're a member of Brookfield Zoo?"

"My nephews love animals. Not as much as I do, which is why I have a membership, but that's my excuse."

"Of course you do. You love everything."

He blushed again, and she mentally kicked herself. It was making her uncomfortable how comfortable he made her.

"How do you feel about guinea pigs?" she asked. "I have two at home named Gale and Peeta."

"The South American cavy? They're fascinating."

"Thank you. That is the correct answer. What else is on your list?"

"The Cummer Museum is also near the Hyatt."

The name sounded familiar. Aunt Lou worked at a museum somewhere around the city high up in the ranks—chief curator or something.

"You can take yourself on a self-guided mural tour, including fifty different ones downtown. There's also the Catty Shack Ranch Wildlife Sanctuary."

"Is that like *Tiger King* but in real life?"

He laughed again, which felt like winning—a thought she tried shoving to the side.

James leaned in, his shoulder brushing against hers. "The coolest place that might be worth the cost of getting there is Little Talbot Island. We're coming to the end of migration season, when massive flocks of birds come through the area, thousands and thousands of them. One of the breeds to look out for is the red knot."

"I've heard of Little Talbot Island but have never been. I'd love to see the coast again, though."

"It's exciting to get to experience something for the first time, isn't it? Tourists get a bad rap, but I like seeing stuff with fresh eyes."

She crossed her arms. "Let me guess—you *love* being a tourist."

James grinned.

The rest of their nearly three-hour flight *flew by,* a stupid pun James was keen on that felt like a throwback to when they first met. The pilot came over the intercom to announce their descent into Jacksonville, and soon after they landed, gathering carry-ons and weaving through the airport to ground transportation, where they would go their separate ways.

Dylan opened her newly downloaded Uber app and typed, "JAX Airport to 331 16th Terrace."

James stood next to her. "What are the chances we booked the same flight *and* the same hotel over the same weekend?"

"I can't believe it either." It was like she couldn't get away. Maybe she didn't want to. "Is that where you're headed now?"

"Yeah. Most of the conference is at the hotel, so I'll be there most of the weekend."

"I'm going straight to my first meeting, but maybe I'll see you around the halls."

"Let me know if you're bored or . . . need anything."

"Like a restaurant recommendation?"

James put his carry-on in the back of his own Uber. "That reminds me of one last recommendation. I hear the riverwalk in front of the Hyatt is beautiful."

"I do love a beautiful view."

"Me too."

Was she paranoid, or was James looking at her when he said that? Her Uber arrived before she could overthink it any further.

"Want me to take your suitcase to the hotel?" James asked when she had one foot in the car. "I wouldn't want you traipsing all over town looking like a tourist."

She nodded. "I'd appreciate that."

The carry-on bumped along the sidewalk as she rolled it to him, mimicking the nerves in her gut. When James took it from her, his hand brushing hers, she swore her skin tingled.

He bit his lip. "See you later, Dylan."

"Bye, Capt—er, James."

She got into her Uber and exhaled. So much for keeping it together. He seemed to be adding to her unraveling. She was proud of herself, though, for making it this far—all the way to Jacksonville. It had required a leap she wasn't sure she could've taken even a year ago.

As the driver headed toward 16th Terrace, Dylan held her head high. Right up until she saw what was waiting for her there.

# 13

## Rub Some Dirt on It

"Are you sure this is the correct address?" Dylan asked as the Uber driver pulled up to the curb.

Behind them was a gorgeous high-rise piercing the sapphire sky; in front of them, another row of distinguished, towering buildings. But where the Uber parked at 331 16th Terrace, there was an open plot of land with a pile of dirt in the far-left corner.

The lot was so empty, except for said pile of dirt, she could see the Saint Johns River sparkling in the background.

The driver tapped a thumb on top of the steering wheel. "I'm sure."

Dylan swiped her phone open and typed in the address again. "But this shows a mixed-use building with restaurants and boutiques on bottom, apartments on top. Not"—she flung her hand toward the sparse landscape—"this pile of dirt."

"Interesting," the driver said, like her dilemma was anything but.

Dylan leaned forward and held out her phone, frantic for what she saw in the pictures to pop into her real-life view. "It's supposed to look like these photos."

The driver gave her screen a split-second glance. "Those are 3D plans of what is going to be built here."

She squinted at her phone. "What? No. They look so real. How is that even legal? I flew all this way—"

"Ma'am." The driver interrupted her spiraling. "Do you want to purchase another ride somewhere else, or do you want to get out?"

Dylan looked at the back of the driver's head. She was bent forward over her phone, probably scanning it for the riders who would be her next source of income. What would it feel like—for just a moment—to be that customer who blamed employees for something that wasn't their fault? She could throw a fit, yell some threat about leaving a bad review, go as far as to renounce the company and the entire state of Florida.

"I'll get out here. Thank you."

She got out and the car pulled away, leaving her alone on the sidewalk under a blinding morning sun. Now that summer had abandoned her back home, she appreciated the warmth. Late September in Chicago was sometimes sixty degrees, followed by an afternoon that soared into the seventies, which morphed into weeks of rainy forty-degree temps. Late September in Jacksonville blazed. According to the weather app, it was eighty-eight degrees outside. Her armpits were beginning to sting, but if she had to go a thousand miles on a wild-goose chase, she preferred this to somewhere frigid. The city of Hell, Norway, for example.

She looked around, trying to get her bearings so she could think straight. An empty bus stop on the corner was shaded by the highrise, and across the street there was a strip of storefronts—a bistro, attorney's office, and a nightclub. Parked vehicles and tall palm trees lined the curb currently peppered with only a handful of pedestrians, customers, and joggers.

Maybe the area would get busier around lunchtime.

She turned back to 16th Terrace. There was no excavating equipment or building materials, nothing fenced off. It was a blank slate. The strap of her purse slipped off her shoulder, so she pushed it back and started walking the perimeter. The bright side of the moment—sponsored by James—was that she didn't have to drag a rolling suitcase behind her. The downside was that she didn't know exactly what she should be looking for.

She needed a sign.

She put on her sunglasses and scanned the area again for some indication she was supposed to be at this exact address at this exact moment like she thought her dad wanted—some reminder she wasn't an idiot for coming all this way. Heck, she'd take a guy on the corner with a sign—THE END IS NEAR: PREPARE TO MEET THY GOD—if he had some sort of wisdom to offer.

"Please," she whispered at her feet, her forehead starting to bead. And then she saw it.

A sign.

A literal sign tucked behind the large pile of dirt. She walked faster so the words would come into focus.

*Coming Soon: Waterway Tower!* it advertised. There were names and photos and phone numbers. Bonus points: The sign wasn't weathered by sun or rain or time—it looked new.

The development was going to feature both income-based apartments and businesses approved by the building's residents. *Royal Cape Companies* was listed next to the phone number, its emblem a scripted *RCC* over top a blue flower.

A familiar blue flower. Where had she seen it before?

She dug into her purse and pulled out the torn envelope she'd taped back into one piece, still holding her birthday card. The flower on the sign and the flower sticker her dad had used to close the envelope were the same. A cluster of small yet vivid blue petals at the end of a gracefully arched branch.

Something about the flower was trying to spark a memory. She pulled out her journal, too, an awkward juggling act to hold everything and flip pages when she had only two hands. She could use a dedicated office with a giant corkboard, yarn, and thumbtacks—her own murder board. The envelope fell out of her hands, proving her point, so she stomped on it with one foot before it could run away with a gust of wind.

Skimming her journal, she didn't come across any writing about the flower. She came across something better. A photo, taped into one of the journal's earlier pages. It was of her and Brooke—she'd guess age six—with both their families, posed in front of a stucco, honeycomb-colored house, the only home she'd lived in that conjured a sense of nostalgia.

She'd pasted the picture into her journal shortly after she was told they were moving out of Jacksonville the first time. Her mom had pulled it off the fridge and was about to throw it in the trash, but Dylan had kept it for herself.

The Turners and the Westmores—all bunched together, happy after another Saturday night eating pizza.

Behind the group, bordering the front of the house, was what she was looking for. Bushes of blue flowers that matched the sticker as far as she could tell. She leaned down to pick up the envelope still wedged under her foot, then pulled out her phone and hovered it over the flower sticker, grateful to live in an era when she could scour the internet for more information.

**Google Lens:** *Royal Cape Plumbago. Nearly year-round, giant clusters of blue flowers are surrounded by evergreen foliage.*

Royal Cape Plumbago.

Royal Cape Companies.

Bingo.

It was strange her dad had used a sticker at all. He wasn't exactly into arts and crafts unless he was purchasing a new painting to hang above the mantel before one of his housewarming parties. "A conversation piece," he'd say to her and her mom, before spending half hours in front of it with guests.

If her dad had too little strength at the end of his life to write anything in her card, it was unlikely he had the strength to hunt down this exact sticker either.

She checked her surroundings again: the empty lot behind her, the sign before her, and the envelope in the hand hanging at her side. Coming all the way here to land at a pile of dirt was a wound, but maybe this sign was enough new information to follow up on. Maybe the flower on the sticker, photo, and sign was her next clue. Maybe her dad was trying to lead her to this property, which would then lead her to the company developing this property.

Maybe.

She pulled out her phone, and at the same time, a V of geese flew over her, honking their arrival. She wondered how far they'd traveled, if they were native to the area or were only here for winter, while also hoping they weren't an omen.

> **Google:** is royal cape companies the next stop on this wild goose chase

She deleted it and tried "Royal Cape Companies" instead, which told her it was an umbrella company for an investment firm, real estate brokerage, luxury design group, and construction management business, among other things.

Yes, Royal Cape Companies was her next breadcrumb.

The thought of breadcrumbs made her stomach growl. She needed food and soon, but ideally from a restaurant within walking distance that wasn't the dark-windowed bistro across the street.

Her phone dinged, and a text notification covered her screen.

> **Captain Jim:** Did you get to your meeting okay?

> **Me:** Minor hiccup but I'm grabbing lunch now.

**Me:** How are your fellow captains?

**Captain Jim:** ☹ about your meeting.

**Captain Jim:** This may surprise you, but everyone seems really excited to be here.

**Me:** A room full of Captain Jims? Excited?

**Me:** Since when did pigs fly?

**Me:** 😉

**Captain Jim:** Lol. Enjoy lunch!

**Captain Jim:** If you want, I can send you a link to Jacksonville's best restaurants???

**Me:** Are you sure your name isn't Tour Guide James?

**Captain Jim:** The Bread and Board Restaurant. Great lunch spot downtown according to one JAX TJ's captain.

**Me:** Thank you.

**Captain Jim:** Also, Five Guys would be an expensive Uber ride from where you are.

**Captain Jim:** ☹

**Me:** Thank you.

**Captain Jim:** I dare you to be a tourist and try something new!

**Me:** I said thank you, James.

**Captain Jim:** Thank YOU for calling me just James.

**Me:** You're welcome, Just James.

According to her map, the Bread and Board was a close walk from her pile of dirt and had great reviews. The menu had something on it called the Crispy Portobello Mushroom Arrabbiata, which sounded like a dish her mom would prepare for a Tuesday lunch.

She didn't need reminders of her mom right now, but maybe James was right. Being away from home was a chance to try something new.

Eleven minutes later, she'd walked the city blocks to the restaurant without any setbacks—a victory considering how her morning was going. The Bread and Board had ceiling-high windows, as well as nooks full of treats, trinkets, flowers, and candles for sale. Not only did it have a welcoming farmers' market vibe, but everyone who left the front counter was carrying large wooden boards piled with food. She was a sucker for generous portions.

She ordered at the register, then waited for her own sandwich bursting at the crusts. By the time she was the one walking away with her own large wooden board, the restaurant was getting noisier, and most of the empty chairs were by the windows, facing outside. Fine for her party of one. Her stomach growled again—this time with a rolling encore. She needed to devour her sandwich before her stomach devoured her. She sat down, took a hefty bite. It wasn't her usual, but the fried portobello mushrooms with spicy red pepper–tomato sauce were heavenly on her taste buds.

Her hunger calmed with each bite, freeing space for her to think about something other than food, like people watching. She looked out the windows in front of her at the pedestrians wearing everything from business suits to Jaguar jerseys. More were interested in checking their reflections than trying to look through, where she was scarfing bites of portobello.

Everyone, that is, except for one person who did a double take. She looked away so he could pass by without her staring at him, but when she glanced up, he was still there—he'd stopped walking. What was this guy doing? He backtracked, turning toward the window to face her straight on.

*Wait. Is that—*

He took off his sunglasses and smiled like the devil he was.

A hurricane of emotions coursed through her. Surprise mixed with shame, laced with resentment. She forced her body to sit completely still, an unnatural lack of motion considering the sudden flare-up of rage she could sprint five miles with.

She would do everything in her power to make him wait, to make him come to *her,* remembering a time when she'd waited—far longer than a day—for him to come back. She swallowed her food, slowly, then set down her sandwich, took a sip of her drink, wiped the corners of her mouth with a napkin—all without breaking eye contact as he watched from the other side of the glass.

For good measure, she crossed her arms, then stared at her past.

He shook his head and laughed. "All right, Turner," he mouthed before making his way into the restaurant and pulling out the chair right next to her.

She kept her arms crossed. "Hendrix Reed. How long has it been?"

She already knew the answer: fourteen years.

His eyes flickered. "Since you last hated me? Probably yesterday."

**Page 103**

## Silent Assassin

### (Sweetly 16)

I was paired up with Hendrix again. And told to apologize.

My instructor said this might be a self-defense class, but my actions technically made me "the assailant."

Hendrix showed up to class with a bruise on his face, but it was much bigger than anything he would've gotten from my accidental punch. I said sorry to Hendrix and I promise I meant it. I don't want to be the jerk. He took the apology but then teased me for going soft on him.

During class, we had to pretend to put each other in a choke hold so we could practice getting out of it. It's scary to think of this stuff actually happening in real life, but I also like how learning this stuff makes me feel strong.

Side note: It's weird standing so close to him.

When my arms were around his neck, he asked, "When you're done beating me up, do you want to go out for ice cream?"

His self-defense worked. I was so surprised I opened my arms and he fell on the ground. Instructor glared at me again and asked Hendrix if he was okay.

I texted my mom to ask if I could go, and she said yes and to enjoy. (Shocking, honestly. My dad was more upset about it than her, which was weird.)

We went out for ice cream and talked for a long time, including why we're taking self-defense classes. I told him my dad thought it was a good idea to be able to defend myself. My mom thought it would be a good way to blow off steam if I wasn't interested in trying any sports and/or exercise. She doesn't get that my high school is huge and we've never lived somewhere long enough for me to learn any sports, so there's no way I'd make a team at school.

After I blabbered on and on, I asked Hendrix. He said he was in self-defense because of his dad too, and then he got really quiet.

We talked for a long time. Hendrix dropped me off. I was twenty minutes late for my curfew.

I think I'm in trouble.

In more ways than one.

## Mon-yay, Wednes-yay, Fri-yay
### (16 yo)

Self-defense class is three days a week, M, W, F.

I think I like Hendrix.

I hate myself for saying that.

**Page 106**

## Record of Raging Hormones
### (Did I mention I'm 16?)

We've been spending every night after self-defense class together.

We went down by the river with a few packs of Hot Tamales. We took turns throwing them up in the air and trying to catch them in our mouths, but if we missed, we had to answer any question the other person wanted to ask.

He asked me about the favorite place I lived (here), and what I want to do when I grow up (don't know yet).

Every time he missed catching his candy, he moved a little closer before answering his question. When he was sitting only a few inches from me, I asked him why he picked Hot Tamales, and he said it's because he thinks I'm hot. But even more, he thinks I'm beautiful.

And then he leaned in the last few inches and kissed me. OH MYYYYYYYYYYYYYYY.

## 14

## Old Flame

Some people say passion sets the world on fire like that's a good thing. What they forget is fire burns. It burned like Hendrix Reed's striking hazel eyes staring into her after fourteen long years.

"If I order myself something to eat, will you still be here when I get back?" He interrupted her inner fuming.

"I'm not the one who's so good at disappearing."

She wanted to be an adult, for self-control to take the wheel, but right then she was okay being a work in progress.

He flinched. "I deserve that, so I'll ask again to make sure. May I join you?"

She softened, trying to ignore how good-looking he still was.

"Sure. You may join me."

It took a good fifteen minutes during the bustling lunch hour for him to order, but he came back holding his board of food looking as pleased as she had.

"The portions here are—"

"Baller," she finished for him, which earned her another devilish grin.

"You remembered."

"Of course I remember. Everything we were obsessed with as teenagers was 'baller.' Ice cream? Baller. The upper-cut back kick Instructor taught us in class? Also baller." Apparently, she could interpret some slang, as long as it was a generation old.

He smirked, then took a bite of his sandwich.

"So, Hendrix, tell me. Did you become someone who sniffs drugs like you wanted to so badly?"

His laugh disarmed her. She remembered it being easy to get under his skin.

"Sixteen-year-old Hendrix was something, wasn't he?"

Something all right.

"Not exactly," he answered. "I did a stint in the Marines. Then after I got out, I had a chance to apply for other federal operations, but I decided it wasn't for me. I do a little investigative work from time to time, but it's typically not with fugitives or hard criminals. Unless you're a fugitive or hardened criminal, Turner."

"Dylan," she corrected, wanting to distance herself from his nickname for her and everything it stirred up. "And, that's a little vague. What are you, a cop? What are you 'investigating' now?"

"I told you. *You*."

Her emotional calendar had no margin for extra nonsense.

When she didn't respond, he said, "Never mind, I guess that's not funny. The truth is I'm sort of between jobs, trying to figure out what's next."

That made sense to her.

"Enough about me, though." He leaned back in his chair. "Where do you live? You said when you grew up you were going to pick a town and never, ever leave. Did you pick Jacksonville and I just haven't run into you yet, or are you breaking your own promises?"

"I don't live here, but I'm . . . investigating a few things too."

"Looks like I'm not the only one whose answers are 'a little vague.'"

The smile she gave him reeked of insincerity. "I don't owe you anything."

He took a bite of his crispy Cajun fish. "Calm down, Turner. I—"

"*Dylan*. And not once in the history of the world has telling somebody to calm down actually calmed them down."

He licked rémoulade residue off two of his fingers, then wiped his hands with a napkin. "Okay, *Dylan*. It feels like we're getting off on the wrong foot with this happy little reunion. Can we please start over?"

"It feels like we started over, Hendrix, and do you want to know why? I couldn't stand you when we first met, and I can't stand you right now."

He finished his drink and set it on the table. "Nice line. Did you read that off an Instagram square this morning?"

"You've changed little." She pushed back her chair and stood up, which must've finally gotten his attention, because he grabbed her hand.

"Wait, Turn— Dylan. Dylan Turner. Please don't go. I'm sorry. I really am. Will you please forgive me?"

"For what, Hendrix Reed? Tell me exactly what I should forgive you for."

He swallowed. "Will you please forgive me for not meeting you at the bridge that night like we planned, never showing up to class again, and never calling you?"

She'd need a week in Norway to cool off completely. "That was good enough. For now."

"What more do you want from me?"

"Nothing." That was a lie. "Nothing right now."

He raised an eyebrow. "Does that mean you'll sit back down and answer my questions?"

"Is that a request or a demand?"

"When has Dylan Turner ever responded to a demand?" He patted her seat. "It's a request. I still want to know where you live."

She didn't want his pleading eyes to charm her into submission, but she sat down, reminding herself she didn't want to leave behind her last bite either.

"I live in Naperville, Illinois, a suburb about forty-five minutes outside of Chicago. It's been twelve years now." A spark of pride lit her face.

"Good for you, Dylan Turner."

"Am I going to be 'Dylan Turner' if I don't let you call me Turner?"

He shrugged. "Old habits die hard. So, what brings you to Jacksonville?"

She sighed. Carrying life's baggage all on her own was getting tiring. James asked why she was here, but he didn't know her dad like Hendrix did. She and Hendrix had history, and familiarity went a long way for her. Familiarity was comfortable.

She looked down, willing back the tears threatening to make a fool of her. "Actually, my dad passed away last week."

"Wow. I'm sorry. That must be hard."

"It is," she admitted out loud for the first time. "He had cancer. He and my mom just moved to Milwaukee, which is about two hours away from me. By the time he was diagnosed, it was too late for treatment and he died four months later."

Hendrix cleared his throat. "How is your mom doing?"

"My mom?" she scoffed. "Not great, but I wouldn't say that has anything to do with Dad dying. She's always been, I don't know, Candis Turner?"

The silence was heavy. Hendrix paused, like he wanted to wade through what she'd just said but was holding back. "What made you choose . . . What town did you say it was?"

"Naperville. I, um, searched online for places people like to live." She'd never admitted that out loud to anyone.

He frowned, wiping his hands with a napkin before tossing it onto his tray. "That's one way. What do you do? Where do you work?"

"Trader Joe's."

"The grocery store?"

She didn't like the hint of condescension. "Correct."

"So, you're here because your dad died and you're investigating something. And that something is what?"

She bit the inside of her cheek. Each question was getting more real, cutting through small talk and catching up to the heart of her turmoil. The question she needed to ask herself was how far she should let him in. It wasn't like her to open up to people; she hadn't since him, three cities ago—three *lifetimes* ago. They'd been teenagers then, their prefrontal cortexes not even fully developed. But he knew her and her parents. She could tell him what was going on, then worry later about how much she'd overshared.

"Right before my dad's funeral, I found out he's not my biological father."

He pursed his lips, the ones she remembered kissing all too well. "Hmm."

"Pro tip: The next time someone tells you that kind of news, at least pretend to be surprised."

"Is this better?" He widened his eyes until he looked like a cartoon. "Nothing surprises me anymore, but yeah, that's quite the bombshell and some pretty terrible timing. How did you find out?"

She fiddled with the scraps of food left on her bread board. "We did a KindreDNA test together so we could build our family tree. It was supposed to be a bonding activity, but he died before the results came in. And, well . . . I think my mom had an affair."

That was more than letting him in; that was admitting one of her deepest fears. It was all so out of character for her, this kind of vulnerability. Her skin felt like it was the wrong size, pulled too tight in some places and bulky in others.

"Hmm," he repeated.

"If you 'hmm' one more time, I swear I'm walking out of here."

"I think it's interesting that your first assumption is an affair."

"'Interesting' as in you think I'm right?"

"'Interesting' as in it could be one of many valid guesses about what happened at your conception."

"Don't use the word *conception*. It sounds weird."

"We're big kids now, Dylan. We can use the word *conception*."

"If it wasn't an affair, then why wouldn't she have told me sooner, Detective?"

For once he seemed to actually be thinking through what she'd said before responding. "People come up with all sorts of excuses for hiding the truth. I'm not saying they *should* hide the truth. I'm saying people don't have a hard time coming up with one or two reasons to."

She tugged at the collar of her shirt. "I can't think of a single good reason to hide this from me, not when my mind is the one being messed with."

"Messed with you enough to get you to travel all the way to Jacksonville, apparently."

The knot in her chest tightened. Sharing what happened last week was easier than trying to explain her current quest. "My dad left a note in my birthday card with what I think is a Jacksonville address. It's only a ten-minute walk away."

"From here?"

She nodded. "The only problem is, there's nothing there except a pile of dirt."

"You flew all the way to Jacksonville for a pile of dirt?"

His smile dug into her nerves. She took out her phone and pulled up one of the pictures. "No. *This* is what I flew all the way to Jacksonville for."

He took the phone and studied it. "Aren't those architectural drawings?"

"Ugh. Why am I the only one who didn't see that?"

"When's the last time you got your eyes checked? Do I need to make sure your Illinois driver's license is revoked?"

"Not helpful." She grabbed her phone back.

The crowd was dying down, which meant the lunch hour was almost over.

Hendrix checked his watch too. "Well, what if I make you an offer that *is* helpful? I don't have much going on the rest of the day, so I could keep you company. Be the Watson to your Holmes and all that. Although maybe I should be Holmes if all you've found so far is a pile of dirt?"

"For the record, I found some really great lunch too." All thanks to James.

"I'll give you that. A pile of dirt plus lunch."

His offer surprised her, though not as much as running into him again. A little help *did* sound nice. "I'm not sure us working together would go that well, as much as I appreciate the offer."

"What are you talking about, Turner comma Dylan? We're having a great time."

"*That* is what I'm talking about." Something in her gut said this was a terrible, confusing idea. She couldn't spend that much time with him again. She shouldn't. "Actually, I'd love your help, Hendrix. Thank you."

"Great." He looked around by her feet, then grimaced. "No luggage or laptop?"

"It's at the hotel with my friend, but I might not be able to get it from him for a while because he's at a conference."

"Friend, huh?"

She couldn't tell if the look he gave her was a question or an accusation.

"He's the manager of the store I work at," she explained, though it didn't feel like the whole story. "He's here for work."

Hendrix didn't nod or *hmm* this time. "The library is only five minutes from here. We could use their computers to research, and I wouldn't even have to move my car."

They gathered their empty sandwich boards and stood up to leave.

"What's his name?" Hendrix asked.

"Who?"

"Your 'friend'?" He even made air quotes with one hand.

"Oh, his name is James, but at work, everyone calls him Captain Jim."

"Your friend is a manager named Jim," he repeated, holding the door open for her. "I'm not sure there's anything more vanilla than that."

She rolled her eyes. "There's the Hendrix I remember."

"The Hendrix you know and love."

He tried to put his arm around her, but she moved away and gave herself a foot of personal space. The heat hit her hard, and she hoped it was the Jacksonville sunshine her body was reacting to, not her gut sounding its emergency siren or her body releasing dopamine.

Yes, this was a terrible idea.

## 15

# The Joy of Discovery

Dylan couldn't look away from the vinyl banner advertisement set inside the entrance to the library. What drew her in wasn't the bold yellow letters saying, *Visit the children's library to experience "The Joy of Discovery" mural!* but the image of two little girls sitting atop a manatee, smiling.

According to the banner, the mural was fifty feet wide, with many more painted images of children riding on top of animals, flying straight out of a book. The palpable delight on the children's faces, their innocent smiles—they captivated Dylan, making her forget she was supposed to be finding signs pointing toward the library's computers.

These must be from one of the murals James had been talking about.

Behind her, Hendrix scoffed.

She glanced back at him. "What? I think it's beautiful."

He nodded at the other image on the vinyl banner, a boy soaring atop a dragonfly, laughing. "*That* was not my childhood."

He wasn't lying. The whimsy depicted in the picture wasn't how she felt about her upbringing either, but something about the kids' joy was contagious. And she hoped to have her own "joy of discovery," once she got her hands on a computer.

She took a picture of the banner and attached it to a text.

> **Me:** Look at me, getting out and seeing things.

**Captain Jim:** *proud tour guide moment*

**Captain Jim:** Looks like an amazing mural!

**Captain Jim:** And lunch???? Did you check out Bread+Board?

> **Me:** Bread+Board=Delicious. Keep the suggestions coming because . . .

> **Me:** you're on a roll.

Ugh, that was too much. She needed to chuck her phone to the other side of the room before she punned anything else.

**Captain Jim:** It's the yeast I could do.

> **Me:** That one crosses the lime.

**Captain Jim:** I agree. We're the worst.

**Captain Jim:** I mean **Worcestershire.

He'd played along, which was the best. Maybe they could both be in Jacksonville without it being weird, minus being a couple of weirdos.

She looked up, expecting to see Hendrix right behind her, but he was already across the room. She speed walked to catch up. Without his number or high chances they'd randomly run into each other again, she couldn't afford to lose him. He led her to a large room—the sign said *Eva Rosier Lamar Information Desk*—where tables were set up in the middle and rows of computers and books surrounded the periphery. Natural light streamed in from the vaulted windows above and swam around them.

They picked two computers next to each other and sat down, Hendrix pushing his chair closer to hers.

"By the way, I have a million more questions for you."

She shook the computer mouse to wake it out of sleep mode. "I'm not sure I have that many answers."

"How exactly did the genealogy test say you weren't related to your dad?"

She yawned, leaning back to stretch a tight muscle in her back. "The results said I had one KindreDNA 'friend' named Darren Turner, which is like having a follower on social media, not an actual DNA match. If he was my biological father, he would've been listed as a 50 percent DNA match, because science says so."

"You trust this company is telling the truth? They aren't messing around with your DNA?"

"Wait." She leaned in, pausing for dramatic effect. "Do we have a conspiracy theorist on our hands? Tell me, Hendrix, is the earth flat? Are pigeons real?"

He swiveled his chair away and opened his browser. "I'm *not* a conspiracy theorist. I simply don't take everything I hear at face value."

"That is literally the definition of a conspiracy theorist."

He shrugged. "It's not wrong to want more information before trusting someone. I've seen too much."

"Whatever. If that's your question, my answer is yes, I trust this company. I don't think they made an error with our DNA or that they're out to get me. Also, you sound like my dad."

She waited for him to react to her joke, but he stared at his screen. "I was surprised he even wanted to do this test in the first place. He wouldn't save a credit card to his computer for faster online shopping, but suddenly he was willing to spit his DNA into a vial for a complete stranger to make a family tree. Maybe he wasn't worried about privacy breaches once he found out the cancer was terminal."

Hendrix typed on his keyboard. "You said the DNA test had something to do with you coming to Jacksonville?"

"Before he died, he must have changed the name of our family tree from The Turner Tree to Jacksonville. My closest genetic match is from the Jacksonville area, and according to her profile, a few people from her family tree are also from the Southeast."

Hendrix clicked his mouse, then typed again. "You've done a lot of work in a short amount of time. Is your dad's body even cold yet?"

His comment hit like a slap.

She pictured the two of them in self-defense class fourteen years ago. More specifically, her fist connecting with his pretty little nose.

"Tell me," she whisper-hissed at a library-appropriate volume, "if you found out on the day of your dad's funeral you weren't biologically related and that the people you trusted most lied to you for thirty years, what would you do?"

He kept typing. "I'd be so happy, I'd dance on his grave."

She couldn't argue with that, not after he'd showed up to almost every class with a new bruise. Still, she'd appreciate a little compassion.

"Everything I thought I knew about my life is a lie, so please excuse me for being a little curious for answers—*obsessed* is probably a better word. I've never been through something like this or known someone who's been through something like this, so I don't know how I'm supposed to act."

He raked his hand through his hair. "If your goal is to find your biological father, does that mean you're hoping to meet him too? Have an actual relationship with him?"

"Maybe? I don't know." It was hard to summarize what she wanted when, in reality, she had no clue. "I want to know where I came from. I want to know my own history—the truth."

"Are you hoping to ask for something from them?"

She glared. "No, I'm not hoping to *ask* for anything. What are you implying?"

"Not much," he said, too nonchalant. "It's just that you work at a grocery store, so I wondered if that meant you were struggling financially or something. Isn't that kind of money hard to live off of?"

"Is that why you're helping me? Because you think I'm poor?"

"Ma'am?"

She looked up. She must've been talking louder than a whisper because everyone's eyes were on the two of them, including the librarian at the information desk who'd just shushed them. "This is a library, not *Real Housewives*."

Dylan shrank into her chair, wishing Hendrix would wipe the stupid smile off his face.

"Somebody's in trouble," he cooed.

"Shut up and do your good deed for the day," she bit back.

"Where do you want me to begin, Holmes?"

"Royal Cape Companies and their new development called Waterway Tower."

"Like what—an address?"

"Anything. A physical address to their office building, what they're about. Any connections to Darren Turner. They are the only lead I have right now, so I need some strategy for how to contact them. While you do that, I'm going to check my KindreDNA profile to see if there are any messages from my relative."

"Got it. I'll do that while you talk to your auntie."

"How do you know about Great-Aunt Kathleen?"

"Lucky guess, I guess."

She wiped her sweaty hands along the sides of her jeans and turned back to her computer, logging into KindreDNA. The message icon in the corner didn't turn red, though. It remained beige. The color that could stop following her around any day now.

She shouldn't be disappointed—it hadn't been even twenty-four hours since she messaged Kathleen. But shouldn't everyone on this planet be submitting their DNA and hovering around their messages? Looking for connections to long-lost relatives? It wasn't fair that the world around her was still spinning while hers had come to a screeching halt, the momentum throwing her face-first into the dirt.

"I have an idea," Hendrix said. "What if we went to Royal Cape Companies posing as a potential business to lease their property?"

"And why would we do something like that?"

He put both hands behind his head, revealing a chest and shoulders that were much broader than when he was a teenage boy. The zesty scent of apricots and eucalyptus wafted from his skin. She couldn't believe, after all this time, she was close enough not only to remember a few of the reasons he drove her mad but also to be able to smell him.

"You can't just walk into places demanding information about their employees and projects, especially from a company as massive as Royal Cape," he explained. "According to this, they're one of the biggest development companies in the area. I wouldn't walk in off the street and say you're looking for private information. I would come with something to offer."

"And the thing you think I should offer them is a fake company?" He couldn't be serious.

"I wouldn't be surprised if RCC is already accepting business proposals that they'll eventually take to residents for approval. If you show up with the 'perfect opportunity' as someone trying to learn about their exciting new development, it might give you an opening to ask if they happen to know a man named Darren Turner. The business proposal works like a buffer. It protects your real questions so you can get your foot in the door before they slam it in your face."

He pushed his keyboard away. "Also, their office is twenty minutes from here."

The idea rolled around in her head like a rock tumbler. She'd need much more time to process it. "What kind of business would I even propose? I don't have ideas for things like that."

"A coffee shop."

She crossed her arms. "I can't believe the way you just say things and accept them, full stop. This is income-based housing, and you want me to propose the first sign of gentrification?"

He threw his hands up. "It doesn't have to be perfect. Besides, everyone loves good coffee."

"It takes months, sometimes longer, to put together a business plan." She rubbed the bags under her eyes that were starting to feel as big as her carry-on.

"What do you think AI was made for?"

She laughed, but he didn't break. "You're serious."

"Look, all you need is a simple document that will get yourself a meeting with someone in the company who might be able to give you a better picture of how your dad is connected to them."

"It's the pretending part. It feels slimy—"

She yawned, interrupting herself. The time in the corner of her computer screen said 2:00 P.M., but with how hard the afternoon lull was hitting her, it could have been A.M. She needed a cup of coffee as strong as Hercules or a nap.

"Can I think about it after some sleep and a shower? If I'm going to put together a business proposal, I'd rather do that on my laptop anyway."

Hendrix checked his watch. "Good idea. I'll call Royal Cape and ask for an appointment. I've been told once or twice I'm a smooth talker."

It was his second kind offer of the day, though she could do without the low-grade flirting.

"Thank you, Hendrix. Really."

"See? We're great together."

He reached for her hand, which she pulled away.

"A great team, not couple."

He laughed, then stood and headed toward the exit. "Let's go. While we walk, we can discuss all the ways you might've been conceived."

# 16

## A Decent Proposal

"That's quite the conversation starter." She yanked her purse strap onto her shoulder, trying to keep his pace as they exited the library.

Outside, the afternoon sun was blinding.

Hendrix put his sunglasses on and scanned the area around them. "All I'm saying is there might be other reasons you aren't biologically related to your dad outside of your mom having an affair."

"Tell me, then. How do you think I was conceived?"

They came to a busy intersection and waited for the crosswalk signal to change.

"I recently watched this documentary on Netflix about a woman who came across an obituary for a doctor who looked just like her. It turned out he used to be a fertility doctor, and—lo and behold—the woman remembered her mom went through infertility before she was born."

"I don't like where this is going."

"The woman contacted one of the doctor's kids to ask if she would be willing to do a DNA test, but she said no because 'sperm donors are supposed to remain anonymous according to the Health Insurance Portability and Accountability Act.'"

"HIPAA. Got it."

The crosswalk signal changed, and they walked to the next block.

"So, the woman did an at-home DNA test, and you'll never guess what she found."

She had no brain waves left for guessing games. That hotel room nap was the only dangling carrot keeping her body moving at this point. "Just tell me."

"She found many, many half sibling matches."

Her stomach roiled.

"This woman alerted the authorities, who investigated the doctor, and found out he inseminated a large number of women with his own sperm instead of the donors they chose, including a few who were trying IVF with their husband's sperm. I'm talking *dozens* of women."

"Disgusting." She could barely get the word out.

"I agree. And then there's the *other* documentary about the guy who has over a thousand children."

"Stop."

"I know."

She waited for him to say more, but he didn't.

"What's your point in telling me that, exactly?" she asked over a car honking its horn.

His brow furrowed into a question mark. "My point is exactly what I said before. There could be many reasons you were conceived without your dad."

"Like, my parents going through infertility and getting IUI or IVF treatments?"

"Maybe."

"Or, my biological father being some nasty doctor who deserves a documentary made about him?"

"I hope not, but you should keep an open mind until you know for sure. Better yet, until you have concrete evidence of what actually happened." He pulled a set of keys out of his pants pocket. "My car's one more block up."

He was walking close enough that if either of them went off course a single inch, they'd bump shoulders. She tucked her hair to one side of her neck and focused on keeping her path straight.

"I guess infertility could explain why I never had siblings. I think I prefer my own conspiracy theory, though."

He stopped in front of a gray Nissan, which wasn't the kind of car she pictured a guy like him driving. Too forgettable for his electric personality. "That your mom had an affair?"

She nodded.

"That's only because it makes your mom the bad guy."

"What does that mean?" She was glad they weren't in the library anymore. Her volume was allowed to match her anger.

"It means you've always hated your mom." He opened the passenger door for her, but she stayed on the sidewalk to argue.

"*Hate* is a strong word. She's always been . . . angry. And I get tired of explaining myself to her."

He raised an eyebrow.

"I don't hate her; I've been hurt by her." She doubled down. "Nothing we've found has ruled out the possibility of an affair, either, so you need to keep your mind open to that possibility too, Detective Watson."

She climbed into the car and looked around, curious how the adult version of Hendrix kept it. There were no wrappers anywhere, no scuffs on the pristine car mats. The only sign the car belonged to someone was a small cooler in the back seat and what looked like a camera bag.

"Going on a picnic?"

He glanced over his shoulder, then buckled himself in. "It's my favorite pastime. That, and taking pictures of birds."

"You seem the type."

He smiled. "The camera is my sister's, but the cooler's all mine."

"How is Junie these days?"

"Living the dream. Married. White picket fence and 2.5 kids."

"What's it like being an uncle to half a child?"

"Less expensive."

She laughed. Was Hendrix as involved of an uncle as James?

Speaking of him, she pulled out her phone and texted about picking up her carry-on. Less than a minute later, she got a reply.

**Captain Jim:** I'll grab it now.
See you soon!

**Me:** Thank you, Captain Jim.

**Captain Jim:** What happened to Just James?

Hendrix set his key fob in the cup holder and started the car. "Is that your boss who's more than a friend?"

"Stop. I have no patience left for you right now." All annoyances aside, she liked not having to fake nice with him. Kept things easy.

"How does six o'clock sound for meeting back up? You can rest and brainstorm a business plan, and then we can talk about it over dinner."

She wondered what kind of restaurant Tour Guide James would recommend, but she decided not to mention it.

"Works for me." She yawned, and he handed her his phone.

"You should add your number so I don't lose you again. Other than that, we have a date."

She stared at his profile, his smile just as striking as ever. Nostalgia was trying to trick her into believing there was still something between them. Some unexplainable, fiery magic.

"As happy as I am to see you, old friend, this is not a date." She put her number in his phone and texted herself.

Dating meant putting *herself* out there, not just the logistical information people wanted to know before going out—like her name and number and if she was related to any prominent serial sperm donors. Putting her heart on a platter where it could eventually be demolished.

She looked out her window, watching the pattern of streetlights and palm trees pass by until he pulled into the hotel's riverfront entrance.

Instead of saying goodbye, he got out of the car and handed his keys to the valet.

She got out of the car and chased after him. "What are you doing?"

"I'm not following you, if that's what you're worried about. This isn't a *date*." He winked, sending a shiver down her spine.

"Then what *are* you doing?"

"If you must know, I'm going for a walk along the river so I can call Royal Cape Companies."

She lifted her chin. "Fine."

"Fine," he mimicked.

"Dylan!" a third, more mature voice interrupted.

She spun around. "James. Hey." Guilt stung the inside of her ribcage. "I'm sorry. I didn't mean to pull you out of your session."

He waved off her apology. "No problem at all. I didn't want to leave you stranded."

She stood between James and Hendrix, feeling crushed by two worlds colliding. "Oh. I should introduce the two of you. Um, Hendrix, this is James. James, Hendrix. Not gonna lie, you guys—this isn't how I pictured meeting Jimi Hendrix."

James laughed, but Hendrix's stone face said she should file that one in her own folder of beige flags.

"I get it. Because he's Jim and I'm Hendrix."

James held out his hand. "Nice to meet you."

Hendrix eyed him, then shook back. "You're also Dylan's boss?"

James beamed at her. "We work at the same Trader Joe's."

"Might as well be Magic Kingdom by the sounds of it. A manager too? That's great."

She glared at Hendrix for making this entire scenario way more awkward than it had to be, then turned to James. "Hendrix is somebody I used to know." Two could play his game. "We randomly ran into each other at the Bread and Board, thanks to your recommendation."

That nap was calling her name. She opened her mouth to say "Good riddance" to Hendrix and "Good day" to James, but a tiny, beautiful woman with a perfectly cut bob walked up and slipped her arm through James's.

"There you are, James. I've been looking all over for you." She wore a button-up shirt with tropical flowers, knotted at the waist, and didn't let go of James's arm. "Hey, y'all, I'm Anna Claire. Captain of Store 368."

"Hi." Dylan waved. Why did she wave?

She glanced at James, who was biting his lip, then Hendrix, who was looking Anna Claire up and down. Goodness, she needed that nap. Neither of their reactions mattered anyway. There was nothing between her and James.

Or her and Hendrix, who was now caressing her elbow.

"Well, this was fun," he said. "I have to go, but I'll see you for dinner." He shoved his hands in his pockets and walked toward the river.

She nodded. "See you then."

"Have a blessed day," Anna Claire called after him. "Who is he?"

"Dylan's friend." James held out the handle of her carry-on with his free arm, and she grabbed it from him.

"Thank you again. I'm going to check in, but I hope you both enjoy your next session."

James took a step away from Anna Claire, who lingered.

"Did your morning get any better?" he asked.

She shrugged. "I didn't make much progress, but I haven't run into any brick walls yet."

Easy enough to accomplish when no brick walls existed at 331 16th Terrace.

"I feel like I hit a brick wall after some pretty exciting sessions this morning."

"Wasn't it great?" Anna Claire chimed in, matching James's bubbliness more than Dylan ever could.

James nodded. He wasn't yawning and had no saggy bags under his eyes. If this was his version of tired, she probably looked like Rip Van Winkle before his twenty-year nap.

"You look no more tired than you ever do."

James shrugged. "It will hit me soon enough. Maybe after we stand in a big open room and all the captains bounce a giant beach ball to each other."

Her mouth dropped open.

"Look at her face." Anna Claire laughed up at James. "He's kidding, Dylan."

Dylan tugged the handle of her carry-on. "Well, I'm going up to my room. You two have fun beach balling, or whatever serious business it is you have to tend to."

She wasn't making sense anymore.

"Bye, Dylan."

"Yeah, bye, hon," Anna Claire chirped.

She turned toward the hotel, feeling them watch her roll her suitcase inside. It took everything in her not to glance back at how James and Anna Claire interacted when it was just the two of them.

She went to the front desk for her keys and took the elevator to the seventh floor, room 714. The curtains were opened to a set of oversized windows, but she didn't worry about daylight keeping her awake. Not even a security spotlight shining in her face could stop her from collapsing onto the plush white bed and crashing hard.

🐦

She didn't sleep long enough to dream, but she woke to the same weight of anxiety that greeted her most mornings.

*Dearly beloved, we are gathered . . .*

Teresa's comment came to mind, the one about the big bash her wedding was turning into and the rare chance to have all her and

August's favorite people in the same room together. Dylan was nowhere near getting married, but so many of Teresa's wedding details mocked her. Who would she beg to sit in the pews if she were the one walking down the aisle? And what about the person who would've walked her down the aisle, if he were still here?

It was hard to picture him, like he was almost faceless. She felt stuck between who had raised her and the mystery of her own biology.

She rubbed the back of her neck, then rolled out of bed to get her laptop and charger. She'd have to sift through her peppered thoughts later, *after* she put a fake business proposal together. When she pulled up Google, she typed "kindred," then yanked her hands off the keyboard. She wasn't supposed to be pulling up KindreDNA. Her involuntary muscles must be as impatient as she was to hear back from Kathleen. Unfortunately, checking her inbox wouldn't make messages appear there.

She opened another tab.

**Google:** business plan for when you have no ideas or dreams or ambitions

She backspaced everything after "business plan" and hit Enter. The first result was an ad for an AI site that could create an outline in only fifteen minutes. All she had to do was fill in a few blanks, and it would compose a description, a target market, a list of competitors, and sample revenue streams. Enough to make it seem like she'd thought it through.

She stood corrected. Hendrix *wasn't* overly confident at how quickly they could piece this together for Royal Cape.

She did another search that would help her fill in those few blanks.

**Google:** businesses that don't gentrify

Two of the first articles listed were from Reddit.

She clicked on them, surprised at the number of users who had thoughts on this topic, though they didn't seem to match Royal Cape Companies' vision for community development. Users' ideas were more geared toward communities already gentrified. A vacation home management company. Dog groomers.

> **pluto_is_a_planet_#9:** Rebottle Costco pickles into mason jars and call them "artisan." They'd go for at least 8 bucks.

She gnawed her cheek, trying to think of something creative. A business, some kind of business, any dumb little business. Maybe she should start a company called Overthinking.

It wasn't like she had to actually start whatever business she came up with, which made this creative exercise all the more frustrating. Even under little to no real-life pressure, her brain was too foggy to daydream a future that didn't include the job she already had.

She closed her eyes and told herself to breathe.

Maybe pouring her sadness into Google would help.

> **Google:** why moms lie

Two days had passed, and her mom still hadn't called.

She deleted it and tried again.

> **Google:** people who discover they were conceived with a sperm donor

The results were wild. Reddit had an open forum for people who'd experienced DNA surprises, and many had chimed in to vent or ask questions.

**The-Sea-Calls89** (2 months ago)
    I try to be a nice person and give people the benefit of the doubt. The fertility doctor had a business to run, so what better way to cut costs than to not have to pay donors? And if my mom was able to finally have her baby, shouldn't that be considered a win-win? But then I remember that only a sicko would do what he did.

She shuddered. Maybe The-Sea-Calls89 was connected to the documentary Hendrix talked about.

She scrolled on. Entry after entry shared people's pain and rage and confusion after learning they'd been lied to. It comforted her knowing she wasn't the only one who'd been through something like this. Her misery loved the company, though she wouldn't wish this kind of surprise on anyone.

**STR4NGRth4nF1CT10N** (1 week ago)
    I had no idea he wasn't my bio dad until I took the test. It's hard for me to ask him about it now—it's hard for me to talk to him about anything besides the weather. But he's getting older, so it feels like time is running out.

A few entries made Dylan want to reach through the screen and hug the soul on the other side of it.

**Cats_R_Bttr_Thn_Ppl** (3 days ago)
    I DID NOT ASK TO BE THE LIVING, BREATHING REMINDER OF MY PARENTS' DRAMA!!!

Fighting back tears, she closed her laptop.

This was why she didn't dream about building businesses, even theoretical ones. It was like Hendrix's reaction to images from the library mural. Discovery was for kids with a different childhood.

*Who am I?* The question nagged. She was grasping for something on the surface—a simple business proposal—without a full grasp of who she was underneath. At least, one half of who she was. Forget dreams—the optimistic kind that didn't torture her sleep. She'd stick to paying her bills. And she'd settle for whatever business idea Hendrix offered, besides a coffee shop. It wouldn't take long to slap together a few slides for Royal Cape Companies after that.

She climbed off the bed and walked to her carry-on for toiletries. She didn't have to do an armpit sniff or breath test to know she was feral from airplane travel. She simply got in the shower to wash away the grime and sweat. The pattering water soothed her loud thoughts while she lathered shampoo into her hair, the argan oil tingling her scalp and nostrils—the job of aromatherapy well done.

When she finally shut off the water and wrapped herself in a fluffy towel, she stared at her open suitcase. She had no idea where Hendrix would take her, so she pulled out a simple black dress and taupe blazer, hoping the outfit paired with a rose-gold chain would be classy enough for wherever they ended up. She used a glob of curl cream and the hotel's hair dryer to put gentle waves in her hair, then added a few swipes of mascara and nude lipstick as a final touch.

After tucking her toiletries away, she took in her reflection.

*Who am I?*

*Does everyone know but me?*

Thankfully, her outward appearance didn't match the wreck she was below the surface.

Her phone dinged twice in a row, as if on cue.

> **That Man:** heading back to my car and will pick u up. R u ready or do u need more time

> **That Man:** also u will not believe what I found

# 17

## The Red Knot

Dylan jumped into Hendrix's car with no patience for pleasantries. "Tell me what you found."

His grin was cocky, which she hoped, besides making his face annoyingly attractive, meant whatever he found was good news. "You'll see." He pressed the ignition and put the car in Drive.

She forced her shoulders back against her seat so she could buckle. "I don't love surprises. Surprises are why I'm here in the first place."

"No surprises. No dating. A lot of fun you are."

They pulled into the heavier traffic of Bay Street, then took a left toward a bright blue bridge.

"What's this one called again?" She hadn't gone downtown much as a kid.

"Its official name is the John T. Alsop Jr. Bridge, but you might remember it as the Main Street Bridge. It's the only lift bridge on the river, and it lights up at night."

She pictured what it might look like in the dark, glowing royal blue over the river. She didn't remember it, but she had other memories of bridges.

"I can't believe after all these years we're finally meeting at a bridge." She wouldn't punish him forever for that night fourteen years ago, but she enjoyed watching him squirm now.

"Main Street wasn't even the bridge we were supposed to—"

"I know. I'm just giving you a hard time."

"How many more hard times before you forgive me?"

She shrugged.

The drive morphed from a bridge over the river to a lively area of boutiques, restaurants, and riverfront mansions. The wall of one church was painted *San Marco* with a massive lion head that looked like it was shedding its outer layer—roaring into a fresh start. Its vivid colors and painted details kept her head on a swivel until it went out of view.

They parked and walked multiple blocks, with Hendrix leading the way, his hand on her shoulder.

"Ta-da." He didn't use any theatrical gestures, and the area was bustling more than she'd expected for a Wednesday.

"What am I supposed to be looking at?"

"There." He pointed.

She connected the dots to a building across the street. It had black doors, cream trim, and a sleek iron sign with the outline of a bird. She squinted to read it.

"The Red Knot?"

"It's a restaurant. Ever heard of it?"

She shook her head, sorry to disappoint him but even sorrier what he'd found was a restaurant when she wanted information.

"It looks like a nice place, though."

He moved his hand from her shoulder to the small of her back, prodding her toward the crosswalk.

"It's considered Jacksonville's best fine dining. Chef Freya Poulter has won multiple awards over the years, though she always gives credit to the trailblazers who came before her. I've always wanted to eat here. Your visit makes it the perfect occasion."

Dylan glanced down at her outfit. "Am I dressed up enough? And can I afford this?"

She remembered his comment about her income earlier and immediately regretted asking. After her all-access membership, plane ticket, hotel room, and car troubles, she had to be conscious of what she was spending.

Hendrix scanned from her lips on down. "This isn't a date, but I'm going to buy you dinner. Also, even though this isn't a date, can I say you look amazing?"

The heat from his hand filled the rest of her body so fast she worried it would singe her dress. She needed air-conditioning.

"Thank you. You look decent too, for someone dressed like a playboy."

His dress shirt was partially unbuttoned, exposing the top of his chest.

"I'll take it," he said.

The signal changed, and they crossed the street, his hand still on her back.

"Where did you change clothes? I thought you were on the riverwalk all afternoon."

"The hotel restroom."

"You had a change of clothes in the car?"

He pulled open the door to the Red Knot and held it for her. "I like to be prepared for all scenarios."

The dining room was dotted with tables, each adorned with multiple candles and a bouquet of fresh flowers, including the table for two where the hostess seated them.

Dylan didn't have to scan the menu or investigate the open kitchen humming with chefs to know the cuisine had a Mediterranean flair. The aroma of rosemary and garlic triggered a memory of when she'd moved from Atlanta to Nashville. The first thing her mom had done was unbox her knives and skillet to make lemon and rosemary chicken.

"It doesn't feel like home, but let's make it smell like home," her mom had muttered amid a furious rhythm of chopping.

Dylan hadn't thought about lemon and rosemary chicken in a

long time. She could almost taste the brief sense of security it had offered then and every move after.

The server arrived, bringing Dylan back to their table at the Red Knot. "My name is Zora, and I'll be taking care of you this evening. Have you had a chance to look at the drink menu?"

"I'll have a Black Manhattan," Hendrix answered.

Zora waited for Dylan.

"I'll stick with water, please." A Black Manhattan sounded delicious, but she didn't want Hendrix to pay for her meal, and staying away from cocktails would help with the sticker shock of her own check.

Hendrix unfolded his napkin and put it on his lap. "So, Holmes, what did you come up with for your business proposal?"

"That's actually what I was hoping to ask *you*. I couldn't think of anything, and the only idea the internet had to offer was reselling pickles from Costco."

He grimaced. "The best idea you came up with . . . is pickles."

She fiddled with the silverware next to her plate. "I know. I'm pathetic. I couldn't think of anything that sounded fun *and* realistic."

"You're not trying to have fun, Turner. You're trying to schedule a meeting. If you can't think of anything, sell Jaguar merch."

"Don't you think it should fit the concept of an income-based development?"

"Sell Jaguar merch at a discounted price, then. People here love the Jaguars."

Zora came back with Hendrix's drink and set it in front of him. "Are you ready to order, or do you need more time?" she asked after talking through the tasting menu, à la carte options, and evening specials.

"We'd like a minute with the menu," he answered for the two of them.

Zora glanced at Dylan, giving her a chance to respond.

"I know what I want already. What's taking you so long?"

"I could ask the same thing about your business proposal."

The server clasped her hands and tilted her head. "I'll check back in soon."

Hendrix sipped his drink, holding the speared orange peel and cherry to the side of the glass. He swallowed, then grimaced.

"Strong?" Dylan asked as he took another sip.

"Probably lethal."

"I know I'm overthinking this business proposal. I want to come up with something I'd actually enjoy doing, and yet I can't imagine doing anything other than what I've been doing for the past twelve years."

"Stocking shelves and working cash registers?"

"Mocking essential workers is lazy comedy, Hendrix."

He swirled the ice cube in his glass, then set it back on the table. "If you can't think of a business *you* would start, think of a business for the kind of person you wish you were. Take the pressure off yourself and play pretend."

"I get what you're saying—I do." The problem was, he didn't get what *she* was saying.

She didn't expect him to. He didn't know her brain had been ricocheting between impulsive choices ever since she opened that KindreDNA email. Why else would she be sitting at a random restaurant in Jacksonville, Florida, with Hendrix Reed right now?

"Were you able to set up a meeting with Royal Cape?"

"Of course. I promised myself I'd never let you down again." He took another sip, looking at her the entire time. His eyes were even more startling by candlelight.

She hoped the dim room would hide her blush. "Is that the natural suave you used with whatever poor assistant was on the phone with you?"

"That poor assistant wanted me to email the proposal, but I knew it would get lost in some crowded inbox. I said your proposal was too good for anything but a face-to-face meeting, and he finally got his boss to relent. Said the meeting was at 9:00 A.M."

"Tomorrow, as in Thursday."

"Yes. Today is Wednesday, which means tomorrow is Thursday. We get fifteen minutes with the vice president of leasing, which isn't an ideal length of time, but I'm hoping, after five minutes on the proposal, you can worm your way into your questions."

She drank her water, which settled into the nervous pit that was her stomach. "You're sure this is more efficient and, more importantly, more ethical than simply asking if anyone in the office knows Darren Turner?"

He shrugged. "Don't hate the player; hate the game. We're trying to navigate the business world, and this forces them to hear out the little guys."

"You should write this proposal. I have no idea what I'm doing."

"I'm the hype guy, not the ideas guy. Whatever proposal you make will be great."

She groaned, swiping her hair back behind her shoulder. "Ugh. Fine. I'll focus, and I'll put together a baller proposal, and I'll stop worrying about getting fired for not being at work in Illinois right now."

Hendrix laughed. "That's the spirit. And as long as you're here with your boss friend, I'm pretty sure you won't get fired."

She picked up her napkin and wiped her sweaty hands.

What were James and all his captain buddies up to right now? Was Anna Claire still suctioned to his arm?

"I think James flies out sometime Sunday, so as long as I book my return flight for then, I should be okay. Which means, tonight I should send another message to blood relative Kathleen, maybe on Facebook this time. It would be amazing if we could meet up while I'm here."

Hendrix grimaced, like, *Are you serious right now?*

"What?" she demanded.

"Or, you could research other angles. You don't want to push too hard; she might get scared at how strong you're coming on."

"Why do you have to ruin everything?" she joked, though it was hard wanting something so far out of her control. Something that seemed so vital to working through the confusing mess of her family.

She looked around the dining room to distract herself. A woman in the open kitchen, wearing a white coat and tall toque, was looking at their table. Their eyes met for a split second, and the woman turned to the man next to her and said something in his ear. The man nodded, then shifted into place where the woman had been standing.

Zora arrived back at the table, blocking her view of the woman. "Will the table be ordering à la carte or a tasting menu? We have both six-course and eight-course offerings."

"À la carte—"

"Eight-course tasting—"

They spoke at the same time.

Hendrix rolled his eyes. "We're doing the eight-course, Turner. I already told you this is on me. Think of it as another way for me to earn brownie points to get back into your good graces."

Again, Zora waited for her to respond, which she appreciated. One person at the table wasn't pushing her around.

"Fine." She set her menu back on the table. "I'll start with the Peekytoe Crab Salad for the first course. And, I'd like a Black Manhattan too." She smirked.

"A fine choice." The young woman turned to Hendrix.

"I'll have the ceviche."

"Yes, sir." Zora nodded to each of them. "I'll be back with those shortly."

With a clear view of the kitchen, she looked for the chef she'd seen earlier, but the woman was no longer behind the protective glass wall.

"About that other angle I was talking about." Hendrix leaned toward her. "I think there's something—*someone*—you may want to spend more time looking into."

"And that is?"

Hendrix opened his mouth to answer, but someone else—not Zora—walked up to their table.

"Excuse me."

Both of them looked up, and Dylan could feel the room of patrons zeroing in on their table, like this person was a magnet walking through a line of paperclips. It was the chef, out from the kitchen. Dylan didn't know much about fine dining, but she knew this was an uncommon occurrence.

"Hello, I'm Chef Freya Poulter."

"*The* award-winning executive chef of the Red Knot," Hendrix added. "Hendrix Reed, and this is Dylan Turner."

"Turner," Chef Poulter whispered, her eyes brightening. "I'm sorry for staring earlier, but you remind me of someone, and the fact that your last name is Turner—well, I have to ask. Are you related to Chef *Candis* Turner by any chance?"

The question pulled a plug inside her, draining all the blood from her face. Had this chef just put *chef* in front of her mom's name? Her mind spun, trying to make a connection between what this woman was saying and the mom she knew.

Chef Poulter must have noticed. "I'm sorry. This must be really uncomfortable. You remind me of Chef Turner, and I thought if you were here, that meant you might be connected to her somehow, but—"

"You're right," Dylan stammered. "Candis is my mom. It's just that she was never a— I mean, she was always a talented cook, and still is, but . . ."

The rest of her brain cells must have circled the drain too.

Hendrix reached across the table, took her hand, and squeezed. Hard. "Chef Candis Turner is her mom."

He was nodding at her so intently, she couldn't help but nod along. "Yes. My mom."

Chef Poulter beamed. "I worked as a sous-chef under her when she was executive at the Prime. She gave me my first real shot in the culinary world, and I know I wouldn't be here if it weren't for her. Your mom changed my life, and many other women's lives. She got how hard it was for us."

Listening to Chef Poulter was like listening to an inside joke she was on the outside of. So far outside, she couldn't even make out its walls on the horizon.

Chef Poulter put her hand on her own heart. "I still can't believe what the press did to her. When I came here, I vowed I would run this place like she did—in honor of her."

The words echoed in the empty cavern of her head.

*"Run this place like she did."*

"The next time you talk to her, will you please tell her Chef Poulter says hello? I haven't seen her since shortly before . . . everything happened."

*"The next time you talk to her."*

Dylan would love to know when that might be. She had to say something.

"Yes." She forced her tingling face to smile.

Chef Poulter bowed her head. "I apologize for gawking earlier, but it's an honor to meet the daughter of an industry legend. Enjoy your meal."

She walked back to the kitchen, the same magnetic pull drawing eyes toward her.

Hendrix cleared his throat. "As I was saying, I think there's another angle you should research."

Dylan couldn't breathe. "What's going on? What is she talking about?"

Hendrix pulled out his phone. "She totally stole my thunder, but that was worth it—it's rare for a chef to leave the kitchen."

"Stop." Why was he being so nonchalant about this? "Give it to me straight. What does my mom have to do with this place?"

Hendrix frowned. "Your mom has everything to do with this place. That's my point. You've spent your time following whatever trail your dad might've left, when your mom is actually a gold mine of interesting information."

"She worked here? She never mentioned *any* of this."

Scallops. Roasted lamb shoulder. Turkish kale salad. These were the kinds of meals Dylan had grown up eating—worthy of a place like this. Sure, Five Guys made a fine enough burger, a symbol of stability, but it was her mom who'd raised her with a palate for things other than macaroni, PB&J, and french fries.

"This is exactly why you should be looking into her more. After I called Royal Cape this afternoon, I did a basic internet search on your mom and found a whole series of local articles about her."

Hendrix typed into his phone, then held it up for her to see.

An article called "Chef's Kiss" was right there on his screen.

"Your mom didn't just work here. She started this restaurant."

## Chef's Kiss: How Talent and Love Are Bringing Flavor to Downtown Jacksonville

**Demetrius Ross,** *The Jacksonville Times*

[Today's From the Archives article features one of Jacksonville's beloveds, the Red Knot, and its first chef, Candis Turner. This article was originally published 35 years ago.]

Boasting Mediterranean dishes with a Florida flair, the Red Knot will undoubtedly please with its sophisticated atmosphere and menu that does not compromise. The genius holding the knives is Chef Candis Turner, who trained at L'Academie de Cuisine in Gaithersburg, Maryland. Upon graduating, she moved up the ranks at the Prime, a prestigious steakhouse near Orlando.

The birth of the Red Knot is a story not only of raw talent but also of love. Turner is teaming up with her husband of six months, Darren Turner, the vice president of finance at Venture-Gold Group, as the restaurant's main investor.

"I couldn't be happier not only to share my passion for fine cuisine with others," Chef Turner says with an infectious smile, "but to also work with the man I love. As an entrepreneur, Darren is smart and driven, and I know my work is in good hands with him at the wheel as general manager of the Red Knot."

"Yes, Chef," Darren jokes. He says he's thrilled to showcase his wife's work. "Wherever Candis is, people want to eat. The Prime was continually named one of Florida's top restaurants, and we expect the Red Knot will be her chance to bring home the AAA Five Diamond Award."

The only thing this power couple seems more invested in than their restaurant is each other.

[Pictured: Candis and Darren Turner. Embracing each other and their strengths.]

# 18

# Perfect Strangers

The article knocked the wind out of her.

"Who are these people?" she whispered.

The two faces in the picture were labeled *Candis and Darren Turner,* but she'd swear they were complete strangers. Certainly not her parents, who, at best, had tolerated each other.

Her dad was sitting on the bar, and her mom was standing next to him, leaning her arm on his thigh. He was bent toward her like he was telling her a secret, the kind of joke whispered in a crowded room between lovers.

The camera had caught her mom smiling mid-laugh, and even in grayscale, she illuminated the page. Unlike any moment Dylan had witnessed under their roof, Candis's tender gaze was all for her husband. Her dad looked familiar—goofing off and throwing one-liners for the room to enjoy—but she'd never seen her parents act like that together.

Her hand was going numb. She gave the phone back to Hendrix. "They never talked about the Red Knot."

"In thirty years, they never talked about running an elite restaurant together? Kind of strange, don't you think?"

She wanted to slam the table. "Obviously, it's strange."

She tried to breathe in the fact that this building held some of her own history, but her lungs were caving in. The sound of simmering dishes and clinking glasses dulled, and everything she'd once seen with twenty-twenty vision started to blur.

She blinked hard. "Wasn't the article dated five years before I was born?"

"*This* article, yes." He typed into his phone again. "They started the restaurant before you were born, but I think you'll want to take a look at these related articles I found. What's your email address?"

"Dylanturner918@gmail.com."

"Got it." He set his phone down. "I'm guessing you won't mind spoilers at this point?"

She rolled her eyes.

"Perfect. The articles say your parents ran the Red Knot until you were a few months old. While there's tons of coverage on the restaurant opening and doing well for five years, I could only find one paragraph about transferring ownership from VentureGold Group and your mom stepping away."

"Do they say why my parents quit?"

"One article claimed they had to be shut down due to health code violations in the kitchen."

She glanced at the Red Knot's open kitchen. Large stacks of white plates lined the walls above stainless-steel commercial appliances and food prep stations. The area was obviously in use from a night of culinary artistry, and yet it glimmered.

"If anyone would run a tight ship in her kitchen, Candis Turner would. She was meticulous. She'd sanitize surfaces before cooking, then again after. Raw meat couldn't touch vegetables—even if they were going into the same dish. Everything got sprayed with vinegar. The few times she let me help, she'd say something about having every ingredient sliced and diced before you start cooking. Something like '*mise en place*'—oh my. How did I not know she was an actual chef?"

Zora arrived with Dylan's Black Manhattan, as well as their first courses, which she set in front of each of them.

"I hope everything is to your expectations."

"It is, Zora. Thank you," Hendrix replied before she spun toward her next table. He tucked his phone into his pocket and picked up his fork. "Anyway, that's why I wanted to bring you here. Another tidbit for your sleuthing."

"Tidbit? Try a *lot* bit. Could you maybe warn me next time instead of putting me on the spot like that?"

He smirked. "Where's the fun in that?"

"I thought we weren't trying to have fun? That's what you said about my business proposal."

"Touché."

She looked at her salad. How was she supposed to eat her plate of crab meat, cucumbers, and pickled grapes draped in an avocado mousse after that?

"Thank you, by the way," she muttered. "Even if your methods are questionable, you've helped a lot, especially because I don't even know what I'm looking for."

He reached across the table and took her hand, caressing it. "Maybe what you're looking for is right in front of you."

"Hendrix," she groaned, but this time, she didn't pull away.

He cocked his eyebrow. "I mean, look at this spread. What else could you possibly want?"

# 19

## The Best Spice

Dylan got quieter with every course, as did the flavor of each dish. Not even the spicy rosemary olives pricked her taste buds. It reminded her of a headline she'd once scrolled past: "Taste Buds Wearing Out? Why Adults' Tolerance for Spicy Food Increases with Age."

Now she understood the metaphor: Adults are slowly dying inside.

She pushed scraps of food around her plate with one of her multiple forks, disappointed in herself for not enjoying this dining experience more, for not being able to focus on whatever it was Hendrix was saying. Something about his time in the military? And a large dog named . . . she couldn't remember now.

Maybe hunger wasn't the best spice, as the old proverb claimed. Maybe feeling awake and secure gave food its flavor.

She nodded and smiled between sips and bites, but her mind lagged.

Zora came back one last time after dessert, without a small leather folder holding their bill. "Tonight's meal is on the house, courtesy of Chef Poulter."

"Wow, thank you." Dylan meant it. Also, this meant they could leave.

Zora smiled. "Thank you for dining with us this evening."

Hendrix put a large cash tip on the table and stood up. "Would you like to go for a walk? It won't be near as hot outside now."

A walk. Outside. She loved summer evenings when the temperatures dropped from stifling to comfortable. She'd often add a mile walk to her five-mile run, the chirping crickets and rustling grass helping her decompress from chatty customers and clanging ship bells. A walk with Hendrix could also be a chance to get more answers. Not about her parents—about other stuff. Like why he'd never shown up that night.

She rubbed her temples. "Actually, I'm tired and I have a lot on my mind with what Chef Poulter said and all. I still have to finish that proposal too."

"Fine. Blow me off for your homework, then, nerd." He sounded like he was teasing, but something sparked in his eyes that didn't look like fireworks.

"You always know the exact wrong thing to say, don't you, Reed."

---

Back at the hotel, she climbed out of his car and leaned into the window. "See you in the morning?"

"Yeah," he muttered. "Good night."

The second she shut the door, his car sped away.

She shook her head, then checked the time on her phone. The clock mocked her. Even if it wasn't already 8:00 P.M. and she had the entire day to research, she didn't have the capacity. Her mind was everywhere and nowhere all at once.

Inside the hotel, the 24/7 market's Starbucks sign glowed like the promise of an oasis. Whatever coffee they had here couldn't compare to the double caffeine of Trader Joe's Electric Buzz, but hopefully she wouldn't need to stay awake the entire night. She filled a cup halfway, added cream and sugar, then made her way to the elevators.

She thought she could hear gears churning and a low murmur of voices traveling down the elevator shaft toward her, but she pressed the arrow button anyway. A bell rang—more delicate than the ones at work—and the door slid open. The cab was full of adults wearing tropical shirts, buzzing with birthday party energy. She wouldn't be surprised if the sea of colorful bodies parted to reveal a clown holding a bouquet of balloons.

She looked down while the line of captains filed out of the elevator, until the last person got off, who was not in fact a clown.

"Dylan." James smiled at her, then turned to the rest of the group and yelled, "Captains, one of our very own crew is here at the hotel."

"We're so blue without our crew!" they responded in perfect unison.

"James. Hello." She tried recovering from the mortifying attention. "Is this what you've been working on so diligently all day? Chants to embarrass your employees?"

"Too much too soon?"

"Maybe a little overkill."

"Hey, Slim Jim," one captain hollered. "Are you coming or not?"

"Wouldn't be the annual treasure hunt without you," another added. Anna Claire.

James had nicknames all over the nation, apparently. And old friends. "Don't let me keep you from your treasure hunt." She stepped toward the elevator.

"It will take them a minute to explain the rules to the newbies anyway."

"Newbies?" The behind-the-scenes details of Captain Jim's life fascinated her.

"Every year, each of us invites a new captain to the treasure hunt as a way to welcome them."

"A treasure hunt. For what—Pirate's Booty?" she joked.

"Sorry—yes, I should have explained that. It's a scavenger hunt around the hotel. No prize except making connections. It helps new captains feel like they can reach out and ask questions if they need help learning their role. Corporate hopes each captain will mentor and develop two other captains."

Dylan took a sip of her coffee. "And you're still positive you're not part of a cult? Or some multilevel marketing con?"

"Oh, we prefer not to mince words. We're definitely a pyramid scheme." He grinned, then pointed at her cup of coffee. "At this hour? What's going on, Dylan?"

"I have a long night of work ahead of me and another meeting in the morning."

"So many meetings. Moving to Jacksonville to start your own business?"

"I can't even come up with an idea for a business, let alone run one. Besides, I'm not exactly a people person. I know why I'm put on registers the least of all the crew."

James adjusted the collar of his tropical button-up shirt, looking ready for work as ever. Outside Trader Joe's, he looked like a handsome guy wearing it to be ironic. "Just think how much louder the world would be if everyone was a 'people person.' Besides, knowing how to talk isn't the only vital skill in this world."

She raised an eyebrow. "Are you this optimistic about everyone and everything, Captain Jim?"

"I just think there's a lot of good in the neighborhood, you know?" He laughed at himself. "Okay, that rhyming was almost as bad as your food puns."

She gasped. "*My* food puns are bad?"

"Yes. Super weir-*dough*." He gave her a second to catch it.

If Anna Claire weren't in the background, she might reach out and touch his arm in protest.

"Anyway," James continued, "the goal isn't to make everyone at work have the same skill set but to highlight what each person does well. You're reliable. You show up and make sure we're not a hot mess all the time. Except around your birthday, of course."

He laughed again. "You're also willing to do the jobs a lot of people think they're too good for. I'd take someone who isn't afraid to scrub a toilet over a smooth talker any day. Okay, this wasn't supposed to turn into a performance review or make you feel like you're at work. I'm sorry—"

"James." This time, she squeezed his arm—just grabbed it without thinking. She couldn't help it. Something about the tagline he'd thrown out a minute ago had unlocked something for her.

*A lot of good in the neighborhood.*

"You did it, James. You helped me figure out my project."

An image of Anna Claire flashed in her mind, and she pulled her hand away, though it helped that he hadn't flinched at her touch.

She pressed the elevator button again. Now that she had an idea to work with, her fingertips were tingling to begin. The door slid open and she walked on.

"Thanks to you, all I have to do is put it together."

"You're welcome." The door started to close, but he put his hand over it to stop it. "Um . . . we should celebrate your successful project, don't you think? *I* think dessert is a fun way to celebrate. How does tomorrow night sound? Do you have any meetings then?"

"Dessert. As in, pieces of cake blended into a chocolate shake?"

He shook his head like some drama queen. "If only. Nobody can blend like Portillo's back home."

*Home.* Dessert with Just James. Two things about the future she didn't dread, though she wondered if they violated work rules. Not if they were just friends, right? This had to be him only being kind again, not, like, a date or anything.

"That sounds nice, James. Tomorrow night should work."

The way his face brightened and the way he tried to temper that brightness made the butterflies come back in legions.

"I'll be in touch." He stepped back and let the elevator close, holding her gaze until the door was all the way shut.

Now it was only her and a burst of nervous energy. Hopefully it would propel her into at least an hour of productivity. She sipped her coffee and opened her phone to the articles Hendrix had sent.

The first headline read, "Fine Dining Favorite Under Fire for Health Code Violations."

According to the journalist, an inspector visited the Red Knot on December 14, a few months after Dylan was born, and found multiple violations "that could endanger the health and safety of the public." Those dangers included dozens of roaches and rodent droppings.

A gagging sensation caught in the back of her throat, making her wish she had fresh air to combat it, not the distinct odor of the elevator—something like grease and ozone. She fanned herself and kept reading. The article explained that emergency shutdowns weren't a punishment, but rather a way to protect the public from safety hazards such as a lack of hot water, sewage backups, fire damage, pest infestation, or inadequate refrigeration. There were no statements from either of her parents in the article, nobody combating the narrative that Candis was careless or thoughtless. In real life, her mom was ruthlessly particular about details—especially ones involving kitchen counters, knives, stovetops, and spices.

The article ended by saying the Red Knot reopened on December 16, after a return visit by the inspector. The restaurant had corrected its violations and once again complied with Florida's Department of Business and Professional Regulation codes.

Dylan went back to her email and pulled up the next article, dated a month after the previous one: "The Red Knot Under New Ownership and New Knives."

Just as Hendrix had described, the announcement said Venture-Gold Group was selling the restaurant and her mom would no longer be the executive chef. The entire article was a single paragraph, with no further explanation.

Dylan clicked the last link. This article was out of chronological order but far longer too—an entire feature on her mom.

The elevator air was even thicker than before.

She braced herself for impact.

# Yes, Chef: Candis Turner's Rise to the Red Knot

**Demetrius Ross,** *The Jacksonville Times*

[Today's From the Archives article is an in-depth interview of the Red Knot's beloved Chef Candis Turner. This article was originally published 30 years ago.]

---

It's my pleasure to go in-depth with one of our favorite Jacksonville residents, Chef Candis Turner. She's taken the culinary world by storm over the past ten years, so we're excited to cover everything from her path to becoming a chef, to her journey opening the Red Knot, to her surprise pregnancy announcement.

**Ross:** Chef Candis, you've become a household name in the culinary world, including here in Jacksonville. Tell us about the moment you knew you wanted to become a chef.

**Turner:** When I was 14, I joined 4-H and did the CERT Program—which is all about emergency response—and learned about food safety. We mastered culinary fundamentals, but I'd always go beyond the basics to make each meal my own unique creation. My teacher kept saying I might not have access to flavor during an emergency, but he always finished the plate I made for him. Our team also entered a state cooking competition and took first place, with the three of us being named Rising Chefs.

**Ross:** There must have been some struggles along your path to becoming such a powerhouse. Can you describe any of those, and what it has taken to overcome them?

**Turner:** It's no secret there's a weight of sexism hanging on this industry. Women are told their place is in the kitchen, except when that kitchen is in a restaurant earning stars or diamonds. We aren't paid equally, nor respected equally, even though the quality we produce is just as good. Did you know 80 percent of women have experienced harassment in this industry?

One thing that helps me is to remember the women who came before me and made my career possible, like Eugénie Brazier. A man was recently honored in the press for being the first chef to win six Michelin stars, even though Eugénie did that over fifty years ago. I want to do the same for other people who've been told they don't belong here when their talent says otherwise.

**Ross:** Interesting, as you've also faced criticism by some who credit your success to your husband. Is it true you wouldn't be in this position, starting a place like the Red Knot, without his financial investment?

**Turner:** Of course, but that's true for every chef who isn't bathing in loads of cash, which is most of the chefs I studied next to. It takes money to open any business, including a restaurant. I proved my talents at the Prime. How I use a knife got me here too, not just the pretty smile I save for my husband.

**Ross:** Tell us more about your love story with Darren Turner.

**Turner:** What can I say? We met while I was working at the Prime. Darren respected my goals, and I understood his drive. He was a rare find for me, someone who saw my potential and even wanted to help me start my own place. We fell head over heels and got married a few months later. Marriage isn't always easy, though.

**Ross:** How would you react to people who say you're too cutthroat in the kitchen? You've experienced some disgruntled employees in the past.

**Turner:** My goal is never to belittle people—that is what I experienced over and over in my training, especially when I worked as a sous-chef. It didn't make me perform my duties better when my boss insulted my mother. My goal is to hold my chefs to a high standard in a typically high-pressured environment, without demeaning their humanity. In fact, I relish seeing my chefs rise to the many challenges of working in fine dining.

**Ross:** You're ambitious, especially considering you have a little one on the way. How will you manage raising a family while running the Red Knot? That is, assuming your baby bump is not from eating your own cooking.

**Turner:** Yes, we are going to have a baby. My husband and I are still figuring out the logistics, but we will work together to raise our family, even in our unique circumstances.

**Ross:** The rumor is you're on track to earn the AAA Five Diamond Award. What's it like to be so close you can taste success?

**Turner:** I try to live by the rule to not count your diamonds before they've been set on your ring finger.

## 20

# Edited to Add

In the time she read the articles, Dylan had ridden the elevator up beyond her floor and then back down several others, ignoring the passengers entering and exiting around her. She pressed the number to her floor again but this time got off when she was supposed to.

Hendrix was right. Again. She'd been so caught up following her dad's clues and waiting for a message from a distant relative that she didn't think to look up more information about the obvious—the two parents she'd known all her life.

She unlocked her door, sat on the bed, and tore open her journal to her list. Next to the first three items she'd written down, she scribbled new notes.

1. Who is my biological father? And mother?
   A RESTAURANT?!

2. Why didn't my mom tell me? About my bio dad
   OR HER RESTAURANT?!

3. Does everyone know but me? Aunt Lou = sus

4. Who am I?

Her parents had run an entire restaurant. Her mom used to be an executive chef. Darren and Candis Turner used to be in love. It all blew her mind, over and over.

Her mom's intensity came through the interview loud and clear. That always hovered beneath the surface, until Dylan said something that poked a hole in the hot air balloon of her mom's temper.

She'd always thought of her dad as driven. He was the one who kept getting promotions in new cities and subsequently outgrowing those promotions. He was the dreamer, the doer. Sure, her mom loved the art she created in her own kitchen, but she'd never spoken a single word about the Red Knot. If cooking food for others had been her happy place, Dylan couldn't imagine a reason she'd quit.

Except for having a kid. Was she the reason her mom had given it all up? Was that why her mom struggled to like her? Restaurant hours weren't exactly conducive to raising a young child. Had her mom felt like she'd had to choose between the Red Knot and Dylan?

Something about the interview seemed off too, like the way her responses got shorter at the end. Speaking of questions, a few of those hadn't aged well.

She rubbed her temples and took a sip of her coffee. Her own questions were mounting, but it was time to knock out this business proposal. She pulled out her laptop and got to work, putting in hours and going as far as to create graphics and a slideshow on Canva for her fake company. It was the most satisfying work she'd done in a long time.

The caffeine coursing through her veins weakened, and her eyelids got heavy so quickly, she didn't remember letting them close.

Didn't even have time to set an alarm for the next morning.

## 21

# Desperate Times

### Thursday, September 25

Dylan's phone dinged with a text. While she clawed at the sleepers in her eyes, a sense of dread wrapped itself around her like a weighted blanket.

Her phone dinged again, and she picked it up.

**That Man:** here

**That Man:** where r u

If Hendrix was here, at the hotel, that meant it was 8:30 A.M. She was supposed to be waiting in the lobby, ready to be picked up. Panic surged from her gut.

**Me:** Be down in five!

She threw off the bulky hotel comforter and sprinted to the bathroom to perform a lightning round of deodorant and mascara and teeth brushing. She settled for last night's outfit too, grateful it could present as business casual. Jeans and a red T-shirt might not have the same effect in this conference room as it did at her day job.

She grabbed her purse, threw her laptop into its flowery protective case, and ran for the elevator.

It was 8:37 when she climbed into Hendrix's car.

"I'm so sorry," she apologized.

He had Royal Cape's address pulled up on his phone and pressed Start on the directions it had given him. He checked his surroundings and pulled out of the hotel driveway.

"I thought we agreed on 8:30." His tone was sharp.

"I know. I overslept. *Sorry.*" She pulled down the visor mirror and checked her face for stray flecks of makeup and dried drool.

He sighed, like maybe he was going to stop holding this over her. "So, what's your business plan? An art dealer? A store for tightrope walkers? Just a whole bunch of hacky sacks?"

She slammed the visor shut. "I'm so not in the mood for this, Hendrix."

"I'm not in the mood for being late," he countered.

She fluffed her hair and settled back into the seat. "For the sake of salvaging the morning, I'm going to ignore that comment."

Her phone dinged. She took it out of her purse. Besides her battery being at 18 percent, she had three other push notifications she hadn't had time to swipe through earlier. An email from KindreDNA advertising discounts for referring friends and family to their testing kits. A calendar reminder that her meeting with RCC was starting in twenty minutes. And a text from James, which she opened.

> **Captain Jim:** How did your project turn out? Everything good in the neighborhood? ☺

She glanced over at Hendrix before replying.

> **Me:** The project came together great last night, but I overslept this morning. Rushing to my meeting now!

**Captain Jim:** *gasp*

**Captain Jim:** So unlike you!

**Me:** Now you have to take back everything nice you said about me last night.

**Me:** None of this "reliable" nonsense.

**Captain Jim:** Never

**Me:** Please tell me the treasure was hunted and found.

**Me:** And more souls were recruited into your cult.

**Captain Jim:** The treasure was found and turned out to be . . .

**Captain Jim:** All of us agreeing to build a compound together.

**Me:** Even better than bags of Pirate's Booty.

**Captain Jim:** THAT'S WHAT I THOUGHT.

**Captain Jim:** Gotta run.

**Captain Jim:** First session starting soon.

**Captain Jim:** Pin the Lei on the Captain.

**Captain Jim:** I'll check in later. GOOD LUCK!!!!!!!!

It was getting harder to hide her grin.

Over the years, her work schedule had taught her to be a morning person, but talking to James outside work was like the perfect cup of coffee at the start of her morning—an extra boost to rise and shine. It was something she'd cherish about this short stint outside their grocery store world of being associates.

She swiped out of her conversation with James to the rest of her messages.

"Okay, my business pla—"

She had another text. One she'd gotten late last night from a 414 number. She opened it.

> this is my
>
> new #
>
> late. I'll call tomorrow

She had no idea who this was. It wasn't a familiar area code to her, as she'd given up memorizing area codes five moves ago. The time stamp on the texts was just after 10:00 P.M. last night. She'd been so busy with her proposal she must have missed them—the same way she'd missed setting an alarm. It was probably someone who had the wrong number.

Hendrix took his hand off the steering wheel to wave at her. "Earth to Dylan Turner?"

Right. Business plan. She was in a car with Hendrix, about to present her business plan. She tucked her phone away.

"Yes, I finished it last night. It's probably dumb, but—"

"Let me stop you right there," he interrupted. "Even if you think your idea is dumb, you better sit down in that room and act like it's the most amazing idea they've ever heard and will ever hear. It's so amazing, they should be kicking themselves for not recognizing this crucial human need you thought of how to fill with your business. *That's* the kind of energy you need to walk into that room with."

If he didn't sound so irritated, she might take his motivational speech to heart.

"I thought it might be—*is*—a good idea to propose an event-planning business and space with room for up to fifty people. So, not huge weddings and stuff, but a community room for birthdays, corporate events, maybe even a co-working space for virtual workers three days a week. I would manage the space and plan the events, organizing logistics with different levels of involvement depending on the price people are willing to pay. I would keep materials stocked, be in charge of setup and teardown."

Why was she so nervous saying it out loud?

"It's called the NeighborGood, 'Bringing the good of our neighborhood together.' Or something like that."

She waited, then stole a glance at Hendrix. She hated herself for it, but she needed his approval on this. He couldn't give her a standing ovation while driving, obviously, but anything on a related note would do.

"Nice," he said, tapping the steering wheel along with the quiet background music, which happened to be Green Day's "Boulevard of Broken Dreams."

Now he was mumbling the lyrics, like he'd forgotten they were even talking about her proposal.

"*Nice.* That's all you have to say. That's your entire reaction to my proposal."

"Yeah. It's *nice.* It's a nice idea. What else do you want me to say about it? Were you expecting applause?"

She scoffed. "Well, no. You could've tried, 'Wow, that's really creative, Dylan. I see the hours of effort you put into this project, Dylan. Thank you, Dylan.'"

"I wouldn't say this is a huge moneymaker or anything, but it sounds like a presentation you thought through enough that it can lead into the real conversation."

There was a strong uptick in her chest, as well as a spark of disappointment that NeighborGood wasn't the real conversation.

"I'm not sure how I'll segue from the NeighborGood to 'Do you know Darren Turner?' Can you help me with that part?"

"Sure." He eyed her flowery laptop case, which was resting on her lap. "Do you have a briefcase you can put your laptop into?"

"No. Why?"

"We're about to enter corporate America, and that laptop case makes you look like a high school intern instead of a serious businesswoman."

"I thought this was a fake business proposal, not the real focus of this conversation. Besides, we already *have* a meeting, so our foot is in the door. We are all the way through the door, Hendrix."

"Whatever." He brooded in the driver's seat like a storm cloud about to rain in her morning cup of coffee.

She could use one of those, though she wasn't sure if she was referring to *coffee* coffee or a text from James.

"What's wrong with you today?" she demanded.

"Nothing."

"If you're going to force me to act like some confident 'boss babe' pretending I have the 'best idea in the world,' I need you to be the not-so-annoying charmer who helps me get the information I need."

He glanced at her, then nodded.

"Seriously, man. I can't go in there with you acting like this. You need to either tell me what's bothering you or suck it up."

"I'll suck it up, then. And for the record, I never called you a boss babe."

"I know. I was reading your thoughts," she retorted. The thought had come to mind when she read the articles about her mom last night. That was what Candis Turner sounded like in her interview. Confident. Ambitious. Trailblazing. Maybe she could pull it together and channel some of that DNA hiding somewhere deep inside her.

She wasn't convinced Hendrix would pull it together with her, but she didn't push any further.

"So, do we need a secret code for while we're in there, in case there's an emergency and we need to book it out? Something like 'Cacaw! Cacaw!'" she crowed.

He didn't laugh.

---

Royal Cape Companies' offices weren't in a traditional high-rise or strip mall but in a stately historic home resting on the banks of the Saint Johns River. They parked on the street in front of it, then followed the manicured walkway to double French doors. Inside, the entryway was warm and enchanting with sprawling wood floors, a sparkling chandelier, and lush green plants tucked in every corner.

Dylan clutched her flowery laptop case to her chest.

The young man sitting at the front desk, whose nameplate read *Braxton—Office Manager*, greeted them with a smile. "Welcome to Royal Cape Companies. How may I help you?"

She looked at Hendrix, who didn't say anything and apparently wasn't going to get a grip, and realized she'd have to do this herself. She took a shaky step forward.

"Yeah, hi. We're here to see the vice president of leasing? Mr. Drake, I believe?"

She scolded herself for not sounding like the women she'd come across on Instagram, the ones who'd go live from their car to "quickly offer sixteen strategies for harnessing empowerment and projecting positivity."

Braxton looked from Dylan to Hendrix. "Oh yes, I spoke to one of you on the phone yesterday."

Hendrix nodded.

She thought about elbowing him, but Braxton was already picking up the desk phone and pushing buttons.

"Mr. Drake? Your nine o'clock is here."

An unintelligible garbling came through the receiver, loud enough for Dylan to guess Mr. Drake was caught off guard by the meeting. Her heart dropped.

The assistant spun his chair toward the wall. "It was put on the books at the end," he whispered into the phone. "I didn't know about the tee time. . . . *That* wasn't on the books, sir."

She glanced at Hendrix, who was still avoiding looking directly at her.

Braxton turned back to them. "Just one second," he mouthed. "Yes, only fifteen minutes," he said into the phone. "I'll bring them to the conference room."

He hung up the phone and tidied a stack of papers on his desk.

She leaned in. "Is Mr. Drake expecting us?"

The young man plastered a polite smile on his face and stood up, leaving the chair spinning. "Right this way."

Dylan and Hendrix followed him to a spacious conference room. There was a large wooden table surrounded by camel leather chairs and canvases capturing Jacksonville's nightlife evenly interrupting the white walls. The room fit the way the "little big town" of Jacksonville marketed itself online—where beach meets city meets a sprawling landscape of parks and music festivals.

"Mr. Drake will be with you shortly," Braxton announced before disappearing out the door.

Hendrix and Dylan had just enough time to pick chairs before a man barreled into the room and sat across the table from them. He had slicked hair and a perfectly ironed shirt tucked into tight, crisp pants.

Her recycled outfit felt cheap and thoughtless.

"Mr. Drake. Vice president of leasing" was his introduction.

If only she were in the forest preserve, an open trail in front of her where she could sprint away. Her lungs froze.

The silence was getting awkward. Unlike on the ride over, Hendrix's eyes were all over her now.

He stood up and held out his hand, which Mr. Drake gripped. The smile on Hendrix's face dazzled like a Christmas miracle. "Thank you for meeting us."

She watched him sit back down, unsure where the sudden burst of charisma had come from but also grateful for the surprise fireworks show.

"We don't need much of your time." The words schmoozed from Hendrix's mouth into Mr. Drake's ears. "My business partner, Dylan, and I are excited to share an opportunity that fits perfectly with the vision of your development coming to 16th Terrace. I'll let her take it from here."

Mr. Drake tapped the screen of his phone, which was sitting on the table, then crossed his arms. The seconds of his attention were ticking away.

*Fake business, fake business, fake business,* she thought. *Confident. Ambitious. Trailblazer.*

The mantras didn't help. She still felt like an unprepared contestant on *Shark Tank*.

She opened her computer and scooted it closer to Mr. Drake so he wouldn't have to squint to read the screen. He didn't seem like a man who ever *scooted* anything.

Wiping her clammy hands on the sides of her dress, she began. "You're building a development that will house people from a variety of incomes, and now you're looking for businesses that will match your vision. What our business wants to focus on is ways we can foster community in and around your complex."

That wasn't the worst start. Maybe she could get the hang of this.

"You're building great spaces for people to live, and what we want is to bring in a great space for people to gather. We envision this being a place where people can do everything from hosting corporate luncheons to celebrating birthdays, and our job is to take care of the logistics. We call it the NeighborG—"

"This sounds . . . sweet and all," Mr. Drake interrupted, looking at his phone again, "but it's basically a restaurant, and we already have plenty of those asking to lease the space. Thank you for your time, Devin."

She gaped. She'd been given only three of the fifteen minutes that were promised.

Hendrix stood and tried to talk Mr. Drake back into his seat, but her desperation sent her in a different direction. She got out her phone and swiped around until it was displaying a picture.

A photo of her dad accepting his Forty Under 40 Award.

"This business is in honor of my late father, Darren Turner. Every time we moved somewhere new, which was often, he would host an amazing housewarming—"

"Is this some kind of sick joke?" Mr. Drake's nostrils flared as he stared at the photo. He'd seemed mid-grade annoyed before, but now he was outright hostile.

"No?" she squeaked.

"Who sent you here?" Mr. Drake's eyes darted around the room. "Wait here," he growled before she could answer. "Don't move." Then he stormed out.

Hendrix looked at her.

They both knew, because it had been indoctrinated into them, that the number one rule of self-defense was to fight *only* enough to give yourself a chance to get away.

"Cacaw?" he said.

"Cacaw." She threw her laptop into its juvenile case and grabbed her purse.

She'd run to get to this meeting on time, and now she was running to get out of it.

Hendrix grabbed her hand and yanked her and her impractical pair of pumps through the large house to the front door.

"Bye, Braxton," he said over his shoulder to the young man, who was stacking more papers.

"Goodbye?"

They made it outside and then down the walkway and almost to the car.

"Dylan? Dylan Turner?" someone hollered at them.

It wasn't Mr. Drake.

"Wait!" the person yelled again.

The voice was familiar, but she couldn't place it.

"It's Mr. Westmore—Brooke's dad!"

## 22

# Magnets Repel Too

Mr. Westmore and Dylan walked toward each other until they met in the middle, halfway between the office she'd just fled and the street she was fleeing toward. His silver temples and web of wrinkles wove a story she hadn't been part of for over twenty years.

He pulled away from their hug. "You're all grown up, Dylan, just like my Brooke."

The fear propelling her earlier subsided. "Mr. Westmore. I can't believe it's really you."

"You're old enough to call me Rob now." He smiled, then tilted his head in concern. "Do you have a minute? I'd love to chat with you back inside."

She looked at Hendrix, who watched them with crossed arms and a steel glare. She couldn't blame him—they still didn't know why Mr. Drake had exploded back there. But maybe they were overreacting. Maybe the news of Darren's death had put Mr. Drake in shock. Shock on steroids.

"I'll meet you at the car in a few minutes," she told Hendrix.

"I can come with you."

For all the ways he'd irked her that morning, she appreciated how protective he was being.

"It's okay. Mr. Westmore—I mean, Rob—is another old friend."

She followed Rob back toward Royal Cape Companies, looking

over her shoulder only once to find Hendrix hadn't stopped watching her.

In Rob's office, it took her all of three seconds to find his nameplate and realize it said *CEO*.

She groaned. If she'd been the one to look up Royal Cape Companies instead of Hendrix, she would've recognized Rob immediately and been able to skip the agony of her fake business that Mr. Drake had zero appreciation for. She'd not only put herself out there to have her ideas squashed—she'd also wasted precious time.

"So, how is Brooke? What is she up to these days?" she asked while Rob settled into his chair.

He turned his phone face down and folded his hands. "She's a busy mom with four kids. Spends most of her time running the PTA and chauffeuring everyone to their activities. Her husband works for me, actually."

Hopefully her husband wasn't Mr. Drake. "And Mrs. Westmore?"

Rob shifted in his seat. "There is no more Mrs. Westmore."

Dylan squeezed her eyes shut and shook her head. "I'm so sorry. How long ago did she pass?"

He grimaced. "We . . . uh . . . split about ten years ago. She's Mrs. Howard now."

He absently rubbed the spot where he once wore a wedding band.

She didn't dare ask what in the ever-loving world had happened to the Westmores' marriage, but she wanted to know.

"What is it *you* do?" Rob pivoted. "Was that your husband outside? Do you have a bunch of little ones at home too?"

She laughed like he'd just told a joke. Married, *with* children, *to* Hendrix, was a joke. She didn't want Rob to think she was mocking Brooke, though. "I'm not married. And, I work for Trader Joe's."

"Brooke's mentioned that grocery chain before. What's your area of expertise?"

In the presence of the successful Rob Westmore, CEO of Royal

Cape Companies, who was currently wearing a tailored navy suit, she really wanted to be able to say something like *marketing coordinator* or *financial reporting accountant*.

"I am an . . . inventory and customer service . . . specialist," she tried.

"Hmm. That's wonderful, Dylan."

She crinkled her eyes and nodded back, wondering if he could see right through her.

"And your parents?"

Her heart ached. "Actually, that's the reason I'm here. My dad . . ." She coughed back the surge of emotion threatening to spill over. "He passed away last week. He was really sick."

Sharing the news with Rob in this way was a crushing reminder of how their families had lost touch. It had been decades ago, but it still confused her why they stopped talking after being so close. The kind of friends you'd expect at your wedding or funeral.

She couldn't read Rob's reaction through the curtain of her own tears.

"I'm sorry for your loss," he said after a moment's pause. "I can't imagine losing a father at such a young age."

"Thank you."

She smoothed her dress to distract herself. She needed to focus, not sob in front of Rob, a potential wealth of information.

*Who am I?*

*Does everyone know but me?*

"My dad gave me a birthday card that had the address *331 16th Terrace* written on it. I flew here yesterday to visit that address, but as you know, it's for a development that's not even built yet. And then I saw Royal Cape Companies' sign, and now knowing you're with that company, it makes me wonder if for some reason my dad wanted me to meet up with you again after he died." She tried to funnel her scattered thoughts into a single question. "Would there be any reason he'd want that?"

She decided to leave out the not-biological part.

Rob's hands were already folded, but they squeezed tighter. "It's certainly interesting he wrote down *that* address, and that he didn't just give you my direct info listed online."

"Is there some sort of connection between my dad and that property? Or to this company, besides you?"

"Your dad never worked for Royal Cape. We worked together at VentureGold Group, but that was many years ago, long before I started this company." Rob fixed his tie, then refolded his hands. "I will say, your father was a sharp salesman. He could sell a block of ice to the peak of Mount Everest if he put his mind to it."

She remembered visiting her dad's many offices as a child. Every time, he had another award on the wall to show them. There was the Forty Under 40 Award—from the picture she'd shown Mr. Drake. Atlanta's Up and Coming. And so on.

"That's right. VentureGold Group," she said. "You worked together when my parents opened the Red Knot."

Pieces of the puzzle were finally coming together.

"Your mom told you about the Red Knot?" Rob's mouth didn't shout, but his face did.

"No. I found out about it recently. Yesterday, actually."

She pictured Hendrix sitting across from her at the Red Knot, illuminated by candlelight.

"I always loved Candis—she was a straight shooter." Rob took another one-eighty in their conversation, unclenching his hands and pressing them flat to his desk. "I've never had cuisine as good as what she used to make either. If it's okay, I'd like to get in touch with your mom to pass on my condolences."

He smiled then, a professional smile she imagined was similar to the one in the headshot he'd have taken for the RCC website. He was staring at her too. Like, really staring—his gaze the microscope and she the specimen.

What was he trying to see?

She hated where her mind went, the way her breathing got shallower. No wedding band. He *loved* Candis, but what did that mean? Like a friend, or like he *loved* her? She still hadn't disproved her mom had an affair and got pregnant with her. An affair could lead to other gross theories.

Like, Rob could be her father.

Brooke, her half sister.

Maybe that was why her mom hadn't wanted her writing letters to Brooke.

"A phone number or mailing address? I'd be happy with email too."

Rob's prodding got her attention. He'd already slid a pen and pad of paper across his desk.

She wrote all of it down—phone, address, email. She'd share all the sensitive intel if it meant not having to be middleman for her mom.

"Did something happen between you and my dad?" The question came out before she could bite it back, but she'd wanted to know for so long. She needed to walk away from this meeting with something. "I know I was only eight at the time, but it seemed like our families were close, and then we never saw each other again. I even tried writing a letter to Brooke after we moved."

Rob inhaled like he was gearing up to tell a long story but there wasn't enough oxygen in his office to tell it.

"I first rubbed shoulders with your dad at a golf outing about forty years ago. We hit it off, so I introduced him to my father, who happened to be the CEO of an investment firm. Your dad nailed his informal interview, and my dad hired him on the spot. Not only was his personality magnetic; his official résumé was also impeccable. Here comes this kid, basically off the street with no personal connections, who'd somehow made his way into some of the largest investment companies and been part of signing two of the largest deals of our day. Honestly, I thought him coming to my dad's firm would be a step down for him. He was almost too good to be true."

Pride swelled up until it threatened more tears. Her dad had always seemed larger than life.

Rob tugged on the collar of his dress shirt. "Your dad and I were a dynamic duo for quite a few years, which was why we set off on our own to start VentureGold Group—much to my old man's disappointment. Your dad was the most confident man I ever met, so I put my faith in him. And then Candis came into the picture."

Dylan's insides curdled. Had Candis ripped them apart? Had she been the prize two competitive, jealous friends had tried to win?

"I've never met such a power couple." Rob stared into the distance, caught up in yesteryear. "There was, however, some disagreement between your dad and the board of VentureGold Group. Your dad's friend was building a music device called ShuffleBeats that he projected would eventually make his company worth nearly $2.4 million. Multiply that tenfold, and it will give you an idea of how much that would be today," he explained. "VentureGold was hesitant about it. They felt like the investment was too big a risk, and a knockoff of some other rising tech of its kind—like Sony's Discman. They also thought Darren had a bad habit of spending money on clients that went above and beyond a little southern hospitality.

"But Darren insisted. He wanted to diversify our investments beyond real estate into technology and medicine. Eventually, the board went along with him and invested a lot of money into ShuffleBeats."

She felt for the hem of her dress, trying to calm herself as the story built.

"ShuffleBeats didn't just struggle; it completely folded in the first year. Millions of VentureGold's capital—gone. The board wanted Darren gone too."

Rob cleared his throat. "I felt bad for your dad. By that time, the Red Knot was up and running and kept your parents extremely busy. So much so, your dad was around a lot less than he used to be—and he missed out on some important deals. The relationship between the board and your dad fizzled. He had a big personality, but that didn't always fit well into the confined spaces of a boardroom."

Everything he shared brought up twenty more questions, but she didn't know how much time she had, so she forced herself to ask the next one.

"Mr. West— I mean, um, Rob, I have something strange and, honestly, uncomfortable to ask you. Did my parents ever struggle with . . ."

She didn't know what to say next.

*Marital issues?*

*Infidelity?*

*A genuine disdain for each other?*

At the moment, the generation gap between her and Rob was a canyon. While her peers talked openly about their private lives online, these were topics their Gen X elders hushed.

She went with "Fertility?"

Rob Westmore, sophisticated businessman, blushed.

Was blushing considered substantive evidence?

"I'm not familiar with that part of their relationship," he answered. "It's possible your mom talked about that with my ex-wife, but you'd have to ask her. Interesting you ask, though, because the address your dad wrote down—"

"Papa!" a little girl with big curls interrupted, running into the room and jumping into Rob's lap.

He melted into a tender hug for his granddaughter. "Annabanana! Does that mean your mommy is here too?"

Dylan turned in her chair just in time to watch two more kids—likely twins—toddle into the room, followed by a woman with her baby held in a carrier.

Brooke Westmore.

Or, Brooke Westmore Whatever-Her-Married-Last-Name-Was.

Her childhood friend had grown up to look like what she pictured if Mattel made a Soccer Mom Barbie. Brooke's long ponytail had finished waves that could have only been made with a curling iron. She was wearing a baseball cap and full face of makeup with lashes, though her concealer didn't cover the tired veins under her eyes.

Dylan was starstruck. This person had lived on the highest pedestal of her memories for a long time.

Rob pointed to her. "Brooke, do you remember Dylan Turner?"

"Dylan? Wow, it's really you." Brooke said it more like a statement than an exclamation, but Dylan didn't know if that was because she wasn't excited or was just distracted. The baby was gripping Brooke's ponytail with a tight fist while one of the toddlers attached himself to her leg.

Dylan couldn't help herself; she needed to embrace Brooke too. She pulled her old friend into a tight hug—hopefully not too tight for the baby—clinging to everything they used to do together. Sleepovers, dolls, choreographed dances, getting pizza on Saturdays, spying on Gavin and Graham, Brooke's big brothers.

Brooke pulled away first. "I'm shocked. It's been a really long time."

*Shocked* as in an amazing surprise, or something else? She hated how much she was overthinking each word, each weary smile. "Yeah."

"Brooke, honey"—Rob stepped in—"Dylan shared that Mr. Turner passed away last week."

Brooke's face filled with pity. "That's awful. I'm sorry for your loss. Hey—Anna. Stop doing that."

"Anna-banana" had climbed off her grandpa's lap and was now tugging on the other twin.

"And," Rob continued, "Dylan works for Trader Joe's. She's a . . . What was it again?"

"A stock and customer service specialist." She raised her voice over the growing volume of children's voices in the room.

Brooke rifled through her diaper bag and pulled out a sippy cup. "That's so . . . neat."

Little hands and voices continued begging for attention, which Rob and Brooke turned to tend to. She was now the guest who'd overstayed her welcome—not exactly how she'd pictured this reunion going. She had more questions, more gaps to fill.

Rob stood and picked up one of the twins. "It was nice to see you again, Dylan."

A polite way to say, *It's time for you to go.*

"Wait. Rob. Can I have your contact information? In case I have more questions later?"

He pulled a business card out of his desk and held it out to her.

"Thank you." She took it and stepped toward the door. "One last thing. What were you going to say earlier? About the address of your new development?"

Rob looked up from his grandson. "It used to be a fertility clinic."

# 23

# Pedal to the Nettle

Dylan waited for Hendrix to react to what she'd blurted, but he took too long. "Did you hear me? I said that property on 16th Terrace used to be a *fertility clinic*."

"Hmm," Hendrix grunted.

"The property had a few businesses after that, then sat vacant for a couple years until Royal Cape bought the land for their new complex."

She buckled herself in, expecting Hendrix would start the car anytime now.

"I still want to point out this doesn't completely eliminate my theory about my mom. The Westmores got divorced a decade ago, *and* Mr. Westmore said he loved my mom, whatever that means."

"In that case, your half sister is here to see you."

"What? That's not funny—"

A knock on the window interrupted her. She turned to find Brooke standing there with no children clinging to any of her body parts. Hendrix didn't seem in the mood to be asked to roll down a window, so Dylan opened the door and got out instead.

"Brooke! Hi. Is something wrong?"

This time, Brooke pulled her into a tight hug, gripping her like she meant it. "Not at all. I'm sorry for being so out of it back there. The twins had me up all night, and there was this big event at school this morning, and my best friend is getting married tomorrow. My mom keeps calling at the worst times—I'm a bit foggy is what I'm saying."

"Oh. You don't have to apologize," Dylan said, remembering when she had a best friend, who happened to be the woman standing in front of her. "I understand. Well, I *don't* understand the brain fog of raising twins plus other children plus those commitments, but all that—it sounds tiring."

"They're lovable little monsters is the best way I can describe it." Brooke chuckled, pulling back. Her smile faded into something more somber. "I know we were really little when our families were friends, so this feels silly to admit, but seeing you brings up some stuff for me. Right after your family moved is when my parents' marriage started crumbling—I think my dad mentioned they're divorced. Part of me associates you with the time my family felt stable. I mean—I *should* be over my parents' divorce by now, but when they still refuse to be in the same room together, I don't know."

The vulnerability took Dylan by surprise, and she didn't know what to say. Instagram's claim was true: Everyone she met was fighting their own battles—even tired, stretched-thin moms who somehow still looked like Barbies. And Rob Westmores, feeling for where a wedding band used to be.

"Family, am I right?" It was the only way she knew how to acknowledge the weight of what Brooke shared without adding to her burden. She didn't want to start some sick round of Suffering Olympics, reciprocating Brooke's woes with her own list of childhood grievances.

"I don't think you're silly at all," Dylan continued. "We moved so many times after we lived here—after you—it was hard to make friends for a while." *Ever since then,* she was too embarrassed to say.

"I wrote you letters," Brooke blurted. "Two of them, actually."

Dylan flashed back to the kitchen. Those crumpled pieces of paper. Her cramped, determined little hand trying to write *Dear Brooke.*

"Seriously? Me too."

"I never got yours," they said at the same time.

It was like Brooke could read her questions, which was the biggest relief she'd felt so far on this trip. She hadn't grown up just dreaming their friendship was mutual.

"Maybe they got lost in the mail or something."

"Weird." Brooke shrugged. "Who knows anymore?"

*Does everyone know but me?* Something churned inside her.

"We were only—what—eight back then? But I cried for a long time after you left." Brooke laughed at herself, as if she felt silly for talking about a friendship that was obviously long-lost. As if they were a couple of kids—now strangers—who simply didn't get the bigger picture, so it shouldn't hurt so bad. "I guess what I wanted to say is that even though life took us in separate directions, I think of you as my first friend. A good one I made some core memories with."

What might have been—if they still lived near each other. If they'd been able to at least send a letter.

"Well, I can't leave my dad with the Monster Jam forever." Brooke gave her another hug—a quick one, turning their moment of fond reminiscence back to the reality of today. "I have to get going too. *Matron* of honor duties and all that."

It was the tiniest glimpse into Brooke's grown-up life—kids, best friend, divorced parents. *Busy.*

"Take care, Brooke. And thank you."

She got back into the car, where Hendrix was scrolling on his phone.

"Well, that was an interesting way to start the day." She buckled herself in, her nerves shot.

Hendrix started the car and sped away from the curb—a little fast for the quiet street they were on, especially when they hadn't talked about where they were going next.

"This isn't the Indianapolis 500," she pointed out.

He clenched the steering wheel, locked in on the road ahead of them. He'd been able to turn on the charm for Mr. Drake, but whatever had been bothering him earlier was back.

"That light you just drove through was very orange, if not fire-engine red."

He accelerated, and her pulse did the same.

"Hendrix, you're scaring me."

They were now at least twenty miles over the speed limit and nearing downtown's smaller city blocks.

"Pull over!" she yelled.

He slammed on the brakes and swerved the car up against the curb.

She put her hand on her chest to make sure she hadn't had a heart attack, then whipped around. "What is up with you today?"

He ripped off his seatbelt and stormed out of the car.

She wrestled her own seatbelt off and followed him to the riverwalk. She'd only seen him like this one other time, which was the last time she saw him fourteen years ago.

"For someone who claims he wants to help, you've sure been acting like a real tool today."

He stopped at the water's edge and leaned his elbows on the faded blue railing.

She stood next to him, putting her shoulder against his. The moving water lapped against the bank, waiting for him to break the silence.

He looked down. "I saw my dad last night."

The pain she felt for him was instant. She'd never heard a good story about Mark Reed.

"He was waiting for me when I got home from the Red Knot. Hadn't seen him in eight years. I've done everything I can to stay away, and somehow he landed on my doorstep like some stork with a sick sense of humor dropped him there."

Dylan put her hand on his back, just like she used to.

"I could tell he'd been on the streets. Too thin, had sores all over his face. He reeked too. He told me he was ready to get help but needed money for the rehab he wants to go to. I begged him to get help my entire life, and he waited until the burden would be on me."

She put her other arm around him and held him tight, resting her head against his back. It gutted her to see him like this, knowing just how deep his dad hurt him. There was no wisdom to share, only acknowledgments.

"You've been through more with your dad than any kid should."

He wiped his nose with a sleeve. "I don't know what I'm going to do. He makes me so angry, and then I get mad at myself for acting so angry, like I'm that scared little kid again."

"Hey, look at me." She put a hand on his cheek to turn his face toward her. The fear entrenched in his eyes scared her too. "You don't have to decide right this second what to do. You can give yourself time to think about it."

She pulled Hendrix into a hug, facing him straight on this time.

"His chaos isn't your burden to bear," she whispered into his shoulder, wondering if that could be true.

Could kids separate themselves from their parents' failures when their actions caused so much pain?

She relaxed in his arms. He was holding her too, his grip desperate and tight. It was intoxicating.

She'd sworn she wouldn't let him in again. This was a chance reunion. He was helping her. But then why did it feel like she'd been thrown back into the deep end of the feelings she had for him so long ago?

Hendrix looked at her, and she sensed the same sparks firing off him.

"Thank you, Dylan. I know I've been, well, difficult today, but it's nice getting to talk to you again. You get me. You know how much he messed me up."

They were connected—by their past, by complicated parents.

There was no rule saying this *wasn't* allowed to happen, that they should remain "associates."

She could even see another one of Jacksonville's bridges in the background. They hadn't met at the bridge like they were supposed to back then, but maybe they were meeting at one now, by some delayed plan.

If she were honest with herself, she'd missed him. She'd missed being *known* by someone like when they were teens. He touched her, and the sensation seeped into the cracks in her heart that had grown with each question of who she was and where she belonged.

*Who am I?*

For once, she was being held rather than having to hold herself together.

He was so close she could smell him, and before she could think—or make any sort of calculated decision—he was leaning in, pressing his lips to hers.

It took her by surprise, but not enough to pull away.

His lips were delicious, and she was suddenly ravenous. She kissed him back, putting her hands on his face and raking a hand through his hair. He gripped her waist and pulled her closer, sending another flood of tingles through her body. It wasn't the shy first kiss of two teenagers. It was the kiss of two people with a giant gap in their story, two people who'd found each other again.

She pulled back, not wanting to make a scene on this public riverwalk. There were other people down the path, including a stranger walking a golden retriever, and—

She took another step back from Hendrix.

James was in the distance. James was on the riverwalk, stopping to bend down and pet some stranger's golden retriever. Anna Claire was with him.

The heat buzzing through her body from Hendrix's kiss cooled into confusion.

Hendrix followed the trail of where she was looking and saw James too.

"Do you like him?" He sounded like a wounded puppy.

"I already told you we work together."

Bills to pay. Jobs to keep. Rules to follow—a rule that was the only red flag she needed. She couldn't uproot the life she worked so hard to keep stable and risk her job for some guy.

James and Anna Claire waved to the stranger and again to the stranger's dog, then followed the riverwalk back toward the hotel. James's hands were in his pockets, and Anna Claire was talking in a way that animated every one of her limbs, grazing James's arm.

Anna Claire walked like she already knew who she was and what she wanted to do with her life. She was bubbly . . . *nice*. She wasn't afraid to put herself out there, obviously, by the way she was dangling from James's arm every time Dylan saw her. She was like James in ways Dylan would never be. Shouldn't she want everything good and wholesome and beautiful for James? A person for him who could be far more than a co-worker?

She turned back to Hendrix. "I think he has a pretty good 'friend' already."

Hendrix nodded. "Looks like it."

"I want to go back to the hotel, follow the lead on this fertility clinic thing. Maybe look up more info on my parents."

He took a step closer to her. "Do you still need your assistant detective?"

She glanced at James, who was pointing at something across the river for Anna Claire to look at.

"Sure," she said, trying to suppress the edge in her voice.

She grabbed Hendrix's hand, leading him away from the riverwalk toward the car.

Hendrix pulled back against her, slowing her down so he could intertwine his fingers with hers. "Are we going this way to avoid James Jacob Jingleheimer Schmidt and his little girlfriend?"

His mood from earlier must've been contagious, because it was starting to cloud her over, much like the rainstorm rolling in and covering the once-hazy blue skies. If they didn't get back to the car soon, they might get poured on. It wouldn't be the first storm she'd gotten stuck in with Hendrix.

She refused to turn around for one last look at James. "Let's just go."

Page 116

## Caught in a Storm
### (16 years old)

Completely humiliated over here!!

Hendrix took me home from class tonight. It was pouring rain. Kind of romantic.

I wasn't ready to go inside, so when he parked in our driveway, I stayed in his car and hung out for a bit. By "hung out," I actually mean we "made out." He kissed me and I kissed him.

It was magical.

By "made out," I also mean we were out past curfew and . . . SO embarrassing . . . MY MOM FOUND US. In the car. In the middle of it.

She knocked on the window and didn't give me more than two seconds to explain myself before she yelled at us both to go in the house. She made us sit down at the counter, which is where she always tells me to sit when she's about to go on a yelling spree. She started chopping onions and then gave a whole long speech. By the time she finished, both mine and Hendrix's eyes were crying from the onions, and she'd pointed her sharp knife at us three times. I think her grand finale was: "Leave enough space between the two of you for your futures."

Finally, Dad stepped in and took the knife out of her hands and told Hendrix to head home.

Before all that EMBARRASSMENT, Hendrix told me he's going to run away from his dad. Says his mom never calls the police and he needs a break. He wants me to come with him. I said I couldn't, that would be impossible, but I still promised to meet up with him tomorrow just to make sure he's okay.

The plan is that we'll meet near the Palm Valley Bridge nearby. He's going to take his dad's car and pick me up.

My parents will kill me if they catch me sneaking out—my mom especially—but Hendrix needs me.

I think I love him.

xoxo Dylan

## 24

# Chron-Illogical

"Isn't it shocking how long you can live with a person and still know so little about them?" Dylan stared at her latest search.

**Google:** candis martin turner

Sitting at the desk in the hotel room, she swiveled to look at Hendrix, who was lounging against the downy mountain of pillows on the bed.

He looked up from his phone. "Again, nothing shocks me. The reason kids don't know their parents' secrets is because they don't ask their parents questions. Either they don't think to ask, they don't care enough to, or they're too afraid. So, secrets stay hidden."

"You forgot one category: The kid asks questions, but one parent dies and the other parent refuses to answer."

Until her mom had a change of heart, she'd have to keep filling in more blanks herself on the timeline she was piecing together on her laptop—a Word doc with dates and paragraphs pasted from the internet, helping her make sense of her family's past.

"It feels like I'm trying to write their biography. I just wish I could pass the work on to someone who'd get me a better grade."

Hendrix laughed. "Like every group project I did in high school."

"Exactly."

She'd started with birth dates but quickly jumped to the years she estimated her parents would've been in college. She already knew her dad was originally from Ohio, that his parents had him later in life and passed away before Dylan was born. How he ended up all the way in Jacksonville, rubbing shoulders with Rob Westmore, was a mystery. Her dad's "impeccable résumé" that Rob had mentioned probably no longer existed.

Her mom grew up in Gainesville, which explained why Candis hated every cold climate they moved to. One article about the Red Knot mentioned she got her degree at L'Academie de Cuisine in Maryland, one of the top culinary schools in the nation. Dylan had thought that might be a promising lead until she learned the school closed a few years ago.

Another dead end.

After culinary school, Candis spent a few years at the Prime in Orlando.

Dylan didn't know what came first—Jacksonville or Darren Turner. With her dad's endless travels, either option was possible.

But just as Hendrix mentioned before, Candis was a rising star, receiving a lot of local and even some national attention for her work as a chef, until she suddenly didn't anymore. The same went for Darren, whose accolades became less frequent the more he aged and the more he moved.

"A good old-fashioned case of ageism?" she joked.

"I don't think you're supposed to talk about ageism and call something 'old-fashioned' in the same sentence."

"Is the point to never call something *old,* or to not view things that are old with such disgust? Especially women?"

"You're getting off track."

"Probably, but none of this explains Mr. Drake's reaction to the picture of my dad."

"Maybe he was also connected to people from VentureGold Group. It sounded like your dad made a few enemies in his life, no matter how 'magnetic' Rob thinks he was. Listen to this—"

"Can I listen while I floss dinner out of my teeth? There's been something stuck in there since we went out last night."

She walked to the bathroom and opened her bag of toiletries.

Hendrix talked loud enough for her to hear from the other side of the wall. "VentureGold and Rob's dad's investment company—the first one Rob and your dad worked for—eventually merged their assets and rebranded into Royal Cape. It's possible a few people around Royal Cape know about Darren and the big loss with ShuffleBeats."

Dylan felt the chunk of food come loose from her molars, then checked her smile in the mirror before walking out of the bathroom. "True. Maybe Mr. Drake held on to some grudge for way too long."

"According to somebody I used to know"—he paused to let her recognize the line she'd used about him earlier—"people might hold on to grudges for good reasons."

She rolled her eyes, which he didn't see because he was flipping through a book.

"What are you reading?"

"Nothing."

She walked closer, and he pushed the book under a pillow, trying to hide the green and blue.

"Wait. Is that my . . ."

He was reading her journal, which she'd left on the bedside table. She ran over to the bed and swung for it, but he held it out of reach.

"How long have you been looking at that?" she demanded, her heart rate skyrocketing.

"Not long." He grinned. "And long enough."

"You may not read my journal."

"And why not?"

She crossed her arms, unsure if the flame inside was from humiliation or rage. Again, she swiped for it and missed.

"It's a violation of my teenage privacy, that's why."

Hendrix's smile was wicked. "How many entries in here are about me?"

"Zero."

"Zero? The journal you're freaking out about me reading has *zero* entries about me? Either you're a terrible liar, or you weren't as into me back then as I thought you were."

She pulled back to reconsider her strategy. Her heart had bled onto those pages, and she didn't want to let him in on the horror show. Maybe if they finally talked about what happened back then, she'd be able to open up about what she'd written.

She stared at Hendrix, who was looking annoyingly good given what he was doing to her.

Then she leaned in close—so close she could almost taste their kiss from earlier. One falter and her lips would be all over his again. After the way it felt outside the hotel, she didn't think she'd mind.

Another moment, staying close, caught in a haze of chemistry buzzing between them, knowing he felt it too.

She wanted to kiss him again, wanted to taste his lips, wanted to go back a few decades to when they were slightly less jaded. She closed her eyes, leaning in a millimeter closer, knowing if she waited just three seconds, two, and then one more second, his grip would loosen just enough—

"Got it." She ripped the journal out of his hand and held it tight to her chest as she ran back to the other side of the room. Her prize was watching how far his jaw dropped. "For a guy who says nothing shocks him, your face says you're pretty shocked right now."

"Not fair, Turner."

"All's fair." She put her hand on her hip, trying hard to pretend she hadn't been interested in her lips brushing his. "Now, I need your help for real. What would *you* do next? I have all this information, but I don't know how to piece it together in a way that makes sense."

Hendrix sighed, clearly disappointed by the turn this conversation was taking, and moved to the edge of the bed. "If you're really asking, here's a few suggestions. First, contact the journalist who wrote the last articles about the Red Knot."

She opened her journal and started taking notes.

"Second, contact a few of your dad's previous companies to see if there was any pattern as to why he moved so often. Third, see if there were any personal connections to the fertility clinic. Just to name a few things."

"Dang, Hendrix, you could be a professional stalker. Also, why didn't you include emailing Kathleen Schulz over and over until she finally responds?"

It had been at least eight hours since the last time she'd checked her messages, which she was sure made her a poster child for self-control.

"What if you never hear back from her?"

The question killed the mood in the room. The silence rang in her ears until the air conditioner sputtered back on.

"I'm serious, Dylan. Have you considered that? Because it's a real possibility. Also, what do you think finding your biological father will fix?"

No, she hadn't considered that. She didn't want to. "I want to know where the other half of me came from. I'm not sure what finding him or meeting Kathleen will fix, but right now it feels like it would help."

He nodded, then stood up off the bed and walked to her. He tugged at the journal she was holding.

"No—"

"Shh." He pressed his finger to her lips. "I'm not going to read it—I promise."

He put the journal on the desk, then wrapped her in his arms. The pressure and warmth quieted the loud thoughts in her head. She rested her head on his shoulder.

"It's only been a few days since I messaged her, but do you think I should already give up? Even if I don't hear from Kathleen, that doesn't mean there aren't other relatives I could get in touch with."

He looked down at her. "I think you can only control what *you* do in this awful scenario, not other people, and you're going to have to make peace with that." He placed the lightest kiss on her lips. "I have to go outside and make a phone call, but I'll be back later. We can continue this conversation then."

Him kissing her and then leaving gave her whiplash, but she'd already taken so much of his time.

"Okay."

"Hang in there, Dylan. I'd bet your breakthrough is coming."

He walked out of the room, and the door shut with a loud click.

Alone in the quiet, she climbed into bed and took the opportunity to check in with things back home.

**Me:** Hey Tara, I know you might be sleeping before work, so no rush to respond. I'm just curious how Gale and Peeta are doing?? I hope they haven't been too much trouble and that Tate is still enjoying them.

**Me:** Thank you again for your help!

She rolled over and reached for the TV remote sitting on the bedside table. After some brief channel surfing, she landed on HGTV to help her brain settle into zombie mode. It was easier than being in overdrive.

Fifteen minutes into a rerun of *Fixer Upper,* her phone dinged.

She checked it, then shot up into a sitting position. It wasn't a text from Tara. Or Hendrix. Or James. It was an email notification.

Maybe Hendrix was right—maybe her breakthrough was coming.

She had a new message on **KindreDNA**.

## INBOX (1)–DYLANTURNER918@GMAIL.COM

**From:** KindreDNA <info@KindreDNA.com>
**Date:** September 25
**To:** Turner, Dylan <dylanturner918@gmail.com>
**Subject:** You Have a New Message on KindreDNA!

### NEW MESSAGE!

You have a new message from: **K. Schulz**
To view this message in the KindreDNA app, click here.

**From K. Schulz:**

Hello Dylan.

It's vital we meet. Does tomorrow morning at 9 A.M. work?

I will meet you at Treaty Oak.

Regards.

**<How likely are you to recommend KindreDNA
to a friend or family member?
Take this 20-minute survey for a chance to
win a $5 KindreDNA gift card!>**

# 25

# Nature Versus Nurture

She thought of Gale and Peeta—the adorable *wheek* noise they made when she brought out a handful of veggies, and the way they popcorned their bodies off their mat when she got home from work. That was her insides now, reading Kathleen's email a second and third time—squealing and jumping.

Sure, it had been only forty-eight hours since Dylan messaged her, not long at all for someone to answer such delicate subject matter, but she felt like she could exhale. Kathleen Schulz had seen her message and responded.

She read the message a fourth time, inspecting each word and analyzing what it might mean. Too bad typed correspondence could only convey so much tone.

"*Vital we meet.*"

"*Tomorrow.*"

"*Regards.*"

She wanted to process it with someone, but Hendrix was still gone.

She looked at her phone, but the email vanished from her screen. In its place were two circles, one red and one green. It was playing her basic ringtone too.

She had an incoming call.

The number was area code 414, just like the texts she'd gotten last night. Whoever this was needed to know they had the wrong number—she'd text and let them know *after* the call ended on its own. She wasn't James, who navigated wrong number conversations in a way that could land him on Upworthy.

Tomorrow—that was what was on her mind.

Tomorrow she was meeting someone from her biological dad's family. Tomorrow she might even have a name, a photo, an answer to the second half of her DNA. She just hoped she would make a better first impression than she had at Royal Cape Companies. That they wouldn't meet her and think she was one big, walking beige flag. Or if they *did* see her that way, they wouldn't think of it as a bad thing. Like James's beige flags, which she saw more like fun facts about him, maybe even green flags.

She read Kathleen's message a fifth and sixth time. It was short, but not everyone was emotive with flowery words and exclamation points when texting or emailing. She shouldn't automatically assume Kathleen was mad at her—that would be ridiculous.

The time stamp was a mere five minutes ago, which was wild. Hendrix would think so too.

She leaned back into the pillows, her mind racing with all the ways tomorrow could go. The TV blared a commercial break, which wasn't helping pass the time. She grabbed her journal from the desk and reread everything she'd jotted down, from her questions to Hendrix's ideas to her new discoveries.

1. Who is my biological father? And mother?
   A RESTAURANT?! Mr. Rob Westmore??!

The way Rob had said her mom's name with such deep respect and a shard of tragedy—it worried her. Did Rob simply feel bad for her mom for some reason? Did he miss her? Was Candis what had happened between him and Mrs. Westmore? His business card was lost in the cluttered sinkhole of her purse. She just hoped and prayed she didn't have anything else from him. Namely, his DNA.

The thought nauseated her.

She scribbled into her journal.

> 2. Why didn't my mom tell me? About my bio dad OR HER RESTAURANT?! About VentureGold Group?
> 3. Does everyone know but me? Aunt Lou = sus. Rob?
> 4. Who am I?
> 5. To Do:
>    - contact journalist who wrote about Red Knot
>    - Dad's jobs—patterns?
>    - fertility clinic—connection??

So little about her past had been solved—not to downplay the fact she now knew about VentureGold Group and the Red Knot or anything, but she had a lot to do. She sat up, brushed the hair off her face, and grabbed her laptop.

The article Hendrix had sent gave her the name of the journalist who'd written the last couple of articles about the Red Knot: Demetrius Ross. The website for *The Jacksonville Times* said Demetrius was still a journalist there. Her second breakthrough of the day. The website's footer had a phone number for their headquarters, which she dialed before a drop of doubt could slow her down. What were the chances he'd remember an assignment from thirty years ago?

"You've reached the offices of *The Jacksonville Times,*" the automated voice recited on the other end of the phone. "Please listen to all the following options, as our menu has changed."

There were eight different "for this department, press this number" options, including one that said, "If this is a medical emergency, please hang up and dial 911." This happened to be the one that applied most to her situation, until she heard, "For all other inquiries, press zero."

The phone rang multiple times. "You are sixth in line," another automated voice finally said. "You can either leave your name and phone number and we'll call you back or stay on the line and wait for the first available operator."

"Ugh." She shoved her computer and journal to the side. The saxophone hold music was interrupted by announcements that might be broadcast in an airport. "See something? Say something, by calling the *Jax Times* news tip hotline . . ."

Her phone beeped twice, so she checked the screen. That 414 number was trying to call her. Again. There was no way she was going to give up her spot in line now. She'd come too far.

"*Jacksonville Times.*" A human came on the line ten minutes later. "How may I help you?"

"Yes. Hello. Hi." Nailed it. She sat straighter so she could focus on the words coming out of her mouth. "I'm trying to reach Demetrius Ross."

"Demetrius is out of town on assignment this week. Do you want me to transfer you so you can leave a voicemail?"

"Yes, please."

Her number of breakthroughs for the day would be limited to two. She left her name, number, and a brief message as instructed, hoping he would get back to her in less than fifty-two weeks.

A notification popped up on her screen for a voicemail. Whoever called from 414 had left her a message. She tapped on it to listen.

Dylan, where are you?

She gasped. It was her mom. But the number that had called wasn't her mom's. The voicemail was still going, so she started it over.

I went to your apartment in Naperville today, but nobody was there. I ran into your neighbor boy outside. Tate? Is that his name? He was holding something that looked like one of your gerbil things, so I asked if he knew you. He said you were out of town so he was taking care of Pita Bread. Anyway, please call me back. There's something really urgent we need to talk about.

Her mom said it as though it was news that merited a call to *The Jacksonville Times* hotline. *Of course* they had something urgent they needed to talk about.

She stood and paced the floor. She'd been waiting for this phone call, and yet, the thought of talking to her mom again sent a wave of anxiety coursing through her. Closing her eyes, she pressed the 414 number to call it back.

"Dylan!" Her mom answered on the first ring. "I was so worried about you."

The sound of her mom's voice moved through Dylan like an earthquake, scaring her but also weakening the walls she'd built up over the past two days of silence.

"Mom, whose phone is this?"

"Where are you? And what did you say to Rob Westmore?"

The questions came faster than she could process.

"How did you know I talked to Rob?"

"He called me this morning."

"You answered *his* phone call but not mine?"

"What are you talking about?" her mom demanded.

"I tried calling you a couple days ago, and it went straight to voicemail. I thought after the funeral you . . . didn't want to talk to me."

"After the funeral, my phone fell in the toilet. As if I needed another logistic to deal with . . ."

That might've been Dylan's favorite thing she'd learned so far today—there was a reason her mom hadn't answered the phone. "But then how did you get a phone call from Rob if your number changed?"

"I finally got my new phone yesterday. The guy at the store set it up so that calls to my old number would be forwarded to my new phone. It was already late by the time I got groceries and got home, so last night I texted instead of calling."

"Even without a phone, there's things like email. If you're ever interested in joining the modern age." The words came out harder than she'd intended.

"I've been a little busy. I was packing your dad's things."

"Packing Dad's things? He just . . ." She couldn't finish the sentence, nor could she blame her mom. She wasn't around enough to have much say over what happened to Dad's stuff. But it was hard not to think her mom was sweeping him out of her life as quickly as possible.

"He just what? *Died*? I'm well aware." Her mom exhaled into the phone, sending a windstorm through the speaker into Dylan's ear. "Look, I've been worried sick about you—"

"I've been taking care of myself for a while now."

"This is serious, Dylan."

The edge of fear in her mom's voice made her pay attention.

"Rob Westmore called. He's angry about stuff that happened between him and your dad a long time ago, and now that Darren is dead, Rob's coming after his estate."

"He's suing you?" The news threw her off balance, like the room had started spinning.

Rob had done exactly what she tried doing to him—schmoozing to get his foot in the door, then swooping in for the kill. And what about Brooke? Either she was a phenomenal actor, or like herself, she had no idea what was going on behind the scenes of her parents' lives.

Goodness, she hated people.

"Yes. Suing for whatever your dad left. What exactly did you tell Rob?"

What she'd told Rob was a whole Pandora's box to pile onto this conversation. Her mom probably didn't know about the birthday card, the address written inside it, or the Royal Cape flower sticker pressed onto the envelope.

"Not much, really, just that Dad died. He told me a lot more than I told him, like that Dad was pushed out of VentureGold Group. After talking a while, Rob said he wanted your information so he could pass on his condolences. He gave me his business card—"

"Wait. You saw him in person? You're in Jacksonville?" Her mom managed to sound shocked and hurt all at once.

"I had no idea he was going to turn around and sue you." She defended herself. "I've been here for two days and ran into Rob by accident. Like I said, he talked most of the time, said Dad had such a magnetic personality he could sell ice to—"

"Your dad isn't who you think he is," her mom blurted.

Her arms prickled into goosebumps. "I know. That's exactly what the DNA test told me."

"No, you're not understanding me." Her mom's vocal cords tightened, like too-taut violin strings that might snap. "*Darren Turner* isn't who you think he is."

She stutter-stepped to the windows, which ran floor to ceiling. She hadn't yet taken the time to admire the view, the vast expanse of water choosing its own route, while braided iron bridges and sleek buildings marked their place in the world alongside it.

She wanted to escape.

Escape the mystery of her body, her mom's voice on the other side of the phone and whatever she was about to say, which didn't make sense to her. All she wanted to know was what her mom already knew. The tug-of-war between her body and will was exhausting.

"What do you mean, Mom?"

"Your dad *was* a talented salesman; he could close any deal. But the thing he was best at selling were his own lies and delusions of grandeur."

The words tried to sink in, but they were like the rain outside pounding against the windows—only a few droplets clung to the glass pane, and even those slid down before being lost completely.

"Think about it, Dylan. Why would he encourage you to do this DNA test instead of sitting you down and having a real conversation with you?"

She slammed her hand against the hotel window. "Who are you to talk, Mom? I've asked you straight up who my biological father is and why I'm not biologically related to Dad, but you still haven't told me. I never even knew you used to run a whole *restaurant* down here. Chef Poulter says hi, by the way."

"Wait . . ." Her mom paused, then cleared her throat. "Rob told you about the Red Knot? *And* you met Chef Poulter . . . how?"

"No, actually. Hendrix did."

"Hendrix? That boy you liked forever ago?"

Her mom was stuck in a time capsule.

"All I'm saying is it's really rich that you call me with accusations about Dad being a liar when you ran an entire restaurant but never told me. You've lied about all the same things he did."

Her mom sniffled. "I know. I get why it's hard for you to believe anything I say."

She yanked the curtains closed and turned from the window. "Was it an affair, Mom? Is Rob my bio dad?"

"How can you even say that when Rob is trying to sue me right now?"

She wanted to scream. Instead, she'd reciprocate her mom's earthquake with a shock wave of her own.

"I'm meeting someone from my bio family tomorrow," she said. "Someone I found on KindreDNA."

"Your *bio* family? *I'm* your bio family."

She spun until she was facing the mirror again, which she could hardly stand to look into. "You're half of my bio family. This person lives in the area, which is why I came down here. We're meeting tomorrow."

Her mom could say anything.

*Your biological father is a guy I knew from college.*

*His name is George.*

*I'm sorry.*

"You're so ungrateful, Dylan," she said instead.

Dylan thought back to when her mom had given her the journal, and how her mom had written a note in it about doing something useful with her anger so it didn't land her in jail. She wouldn't mind a journal burning, followed by jail.

"You might have lost your husband this past week—who, might I add, you never seemed to like a day in your life—but I lost my dad *and* the entire story of my family. I learned my whole life has been a lie. So, don't tell me I'm ungrateful, because no amount of gratitude could change what your lies stole from me."

Her mom was crying now. "You've made me the enemy all these years, but you can't see that—"

"By the way, I *am* grateful for my life—"

"You don't have a life, Dylan. You have a routine."

"It's *my* routine!" she screamed. "It's safe, and I'm no longer getting jerked around every year and a half to new cities and new schools full of new people I don't know. I'm *grateful* I have a job and an apartment that's mine. I'm *grateful* I finally have just a tiny bit of control, so I can choose to be away from you and your secrets."

"I didn't know when to tell you!" her mom yelled back. "Or how to tell you. You were just a child. There was never a good time to ruin your life more than it was already being ruined. The least I could do was give you a semblance of normalcy."

"You should have let me decide how to handle the truth. Instead, you kept it from me."

Her mom exhaled. "I'm sorry. I have so many regrets, and they all have to do with me not being who you needed as a mom. Things were taken from me too. Even though we might never see eye to eye, I wish you could see *I'm* the one who tried to take care of you."

"This is unbelievable. *You're* unbelievable. Dad had his flaws—he was human. But at least he liked me."

"That's because he didn't parent you. He would watch you and me argue, and then he'd go from ripping me apart for being a bad mom to taking you on a shopping spree. He made me look like the bad guy, constantly, while he got to be the cool friend. He'd whisper sweet nothings in your ear while stabbing me—*and* others—in the back."

*Click.*

Dylan ended the call and chucked her phone onto the bed.

## HTTPS://WWW.REDDIT.COM/DEALING-WITH-NPE/ COMMENTS

**with_my_gnomies** (1 month ago)
I'm shook. Just found out my parents did IVF to have me, but my dad was infertile so they used another dude's sperm. I kinda feel like I was their second choice for a kid. Now I just wanna know who that dude is, you know? What should I do?

**hakuna_chihuaua** (1 month ago)
Same here except my surprise wasn't IVF—it was an affair. My mom totally denied it until I showed her my DNA test results. There goes my life. (And my parents' marriage.)

**free_kitten_hugs** (1 month ago)
No advice to offer, but I'm really REALLY sorry! *HUGS*

**hoosier_daddy** (3 weeks ago)
I donated my guys at least fifteen times in college when I was strapped for cash, and now, because everyone in this country is screws-loose over their feelings, I'm supposed to be responsible for whatever was made in those petri dishes? I'm sorry, but if you have my DNA and come knocking on my door, you can call me DONOR not DADDY.

> **with_my_gnomies** response to **hoosier_daddy** (2 weeks ago)
> But doesn't donating "your guys" lead to making people? Why are you promised anonymity while I'm left with secrets?
>
> **hoosier_daddy** response to **with_my_gnomies** (2 weeks ago)
> shut up snowflake
>
> **free_kitten_hugs** response to **hoosier_daddy** (2 weeks ago)
> Sounds like someone REALLY needs a hug! *HUGS*

**AI-Generated Summary of Thread:**
The expansion of fertility treatments created a market for sperm from healthy, usually college-aged men that lasted nearly thirty years before the first at-home DNA test was made available. It's important for people to know their role when DNA connections are made and to respect the wishes of whether or not each party wants a hug.

# 26

# Five Guys Is Too Many

In the three days since her dad's funeral, Dylan had adopted a new form of doomscrolling—reading online forums. Specifically, entries written by NPEs, followed by comment sections full of usernames who thought their opinion deserved the biggest microphone. What better way to cope with your own mess than reading about other people's?

"Misery loves company" and all that.

She didn't know anyone in real life who'd gone through this, someone she could call up and force her miserable company on. If she did, they kept it a secret by not wearing a *Hello, my name is NPE* nametag.

People like with_my_gnomies who were willing to talk openly about this stuff on the Web reminded her she wasn't alone. Maybe her spiraling thoughts, ravenous questions, and, yes, even some of the self-hatred were normal in situations like this. Maybe there were others in the world with unanswered questions.

*Who am I? Why didn't my mom tell me?*

Lying in bed at the hotel, she was still reeling from the phone call with her mom. Her hour of doomscrolling naturally led to a solid nap, which led to an episode of *Property Brothers* and then reruns of *The Amazing Race*, all while shoveling M&M's into her mouth. The exact number of hours she stayed in bed, snacking through her numbness, she wasn't sure. It must have been a long time, though, because when she woke up from another nap, shadows stretched in child's pose across the walls and carpet.

*Ding.*

The chime from her phone came from deep inside the folds of the comforter. She dug for it, then had to squint against the blue light piercing her retinas.

> **That Man:** sorry. got caught up w/ work
>
> **That Man:** interested in dinner?

She pulled her dead weight up into a sitting position. Her head began to throb.

*Ding. Ding.*

> **That Man:** jk silly question
>
> **That Man:** what do u want for dinner

She yawned. Her breath tasted rancid.

Hendrix was right about her wanting dinner, and she had plenty of news and feelings to process with him—not that he'd be super interested in the feelings side of things.

But Kathleen's message—he'd listen to her talk about that for sure.

> **Me:** It might be a bit far, but can we eat at a Five Guys? I could really go for some comfort food right now.

**Me:** Also, guess who I heard back from (!!!)

She went to the bathroom and set her phone on the counter. After taking an extra-long time at the sink to brush her teeth and splash water on her greasy T-zone, she dried her face and hands with a towel. It was getting harder to look at herself in the mirror. That, or the mirror was telling her less and less each time she looked into it.

*Ding.*

**That Man:** 5 guys is all the way across the ditch

**Me:** The ditch?

**Me:** It's been a minute since I lived here.

**That Man:** In Jacksonville, the Intracoastal Waterway separates the city from the beach. Locals often refer to it as "The Ditch." City folk look at people who live at the beach differently, and vice versa.

**Me:** Capital letters. Punctuation.

**Me:** Tell me you copied something off Wikipedia without telling me you copied it off Wikipedia.

**Me:** Fine. I'll ask nicer. Will you PLEASE take me across "The Ditch"?

**That Man:** 😒 b there in 10

She rummaged through her carry-on, which was quickly dwindling from two neatly folded columns of clean clothes to one crumpled pile that needed laundering. She put on a taupe midi skirt with a fitted tee she tucked in, and grabbed a cardigan in case the night got chilly. She threw her hair into a ponytail, then grabbed her shoes and room key and headed to the elevators.

Adding some normalcy to her Thursday night would balance the otherwise-shifting sands of her life. Not that crossing the Intracoastal Waterway was a normal part of any day of the week for her, but a fresh patty off the grill with applewood smoked bacon placed on a soft toasted sesame bun? One of her personal favorite "normals."

She left the hotel through the lobby and was greeted by fresh air, as well as Hendrix leaning against the passenger door of his car, arms crossed. It still took her by surprise to walk outside and see rows of palm trees instead of maples at the end of their growing season. And the guy she'd fallen so hard for back before she was all grown up.

She lowered her sunglasses. "Excuse me, sir. I believe that's my seat, and you're in the way of me getting dinner."

Hendrix smirked and grabbed one of the belt loops on her jeans, then tugged her closer until she was leaning against him. Hands on her hips, he kissed her, reminiscent of their heated moment by the river that morning. She wasn't used to being desired like this—especially outdoors, where anyone could see them.

When she pulled back, she was sure her cheeks were on fire. Hendrix Reed was kissing her again.

"Hello," she whispered.

"Hey."

"I think there's some things we still need to talk about."

"I know." He raked a hand through his hair, like he wasn't ready to talk just yet. "It's just really nice being with you again."

He brushed a piece of hair out of her sight line and cupped her face with his hands. This tender gesture was even sweeter to her than his deep kisses. There was something so intimate about it.

He leaned in one more time to brush his lips against hers, gentler this time, though his hands were starting to wander.

"Hendrix." She grabbed his hands and held them in place.

"Sorry." He stepped back and walked to his side of the car. "You just look so good. Even when your life's in crisis mode."

She laughed off the compliment and got in the passenger seat. "Are you sure you're okay with going from fine dining last night to fast food tonight?"

He shrugged. "A woman of many tastes. It's over twenty minutes to get there, though."

"How about I find us something to listen to?"

"I'll control my radio, thank you very much."

She couldn't tell if he was serious or not, so she decided not to mess with it.

Her phone dinged. She opened the notification to a text from Tara with a picture attached. It was of Tate holding Gale while Peeta sat on the floor next to them. The little boy sparkled on the screen.

> **Tara:** Sorry it took me so long to get back to you. Work, and all that. Tate is never going to let you have these two back. ☺
>
> **Tara:** Gale and Peeta are doing great, and Tate is working really hard to follow their routine. I'm sure you miss them, but thank you

for letting him take care of them
for a few days!

Dylan replied with many thanks and heart-eyed emojis, then held up the phone for Hendrix to see.

"My neighbors are taking care of my two guinea pigs, Gale and Peeta. Isn't this the sweetest picture?"

She felt like how Tate looked in the picture—proud of what she had a hand in taking care of. Tara was right. She missed holding their small, soft bodies.

Hendrix glanced at the picture.

"Pet rodents? You've got to be kidding, Turner." He laughed, its sharp edge leaving a paper cut on what started out as a sweet moment.

She needed to stop being surprised by Hendrix's reactions to things that were soft and cuddly and joyful, though. At least he wasn't faking nice to impress her. She tucked her phone away.

"You're the worst, but I'll let that one slide. Also, I have things to tell you. The first is that my mom called."

"And the two of you talked through everything and worked it all out and you're back to having a loving mother-daughter relationship?"

"Not even close. Rob Westmore is suing my dad's estate."

"You're kidding." His jaw clenched, and he raked his hand through his hair again. "I have a few choice words I'll keep in my head."

"You have better self-control than I do. I have no idea what my mom's going to do."

He glanced at her. "You sound upset, but not *that* upset."

"I'm plenty upset. It's just that the second half of my news is good, because Kathleen Schulz messaged me. I'm not kidding—it was less than fifteen minutes after you left."

"Wow." The way he said it was on brand. Nothing actually wowed him. "What happens now? Kathleen Schulz agrees to send over some medical history and you both go about your lives?"

"You're really bad at guessing games. No, Hendrix. We're meeting in person. Tomorrow morning."

He shifted in his seat. "Where are you meeting her? What time?"

"Treaty Oak. Nine o'clock. That's close to the Hyatt, right?"

"Really close."

Her phone dinged again. Maybe it was more photos from Tara.

> **Captain Jim:** We're done with our sessions a little earlier than I thought! Are you still up for a celebratory dessert tonight?

She leaned her phone away from Hendrix.

If she were alone, she'd palm her forehead. She had totally forgotten about dessert with James, which made her mad—no, disappointed?

She thought about how to reply.

> **Me:** Captains finishing a party early? I don't believe it.

> **Me:** Is it okay if I ask for a rain check?

> **Captain Jim:** Of course!

> **Captain Jim:** Are you okay? Can I still come by—say hello??

Maybe she should give him an excuse, say she wasn't feeling well. After all, she'd lain in bed all afternoon and was now on her way to stress eat Five Guys. There was the funeral, the news, the fight with her mom. Cortisol constantly mounting in her bloodstream, probably related to her meeting with Kathleen tomorrow.

**Me:** I'm okay. Thanks though, and I'll see you soon.

**Captain Jim:** Hold on tight to that rain check. Wouldn't want you to lose it.

**Captain Jim:** ☺

**Me:** *holding on tight*

That wasn't completely false, though the thing she was currently holding on tight to was Hendrix's hand. He'd reached over and laced his fingers with hers.

Three dots blinked in the corner of their conversation, then disappeared.

At Five Guys, she ordered her bacon cheeseburger, a greasy pile of fries, and a chocolate milkshake.

"Make that two," Hendrix said to the cashier.

When their tray was ready, he took it to a table for four next to one of the red-and-white-checkered walls, then patted the chair next to him. Between massive bites of their perfect burgers, the conversation shifted to their shared memories.

"I still can't believe you beat me up. *At* self-defense class." Hendrix stole one of her fries and slathered it in her ketchup before putting it in his own mouth.

"*I* can believe it. Do you know how annoying you were, flirting with every XX chromosome in the room and acting like you were better than everyone?" She stole one of his fries back. "You went out of your way to make me miserable, one comment at a time."

"You must've forgotten the rule that if a boy is mean to you, that means he likes you."

"And you must've never learned that being mean is not an acceptable way to show affection."

"I think I've been pretty nice to you the past couple days." He put his hand on her thigh, the wryest smile tugging at the corner of his mouth.

"If you were ever surprised by things, you might be surprised to hear I think the nicest thing you did for me so far was drive me here tonight. Thank you."

She took a long sip from her straw, savoring the sweet, cold cream of her milkshake. The restaurant was getting busier, which made it easier for her to bring up the one thing she'd been waiting to ask him ever since he spotted her through the window at the Bread and Board.

"Hendrix."

"Dylan." He mimicked her serious tone, then waited for her to go on.

"You're visibly squirming."

"You're staring at me like you're about to scold me."

"It's time to talk."

"We *are* talking."

"You know what I mean." Her voice wavered. Why couldn't courage be bottled and spritzed? "I need to know why you didn't show up that night."

Hendrix fanned his face. "It's hot in here. Is it hot in here? Are we about to get hit by Hurricane Dylan?"

She didn't laugh. "We have to talk about this sometime."

"That was fourteen years ago. We were sixteen. Can't some things stay in the past?"

"I agree—we were silly teenagers who had a few things to learn about life and . . . love. But, I really cared about you."

The last words caught in her throat.

"Fine." He straightened in his seat, balling his hands into fists. "The reason I never showed up that night is because your dad made it clear I should never see you again."

"My dad," she repeated. "Don't you mean my mom? I know we got caught the night before, or whatever."

Her mom's rambling about curfews and futures in front of Hendrix had been embarrassing.

Hendrix shook his head. "No, I mean your dad."

"What do you mean? My mom yelled at us and then you went home."

He uncurled his fists and fidgeted with the last mushy fry on his tray. "We remember a lot of the same things. I took you home from class that night."

"Yeah."

"And then, like you said, we . . . hung out in my car, got yelled at by your mom. But the next day, an hour before we were supposed to meet at the bridge, your dad showed up on my doorstep."

She tried swallowing, but the lump in her throat got in the way. "What? How did he even know where you lived?"

"It's not that hard to get people's addresses."

"True, but—"

"I was ready to meet you that night—I promise—but somehow your dad figured out what we were going to do and came by my house to stop us."

She sifted through files of memories to think about how her dad might've found out about their plan. Had he snooped in her room and read her journal?

"I told your dad I wouldn't do it, I'd call off the plan, but that wasn't enough. He wouldn't let it go." Hendrix looked down. "He kept saying he loved you, and that I'd never be able to take care of you like he did because you were his little girl. I told him I cared about you, but he went even further. He started saying some really dark stuff, like a bunch of reasons why I didn't deserve you, how I was just fatherless white trash who'd never amount to anything."

Noise from the surrounding tables started to ring in her ears. She tried to make sense of what Hendrix was saying. Tried to connect it with an actual memory of her own.

"I've never heard him talk like that," she whispered.

"He said you were just a confused teenage girl who didn't know what was good for her." Hendrix touched her hand, but her skin absorbed it like an electric zap. "So, I didn't show up that night. I was scared of another scary dad, *and* a lot of what he said was probably true—you *are* too good for me. The night he came and yelled at me on my front doorstep, my mom was working late and my dad was passed out on the couch."

She looked at her tray. Mangled tomato, soggy lettuce, and slippery onions combined into a raw mess she was sure resembled the pit of her stomach. She couldn't stop staring at it.

"I'm sorry. . . . I—I want to go back to the hotel."

Hendrix threw his hands up. "You said you wanted the truth, and that's the truth. Why are you acting like this is my fault?"

The couple at the table next to theirs looked over at them, so she lowered her voice. "I never said this is your fault. You were just a teenager too. It's a lot to take in is all, and I'm still . . . *angry.*" She pushed back her chair, which grated against the floor. "Will you please just take me back? I need time to think."

"You need to do more than think." He pushed back his own chair and walked toward the door.

"What does that mean?" she called after him.

"Nothing. Let's go."

The ride back to the hotel was quiet, minus the rage waging war inside her.

The things her dad had said were awful, *and* Hendrix had never tried to get in touch with her again. In all the wild, emotional details wrapped up in the night they were supposed to meet, the one thing lost in the mix had been *her*. Nobody had considered how their scolding, defending, and ghosting might affect her. She'd been shushed and sent to her room. Taken to self-defense class the next day but left alone.

Hendrix pulled his car up to the sliding doors of the hotel lobby and stormed around the front of the car to open her door.

She grabbed her milkshake, got out, and stood literally toe to toe with him.

He looked down at her, the ache in his eyes unmistakable. "I don't think it's a coincidence we crossed paths after all these years. I like you, and you like me, and maybe that's enough to start something again, to forget about the past and our mistakes and our parents' mistakes and move on. A clean slate. I cared about you then, and I still care about you now."

It was no small thing for him to say something so vulnerable.

She tucked it away to savor later.

"I care about you too. I just need a minute. Everything in my life is piling up at the same time." She stretched onto her toes and kissed him, briefly. This time, she didn't worry whether the valet was watching. "I'll call you tomorrow, okay?"

"Okay." His sad smile blinded her anger for a moment, reminding her there was still good in the world if he was going this far to help her. To say he cared about her.

She watched him drive away, ready to go to her room and finish her milkshake, maybe watch an episode of anything the TV would throw at her.

She spun toward the lobby. The only problem was, she spun right into another person, squashing her paper cup and splashing milkshake all over her hand.

"I'm so sorry—" she started to say.

"That was my fault—" he said at the same time.

She looked up, horrified. "James."

He wiped at the splatters of milkshake on his own hands, as well as the large glob on his shirt. "I was just up at your room checking on you. I thought maybe you weren't feeling well."

His eyes landed on the milkshake in her hands. It was only three seconds, but it felt like three million. She wanted to crawl under a rock.

"I, um, wanted some Five Guys."

He grinned, but it fizzled quickly. "You don't have to explain yourself."

"I know. I—"

"I'm just glad you're okay," he said, taking a step around her, toward the riverwalk.

"I'm still holding on to that rain check," she called after him, holding the dripping cup away from herself.

James was well on his way now, far enough he probably couldn't hear her.

She closed her eyes and groaned on the inside.

He was right—she didn't owe him anything, but she'd made plans and forgotten them, and it tore her up. She wasn't used to navigating people with their different personalities and contradicting calendars and hurt feelings when her circle back in Naperville was so . . . small.

It was like her loneliness was making a mockery of her. Even when she was finally around other people, connecting with other people, she felt out of place or like she was doing it wrong. She thought she wanted to be known by other humans like Brooke and James and Hendrix and Teresa. It seemed almost superficial to want to be loved without letting them in. But what if she *did* let them in? What if people knew her—like, *really* knew her and all the ways that first KindreDNA email had ripped her apart? What if they knew her suffocating fear of change, and that she didn't get along with the only *biological* parent she knew, and that sometimes it was hard to look at her own eyes and ears and mouth and nose in the mirror, and that she sometimes blew people off who actually wanted to celebrate her?

She found the nearest trash can and chucked the sloppy paper cup into it, then went up to her room. Her hands were still gross, so she washed them in the bathroom, cursing the sticky residue and the painful conversation with Hendrix and the way she'd left James hanging.

Then she fell onto the large bed and let herself be exhausted by everything she couldn't get right. Tormented by the intrusive thought that she'd probably mess up tomorrow too, when it meant so much to her.

## 27

# Treaty Oak

Friday, September 26

Her alarm felt like a downed wire in the puddle of her mind. Her body jolted from the shock, forcing her eyes open from a deep, troubled sleep. She couldn't remember what she'd been dreaming about, but Freud might've been right: Dreams were her primal urges, repressed memories, and unresolved conflicts turned into blockbuster entertainment for her subconscious.

Stretching the kink in her neck, she pushed back the covers and put her feet on the floor. Today needed her to be clearheaded, to be the grown-up, fresh thirty-year-old she was.

She'd learned to be self-sufficient at a younger age than most. There hadn't been time to be afraid of doing laundry and making her own dinner and paying rent—it was that or go back to moving all the time. After twelve years, taking care of herself was starting to feel like the time she went for a run and twisted her knee on a divot in the forest preserve trail. Sure, she'd survived and helped herself until it healed four weeks later, but she'd limped the entire way.

She grabbed her phone off the bedside table and busied her thumbs to call in backup.

**Me:** Reminder. I'd *love* your friendship and support at this meeting.

**Me:** I promise I won't tease you for changing your mind.

**Me:** In fact, I'll deeply admire your humility.

**Hendrix:** cant. working this morning

**Hendrix:** sorry

**Hendrix:** pick u up after?? text when ur done

Last night, after her first round of texts asking if he'd go with her to meet Kathleen Schulz, she'd changed how his name was stored in her phone. If she were trying to be open about what this reunion with Hendrix meant for them after all these years, she could start by not referring to him as That Man.

He'd replied with the same excuse both times: *Working.*

She really needed to be a better human and ask what his work was now that he was technically between jobs. She'd been so absorbed by her own stuff, she hadn't asked him basic questions.

She scraped the hair out of her face and dragged herself over to the coffee nook. After putting a pod into the Keurig, she filled the water canister with bathroom tap water—something she decided to not think too hard about—and hoped the caffeine wouldn't send her from foggy into full panic. Throughout the past five days, there seemed to be no third option.

While the coffee maker burbled, she brushed her teeth and looked at her suitcase of dwindling clothes. Thinking about what to wear intimidated her. She put on her second-to-last outfit, added an extra swipe of mascara and brow gel in the bathroom, then repacked her purse, which consisted of removing gum wrappers, pamphlets, and even the torn birthday card envelope with her footprint on it. This tiny reset seemed like a good idea before presenting herself, Dylan Turner, as a capable, curious, but competent human being to her biological relative.

She poured her coffee into the hotel's Styrofoam cup and headed out of her hotel room to the elevators. She didn't feel psychologically ready for this momentous occasion, but she probably wouldn't feel ready until after the day revealed all its secrets. This was a day for her to fake it until she made it back with all the information Kathleen could give her, which was the gist of the pep talk she gave herself in the elevator. She didn't need Hendrix to drive her; she didn't technically need an Uber either. The same blue bridge they'd driven over to get to the Red Knot would take her to the vicinity of Treaty Oak, as long as she could handle twenty-five minutes of walking in what the internet claimed was seventy-five degrees and sunshine. The low-impact exercise would do the anxious swarm in her stomach some good anyway.

She'd arrive on her own—with a little help from Google Maps—just like she'd been doing for the past however many years of her life. Even if she did limp through it sometimes.

As if her life were a musical, the elevator door opened with a ding right on cue, and bright sunshine from the lobby's glass doors beamed onto her like a spotlight.

She could do this, and she was proud of herself for it.

That same pride proved fragile to the pinpricks of real life outside the hotel lobby's doors. By the time she got to the Main Street Bridge, she was sweating through her shirt, intrusive thoughts yelling at her.

*Empty pews.*
*Nobody dearly beloved.*
*Alone.*

The thoughts were recurring ever since the conversation with Teresa about her guest list. Dylan kept picturing herself at her own wedding, but she couldn't recognize the man holding out the crook of his elbow to walk her down the aisle. And, of course, there was no groom standing at the front of the church, waiting for her. But neither of these things was what truly haunted these spiraling thoughts. It was that when she got down the aisle and the reverend said, "Dearly beloved, we are gathered here today in the presence of God to witness and bless this *blah, blah, blah,*" she'd turn around and realize nobody was there. And the reverend laughed at her. A laugh that pounded her eardrums.

*Empty.*
*Nobody.*
*Alone.*

The spiraling thoughts didn't help when, right in the middle of the bridge, she also learned she was terrified of heights. The railings were stupidly short, and she kept having to pivot to the right side of the walkway—the side closest to the edge—for people running in the opposite direction. She couldn't even glance over the railing at the water without feeling like she might faint or take one clumsy step and fall between the bars to the river below.

Both options sounded tragic and set her pulse on fire.

*Alone.*

Her breathing got shallower. She couldn't afford a full-blown panic attack in the middle of a bridge in a state she didn't live in. She squeezed her eyes shut, trying not to give the panic any more airtime, to escape the prison her mind had become. Grabbing the railing with one hand, she used her other hand to fish out her phone and one earbud. Somehow she connected them with Bluetooth, pulled up her favorite podcast, and pressed Play, all without slipping off the Main Street Bridge into the Saint Johns River.

> Welcome to *Fencing Your Fury*. This is your host, Dr. Lionel Cain, here to remind you for ten minutes each day to exhale your anger and inhale peace. This is season 6, episode 271.

The familiar gravelly voice crackled like vinyl on a record player, its slow, soothing rhythm cooling her desperate thoughts.

> Let's start with one long, deep breath. Inhale and say, "It's a bad day."

She did as she was told, though Dr. Cain's pause was two seconds longer than she needed.

> Now, exhale and say, "It's not a bad—"

*"You have one new text message."* The voice changed pitch, from late night radio host to a robotic-sounding female. It was her phone's AI assistant, who had all the information of the internet in its microchip, but no concept of good timing.

"It's not a bad what? Tell me what's not bad, Dr. Cain," she yelled in the middle of the Main Street Bridge in Jacksonville, Florida.

*"I'm sorry. I couldn't hear that,"* her phone went on. *"Would you like me to read your text message? If yes, say 'Read it—'"*

"Read it," she groaned. It could be Hendrix, in his car, on his way to pick her up.

**Mom:** working through some stuff

**Mom:** I want to

**Mom:** talk again soon

**Mom:** I love you Dylan

Her mom's texts sounded more robotic than AI.
"*To replay the text message, say, 'Replay.'*"
"Replay," she said. Once, twice, then three times.
"*I love you, Dylan.*"
"*I love you, Dylan.*"
"*I love you, Dylan.*"
Whether or not she believed the words, they helped her focus less on the river below and more on putting one foot in front of the other. She made it over the bridge, already a miracle in her mind, plus down a few more blocks until she passed under a large iron sign supported by two pillars: *Treaty Oak at Jessie Ball Dupont Park*. She was so relieved, she jogged the last steps like she was running through finish-line ribbon.

Nearby, someone clapped for her—a man wearing a bucket hat, standing on the grass by a group of trees, not far off the cement sidewalk. She pulled out her earbud and threw it back into her purse.

"Thank you," she said.

He pointed into the trees. "A red knot."

"Oh?" It took her a second to realize he was talking about a bird. She tuned in and soon picked up the sound of the bird's yodel: *Yeh-yeh-yeh*.

"It's out of place here," the man said.

"That's not good." She didn't know anything about red knots. Or any bird, for that matter.

"This time of year, you might see up to ninety percent of this species on Little Talbot Island, which is on their typical migration route and schedule. To see one red knot all by itself, this far inland—across the Ditch, mind you—that's not good."

"What's going to happen to it?"

"I called conservation to see if they want to try and reunite it with the flock on the island, and they said they might come out here. But who knows? This bird could fly off on its own again any time and put itself in danger."

She looked into the trees one more time but was eager to start looking for Kathleen. "My friend mentioned visiting Little Talbot Island."

"Wise friend. Don't wait until you're my age to consider the birds. They have a lot to teach us."

It felt like one of those times she was standing at her register, unsure how to respond to a customer.

"Okay. Thank you." *For that sage advice?*

She followed the sidewalk toward the back of the park, then took a right onto the boardwalk that led her under Treaty Oak. Stepping under its canopy of shade was both a relief from the sun and like stepping into a completely different world. The oak's massive trunk tossed branches out at every angle—some overhead and some so large and sprawling they were resting along the ground in thick green grass. It was a glorious masterpiece, an octopus-like creature but with skin of bark and moss.

She surveyed the area for someone resembling Kathleen Schulz, acutely aware that matching people's faces in real life to their online photos was one area where the internet fell short. Thankfully, even though the park was home to the city's biggest tree at seventy feet tall and twenty-five feet in circumference, according to the plaque at the end of the boardwalk, the park itself was the city's smallest. She'd only read the tree's dimensions before moving along, which she now regretted because plaque-reading was a great way to ward off the compulsion to throw up. Give her all the dates and histories and random facts to make her mind forget what she was here to do.

"Dylan?"

A woman wearing dark sunglasses, a knee-length sundress and trench coat, and chunky gold hoops walked the boardwalk toward her. Tucked under her arm was a large envelope.

"Kathleen?" Her body begged to jump out of its own skin.

Was she supposed to open her arms for a hug? Shake hands? Curtsy?

Kathleen held out her own hand first, which Dylan shook, grateful for the clarity.

"Yes, I'm Kathleen. Welcome to Jacksonville. Shall we have a seat on the bench right here?"

"That sounds great." She liked that Kathleen was taking the lead.

"Remind me where you're from, Dylan?"

"I lived here until I was eight, and another year when I was sixteen. Right now, I live in Illinois. Naperville."

"That's quite far. How were your travels? I assume you flew?"

"My flight was smooth, and I was able to travel with a friend. Thank you, by the way, for being willing to meet on such short notice."

She hoped she didn't sound as awkward as she felt.

"You're welcome, honey." Kathleen smiled, taking off her sunglasses and tucking them into her purse. "I'm sure finding out this news about your DNA was . . . difficult, and you have a lot of questions."

She squeezed her hands together to keep from fidgeting. "Do you know exactly how we're related?"

"I did some digging on my end." Kathleen didn't smile. Didn't twitch. She seemed like the kind of person who was going to give it to her straight, but her face offered no clues in the meantime. "I think I figured some things out."

Dylan almost squealed but reminded herself she was thirty years old, not some coming-of-age emotional wreck. At least, that's not how she wanted to present herself. "Does that mean you know who my biological father might be? I tried finding pictures on Facebook—"

Kathleen flinched then.

If she could, she'd hook, pull back, and swallow her comment, but it was too late. While internet stalking was a socially acceptable "crime" to commit, it wasn't socially acceptable to admit out loud, especially to her victim.

She grimaced, but Kathleen gave her a sympathetic smile.

"I think it's natural to be curious about all this, Dylan, which also confirms why it was so important for us to meet today."

*"Vital we meet"* was how she'd worded it. Maybe Kathleen also believed it was vital for Dylan to know her own roots.

"Again, I have so much sympathy for you, Dylan. It's just that . . ." Kathleen faltered, then looked away, like whatever she wanted to say was lodged in her throat. Like a cashew.

Dylan's gut, on the other hand, was freaking out.

"My family prefers not to share any more information about our biological connection," Kathleen finally said.

The fog in Dylan's brain swelled. Her body was frozen to her seat, but her insides hovered above, kicking and screaming and pounding her fists, demanding the woman in front of her open up.

"Can you explain why? Is it because my biological father doesn't want to meet me?" She eyed the envelope tucked in Kathleen's arm.

"What you need to know is that literally none of this is personal. The man who is technically your biological father was, shall we say, a bit of a wild card when he was younger. He donated his . . . samples . . . for extra spending money his dad wouldn't give him. A few times, apparently."

It was the sugarcoated version of the thirty-year-old phenomenon Reddit described: A bunch of college-aged guys used to donate sperm for beer money.

"The thing is"—Kathleen brushed an imaginary piece of hair from her face, like it was her way of fanning her cheeks from embarrassment—"you are not the first biological family member to come forward with connection to this man. Now that money isn't as tight as it used to be, the money has become a target. Once these people found out they were related to our family's enterprise, they attempted all kinds of shakedowns."

"*These people.*"

"*Vital we meet.*"

Kathleen's words, the breeze in the branches above her, the birds twittering happily like they couldn't read the room—all the sounds were garbled, like she'd sunk underwater.

And what was in that envelope?

"How many others?" Dylan asked.

"Excuse me?"

"How many others have come forward? Are we talking thirty, like a Netflix documentary, or—"

"Two others have come forward. We matched through different genealogy tests. We took a couple."

Two half siblings. *Two* people she shared that much DNA with.

"Again, this is not personal. While this may be difficult to hear, our family hopes you'll understand that."

She was suddenly over Kathleen taking the lead. "*Why* did you do the tests?"

The woman sighed. "My kids gave them to my husband and me for Christmas, just for fun. We were interested in building our family tree backward in history but didn't realize it would open such a difficult can of worms."

Was she the worm in this scenario?

"Your biological father is a good man. He didn't understand the ramifications of what he was doing. I don't think anyone could've predicted or understood what all of this would lead to or how genealogy tests might blow it up in our faces."

*It would lead to me—a human being.*

Her body returned to her, and though words were hard at the moment, she forced them out. "Just to be clear, you know who my biological father is, but you won't tell me because you're afraid I'll come after your money."

Kathleen's eyes narrowed. "He was promised anonymity. Look, you seem nice, and from what I've been able to learn about *you*, you're doing just fine on your own, which is part of the reason why I was compelled to meet you in person instead of telling you this in an email." Kathleen, an admitted mutual stalker, grinned.

*"Just fine on your own."*

The sentiment rang familiar, probably because it was the same lie she'd told herself in the mirror only an hour ago. Before she got stuck in the middle of a bridge and needed other people's voices to walk her down.

"It's not only that I can't tell you about your biological father," Kathleen continued, taking the envelope from under her arm and setting it on her lap. "It's that I don't want you to talk with others about our connection either."

The only thing keeping her from ripping that envelope out of her hands and tearing it open was her last tiny shred of dignity.

Kathleen patted the envelope with both hands. "One of these documents is a nondisclosure agreement we would like you to sign. Not for nothing; we would pay you ten thousand dollars. All we ask is you don't speak publicly about being related to anyone in my extended family or that you came about by artificial insemination."

Ten grand.

This couldn't be real.

Was it a hefty consolation prize or a stab in the back?

"I'm so sorry you're going through this, Dylan. My extended family has been quite shaken by these episodes as well, so I understand."

No, she didn't. Nobody understood.

Kathleen held out the folder of documents. "The other one is a family medical history. You have a right to know, though you'll be happy to find a clean bill of health."

Like it was some cherry on top of her currently crappy life sundae.

"Minus a few insomniacs in the bloodline," Kathleen added. "I hope you sleep better at night than most of us."

She laughed and shook her head, not as a reply but in delirium. She tried to grab the envelope, but she couldn't move her hands. It was like reading that KindreDNA email all over again. A new wave of pain paralyzing her.

Kathleen set the envelope between them. "So, what do you say, Dylan?"

She needed more than two minutes to know whether she should sign a legally binding document. Ironic, considering she'd wanted to give Kathleen no more than two minutes to respond to her initial message. The world was a merry-go-round, spinning too fast for everyone to stay on. Especially the children inheriting their parents' messes.

"Doesn't an NDA have to be signed with a notary public or something?" It sounded like an adult thing to know.

"Our lawyers made sure the document has everything it needs to be legally binding."

Lawyers. Plural.

"Online too?" She thought about the forums she'd love to pour her heart out to but hadn't had the courage to yet.

"Yes. Online is considered public domain."

She was dizzy. Too much coffee and not enough breakfast. Or her long lost family shutting down any hopes she'd know the other half of her DNA beyond his medical history.

"How would I speak in public about a person I don't even know?"

Kathleen paused and looked up at the giant tree looming over them.

"Do you know the history of this tree, Dylan?"

Its branches, once magnificent, now looked like a tangle of claws reaching out to grab her. "I don't."

"Nearly a hundred years ago, someone wanted to tear down this tree and develop the property, but because it was the oldest living thing in Jacksonville, one individual was bent on saving it. A reporter. He wrote a newspaper article claiming, falsely, that a treaty had been signed 'beneath the tree's bountiful limbs' between early settlers and an indigenous tribe. Up until then, the tree had been called Giant Oak, but he called it Treaty Oak. People read the article and joined in his efforts, and the city gave in. It decided to preserve the land and leave the tree alone."

She hated her instant connection to the tree. Its story built on a lie.

"Is that why you asked to meet me here, because I'm a sham? Because you think we're supposed to tell lies for the greater good? To preserve our families?"

Kathleen put her sunglasses back on, then stood up from the bench. "I can see you need time, and that makes sense—this is a lot to take in. I'll get in touch in one week to see where you're at. Remember, these are simply precautionary measures. None of this is personal."

Kathleen left, and Dylan stared at the envelope in her lap.

"It's personal for me," she whispered.

She'd hoped with all her heart that inside it was a picture.

## 28

## Wild, Wild Wrest

Kathleen had meant to disclose nothing, had tried to make herself sound perfectly reasonable for not giving her one single name. Yet, even with a case of brain fog, Dylan was able to yank Kathleen's lines apart like flimsy blinds and read between them. To comb through each sentence for details she could flesh into leads.

Her butt and back ached, probably because she was still sitting under Treaty Oak's thick network of branches on a hard wooden bench, but she wouldn't leave until she'd added all this new information into her journal.

- "Wild card" = partier?
- "Enterprise" = business-driven family = maybe went to college??
- TWO HALF SIBLINGS—why didn't they show up on K-DNA??
- *****INSEMINATED*****

That half siblings bit, though. She didn't know how to feel about it. Curious? Disturbed? Like she should spit into more vials for more DNA websites to try to find them?

That detail was what finally forced her to eat the venomous words she'd said to her mom. She wasn't the product of some affair. Her "wild card" bio dad had donated his stuff a bunch of times for "extra spending money." Rob Westmore was out of the picture now, besides him trying to sue her mom—another detail she needed to shove into her boiling cauldron and force the lid over top of.

She now knew her bio dad was part of a business so lucrative, Kathleen had gone as far as to call it an "enterprise." Strangely specific wording that might help her draw lines backward from Kathleen to her maiden name and its connected company. Who called their business an enterprise unless *enterprise* was in the name? And, if the family was that driven and needed "extra spending money," it's possible her bio dad went to college, something that wasn't nearly as common thirty years ago as it was today. That fact alone might narrow her leads.

She rubbed the right side of her jaw, trying to get it to stop grinding her innocent molars to dust.

She gave Kathleen credit—this was one meeting that could've been an email, but she'd taken the time to meet her in person to shut her down. Not even her own family of origin had given her that courtesy.

One thing hadn't changed, though, and that was her craving for answers. Kathleen had mentioned not *talking* about her connection to their family, but she hadn't said anything about *researching*. She would use the coming week to consider signing the nondisclosure agreement, *and* she'd sleuth her way to as much information as possible.

And then there was the ten thousand dollars—so much more than pocket change. It was a new-to-her car. Part of a down payment on a house. Start-up cash for NeighborGood. An all-access membership to KindreDNA for the next fifteen years.

Who was she kidding? It was hush money. She would have to sit down and really think about it, just not right now.

Right now, she had to see what internet stalking could be committed from the palm of her hand. Once she'd opened the Facebook app, she typed "Kathleen Schulz" in the search bar. The results looked different than the day before, though, because none of the profile pictures were of the person she was related to. There was a new Kathleen Schulz profile, but it had a blank picture and no other identifying information, like a city or Instagram handle.

She rushed to KindreDNA.com and clicked through to her message to Kathleen's name, only to find the same thing. Her profile and family tree had been set to private. Kathleen wasn't playing games.

Dylan couldn't take it anymore. Her anger needed a place to go besides around and around in an endless circle. She needed a break from vague nonanswers. She wanted the truth; she deserved the truth. She shouldn't be the only one in her life who didn't know where she came from.

There was one other place nearby that might have answers.

Her brain was coming out of its fog and going into overdrive. Her gas pedal was to the floor, like yesterday when Hendrix had been driving.

She pulled out her phone and opened the Uber app, typing in the address of where she wanted to go.

Dylan tore open the door to Sunshine Fertility Clinic. She'd found the name of the fertility clinic that used to be on 16th Terrace and was delighted to learn they still existed in a recently refurbished office in an all-new location.

She stopped short of charging at the welcome desk when she saw what was inside. The waiting room on her left was full, and the couples scattered around it were either quietly whispering or staring silently at the walls ahead of them.

A space weighted with sorrow and desire.

The administrative assistant was staring at her with an almost-aggressive smile. "Hello. How may I help you?"

She wouldn't weasel around with fake business proposals anymore. She'd use the truth to get to the truth she wanted. "Yeah, hi. I'm here because I'm looking for information about a former patient."

The assistant's eyebrows levitated with suspicion. "Are you listed on the patient's disclosure forms or on file as the patient's healthcare power of attorney?"

"I'm her daughter. The patient's name is Candis Turner."

Technically, that made her the *outcome* of Candis's treatments.

"I see." The woman leaned back in her office chair and tapped a pen on her chin, her sunny demeanor turning overcast. "So, you're trying to access files from four decades ago?"

"Three."

"Hmm." The woman glanced up at her before typing into her keyboard, then reached behind her back and pulled a piece of paper from the printer. It took thirty seconds, which felt like thirty business days.

The assistant slid the paper across the desk to her. "This is what's called a disclosure form. *If* your mother fills it out and lists you as a trusted person who can receive her medical records, or *if* you come into the office *together* and she fills one out, *then* you can ask for her records. Otherwise, I'm not at liberty to share any information with you. Your third option is to bring in a court order."

Dylan could feel her thin, polite façade cracking. Maybe leveling with the woman would appeal to her compassion.

"Listen, I just did a KindreDNA test and found out my dad is not my biological father. Does that make sense? It doesn't make sense to me either. I think my mom may have had treatments here or, rather, over on 16th Terrace when the clinic was there. Anyway, it would really help me out if you could let me know the name of her donor so I can meet my biological father."

The assistant wasn't wearing glasses, but she peered over at Dylan like she was. "I'm sorry for what you're going through, but you have to understand that all of our donors—including the ones who donated samples at our previous location—were promised anonymity."

"I get there's rules and all that. I just . . ." She coughed and wiped at her eyes. She couldn't crash—not yet. She needed more time, more information.

The front door opened. A couple walked in and got in line behind her. The man nodded at her, while the woman stared at the floor.

"I'll be right with you," the assistant assured them, then patted Dylan's hand resting on the desk. "Wait here. I'm going to get someone who can help you. What's your name?"

"Dylan."

"Got it." She stood and walked through the doorway behind the welcome desk.

Dylan could hear faint voices.

"Just the person I'm looking for."

"Another genealogy test gone wrong."

"Have five minutes?"

The assistant reappeared, a man holding a clipboard following her. "This is our resident social worker, Raj. He's a great person to talk to about your situation."

Raj smiled with just the right amount of pity. "Hello, Dylan. I have a couple minutes before my next appointment. Would you like to talk?"

"That would be nice. Thank you." She somehow summoned her calm and collected voice.

Adjusting her purse strap higher on her shoulder, she walked through the door to the right of the desk that led to the back offices. Raj took her into a room painted the softest teal and motioned for her to sit in one of the light gray chairs facing his desk, which was garnished with a vase of fluffy white flowers. The aesthetic screamed, *Your life is a lie, but don't worry: We put this calming paint color on the wall!*

Raj sat down at his desk, which had a pen and notepad on it, opened to an empty page.

"Carmen tells me you recently took a genealogy test. Would you like to share what happened?"

She went through the bullet points of the last week of her life, ending with, "I came here looking for answers, which I know was stupid—"

"You aren't the first person to come here looking for their biological father," Raj interrupted. "And, you certainly won't be the last."

She looked up. "So, you can help me, then?"

"Probably not in the way you're hoping. You have to understand that, a few decades ago, fertility treatments were a lot less regulated than they are today. Sometimes we refer to that time as the Wild, Wild West of fertility. Even if your mom came for treatments to this clinic, the doctor may have chosen her donor for her, without writing it down in her file. Doctors didn't keep medical profiles or genetic histories of donors either. The one thing doctors promised—or *thought* they could promise—was anonymity."

"Can I say something off the record?"

"None of this is on the record, technically."

"Everyone loves that word. *Anonymity*. And sure, it's great for the donors and healthcare laws and all that, but what about me? Why do they get privacy, while I have to be on the outside of all these secrets that are *about* me? Don't doctors understand they're making people?"

She was out here regurgitating Reddit user with_my_gnomies to Raj the social worker, but she couldn't help it. He'd articulated her turmoil.

"That's what we're learning," Raj noted. "When it comes to biological relationships, there is no such thing as anonymity anymore—not in this day and age. People lie. Public records even lie. But DNA doesn't lie."

He shuffled papers around on his desk, then set a few brochures in front of her.

With the barely teal walls closing, she half expected the title to be in all caps and say something like SO, YOU'RE A SPERM DONOR KID.

"I'm truly sorry for what you're going through, Dylan. You're at the beginning of a difficult journey, and navigating such sensitive, complicated stuff with family is hard. Sometimes these mysteries take years to be solved. And sometimes these mysteries never get solved, and you have to learn how to live with the unknown."

He opened his laptop and typed something, then turned it around for her to look at. It was a picture of a traffic circle, but two of the four street exits were blocked by walls.

"This figure is inspired by Dr. Neufeld's Traffic Circle Model of Frustration," he said. "It's meant to be a metaphor to describe frustration from an attachment perspective, so it often applies to people who've gone through adoption. A nonpaternity event isn't exactly the same, but I think some of the psychological effects are similar."

He already knew the lingo. For once she was in a place where everyone understood the acronym NPE.

He pointed to the two blocked roads. "When a person first learns about their nonpaternity event, they will experience grief and deep frustration. However, if their grief or frustration has no healthy exit—let's say they've built up walls around themselves to suppress it or they're never given a chance to grieve—their frustration will build until the one thing it thinks it can do is leave through this last exit. But this last exit is where grief turns into attack mode."

What he was saying made sense so far, but it was embarrassing to hear. She was trying to hold it together, but her "frustration," to put it lightly, was turning foul.

"Some people direct their attack at others, while some attack themselves or seek other numbing escapes."

"Will this get any easier?" she whispered, picking up one of the brochures. The words *anger* and *search for identity and roots* stuck out on the page.

"None of this is easy," he replied, "but I think with the right support, you'll come to a place where you can integrate this part of your story with the rest of your life. You might see that all the branches, even the splintered or broken ones, have a place in your family tree."

Raj stood up, so she did the same. "I don't mean to rush you, but I have clients arriving soon."

She nodded, but her head was starting to feel heavy.

"Can I offer one piece of unofficial advice, though? First, your father died five days ago. Second, you found out you're not biologically related. Third, you found that out from neither of your parents. Fourth, you traveled a thousand miles from—where did you say you live, Illinois?—looking for answers. Fifth, some of your bio family members aren't ready to meet."

He didn't even know about her car.

Her half siblings.

The NDA.

"My advice is, it might be time to let yourself press the brakes."

## 29

## Who's the Bad Guy?

Pressing the brakes wouldn't help if they'd already failed. It reminded Dylan of her family's short stint in Denver, where each downslope of mountain interstate had a runaway-truck ramp in the case of a brake failure. Large pits of sand and gravel meant to stop eighty thousand pounds of engine using friction alone.

Standing outside the clinic, the sun beating down on her, she was starting to think she needed more than brakes to stop her careening down the path she was on. Though maybe if she allowed her frustration to barrel on at maximum speed, she could use the momentum to crash through one of the walls blocking her "healthy exits" from the traffic circle. Surely one of Raj's brochures would mention that.

Her stomach growled.

The other certainty beyond death and taxes—and frustration—was her own hunger. She took out her phone.

> **Me:** Can you pick me up?

> **Me:** Sunshine Fertility Clinic. I need food asap.

**Hendrix:** SFC? seriously dylly?

**Hendrix:** on my way

**Me:** "Dylly" is so not happening.

Ten minutes later, he pulled into the parking lot, and she dragged her heavy limbs into the car. Hendrix set a fresh banana and box of Hot Tamales on her lap.

"Do you still like these?" he asked.

She lifted the box of Hot Tamales to her nose and let the strong smell of cinnamon work its nostalgia on her senses. She hadn't eaten them in nearly a decade, but she hadn't forgotten them either. "You remembered. Thank you."

She leaned over and kissed his cheek, catching the scent of citrus and sandalwood.

"So? How'd it go?"

She leaned back against the headrest and flopped her head over to look at him.

He laughed. "That good, huh? I thought medical facilities gave out private records like Smarties at a parade."

"I didn't have energy to put together a fake court order before asking for my mom's records." She ripped open the banana and scarfed it.

"Not a bad idea. Now you're getting the hang of investigative work."

"As if you're some expert. What about your morning? What have you been up to?"

He put the car in Drive. "I had a couple work things to do."

"What kind of work things? You keep mentioning work without saying what that means. I thought you said you were between jobs."

"Exactly, so let's talk about you. I want to hear how things went with Kathleen."

"I'm trying to be a better person who takes interest in other people's lives besides my own."

"I think you're a better person when you're not being nosy."

Maybe all the "work stuff" was related to his dad, which was why he didn't want to talk much about it.

"Maybe I don't feel like talking about Kathleen Schulz—did you ever think of that?" That wasn't true. She'd need to verbally process this one for a long time, especially because the calm she'd absorbed from Raj's walls was fading fast. "She wouldn't tell me who my bio dad is. Also, she said she'd pay me ten thousand dollars to shut up about it."

He gripped the steering wheel and glanced at her. "Ten grand. That's not an offer you get every day. Are you going to take it?"

"I don't know."

"You don't know?"

"This isn't only about the money. It's about shutting down future possibilities too."

Like finding her half siblings. Maybe introducing them to Gale and Peeta. Would a half sister think they were more than lab rats?

Hendrix scoffed. "Who cares about possibilities when ten grand is a sure thing? Don't be crazy—take the money."

"It's not that simple. Even Kathleen knows that, because she gave me a week to think about it, a week I plan to use. I need to slow down anyway," she said, repeating Raj's professional advice.

"Just don't throw away ten grand for some pretend relationship with a half sibling," he muttered.

Her heart dropped, like it had been swallowed by a sinkhole.

"I never told you that," she whispered.

"Never told me what?"

"I never told you I have half siblings. I *never* told you that. How did you know that?"

He shrugged. "It's a joke. We were joking about that documentary and having all those siblings or whatever. Why are you acting so paranoid?"

Was she paranoid? Maybe.

She looked around his car, his nondescript car with tinted windows that would blend in with its surroundings wherever it went. She thought about him keeping changes of clothes in his trunk, how he'd been "working" when he was actually hovering nearby.

The camera, still on his back seat.

The cooler of food, for long hours in the car.

If she opened his glove box, would she find a pair of binoculars?

He'd been so insistent on how they should get information from Royal Cape Companies, acting like he knew how all the investigating should be done.

It *was* strange how he randomly, out of the blue, had run into her at the Bread and Board the other day.

Hadn't Kathleen made some comment about what she'd found out about Dylan?

What if . . .

Could that actually mean . . .

Could she be that big of an idiot to not have seen it before?

"You're following me." She couldn't look at him, could barely say the words. "You're following me for Kathleen, aren't you?"

He glanced at her, then scraped the side of his scruffy jaw. "It's not what you think."

She whipped her entire body around so her wrath could face him. "Oh really? Then humor me, Hendrix. Tell me exactly what it is I'm thinking and how it's *not* that."

The way nothing surprised him.

The way he was suspicious of everything.

The way he talked about keeping an open mind until they had concrete evidence.

"Pull over," she demanded.

He shook his head, gripping the steering wheel tighter. "Not until we're all the way over the bridge."

"Pull over, or I will throw myself out of this car!" She screamed so loud she almost believed her own threat. The last piece of banana was squished in her fist.

He waited until they'd crossed the river, then pulled up next to the curb.

She chucked the banana onto his clean car mat. "If you pretend to care for me at all, you will tell me the truth and you will tell it to me right now."

He held his hands up, like he was protecting himself from her outrage. "All of this was pure coincidence—I promise. Kathleen reached out to hire me to learn more about you. She didn't know I knew you, and I never told her."

"You're a private investigator. Say it."

His shoulders fell. "I'm a private investigator."

"No. No, no, no." While she was trying to dig up her own past, he was keeping tabs on her. She was his job.

She couldn't believe how stupid she'd been.

"Kathleen contacted me right after you reached out to her about meeting. Their family was nervous because of the other half siblings who showed up on their doorstep. Frankly, I think they're overreacting about the other two wanting to take all their money, but it's not my job to determine that. It's my job to investigate who I'm asked to investigate."

"I can't believe this entire time I thought you were trying to help me." She couldn't see the hotel from her window, which unnerved her.

Hendrix banged the steering wheel. "I took the job *because* it put me in a position to help you. I wanted to make this a gentler letdown for you. And, I wanted to see you again, Dylan. When I heard your name, I knew this wasn't a coincidence."

"You thought lying to me would help me?"

"When I left your hotel room yesterday, I called Kathleen and told her to message you back. I told her you weren't some scumbag trying to shake her down. I told her she should meet with you and see for herself you're a great person."

"That doesn't erase the fact you were lying to me. Once Kathleen contacted you, you could have easily found me and given me a heads-up. Instead, you lied to both me *and* your client. Isn't there any code of ethics for PIs?"

He reached across the seat to try to touch her, but she pushed him away.

"This isn't happening." She threw off her seatbelt and reached for the door handle.

He shook his head. "You're mad I lied to you, but this entire time you've been lying to yourself."

She turned around and glared. "What are you talking about?"

"Your dad, Dylan. He was insane, and you refuse to see it even though everyone else around you can."

"My dad was complicated, sure, but isn't everybody? Who are you to talk about dads being insane? Isn't yours underneath a highway somewhere, bumming for his next fix?"

As soon as she said it, she wished she could take it back. "I'm sorry, Hendrix."

He glared at her. "This is different. My dad is obviously out of his mind. He's always been an angry, abusive addict for everyone to see. *Your* dad, on the other hand, reeled people in and then ripped them apart from the inside. You didn't move seven times because he outgrew his job. You moved because he got fired for being manipulative and obsessed with himself, over and over and over."

He reached into the back seat for a folder, which he slammed onto her lap. *Another freaking folder.*

"What's this?" she demanded.

"Receipts," he answered. "I'll bet my entire career that Darren Turner is the reason your mom was forced to leave the Red Knot."

She looked down at the folder, which she swore had an electric current running through it.

"Your dad was the roach in her kitchen."

# 30

# Receipts

|  | Employer: | Boss/HR: |
|---|---|---|
| Jacksonville | VentureGold Group | Forty Under 40?? self-obsessed, misused funds |
| Atlanta | Atlanta Capital | boss: "Atlanta's Up and Coming Annihilator" |
| Nashville | Bluegrass Assets | took credit for co-worker's investment plan, threatened same co-worker into silence, co-worker kept paper trail |
| Dallas | WindCorp | threatened his boss when not chosen for promotion |
| Boston | Bayside Partners | blamed co-worker for losing investor's entire retirement fund on bad deal he made unilaterally |
| Cleveland | Shale Advisors | constantly complained about the board to investors, poached clients to MATRIC |
| Jacksonville | MATRIC | overspent investor budget by 50K |
| Denver | Summit Investors | DT's stories didn't line up, SI decided to call past work references and found out he'd faked his résumé |
| Other cities?? |  |  |

## 31

## Up to Code

DNA didn't lie, but did spreadsheets? Dylan stared at the three columns Hendrix had made. It was all there—the cities she'd lived in, the companies her dad had worked for, and the comments about what it had been like to employ or work alongside Darren Turner. The content must have taken hours to collect. All the random hours he'd told her he was "working."

"I realize it was your idea to call all these people in the first place, but you actually called all these people?"

"Every last one," he said like he was giving closing remarks for his defense. "It took much longer than I thought it would. Each phone call turned into a therapy session. People venting all the ways Darren Turner messed with their companies and their minds. Many of them were talking about things that happened decades ago, and they still hadn't recovered."

"How did you even know I lived in all these places?"

"The internet is a vast—"

"Don't. I know I spend a ton of time online, but my actual footprint is tiny. Please, no more lies." She hated how desperate she sounded.

He looked down at his hands. "When we were in your hotel room and you caught me with your journal, I'd flipped toward the back and came across the entry listing all the places you lived. I had to start somewhere so I could get all of this information for you, but I swear I didn't read any other entries."

"Hendrix—"

"If you're seriously mad at me about that, I don't even want to hear it. Don't hold me to some code of ethics you won't even hold your dad to. It's the dumbest kind of hypocrisy."

So, he wanted to fight. She wouldn't mind throwing the gloves off. But she was just so tired, like her body was slamming itself into one of those walls Raj had talked about.

"I need to go."

"Dylan—"

"I have to make sense of all this. My brain has been in and out of this debilitating fog the past five days. I think it's because, right now, I'm trying to figure out the difference between my memories and all the lies I've been told. I need to slow down and actually process everything."

For a second, she thought he might argue, but this time he only nodded.

She shuffled the papers together, tucked them into her journal, and grabbed the door handle. "Thank you for getting all this info, Hendrix."

"Dylan, I—"

"By the way, I think you're right. I haven't been holding you and my dad to the same standards. I'm done with liars."

She left the box of Hot Tamales on the seat.

Page 117

## Worse Than Rage
### (16)

Hendrix didn't show last night.

I was so worried—what if his dad hurt him? I had to go and check to see if he was okay. Hendrix gave me his address before. In case I ever wanted to "sneak out and say hello" was how he put it. I reminded him my nerves had limits, even if it sounded kinda fun.

I went to his house and saw him in his window. I was so excited, and so relieved.

But when I knocked on his door, his mom answered. It was the first time I met her. I told her I was Hendrix's friend and asked if I could say hello. She went to go find him but came back and said he wasn't up for company. She seemed really sorry about it, but I could've died of embarrassment.

Hendrix didn't come to class today either.

This isn't rage. Rage means you still have energy to feel angry, and if nothing else, anger can give you forward motion. It can give you the power to not let someone hurt you.

This is something worse than rage. It's sadness, and sadness is just that.

It's sad.

It means someone had enough power over you to hurt you.

Page 118

## Getting Off the Carousel
### (18 FINALLY)

Jacksonville.

Atlanta.

Nashville.

Dallas.

Boston.

Cleveland.

Jacksonville.

Denver.

Leaps and bounds around the country.

The carousel circles.
    But I'm jumping off.

# 32

# Rat Race

Dylan ordered an Uber back through the maze of square city blocks to the hotel, feeling lost in the horde of cars and pedestrians scurrying around corners and through stoplights. She was merely another in the crowd, searching for her own scrap of life. Hitting dead end after dead end, while a few key players stood nearby and watched.

Hendrix had accused her of being paranoid, and he was right, but why shouldn't she be? Her parents had lied. Rob Westmore had lied. Hendrix had lied.

She wondered if there was a prize for finding her way out of the maze, a metaphorical piece of cheese. Even more than ten grand, she wanted the truth of her past, a better definition of who she was, or maybe a sense of connection with one of the other billions who existed on the planet.

She had a sudden urge to compare notes. She opened her journal to the entry Hendrix had mentioned, the last one she'd written as a teenager. Holding it up to the spreadsheet, she could see the lists were identical, like he'd admitted.

Was it true—was she stuck on some version of her dad that wasn't real? And how did this all tie in to him not being her biological father?

*Who am I?*

*And who is Darren Turner?*

The Uber dropped her off at the hotel, and when the lobby doors slid open, a wave of air-conditioning blasted her.

She had to slow down. She had to stop looking for clues and evidence and truth all over the city of Jacksonville and sit with her own thoughts. If her dad was truly that manipulative of a person, why had her mom stayed with him? And why hadn't she talked about it with Dylan?

She waited for the elevator doors to open and the people inside it to empty out.

"Dylan?"

She winced at the sound of her name, not ready for James's sunshine.

"What happened? Are you okay?"

"Hey." She tried to smile, but her face didn't cooperate. Whoever said it took fewer muscles to smile forgot sometimes life deserved a frown.

He reached out but then pulled his hand back. "I'm sorry. It's just that—you're crying."

She wiped her cheek, wondering when those tears had spilled. "Yeah, I'm not doing great right now."

"Thanks for being honest."

"Sure." She'd braced herself for a pump-up speech, so his answer surprised her. She walked around him and into the elevator, which James held open.

"I'm going to check in on you later. You don't have to answer if you don't want to. Just know I'm here if you need anything."

He let the door close, and the elevator lurched upward. She wasn't hungry anymore; those pains had been shoved to the side by other pain.

*Does everyone know but me?*

Inside her room, she didn't doomscroll internet forums for answers, even though that was what every nerve in her thumbs wanted to do. Instead, she pulled up the Notes app on her phone, ready to finally read the short eulogy she'd written with the world's largest blind spots.

## Dad's Eulogy

The first thing my dad did when we moved to a new city was invite his co-workers and their families over for a housewarming party. He said a party was the perfect motivation for us to unpack our stuff and put it away quickly.

"Besides," he'd add, "then Mom can make me look good with her cooking, and you, Dylan, can make me look good by telling everyone how awesome your dad is."

My dad had a sense of humor, which is something I admire about him because it showed how resilient he was. Even though he worked in tough environments, including a few places that didn't appreciate his confidence and ambitions, he was able to move on, pick up the pieces, and start fresh. Fresh enough to be the new guy and still throw a party where he made everyone around him laugh and enjoy themselves.

He was generous. He made me feel special. He didn't focus on my flaws.

I wish I was more like my dad. I wish I could bottle his energy, determination, and zest for life. He was so driven—he didn't let anything or anyone stand in the way of reaching his goals.

I miss him already.

## 33

## Fool Me Thrice

**Google:** how to let go of a fantasy

Dylan had used words like *resilient, generous,* and *driven* in her short eulogy for Darren Turner, but she was starting to believe those were the masks he'd worn. The other people in his life would've chosen antonyms. *Manipulative. Thief. Bully.*

After every firing and every move, her dad had painted himself the victim. He wouldn't even call it a firing—he'd tell her he'd done nothing wrong and had been pushed out; his bosses were too small-minded for his big aspirations. She'd said he "didn't let anything or anyone stand in the way of reaching his goals," but did that mean he plowed through a pile of bodies to reach every new job, milestone, or award?

Hendrix's receipts said yes.

How had she not seen it before? She thought back to everything she'd read in her journal before coming to Jacksonville. Her dad had praised her in ways that built up his own ego but belittled her mom. He'd taken Dylan's ordinary frustrations as a kid and used them to turn her mom into the bad guy, the scapegoat for his own mistakes. He'd played the victim while yanking their family around the country to chase his grandiose dreams. He'd sowed lies and reaped thorns that choked out the truth.

The first time she'd read those entries, she'd thought of the quote about how we forget what people say and do but we don't forget how they make us feel. He'd made her feel special. He'd showered her with gifts even after she acted like a brat to her mom. He'd left her mom to unpack moving boxes, while he took Dylan to the nearest museum. The evidence of what he'd said and done had always been there. Her interpretation—the way he'd made her feel—was off.

Shame filled her gut like lead. Maybe the worst part of all this wasn't even the light it shed on her relationship with her dad but how it also repainted her relationship with her mom. Her mom had been busy trying to take care of her, trying to be a parent. What did it mean that Dylan had never gotten along with her biological parent? What did it mean that her non-blood parent, the one she thought she got along with, had turned out to be so awful?

Dylan backspaced her Google search and typed in a question that would give her a more relevant answer.

The first result was an article called "Seven Signs You're Dealing with a Textbook Narcissist."

It wasn't like everything in her life suddenly made sense. It was still a serious, if not unbelievable, accusation that her dad had sabotaged her mom's restaurant. But now she had a theory to go off, at least until she talked to someone with a higher degree than Google.

She stood up from the desk and walked over to the freshly made bed. After pulling open the heavy comforter, she climbed in and curled herself into a ball.

A tear fell. And then another. And then five more.

She pictured each big drop of salt water rolling down the side of her face as a lie she'd been told. A lie she'd believed.

Like her body was trying to detox.

# 34

# Just James

### Saturday, September 27

Light pierced through the cracks in the hotel room curtains, like an alarm clock for her anxiety, announcing it was a new day and there were internal organs to torture. She checked the time on her phone, 7:46 A.M., *and* found text messages marked 11:13 P.M. she'd never heard come in.

> **Captain Jim:** Have you eaten? Taken a drink of water? Slept?
>
> **Captain Jim:** (No need to reply. Just checking in.)

No, she hadn't eaten. Her mouth was so dry it tasted like an expired mushroom, and she must have cried herself to sleep. She wasn't sure what James's grading scale on self-care was, but it was likely she'd failed.

> **Me:** Thank you for checking in.
>
> **Captain Jim:** Can I get you breakfast? We could meet in the lobby.

She was a disaster, still wearing her clothes from yesterday, but she couldn't shake the idea she needed more than self-care. She needed help.

**Me:** Can you give me 20 minutes??

**Me:** Thank you.

**Captain Jim:** See you in 21 ☺

Dylan dragged her numb limbs to the shower. The hot water was so soothing she thought about sitting on the floor and crying. Instead, she put globs of shampoo in her hair and dug her fingers into her scalp. There was so much about the past week—and the past thirty years—to unpack, the burden was suffocating. Even when she separated her dad's careful character assassination from her rocky relationship with her mom, it didn't erase her mom's lies. Or give her the name of her biological father. Or remove the sting of the thousand paper cuts from Kathleen's NDA.

She turned off the shower and dressed herself in her last clean pair of clothes. It took at least five minutes to get through her tangled hair, and when she brushed her teeth, her strokes were so weak she was sure her dentist would praise her. Her gumline finally got the break it deserved.

Most of her twenty minutes were gone, so she plodded around the room faster, then finally headed to the elevator. She'd already decided this was her last day in Jacksonville, away from Gale and Peeta. She'd book a flight home and ask Tara to keep the pigs for one more day.

The door slid open, and she spotted James in the distance, his arms filled with bananas, yogurt, a drink carrier with two coffees, and a bag of what she hoped was carbs.

His smile was warm but, thankfully, not insufferably cheerful. "I didn't know what you like for breakfast."

She almost smiled back. "It just so happens I like food for breakfast, so you did great."

"Glad I couldn't go wrong. Want to sit by a window?"

James led them to a set of armchairs with a small table nestled between them. He grabbed a banana while she took one of each item, including one of the blueberry muffins in the bag. He was quiet, like maybe he didn't want to pry after running into her last night.

"How are all your captain-y things going?"

He yawned and wiped his eyes. "Amazing. I'm tired and ready to go home tomorrow, but I love this conference. It's special when we only see each other once a year."

"Are they like family to you?" She stopped chewing, annoyed her filter had malfunctioned. "Sorry. That was a weirdly personal question."

"Depends on what your definition of family is." He didn't seem weirded out at all. "Is family the people who know and love you or people who cause a lot of chaos and pain? Or maybe a complicated mix of both?"

She tried to picture a family of Jameses growing up, like the Bradys or the Winslows. She wondered which TV family she'd relate to. According to that librarian—*Real Housewives.*

"My friends from Trader Joe's understand the ups and downs of my work, and that's something not every friendship can offer. But they also don't get to be in my life every single day. I need people to eat dinner with on a somewhat regular basis. Who do you think of as your family?"

"I think that's why I'm in Jacksonville. To figure that out. I'm definitely in the camp where family is chaotic."

He nodded. "My dad wasn't a nice man. In fact, my sisters and I spent some time in foster care." He must have seen the shock all over her face. "I've had to work through all the ways that messed me up. *Still* messes with me," he added.

"I'm really sorry you went through that."

"Thank you. Kids shouldn't have to go through what so many kids have gone through. Did that even make sense?" He laughed at himself, then set his yogurt on the table.

"I agree." She started peeling her banana.

"I'm sorry. This is probably a lot to put on you, especially with whatever has been going on. Are *you* okay?"

She shook her head. "But it's good to remember I'm not the only one who's gone through stuff."

"Does that mean I can ask why you're in Jacksonville? For real?"

She blushed. Of course he'd seen through all her vague answers. "I wasn't off work for my birthday. I mean, it was my birthday last week—I turned thirty—but I wasn't exactly celebrating."

She started sharing the whole story, and at first, it was like pouring it through a tiny crack, only the necessary details coming out, but as she kept going, the crack fractured into a sinkhole. Everything spilled. The only detail she couldn't give voice to yet was Hendrix.

His heavy kisses. His lies. Her heart stung at the betrayal.

She put the last bit of muffin in her mouth and brushed the crumbs from her hands. "That's why I'm here. I'm trying to figure out who my bio dad is and why my parents never told me. And that's a lot to put on *you*."

"I just wish we could've supported you better at work. There's family leave for stuff like this."

She thought about when Teresa's beloved grandma died. Crew and mates brought cards and flowers. Olivia took Teresa's shift on a day she was struggling. Dylan wondered if that kind of support was only for irresistible personalities like Teresa.

"I'm not great at opening up to people."

"You?" James smiled.

"I've lived in Illinois for twelve years, but I don't know. It's hard to even know *how* to let people in."

"Especially when some of the key people in your life let you down."

"Exactly."

He fiddled with his own coffee cup. "What if you don't ever find out? Either who your bio dad is, or the answers to any of your questions, like why your mom didn't tell you?"

"I don't know. It's hard to explain, but I feel like I would do almost anything for answers. It's why, out of nowhere, after not traveling more than two hours away from my apartment in the past twelve years, I jumped on a plane."

He nodded.

"Anyway, I'm flying home tomorrow too."

"How are you going to spend your last day?"

She shrugged. "I still have to figure that out, but now that I'm thinking about it, you should know you were the first of *two* people who said I should go look at birds."

"Little Talbot Island." James lit up. "You have to go, and you have to take pictures for me."

Her eyes met his, and something sparked. But sparks weren't everything, she'd learned.

He checked his watch, then gathered their trash. "Our first session starts in five minutes, so I have to go. *You* should decide how you spend your last day, but no matter where you go, do you promise to take a few pictures like a proper tourist?"

"I'll do my best." She watched him walk away, then pulled out her phone.

She was scared to send her next text, mostly because she didn't know how it would be received, but it was worth a shot.

> **Me:** Hey. I'm wondering if you're around and would possibly be up for taking me to Little Talbot Island??

# 35

# Tied Up in Red Knots

It was a coin flip whether or not Dylan would get a reply. The worst she'd get was a no, which wasn't nearly as bad as *I'm sorry, but your blood family doesn't want to know you. By the way, will you sign this NDA?* She could handle no just fine, but she smiled when her phone dinged with a reply saying yes.

Waiting in the lobby, she used the half hour to book a flight home, then watched as a car drove up to the doors and parked. It wasn't a gray Nissan, though. It was a Subaru, and Aunt Lou was in the driver's seat.

Aunt Lou's phone number hadn't changed, which she guessed might be the case. Lou was the type of person who traveled five new places every year but kept the same classic black blazer for twenty.

Aunt Lou ran around the front of her pearly blue car with arms wide open, hugging Dylan so hard all four of their lungs grunted.

"I'm so glad you reached out. I wanted to give you space, but I've been worried sick about you since the funeral." Aunt Lou leaned back and scanned her head to toe, then pulled her in for a second hug. "Who am I kidding? I've been worried sick about you most of your life."

She hadn't seen Aunt Lou much since she turned eighteen, and before that, it was typically once or twice a year—when Aunt Lou visited whichever city they'd moved to. Dylan recognized her earthy perfume, a comforting scent given she was the one human her mom seemed to relax around. Whenever she came by, world peace did too.

"I'm just glad it worked to meet up without any notice. Are you sure you don't mind, though? You can always leave the island early, and I can Uber back too."

Aunt Lou scowled. "Stop it with your Midwest nice, child. I would never miss out on this once-in-a-decade chance to spend the day with my favorite niece."

"I don't think you're allowed to say that when you have real nieces."

"Probably not, but they can't hear me. Plus, they don't even know who Mick Namarari Tjapaltjarri is."

"The coolest artist in the world?"

"See? You at least fake like you're interested in my work. I can't say the same for 'princess' Charlotte."

"How old is she again?"

"Five. She's my great-niece." Aunt Lou winked, then headed back to her car. "Anyway, Saturdays are for fresh air and looking at birds, so I've been told by my latest AARP magazine. You picked the perfect spot—Little Talbot is teeming right now."

Dylan opened the passenger door and got in. "You're the third person to tell me that this week."

---

They drove to Aunt Lou's apartment first, tucked just north of downtown. From the curb all the way to her door, Lou called everyone by name, including the neighbor's black cat. "Why hello, Paula Kelly." Aunt Lou brushed her hand under the feline's chin. "On a scale of hissy to cuddly, how are we today? I was feeling hissy until my niece here texted me."

Meeting Paula Kelly made Dylan miss Gale and Peeta even more, so she also petted the cat before going in.

On the other side of the narrow entry hallway was a living room strewn with maximalism—every flat surface covered in picture frames and small trinkets, while the walls boasted woven tapestries, painted canvases, and more framed memories.

"Pretend you can't see all my clutter, because I'm not asking for forgiveness," Aunt Lou trilled, disappearing behind a beaded curtain that swung and clacked together.

Dylan rotated in a circle, guessing there might be hundreds, maybe even a thousand, different things to look at. "I don't have to dust, so it doesn't bother me. Besides, it screams 'Aunt Lou.'"

"Emotional? Vibrant? Lush?"

"That, and adventurous. Enchanting. Curious."

Aunt Lou reappeared through the curtain. "I know this will all get thrown into a landfill after I die, but every piece reminds me of someone. Strangers. Creatives I admire. Dear friends. A lot of the people who've shaped me over the years."

Dylan wondered what her living room would look like if she decorated that way. Aunt Lou's list of dearly beloved was large.

"I'll be back here in the kitchen. The bathroom is around the corner if you need it."

"Is the bathroom door made of beads too?" she called back. "If that's the case, I'll hold it until we get to the park."

"I'm a curator, not a monster. You should come by the Cummer sometime. I'd love to show you around."

*The museum James mentioned.* "I'd love to, but my flight leaves tomorrow morning."

She walked the perimeter of the living room like it was its own museum of tiny exhibits. She recognized a few landmarks—Machu Picchu, Taj Mahal, the Colosseum—but many of the photos and souvenirs were stories Aunt Lou would have to tell herself.

A frame resting on one of the side tables caught her eye. She stopped strolling and picked it up, feeling the ornate ridges of the wooden design, while staring at the faces of her mom and Aunt Lou. They were standing in front of a building with a sign that said L'Academie de Cuisine. Her mom had said the two of them met in college, which Dylan now knew meant culinary school. The two women looked older than freshly enrolled eighteen-year-olds, though.

She opened the frame and flipped over the picture. The Kodak emblem was printed on the back, along with a series of letters and numbers. *JAN,* likely for *January,* but she couldn't remember if that meant the month it was taken or the month the physical copy was printed. The sidewalk in the picture was carpeted with snow, so maybe it was both.

"Dylan, will you grab the cooler for me?" Aunt Lou hollered from the kitchen. "It's in the bathroom closet next to the washing machine. Looks like a backpack."

"Yeah, no problem."

She tucked the picture under her arm while she fetched the cooler, then brought both objects to the kitchen where Aunt Lou was chopping peppers.

She set the frame right next to the cutting board and crossed her arms. "What's the story behind the photo?"

Aunt Lou squinted to look at it. "That's a famous culinary school in Maryland. We visited on one of our annual girls' trips back East. That was our first, I believe."

Her chopping never slowed, and somehow each strip of pepper came out the same size.

"Did you master that skill at L'Academie? I didn't realize you set out to be a chef before becoming a curator."

Aunt Lou tossed the knife to the side. "It's a French knife cut, and you're saying that like it's an accusation, which I'm guessing means your mom didn't have the sit-down with you like she promised."

She shook her head.

"Oh, Candis." Aunt Lou wiped her hands on a towel, then covered the glass container of peppers. "Look, your mom is a dear friend, and I don't want to come between you and her. I'm just more than annoyed she hasn't talked to you yet. You're—what—twenty-eight?"

"Thirty."

"Exactly. You're a big girl, and it shouldn't have taken Darren's death to bring all of this up."

Dylan bit her lip. "She *has* tried to get in touch a few times, but we keep . . . missing each other. In more ways than one."

Aunt Lou eyed her. "What does that mean?"

"It means I may have hung up on her when she called last time."

Aunt Lou grabbed her shoulders. "I guess I need to shake both of you, then."

Dylan leaned back against the counter. "I found out about the Red Knot and my dad getting fired everywhere, but is there anything *you* can tell me? Like why I'm not related to my dad?"

Aunt Lou opened the fridge and started chucking cheeses and spreads and fruits into the cooler. "The truth is, I don't know."

"She never told you?"

"Not the full story. I knew she was trying to get pregnant, and then suddenly, after our first girls' trip, she was pregnant."

"Does it bother you that she never told you?"

Aunt Lou pinched the bridge of her nose. "It's not that I don't want to know. It's that I love your mom enough to believe if she's not telling me something, it's for a reason that matters to her." She zipped the cooler and threw it over her shoulder. "Can we go to the island now? I'm worked up, and I think someone wise once said looking at birds is supposed to reduce midlife rage."

Magnolias, live oaks, and cabbage palms sheltered Little Talbot's Dune Ridge Trail from the harsh sun. Dylan and Aunt Lou walked side by side on the broad path, allowing them to talk without the added burden of eye contact.

"Your mom was a force of nature at the academy," Aunt Lou began. "That doesn't mean it was easy. It was punishing, being expected to 'yes, chef' this and 'yes, chef' that. We couldn't be precious about anything, not our feelings or joints or being with loved ones on the holidays—all of it was sliced and diced and burned at some point. It was even harder for women. Candis somehow found a way to let everything roll off her back. Her only goal was to be the best."

It sounded like the articles she'd read about her mom.

"Is that why you stopped?"

Aunt Lou tucked a chunk of frizzy hair behind her ears, which, in protest, bounced out again. "I had an unfortunate encounter with a male student. It was too much for me, and I dropped out after the first year. I stuck around the area and lived with your mom, then started the uphill climb to get my master's degree in art history. I decided if I couldn't make my own art, I'd collect other people's and share it with the world instead."

Dylan kept her eyes on the trail with its padding of grapevines and greenbriers. Every so often she kicked up sandy debris. "It's hard to picture Mom like that—everything rolling off her back. I don't think she ever let go of one annoying thing I said."

"Back then, she was the life of the party."

"Which sounds like my dad. At least, how I *thought* of him."

Aunt Lou patted her back. "I thought the same thing when I first met him, but people like your dad don't always go after the submissive, quiet ones. They pull in and destroy the strong because it makes them feel stronger. They want to be the thing everyone else orbits around. All relationships will go through tough times or life's storms or whatever you want to call them. Even healthy ones. The thing that kills me about Darren is that he *was* the storm, ripping apart your home from the inside."

"Did anything seem off when they were dating?" she asked, desperate for every explanation, motive, or decision that made up her parents' history.

"When I saw your parents together the first time, I thought the stars aligned for one of those once-in-a-generation couples. There was your mom, taking the culinary world by storm. And her new boyfriend, a development tycoon."

Aunt Lou's responses were getting breathier, which seemed to correlate with the sand getting deeper. Not only was the conversation weighty—each step forward was also asking more from them, making their muscles burn and their brows glisten.

Dylan wiped her sweaty forehead with the back of her hand, then took a swig from the water bottle she'd tucked in her purse. The water helped her overheated body, but she hoped the ocean breeze would reach them soon.

"I feel like I should've noticed a bunch of red flags," Aunt Lou said, "but Candis seemed happy, so I was happy for her. It wasn't until she started making headlines that Darren's other side surfaced."

"He started acting strange?"

"Jealous. He would go on long trips, then come back and complain about how busy your mom was. He'd name-drop in conversations where other people were celebrating her. He'd cut her down in front of her sous-chefs. It felt like a flashback to culinary school, but just like back then, Candis let it roll off her back and kept most of it to herself. I saw glimpses of it but had no idea the full scope of what was going on until years later."

The canopy of trees parted, and the path climbed higher. The women walked in silence, saving their energy for walking and breathing.

Someone came up from behind and fell into step alongside them. Her sleeves were sewn full of park badges. "Y'all are in for a real treat once you round the corner. The red knots are out in full force."

"Red knots? Like the restaurant?" Dylan muttered to Aunt Lou, who elbowed her.

"It's only the size of a robin but flies over eighteen thousand miles round trip, from the Canadian arctic to Argentina, every year." The ranger didn't skip a beat. "That's longer than going from planet Earth to the moon."

"Tenacious little birds," Aunt Lou marveled.

"I heard one inland this morning, all by itself," Dylan said.

"Hopefully it will rejoin the flock soon. It needs them to survive." The ranger picked up a piece of litter off the trail and shoved it into her pocket, then picked up her pace into a jog. "Enjoy your day and these gorgeous views!"

How did she keep that pace in this stifling heat in those thick, long pants? Dylan's own midwestern tolerance for southern heat was showing up in large rings of sweat on her T-shirt.

The trail turned east and climbed steeper. Finally, their view changed, and forest gave way to dunes and grasses. They could see not only the ocean with its majestic shoreline of waves crashing against it, but also masses of red knots sprawled along the coast. It was low tide, so from that far away they looked like a swarm of bugs bumping into and bouncing over one another for food. They had cinnamon bellies that contrasted the peppery feathers on their backs, which were held up by legs that looked like black spindles.

"There must be thousands," Aunt Lou said. "It's mesmerizing."

For a while they simply watched, the breeze cooling the sweat they earned on their hike. It seemed wrong to take out her phone while secluded in such breathtaking nature, but James specifically asked for a photo. She couldn't *not* send him one, though it took a minute for cell service to deliver it.

**Me:** The view here is im-peck-able

**Captain Jim:** Threw up in my mouth that pun was so . . .

**Captain Jim:** hawkward.

**Captain Jim:** But seriously, thank you for the picture!! I'm jealous, and that's saying something because we are currently taste testing next month's product release!

**Captain Jim:** New fav might be the zany zinger cashews

**Me:** Heading back to the birds. Cashew later . . .

The text wouldn't send, so she tucked her phone away and lifted her face to where sand met water. Even together as a sprawling flock, the red knots were miniscule against the Atlantic Ocean behind them. They knew it too, because every time a wave came close, the birds nearest the water turned and skittered farther inland, sending ripples through the entire assembly.

"Hungry?" Aunt Lou asked, turning off the trail to the open beach.

Dylan followed, then grabbed the thin blanket tucked in the mesh pocket on the side of the cooler and unrolled it for them to sit on. Aunt Lou pulled food out of the cooler more gingerly than when she packed. "Are the birds speaking to you yet?"

"Funny." She said it like it was the least hilarious thing she'd heard in a while, then grabbed a cracker and spread it with spiced apple jam. "They're not speaking to me; they're confusing me. I mean, how does a group this size learn to live as a flock? That doesn't compute in my brain. I relate more to lone wolves. With a dad who turned out to be a wolf in sheep's clothing."

"And your mom?"

Tears stung the corners of her eyes. "The one who never cried wolf?"

Aunt Lou sliced a piece of cheese and nibbled on it. She looked like she was about to say something but sighed, as if there wasn't a good enough response to capture the complexity of what they were dealing with—it would all ring empty, like platitudes.

She stared at the water instead, and Dylan stared with her.

"I keep having these awful, spiraling thoughts," Dylan blurted, not knowing exactly where she was going with it except somewhere personal and humiliating. "My co-worker Teresa said something about her wedding that I can't stop thinking about. She said she likes the thought of it being the day that all the people she and her fiancé love are in the same room together—how that pretty much only happens at weddings and funerals."

The look on Aunt Lou's face said she didn't know why exactly Dylan thought this was awful. "That sounds . . . lovely."

"Yes, it does, but my spiraling starts when I picture *my* wedding. And obviously, there's no groom and I don't know who's walking me down the aisle, but that's not the awful part. The problem is that the pastor says his 'Dearly beloved' speech, then laughs and tells me to turn around, and . . . there's not a single person there. It's supposedly one of the happiest days of a person's life, but I have nobody to celebrate with. I'm alone."

Aunt Lou bit her lip. "I get why that hits a nerve. I've been what many would technically think is 'on my own' for most of my life too. A lot of that time has been lovely—doing a job I love, traveling, flexibility—but there's times when it's not so great, like when you're too sick to make your own soup. Those are the days when you realize you need some sort of flock. Or pack, if you happen to be a wolf."

She felt Aunt Lou's hand on her back.

"You have some hard stuff to work through, but what worries me is that you'll let these thoughts become some self-fulfilling prophecy."

"What do you mean?"

Aunt Lou's brows arched with worry. "You believe you're alone and you'll never *not* be alone, so you isolate yourself until you're right. You might never find 'the one,' but I guarantee there are a few people out there who are worth letting in. Sure, you might get burned; some decide they don't like you; you realize *you're* not always a nice person and need a dose of humility. But meaningful connection is out there in all sorts of places, and we weren't wired to be *alone* alone." Aunt Lou took a bite of another flawlessly sliced pepper. "That includes your mom. After a big conversation and a lot of time to process, that is."

She thought of her mom's text message from yesterday, which she still had no idea how to respond to. "I'm out here talking about how alone I am, and you want to talk about working it out with my mom?"

"I'm not saying you have to accept anyone's actions, or that it's even possible to reconcile. I'm saying you can't let bitterness steal from your life and leave you lonely either."

Dylan paused, her cheeks burning. "I'll think about it."

"That's all I ask." Aunt Lou finished her cracker, then wiped the crumbs from her hands. "Actually, it's one of the two things I ask, but the second one isn't as hard."

She arched her eyebrow to let her aunt know she didn't believe her completely. "And that is?"

"When your mom finally sits you down, you need to keep your butt in that chair and not throw a fit this time. Just listen to her entire side of the story. Can you promise me that? Listen, and then give yourself space to blow up about it all. After that, decide what to do next."

She grinned. "Are you asking so I can report back with the tea?"

Aunt Lou pinched her cheek. "You're so funny. And I'm so sweaty—this sun and these hormones and all that. I'm going to stick my feet in the water, and while I'm gone, let yourself be sad for a minute. Maybe you keep ruminating on your fake wedding guest list because you haven't let yourself grieve yet."

Dylan hadn't considered that. "Aunt Lou?"

"Yes, darling?"

"Thank you."

"I love you too."

As Aunt Lou said it, the flock of red knots took flight. Thousands and thousands of birds sprang into the air with a chorus of twittering. Their movements as a flock were so fluid, so synchronized, they looked like a dancer lost in his own choreography. After dipping once more in the air, they settled back onto the beach to forage.

Dylan opened her journal, past her lists and notes to its last empty pages, and let her emotion pour into it like waves. Salty tears crashed down her face, and she let herself sob—trusting the ocean to drown out the sound.

Page 120

## Dark Night of the Soul
### (age 30)

I'm sitting on the beach at Little Talbot Island, the waves wrecking the shore in a way that reminds me of the past six days of my life. I thought I would have more stuff figured out by now, be more sure of myself. I'm calling it "Turning 30's Best Kept Lie," because the thing I'm most unsure of IS myself.

My story is a lie.

Dad was a nightmare. Even though I'm starting to see the signs, it goes against all my memories of him, which scares me. Also, he died. He's gone and he's not coming back. I'm supposed to be mad at him, and I am, but I'm also so sad. I miss him, which feels gross to say out loud knowing he hurt so many people.

And me—what's wrong with me? I want the truth, but I can't hear it without imploding. I'm mad at all these people, and yet even as I'm trying to write the anger out of me, it's like I'm breathing the inky pollution of rage burning off my pen back in through my nostrils, its dead weight settling at the bottom of my lungs.

I've been fine with my modest place in the world. I've minded my own business, kept my hands busy, managed to suppress some of my anger and keep from having to move states every ten to eighteen months. Mom said my life was just a routine—directionless. I liked to think of it as quiet.

But I remember Debra coming back to work from maternity leave, complaining about the cliché "the days are long but the years are short." She'd rubbed the bags under her eyes and said on the one hand every day felt like an eternity of being tired, while on the other she couldn't believe her baby was already four months old. She'd said, "Time sure is strange—a thief."

I wonder if I've done that to my life—merely survived the days only to realize twelve years have gone by. I can't remember what I said I wanted to be when I grew up, but I don't think it was Alone and Allergic to Change.

I'm afraid exposing my parents' lies is exposing the lies I've told myself too. I don't have answers, but for the first time I'm asking real questions. Is Mom right? Is my life just a routine? Am I living, or living out survival responses to my life?

How would I actually like to spend my thirtieth birthday?

"What if you don't find out?"

The question still haunts me. I hate to admit it, but James is right. There's no guarantee I'll ever know who my bio dad was. How will I begin to make peace with that?

I'm waking up, but waking up is like ripping the scab off the burn wounds I've accumulated.

I think I want different. I'm not talking about work as much as twelve years of putting down roots without ever learning how to connect with the rest of the world. I've kept a safe distance, but being this alone doesn't feel safe. I need more than Gale and Peeta and five-mile runs, but I don't even have the guts to ask my co-worker if she'd like to get supper together sometime. Or the decency to remember the one invite I've gotten from someone who is good and kind.

And yet, everything in me screams that red knots are liars. Nobody has the resilience to fly that long of a marathon through different climates and storms with the same flock, year after year. Taking a breather at a quiet, inland park sounds nicer. I'll just leave again, or other people will. Worse, they'll lie. What's the point?

I'm lonely.

So lonely.

## 36

## Life and Other Mysteries

Inside her purse, her phone rang. The number had a Jacksonville area code. She didn't want to answer it—the birds and the waves and the fresh air were doing wonders—but curiosity got the best of her.

"Hello, this is Dylan," she answered.

"Dylan Turner? Daughter . . . and Darren Tur . . ." The words garbled with static.

"Hello? Can you hear me? Yes, this is Dylan."

"Demetrius . . . Jacksonville . . . *Times* . . ." His responses kept cutting out.

Her heart pounded. She couldn't believe he'd called her back so soon. "I can't hear you. I don't have great cell service here."

"I can't . . . thing . . . I'll try . . ."

The line cut out.

"Seriously?" she groaned.

Aunt Lou's shadow hovered over her spot on the blanket. "What's going on?"

"I reached out to this reporter at *The Jacksonville Times* who wrote a lot of stories about Mom and the Red Knot. He just called back, but cell service isn't great. His name is—"

"Demetrius?" Aunt Lou shook her head. "That little worm."

Her phone dinged again.

> Dylan. This is Demetrius Ross with The Jacksonville Times. I have something for you that I'd rather talk about in person. Are you in the Jacksonville area? Would you be able to come by the Times office today?

She held it out for Aunt Lou to read. "He said he has something for me."

"A whole bunch of lies, that's what." Aunt Lou picked up jam jars and twisted on their lids, then threw boxes of crackers into the cooler.

Dylan thought she heard her mumbling a few other choice words, but Aunt Lou's jaw was clenched so tight Dylan couldn't understand them.

"What should I say?"

"Say you'll be there in about an hour, and Lou will be with you."

"But, you took me all the way out here—"

Aunt Lou stopped shoving things into the cooler and looked at her. "On the days I'm around, let me help. I promise I'll keep my mouth shut. Some of the time."

Dylan couldn't help but smile. She wouldn't be alone for this one.

> **Me:** Thank you for calling me back, Demetrius. I can come by in an hour. Lou is with me.

> **Demetrius Ross:** Couldn't call back soon enough. I'll have security waiting for Lou.

> **Demetrius Ross:** Just kidding.

She decided not to relay the message and instead helped refold the blanket.

"I thought you wanted me to talk to Mom first?"

Aunt Lou sighed. "This might be something you can do *for* your mom."

They walked the two miles back along the shore fast enough to kick up sand, not exactly the pace for considering birds and their natural habitat. This was the pace of business, which Aunt Lou carried over on the drive to the *Times* office.

"Demetrius followed your mom's career from start to finish," Aunt Lou said in the car. "Press is important for chefs, and good press *crucial* for a female chef to succeed. Every article Demetrius wrote about the Red Knot was supportive of Candis."

Through her window, Dylan watched the island's forest give way to more pavement and infrastructure. "Isn't that a good thing?"

"It was great, because none of it was forced. Demetrius loved Candis's work, so his coverage was genuine. They became friends, and I was their happy third wheel by association. But then he published that report. There wasn't a single sign of widespread roaches or rodents in that kitchen except for the few bugs and pieces of feces they found, but he went and published it anyway."

"Did he ever explain what happened?"

"He claims his boss pressured him to publish it, but he lost all credibility with me."

Inside the *Times* lobby, a man was sitting in a chair, eating a muffin.

"Lou," he said, like he wanted to address the elephant in the room right away.

Aunt Lou didn't offer the kind of reunion hug she'd given Dylan earlier, but she did give the courtesy of a cold nod. "Demetrius."

"I'm surprised you came along."

He stood up and brushed the crumbs off his pants while Aunt Lou put her hand on Dylan's back.

"Couldn't feed my niece to the wolves."

He turned to her. "Yes, Dylan. I had no doubt it was you. You look so much like your mom."

Coming from him, it was a neutral statement, but the words stung.

"Your voicemail resurrected a few ghosts I've been haunted by for thirty years now, some I'm guessing Lou filled you in on. I know I can't make everything right, but I hope what I have for you will help."

She looked between Demetrius, who was clasping his hands, and Aunt Lou, whose arms were crossed—the air tense with history.

She leaned toward Aunt Lou. "I think we should go and just 'listen to his entire side of the story,'" she whispered.

"Do as I say, not as I do," Aunt Lou snipped, but she let her arms fall to her sides.

"It's okay, Lou. I don't expect to get off that easy. Follow me, ladies."

He led them through a door that required a passkey, through a wide, open room of cubicles where heads hunkered over keyboards.

"News never sleeps," he said, taking them into a small office. He pointed at a couch for two. "Make yourselves comfortable."

Aunt Lou sat first. "You've moved up the ranks."

The office was tidy, except for a rolling dune of paperwork on his desk, and had a soft floral scent, which she traced back to a diffuser on the windowsill.

Demetrius nodded at the light puffs of steam. "It's ylang-ylang," he said, then pulled his chair around his desk in front of the two of them to form a triangle. "My wife claims essential oils and live plants will keep my heart rate down, but I'm not sure that's possible in this business."

She smiled, but the urge to run tingled at the bottom of her feet. She thought of Aunt Lou's request—that she sit and listen like a big girl. Patronizing but effective.

Demetrius cleared his throat. "I want to start by saying I came across your dad's obituary online, and, well, I'm sorry. I wouldn't wish cancer on my worst enemy."

"Thank you." She had a hunch who the enemy was in this scenario.

"I'm assuming from your voicemail you saw some of the articles I wrote about the Red Knot, including the one about the temporary closure."

"Your last two articles had a different tone than the others."

Demetrius gripped his knee, which until then had been bouncing in place. "Brief and straightforward, yes. After the article about the sanitary reports, I tried convincing Candis to sit down for a follow-up interview, almost like a rebuttal to explain what happened before she got reviewed in the coming months by AAA. The offer was too little too late, but it was the only way I knew how to try to make things right. She finally agreed to meet, but she'd had some sort of breakdown, like she'd been pushed past her limit. Until then, I didn't know she had any."

For as many people with grievances against her dad, there were strangers in awe of her mom. Dylan would appreciate them more if her own memories would stop interfering.

Demetrius grabbed a small contraption from his desk. "My vintage little friend here is called a Sony Portable MiniDisc Recorder. It's logged a lot of conversations that became news over the years."

He opened a plastic case and pulled out a small disc labeled *Restricted*.

Aunt Lou uncrossed her legs and leaned forward. "Wait. Does this mean . . ."

Demetrius nodded. "With Candis's permission, I recorded the interview. I'd like to listen to it together if that's okay." He fiddled with more settings. "She gave me a hard time at the beginning of the interview, too, but that was Candis. She did everything with excellence."

Saying it in past tense made it sound like a eulogy. Dylan wasn't ready to think about another one of those.

"Dylan? Are you ready?"

Aunt Lou and Demetrius were both staring at her.

"Yeah. I mean, yes," she fumbled.

Demetrius pressed Play.

## Audio Recording: Candis Turner Interview

**D. ROSS:** My name is Demetrius Ross, and today is January 16. This interview is with Candis Turner regarding—

**C. TURNER:** What are you doing?

**D. ROSS:** I'm marking the recording. It helps me keep my interviews organized.

**C. TURNER:** I don't remember you recording any of our other interviews.

**D. ROSS:** It's a new thing for me. I thought it would be a good idea. Ensuring accuracy and all that.

**C. TURNER:** You want to cover your tail.

**D. ROSS:** That too. I mentioned the idea of recording this when we spoke on the phone, so I'm not sure why you're making such a big deal of it now. Are you still okay with it?

**C. TURNER:** Sure.

**D. ROSS:** Yes or no, Candis.

**C. TURNER:** Yeah, I mean *yes*, I consent to you recording this interview.

**D. ROSS:** How proper of you. Now, give me a second to finish marking.

**C. TURNER:** Fine.

**D. ROSS:** This interview is with Candis Turner regarding the reports—

**C. TURNER:** I think you mean *accusations*.

**D. ROSS:** Excuse me?

**C. TURNER:** *Accusations* is more accurate than *reports*.

**D. ROSS:** Candis.

**C. TURNER:** Don't shake your head at me. You claimed you wanted to improve your accuracy.

**D. ROSS:** I didn't say "improve" accuracy. I said "ensure." Now, please let me do my job.

C. TURNER: I did, Demetrius. I let you do your job and you published a false report. Therefore, you made an *accusation* about my restaurant. You—quote—doing your job—end quote—is exactly why we are here.

D. ROSS: Can I just finish marking the interview? Please?

C. TURNER: *incoherent muttering*

D. ROSS: Demetrius Ross. January 16. Interviewing Candis Turner about the *accusations* made by *The Jacksonville Times* about the sanitary conditions of the Red Knot.

C. TURNER: Are you finished marking the interview?

D. ROSS: Yes.

C. TURNER: I thought we were friends, Demetrius.

D. ROSS: Here we go.

C. TURNER: I'm serious. I thought we were friends, and not just because you like my food.

D. ROSS: This is being recorded.

C. TURNER: Why did you run the story? Why didn't you at least run it by me first?

D. ROSS: I asked my boss to not run it, to at least wait until we had more of the story before putting it in print, but he said I've followed the Red Knot from the beginning so it wouldn't be fair to *not* run the story. He said my bias was showing. The report came right before the paper was being sent to the printers. I was given ten minutes to produce something or get fired. I panicked—my job was on the line.

C. TURNER: *Your* job was on the line.

D. ROSS: This is what I don't get, Candis. The reports—as in multiple reports and photos—were legitimate. There were roaches and rat feces.

C. TURNER: I had the building inspected so many times, Leo Martinez told me this was the one public establishment in

|  |  |
|---|---|
| | all northeastern Florida where he wouldn't be afraid to lick the floors. |
| D. ROSS: | That doesn't make this one bad report false, so how— |
| C. TURNER: | They could have been planted. The roaches and feces had to have been planted. |
| D. ROSS: | That implies someone did the planting. Who in the world would— |
| C. TURNER: | Darren. |
| D. ROSS: | What? |
| C. TURNER: | I think . . . Darren planted them. |
| D. ROSS: | Are you serious? |
| C. TURNER: | Or . . . he paid someone to plant them and report the Red Knot to the city. |
| D. ROSS: | Candis, that's insane. |
| C. TURNER: | Don't call me insane, Demetrius. Don't you dare call me that. I'm *not* insane. I'm not— |
| D. ROSS: | I just mean that's a serious accusation. Of course you're not actually— |
| C. TURNER: | I'm a professional. I've worked myself into the ground to get where I am today. I've pushed through being told over and over I don't belong in this kind of kitchen, even though I have the trail of stars and diamonds and "best of" articles to prove it. But then Darren came along, and I think . . . |
| D. ROSS: | What is it, Candis? |
| C. TURNER: | I think he's trying to make me feel insane. |
| D. ROSS: | Don't cry. Um, here's a tissue, Candis. Do you want me to turn off the recorder? |
| C. TURNER: | *sobs* |
| D. ROSS: | I'm so sorry. I just don't get it. You and Darren are . . . |
| C. TURNER: | I know. |
| D. ROSS: | He seems like a really supportive guy is all. I thought |

| | |
|---|---|
| | the two of you were—I don't know—wildly in love? You seem perfect together. |
| C. TURNER: | Love isn't always so easy to define. |
| D. ROSS: | It's still recording. I can turn it off— |
| C. TURNER: | The Darren you know is a powerhouse. That's the guy I first met too. I'd never met anyone like him. |
| D. ROSS: | Was that when you were at the Prime? |
| C. TURNER: | He was in Orlando for a business meeting and came in with the same group, a table we were waxing hard because of the bigwigs there. Darren asked to meet the chef, but I'd never heard of the guy, and we were in the weeds that night—low on servers, plates dying on the pass. I almost never come out to see patrons, so I said unless it's the president of the United States of America or Michael the archangel, don't bother. But somehow he snuck into the kitchen to meet me. |
| D. ROSS: | Bold. |
| C. TURNER: | And rude. And . . . fearless. It got heated. I couldn't believe he had the audacity to barge into my kitchen like that. But every time I told him off, he asked me out. |
| D. ROSS: | And that worked? |
| C. TURNER: | Eventually. You have to understand—all the other men I'd dated turned out to be insecure boys. They didn't know what to do with someone like me—driven and successful. Darren was so confident. He didn't waste his breath telling me how beautiful he thought I was. On our first date he said, "I feel so lucky you're giving me your time." |
| D. ROSS: | Who needs flowers? |
| C. TURNER: | He understood what the restaurant required of me— how selective I was about who I spent my small slivers of free time with. There were flowers too. And coffees. And expensive jewelry. He started coming by every |

|  |  |
|---|---|
|  | night after close, talking about our future together. And he was fun. I've never had so much fun. |
| D. ROSS: | So, what happened? |
| C. TURNER: | He proposed to me, but it wasn't what you're thinking. He took me to my favorite park and unrolled a blueprint of a restaurant—exactly like the one I said I wanted to build one day. He was proposing we open a restaurant together, with him as my investor. |
| D. ROSS: | Whoa. |
| C. TURNER: | I hesitated at first. I told him all the reasons why this could backfire and why it was such a big decision to make, and he said, "How could any downside compare to your biggest dream coming true?" |
| D. ROSS: | Swoon. |
| C. TURNER: | I still hesitated, said we weren't even married, so he pulled a ring out of his pocket. We hadn't been dating that long, but I couldn't imagine my life without Darren. I thought I hit the jackpot because I found someone who understood my work *and* who I liked being around. |
| D. ROSS: | So, you got married and moved to Jacksonville. |
| C. TURNER: | He told me his time in Orlando was coming to an end, he was outgrowing his job, so why not get a fresh start together here? He wanted to live closer to the coast too. I had my dream job, my dream man. But . . . |
| D. ROSS: | Take your time, Candis. |
| C. TURNER: | It seemed like the more successful I got, the more I realized Darren's charm and support were a mask, and that mask was starting to come off. It was after the first article you wrote about us, actually. Something about a chef's kiss. |
| D. ROSS: | I thought that was a clever title. |
| C. TURNER: | Of course it was. You're a great writer. |

**D. ROSS:** That's the first time you've ever said that.

**C. TURNER:** I thought it was implied by our friendship.

**D. ROSS:** Right. It doesn't hurt to say nice things out loud to your friends sometimes.

**C. TURNER:** My way of being a friend is letting you try my new dishes.

**D. ROSS:** It's putting you in the running to be my best friend, actually. I didn't mean to interrupt what you were saying, though. About Darren.

**C. TURNER:** This is hard to say out loud. I'm not even sure I understand it.

**D. ROSS:** What happened?

**C. TURNER:** A lot happened, but like a slow boil. One night, he brought friends to the Red Knot and asked the waiter to send me to their table. We were slammed that night, so it took me about twenty minutes. One guy was running late for his flight and had to leave before I could get out there. At home, Darren reamed me out, saying I'd embarrassed him and how I think I'm better than everybody—how it's always my way or the highway. He started complaining about how busy I was.

**D. ROSS:** Was that when . . .

**C. TURNER:** Yes, right before we applied to AAA to consider us for a Diamond rating, which meant we might have a surprise visit from an inspector any time in the next year.

**D. ROSS:** I thought Darren was convinced you'd get Five Diamonds.

**C. TURNER:** Me too. I was nervous, trying to focus on getting the Red Knot ready for inspection, and suddenly he was angry about how much I was working. Whatever I tried to do to work through our differences, including cutting back my hours, it was like he didn't want to talk.

**D. ROSS:** That's confusing.

**C. TURNER:** Not as confusing as him, out of nowhere, demanding we have kids. I told him, over and over, every day leading up to our wedding, that the Red Knot was my baby, and it would always act like a baby. It would never grow up and leave the house, and it would cry every time I wasn't looking at it. Restaurant life was not compatible with family life, and I needed us to be on the same page about that so I wouldn't make a child miserable by me being her mother. He said he was okay with that.

**D. ROSS:** Until he suddenly wasn't okay with that? What did you do?

**C. TURNER:** I decided if Darren wanted kids and that would make him happy, then I'd try for the sake of our marriage. You have to understand: I love him so much. Loved? *Love.* I thought, I would die for him, so I could have children for him. I withdrew our application to AAA.

**D. ROSS:** But that was over four years ago. Dylan's only—what—a few months old?

**C. TURNER:** We couldn't get pregnant. When I first agreed to try, he was so happy. It was like we were dating again—dreaming about running a place like the Red Knot. We were in love, crazy about each other instead of him constantly at my throat. But then every month was a horror show of not getting pregnant. He blamed me, said I let myself get too stressed about work. He'd give me the silent treatment for days at a time. I started to get panic attacks after each test.

**D. ROSS:** That's awful.

**C. TURNER:** Things at the Red Knot started to get worse behind the scenes too. Supplies stopped arriving on time. Sous-chefs and managers quit unexpectedly.

**D. ROSS:** You never mentioned that.

**C. TURNER:** I thought as long as the food was good, I could handle it, but watching so much be out of my control, along with Darren's rollercoaster treatment, was starting to get to me. I thought if I could just get pregnant, then I'd have nine months to focus on the Red Knot before a baby. I brought up the possibility of seeing a fertility doctor, but Darren flipped. He said there was nothing wrong with him and I must think some random sperm donor would be a better father than he was.

**D. ROSS:** So, how did Dylan—

**C. TURNER:** What am I doing? I've said too much already. If Darren finds out—

**D. ROSS:** Candis, wait. It's okay. You can talk to me. Don't leave.

**C. TURNER:** You may not publish any of this, Demetrius, you hear me? Not a single word. Don't even tell Lou.

# 37

## Kicking Oneself

Dylan agreed with Demetrius—the puffs of fragrance coming from the diffuser didn't protect the heart from hard-hitting news. Today's headline: Her mom hadn't wanted her.

Demetrius removed the disk from the player and put it back into its case. "And then, as you heard, Candis up and left. Ran out of the room—all the way out of downtown to the suburbs, in fact. You remember, don't you, Lou?"

Aunt Lou's face clouded over. "I remember."

Demetrius returned the device to his desk and grabbed a stack of papers, shifting the documents enough to spill one file to the floor. He ignored it, but she couldn't look away from its splayed insides.

"My boss told me to write one last article on the Red Knot transferring ownership, and you'll never guess who called in with the tip."

"My dad."

"Darren."

She and Aunt Lou answered at the same time.

He nodded. "He said VentureGold Group was selling the Red Knot. I asked for more details, and he claimed there weren't any worth sharing. Candis wanted to stay home with Dylan, and he had a new job. He was moving your family to the suburbs."

Her jaw clenched. "That sounds nothing like my mom."

Aunt Lou reached over and squeezed her hand, the force coursing up her arm and through her shoulder to push a single tear over the brim. She clawed it away from her cheek.

"I wrote the article, but the entire situation haunted me. I decided it was time to start digging, and what I found was complete and utter sabotage. It's all here." He tapped the stack of papers he was holding, then handed her one. "That one shows phone calls to the trucking company from Darren. He called and changed the Red Knot's delivery dates to later than what Candis ordered, sending the kitchen into a frenzy on more than one occasion."

He passed over the rest of the stack. "Those have comments from former employees who'd been harassed by Darren, including one anonymous hostess he flirted with enough to convince her to plant the roaches and feces *and* call the city inspector. The only reason the young woman was willing to admit her part in it was because of how angry she was at Darren for leading her on and then dumping her."

Dylan looked at the papers, each sheet light as a feather in her hands but heavy as iron on her chest. What was she supposed to do with such sensitive information—mentally and logistically? Maybe she'd add them to the papers in the folder Hendrix had given her and then put the folder in her memory box back home. Maybe she'd take a trip to the Grand Canyon and throw the box into it.

"Why didn't the paper run *this* story, Demetrius?" Aunt Lou demanded.

"Believe me, Lou, I tried. I must have called a dozen times before we finally connected. She didn't want to hear any of it—the article or the evidence. She said I had to let the Red Knot die. For the sake of her family."

Aunt Lou closed her eyes. "Oh, Candis. She made me promise to never talk about any of her professional life in front of Dylan too."

The small office filled with a raw quiet. There they were, friends and daughter, stifled by shared frustrations and regrets. Two who'd tried to help and one who'd been collateral damage. As the silence trudged on, it became clear none of them knew how to end a meeting of this nature. Dylan was ready to leave, though, to limit the amount of new, devastating information she took in each day.

"Thank you for letting me listen, Demetrius. And for your time."

Demetrius put a hand on his chest. "Candis was my friend, and I know I had a part in everything that happened. I'm just grateful I could pass this on to someone else who cares about her and knows about Darren's . . ." He let the sentence trail off, then cleared his throat. "None of this can be easy to hear about your family," he tried instead.

She and Aunt Lou stood up, and Demetrius escorted them back to the entrance. "If it's not too strange to ask, will you please tell Candis I say hello?"

Dylan shook his hand. "I'll let her know."

"And, Lou, if you ever forgive me, please call sometime. I've missed you too."

Aunt Lou patted his shoulder. "I forgave you a long time ago, Dem. Maybe I'll see you around."

Outside the *Times* office, Dylan told her lungs to take deeper breaths. They wouldn't listen, leaving her a mess of shallow gasps and tears on the sidewalk.

Aunt Lou grabbed her shaking hands and made Dylan face her. "Look at me. I know how all that sounded, but your mom wanted you. I know she did."

Dylan ripped away from Aunt Lou's grasp and took a step back, her anger spilling like molten lava. "Does it matter?"

Aunt Lou blinked. "What do you mean?"

"I mean does it really matter when the damage has already been done? When all my life my mom has *acted* like she didn't want me?

When she was always happier in her kitchen with her knives and oils and spices than she was trying to help me understand why we were constantly throwing our lives into a moving truck?"

Her aunt didn't flinch.

"What's wrong with me, Aunt Lou?" she demanded. "Why couldn't I get along with my biological parent, while the parent I liked turned out to be some monster we were chasing around? How do I reconcile that, and what does it say about me?"

The wind picked up, rustling the fronds at the tops of the trees. The sound caught her off guard.

Aunt Lou unlocked her car and opened the passenger door. "Get in."

"Why?"

"Don't cross your arms at me. Get in because I want to show you something, that's why."

Dylan did as she was told. While Aunt Lou wove through traffic, she leaned against her headrest and looked up at the palm trees—the starkest reminder she wasn't in Illinois anymore. What were the maple trees next to her apartment building up to at home? In her short time away, had autumn started turning them gold or flaming red?

Aunt Lou pulled up to the curb in front of her apartment and turned off the car. "Follow me. If you stay in the car too long, you'll fry."

This time she knew where she was going: up the stairs and past Paula Kelly, into Aunt Lou's apartment. Inside, Aunt Lou dropped her cooler and shoes and went straight to her living room, over to the far corner. Dylan followed, wondering what in the treasure trove of knickknacks her aunt was after.

"Here it is." Aunt Lou picked something up and came back to place it in Dylan's palm.

It was a tiny porcelain teacup—no larger than a nickel—with a detailed purple flower painted on each side.

"It's okay if you don't remember this, but when you were about five, you asked me to have a tea party with you. We spread a blanket on your bedroom floor with pretty teacups and teddy bears and dolls, and you did our makeup. I think your mom made us fancy scones to eat."

Dylan racked her brain for the memory. "It sounds adorable."

"During the tea party, you went on and on about this little butterfly you'd found outside in your backyard. You said it was the color of dandelions and had only one wing, so you decided to give it a funeral. You buried the butterfly, put a rock by its grave, and sang a song. I thought it was the sweetest thing I'd ever heard, until I asked, 'Was the butterfly dead?' and you said, 'Practically.'"

She covered her mouth to stifle her shock. "That poor butterfly."

"Yes, that poor butterfly, but it was such a sweet time with you that, on my next day off, I scoured Blossom's Antiques for something to remind me of that day. To remind me of you."

Dylan turned the tiny teacup in her hands. It was somehow both insignificant in the room crowded with beautiful mementos and wondrously captivating all on its own.

"Dylan, I love you so much. I won't say nothing is wrong with you because, in my opinion, I think there's probably one or two things even the coolest humans need to work on—and you have a thing for murdering butterflies." Aunt Lou nudged her with an elbow. "I will say this, though: You are many things, but you are *not* the wrong that's been done to you."

*Who am I?* She balled her fist around the teacup to keep it safe from her fresh tears.

"Come here." Aunt Lou wrapped her arms around her. "I love you because you're this cool kid who calls me 'Aunt Lou,' and growing up, when you weren't throwing a fit at your mom, you said things so funny it split me. I only got to spend short days with you once or twice a year, mostly when I visited whatever new city you were in, and yet you impacted me. You're part of something bigger than you, *and* all the details of your life—small like this teacup and big like your parents' struggles—they matter. They matter because *you* matter. No matter how you got here, you are *not* an accident."

Aunt Lou let go, walked across the room, and grabbed another object, an identical teacup. "Take that one home with you. You've been hurt in many ways you'll be forced to remember, but I hope when life is hard and grief is complicated, this will remind you that you've also been loved—even in ways you might not remember. If I'm lucky, it will remind you to buy a plane ticket and visit me every once in a while. Heck, *I'll* buy your ticket."

Dylan wiped her face with the back of her hand, then reopened her hand. "I love this, Aunt Lou. Thank you."

Aunt Lou clinked Dylan's tiny teacup with the one in her hand. "Cheers."

## 38

# There's No Place Like—

"Home." The word fell out of Dylan's mouth, not like bitter tears or spewing lava, but like a flock of red knots, falling from its dance in the sky down to shore for more insects and crab eggs. It fell toward an instinctual need.

She wasn't the only one caught off guard.

"What?" Aunt Lou asked.

Dylan bit her lip, trying to turn the word into a complete thought. "I want to go home, then to Milwaukee so I can talk to my mom. And is it stupid I want to go right now?"

"I like hearing you call a place 'home.'" Aunt Lou set her tiny teacup back in its place on the end table where it once rested in a set. "How can I help? Do you need a ride somewhere—the hotel or the airport? I don't have to work until Monday, so you have a glorified Uber driver."

Dylan looked around the apartment, then squeezed her eyes shut to see if that would help her focus. "First, I should see if I can even change my flight to tonight."

"Good call. I'll unpack the cooler while you figure out what's next. Do you want some tissue paper for your new BAE teacup?"

"Bae teacup?"

"Best Aunt Ever."

"I don't think that word means what you think it means."

"It means what I want it to mean."

"Then yes to the tissue paper."

She collapsed onto the couch and rummaged through her purse for her phone.

After pulling up her email, she clicked through a series of links that led to the airline and her specific flight. It turned out there was one open seat left on tonight's flight that could be all hers, and she didn't even have to pay a premium fee, because it was cheaper to fly on Saturday night than Sunday. A few clicks later, she was scheduled to leave in four hours instead of twenty.

Pictures of Gale and Peeta flashed through her mind. And another of her own bed. And then her usual cash register, and Teresa, and a burger from Five Guys, and her afternoon sprints through the forest preserve.

Then she thought of how much she'd avoided her mom over the years.

It was time to get back and sift through what was hers because she loved it and what was hers only because her pain had trained her to choose what was familiar.

She also had to think about Great-Aunt Kathleen Schulz and her NDA. She'd have to figure out what to do with Rob Westmore's threats. She'd have to grieve her dad—both the man she remembered and the man he'd turned out to be. Her current state of affairs would require her to dig deep. Limping through her escalating to-do list would have to be enough.

She pulled out her phone and finally responded to the text she'd left unanswered since the middle of the Main Street Bridge.

> **Me:** I'm flying back tonight. Hoping to come up and visit you tomorrow so we can finally talk—just have to figure out a few things with my car first.

When Aunt Lou pulled up to the hotel, Dylan gripped the door handle. "I only have a carry-on, so I shouldn't need more than ten minutes. Maybe fifteen if the elevator is slow."

Her aunt put the car in Park and unbuckled her seatbelt.

"It's okay," Dylan said. "You don't have to—"

Aunt Lou waved her off. "Don't you dare. I'm coming in and soaking up every last minute you're here."

Aunt Lou's decision was final, and her own relief tangible. Taking life's sucker punches—and figuring out stuff like rides to the airport—was so much easier with an Aunt Lou by her side. An Aunt Lou who was actually an Aunt Lou and not a Great-Aunt Kathleen or a Hendrix. Her chest panged.

Once Aunt Lou handed her keys to the valet, the doors to the hotel entrance parted for them, and they made their way through the cheerful lobby toward the elevator.

"Hey, Dylan," a familiar voice called.

She squinted, trying to confirm it was actually James, because the man walking up to her wasn't wearing a red T-shirt or a button-down with hibiscus all over it. This guy was wearing a dark suit, his hair styled like he was about to meet the mayor.

"I almost didn't recognize you." She hoped her eyes weren't puffy from the on-again-off-again crying she'd been doing all morning.

He looked down at his outfit. "Because of this old thing?"

She grinned. "What's the occasion?"

"Tonight is our last event before everyone heads home tomorrow, a banquet of sorts." He turned to Aunt Lou. "And this is?"

Dylan caught a hint of his aftershave, similar to but also very different from the ylang-ylang oil in Demetrius's office, and her heart rate skyrocketed. She had to yell at herself on the inside: *Don't blush, don't blush, don't blush.*

Aunt Lou tapped her shoulder. "Dylan?"

"What?"

"Are you going to introduce me?"

She blushed. "Yes. Sorry. James, this is my aunt Lou—by friendship. Aunt Lou, this is James. He is my captain." What the heck. "I mean, he's my James." She wished the earth would swallow her whole. "James is my boss."

Her blush exploded through the rest of her body. And yet she'd wanted to add *kind* and *kind of hot* to his introduction. She wondered if HR would be on her back if she said something like—

"I'm sorry, but I can't see very well, Dylan. Did you say Captain James or James Bond?" Aunt Lou winked at her, then accepted James's handshake.

Apparently, this was also the cost of having Aunt Lou around. Dylan shook her head, her face burning.

"I'll respond to either." He grinned. "It's nice to meet you, Aunt Lou by Friendship."

Her aunt was clearly amused, looking back and forth between her and James with a dumb smirk. "How did you both end up in Jacksonville at the same exact time?"

"Our Annual Captains' Meeting happened to be here. We were even on the same flight."

"James was one of the people who recommended Little Talbot Island," Dylan explained.

Aunt Lou's many animated faces were starting to make her feel like a mortified teenager. "Great taste, James. Birds and nature and all that."

"Hey, y'all."

Her shoulders clenched twice. First, when she heard Anna Claire's precious voice. Second, when she saw how gorgeous Anna Claire looked in her glittering shift dress. It popped against her complexion perfectly, as did her lip gloss and lashes. Having sweated and cried around the entirety of Little Talbot Island, Dylan was immediately self-conscious of her current look, which could probably be described as *grunge*.

Anna Claire slid her arm through James's, and Dylan's shoulders clenched a third time.

She tried her best unbothered smile—something James could summon with no effort. "Hi, Anna Claire. You must be going to the banquet too."

"I am," she drawled. "I wouldn't want to miss James being honored as Captain of the Year tonight."

The woman was visibly swooning.

Dylan wanted to kick herself for not asking James more about the banquet and the award he'd mentioned before.

He patted Anna Claire's hand. "That hasn't been decided yet."

She couldn't read if his gesture was a boundary or a display of affection, but Anna Claire took it as an invitation to rub his arm from shoulder to elbow.

It was better this way, really. With all she had to think about at the moment, her boss shouldn't be added to that list. She swallowed every last ounce of desire for James, as well as her bristling resentment toward Anna Claire, who deserved none of her wrath.

"Congratulations, James. I'm really happy for you. They better ring at least three ship bells in your honor."

He laughed, taking a step away from Anna Claire, who finally let go of her choke hold on his arm. "What are you up to? Any more meetings?"

Was he insinuating something about Hendrix? "No more meetings. I actually rebooked my flight for tonight. I'm here to pack, and then Aunt Lou is driving me to the airport."

"Wow. Well, I hope your travels go smoothly. And, I'll see you soon?"

"Yeah, bye, Dylan," Anna Claire inserted before Dylan could say, *Yeah, see you soon.*

She looked back at James one more time but had to tell herself to stop analyzing what his lingering smile meant. Instead, she focused on walking to the elevator, climbing on, and pressing the correct buttons.

The moment the door closed, Aunt Lou turned to her. "So—"

She held her hand up. "Nope."

"James—"

"Don't."

"He clearly likes you."

"He clearly has enough arm candy to give him a sugar high."

"Is he nice?"

The doors slid open, and Dylan led them to her room. "If there's one thing I learned this week, it's that I can't always trust *nice*. It might be code for *sociopath*."

Aunt Lou followed her inside. "I hear you, but *nice* isn't an immediate red flag either."

"My co-worker called James a walking beige flag."

"I thought there were only red and green."

"According to her, beige means 'boring.'"

Aunt Lou pushed the curtains open and took in the view of the river. "Or stability and fidelity? Besides, I thought you liked boring."

"I do." At least, that was what she had to figure out.

"Okay, then, want to know what else is a green flag?"

"What?"

"James in that suit."

"Aunt Lou. Stop," she groaned.

Aunt Lou huffed. "Youth is wasted on the young, but I'll leave it alone. For now."

Dylan showered and packed, throwing dirty clothes and toiletries into her suitcase with less care than she shelved bags of cashews or boxes of tea. Before she knew it, they were back in the car, pulling up to Departures at Jacksonville International Airport.

"Next time, we'll do Little Talbot Island right," Dylan promised. "We'll bird-watch so hard, the birds won't know what hit them."

"I just like that you're saying there will be a next time. You're always welcome to stay with me. I'd love to show you the Cummer too."

Cars wove around them, as did streams of passengers with luggage heading from the curb to the terminal. A security guard eyed their car.

"Can I say one last thing before I'm told I have to move?"

Dylan let go of the door handle. "Sure."

Aunt Lou's eyes brimmed. "You're going through your own version of one of life's toughest lessons, which is getting comfortable with everything you *don't* know—about your parents, your bio family, yourself. So please, be patient with yourself."

It made her think of the question James had asked, the question she'd written down in her journal: *"What if you don't find out?"*

"I'll try."

Aunt Lou nodded. "That's all I ask. On the days it's hard, make yourself a tiny cup of tea. I hear that helps."

Dylan checked in and made her way through security, then found her gate with twenty minutes to spare before boarding. The thrill of going home was turning into an ache—she wanted to be there now, not four hours from now.

She pulled out her phone but didn't know where to go on it. There was Instagram, where she was a longtime lurker, never-poster. Reddit might offer more thoughts from other NPEs. She could search for credible therapists in the greater Naperville area, maybe follow it up with some vision-board dreaming on Indeed. She clicked around for a few minutes, then exited all her apps. She had an entire two-dimensional world at her fingertips, and yet none of it gripped her.

It wouldn't let her savor a bite of her mom's lemon and rosemary chicken, or stroke her guinea pigs' silky fur, or experience the intoxicating fragrance of James walking up to her. The dimensions she craved were inaccessible from the palm of her hand.

One idea crossed her mind, though, captivating enough to keep her phone out of her purse. She glanced around the terminal. The sitting area was full, and two gate agents were shuffling around the desk.

One last search, and then she'd take a break.

**Google:** kathleen schulz enterprise florida

If Kathleen's business was as massive as she'd hinted and her family so worried about Dylan shaking them down they'd attempt legal bribery to silence her, then her other biological relatives might not be that difficult to find. She scanned the results and saw five URLs tied to a company called Berk Enterprise. A few more clicks, and she was on the Berk Enterprise page listing its management with names, titles, brief bios, and, yes, even pictures. Including one Kathleen Schulz.

She wiped her clammy hands on her pants, then chewed on a fingernail. Four of the executives had the last name Berk, which could be Kathleen's maiden name, and they were possibly Kathleen's siblings, cousins, or nephews.

She read each bio, her mouth going dry.

Three of the Berks were men.

Two listed a university degree in their bio.

But only one made her gasp.

## Christopher T. Berk
*Executive Vice President and Chief Operating Officer*

Christopher T. Berk is the Executive Vice President and Chief Operating Officer, responsible for overseeing Berk's operations strategy and coordinating all aspects of the company's production performance. Before becoming COO for Berk Enterprise, he oversaw the completion of forty-six capital projects.

He earned his MBA from the Robert H. Smith School of Business at the University of Maryland.

## 39

# The Screenshot Heard Round the World

The itch to stare at Christopher T. Berk could always be scratched now, thanks to the photo of him saved to her phone. It was hers. What she meant by *hers* was that pieces of Christopher T. Berk might be hers. He might be her biological father. The other half of her DNA.

Could it have really been that easy—a couple of assumptions and a simple Google search? Or was she way off?

"May I have your attention, please?" the gate agent called over the intercom. "We will now begin boarding Flight 2659 for Chicago O'Hare by welcoming our Premier Platinum and Gold Members, as well as any active military members."

Her only membership was to KindreDNA, and her ticket said Group 6, so she zoomed in on Christopher Berk's features, which had been captured in high-resolution by a professional with a powerful camera.

It had to be him.

She resembled her mom a lot, with Candis's apple hips and upturned brown eyes. Once upon a time, she'd thought her dark hair and pointed nose were her dad's. But now that she had actual DNA to go on, she realized she and Darren Turner were the kind of reflection made in a fun-house mirror. Similar, but not duplicates. Not blood.

Christopher Berk, on the other hand, had features that weren't a coincidence, like the exact same dimple in his chin, the matching full bottom lip, and an identical mole under his left eye.

She touched the tiny mark under her own eye, flashing back to a long-forgotten memory. She couldn't remember the city they were living in at the time or the dish Candis was making, but her mom came around the kitchen table, brushed a kiss on her mole, calling it her little peppercorn. It happened a few other times—when she caught her in a good mood—her mom saying she needed some pepper, and Dylan holding up her cheek. Why *that* tender memory hadn't stuck itself near the top of the pile, she didn't know. She should have journaled some of the good parts too.

She looked closer at her phone's screen. What else had Christopher Berk passed on that was all nature versus how she'd been nurtured? Did he also drum the steering wheel when he got impatient? Was he more partial to people's pets than their owners?

"This is the final boarding call for Flight 2659 to Chicago O'Hare . . ." In all her staring, she almost missed the agent's announcement. She raced to the back of the short line, where the gate agent sent her down the Jetway, onto the plane, and into her middle seat in row 29—cloaked in big family secrets. She took one last look at her phone before the stewardess encouraged passengers to put away devices.

Christopher Berk. She dreamed up an entire life for him: He was the top of his university's graduating class—after he finally gave up donating sperm samples for thirsty Thursday's beer money. Even though he hit it big financially, he was one of those people who looked up from power walking down the sidewalk to watch a busker play her violin, then drop a hefty tip into her case. He had no idea his bossy aunt Kathleen was trying to bribe Dylan to sign an NDA, and he really wanted to get to know her.

Her theories—better said, *hopes*—led to more questions, of course. Did he understand the ramifications of his actions thirty-plus years ago? Would he say the beer money was worth it?

Google might refute all her theories in a matter of seconds, but she couldn't bear the thought of her version of Christopher Berk being blown to bits like her version of Darren Turner. For the next few hours, his name and picture were enough details, and she'd let every last one of her theories live in their fragile bubbles. Only when she got back to Chicago, found her suitcase at baggage claim, picked up her car from the shop, and drove to Milwaukee, would she beg her mom to connect the dots for her. She might even scream at her mom for admitting to someone that she'd never wanted to be a mom.

That was her plan.

A plan that changed the moment she got off the escalator that had brought her to the baggage claim area. She didn't have to go to Milwaukee, or even pick up her car.

Her mom was here, waiting for her.

# 40

## Greater Love Has No One

Under different circumstances, including an entirely different family history, Dylan might've let her own wave of emotion carry her from the bottom of the escalator to where her mom was standing. But utter shock glued her feet to the terrazzo floor, so she waited for Candis to pick her out of the crowd. A split second later, her mom's face warmed into a soft smile, and Candis jogged the last ten meters between them.

"Dylan. Hi." She sounded out of breath, not from movement but from nerves.

"Hi, Mom."

Their eye contact burned to the point of being awkward.

Her mom cleared her throat. "We, uh, have a lot to talk about, but is it okay if I hug you first?"

Dylan nodded, that wave of emotion pounding harder now that it smelled like her mom's signature English Pear & Freesia. Another memory she didn't realize she'd tucked away.

"Mom, what are you doing here?"

Her mom pulled back, holding her elbows tight to her body. "When you texted that you were flying in tonight and had car trouble, I asked Aunt Lou for your flight info. It's silly, but—"

"It's not silly at all. It's just that you already came here once and I wasn't here, and grand gestures aren't exactly your style." She hoped that came across as matter-of-fact instead of as an accusation.

"I know. Dylan—" Her mom looked down, wiping at her eye. "I'm sorry. I'm so, *so* sorry."

Dylan's shock was wearing off, so this time, she let the wave push her forward and hugged her mom as hard as she could.

"I have so many questions," she whispered into her mom's shoulder while her mom rubbed the back of her head.

"I know. I think I'm finally awake enough to answer them."

Candis pulled a tissue out of her purse pocket and wiped at her nose, scanning the bustling crowd around them. "Is it okay if we go somewhere else to talk?"

"Somewhere that's not a busy airport? Sure, I just have to grab my suitcase from the carousel."

After, they tracked down Candis's car in the parking garage.

Her mom fidgeted with her car keys, which had no keychains or reward cards attached to them. "Is there somewhere specific you want to go, like your apartment? Are you hungry?"

"I don't know if I can eat yet," she admitted.

"Yeah, okay." Her mom pulled the collar of her coat closer around her neck, which she then kneaded with the back of her palm. "Is there a park nearby, or . . ."

Dylan waited for her mom to finish her sentence, wanting more than anything for her to take the lead like Kathleen had. But also, *not* like Kathleen. "I can look one up on my phone. My apartment's about thirty-five minutes from here."

"I'm going to drive you home; I just don't want to wait any longer. To talk, that is." Her mom twisted in the driver's seat toward her.

"I don't need candlelight and chocolates, if the ambience is what you're worried about."

Her mom grinned.

"Seriously, Mom, a parking garage is as good a place as any to have this conversation."

"Okay." Candis set her keys in the cupholder and folded her hands in her lap. "First, I wanted to tell you that the day after the funeral, I checked myself into a psychiatric hospital for a couple days."

Dylan blinked, not sure how to process the information.

"I know," her mom added before she could reply. "This is a lot, but we haven't even scratched the surface, and I want to get through everything."

Dylan fidgeted with her purse. "Is that where you called me from the other day?"

Her mom nodded. "I'm still doing intensive outpatient therapy, but after your dad died, I could tell everything was finally coming to the surface, and . . . I needed help.

"During my downtime at the hospital, I read more about genealogy and . . . well . . . I wanted to apologize for the things I said at the funeral. I was so dismissive, acting like my lies shouldn't affect you. The truth is, I haven't been who you needed me to be as a mom for a really long time. Life with your dad was—"

"Mom." She reached across and squeezed her mom's hand. "I promise not to interrupt you every time you talk, but about Dad . . . I believe you."

Watching her mom react to that simple phrase made her want to sob. She wanted to rip off all the grief and secrets they were both shrouded in.

Her mom rested a hand on top of hers. "It means so much to hear you say that. For so many years, he made me feel like I was going crazy, but everyone loved him so much. At least, they did at first. Back then, I didn't think anyone would believe me. Some people *didn't* believe me."

Dylan looked around, grateful for the dim parking garage and tinted windows. For some reason it was easier to whisper hard things in the dark.

"When I found out Dad isn't my biological father, it felt like I'd lost all my memories. I kept looking in the mirror wondering who I am and why nobody told me. I learned a lot about Dad in Jacksonville, though. Hendrix contacted a bunch of his former employers. Mr. Westmore obviously has some unresolved issues with him. I even met Demetrius Ross."

The dim lighting didn't keep her from seeing her mom's jaw drop. "You met Demetrius?"

"He let me listen to your interview."

"Demetrius," her mom scolded.

"Why didn't you let him run the story or—I don't know—take the evidence to court?"

Her mom coughed to clear her throat. "It all happened so fast. First, the roaches and mice. Within a month, Darren told me because the restaurant was having issues, it was being sold to a different investment company. The cherry on top was him telling me he had a new job in the suburbs, so it was perfect timing for our family to 'get a fresh start.'

"I saw right through all of it. I said I was going to fight him for the Red Knot or leave him, but then I found out nothing was in my name. The thing I'd built and loved didn't even legally belong to me. I knew if he was able to cause chaos and still get new jobs everywhere, a jury would believe him over me too. Back then, narcissism wasn't a diagnosis. It was called charisma and passion. The worst part, though, was that he said if I did go to court, he'd make sure they took *you* away too."

Dylan closed her eyes. "Basically, you had to choose between the Red Knot and me."

"Oh, sweetheart—"

"I was the reminder of everything you gave up."

"It's not like that—"

"Do you think that's the reason we never got along?"

Her mom tugged at the tight bun in her own hair, freeing wisps near her face. "I wasn't a good mom. I got more depressed and checked out with each move—and worse, I took my anger out on you. Probably because you couldn't retaliate."

"And you didn't even want to be a mom? That's what you told Demetrius, at least."

Her mom kept shaking her head, not like an answer but like a reaction to the domino effect of pain that was their family's story.

"You have to understand—I *loved* my job, yes. A kitchen is a wild beast I was good at taming, unlike motherhood, where I felt like I was playing with fire that couldn't be controlled, in conditions that wrecked me. I didn't want to be a mom, but then . . . I had you." She choked on the words, then wiped at her face. "I didn't leave Dad because I knew he'd do everything he could to take you away from me. As much as it killed me to leave the Red Knot, you were far more important. I just wish I'd been able to show you that." She paused.

Before courage left her, Dylan had to ask. "Mom, how did I get here?"

This was it. Her mom was cornered. She was too—she would listen without hanging up or interrupting or running away, just like she'd promised Aunt Lou.

"I know it might not be easy to tell me," she added.

"I know it's absurd you have to ask."

"I just don't think the lies are working out great for us."

"I agree."

"But, you can tell me. I—"

"I used a sperm donor without telling your dad."

In her mom's car, tucked deep in a parking garage at Chicago O'Hare International Airport, the silence was loud.

"What?" Dylan whispered.

"That's the short version of the story."

"Well, can I have the long version? A little more context?"

Her mom exhaled a sharp breath. "I couldn't get pregnant. I was checked by a fertility doctor who said I looked healthy and wondered if my husband would come in as well. Your dad flat out refused and basically freaked out. At that point, I still thought our relationship had a chance. I was so in love with him, and I thought he was acting strange because he was grieving not being able to get pregnant. I felt awful for him—so awful I thought I'd do anything for him to feel better, for us to get back to where we were at the beginning of our relationship. *Anything.*"

It felt like listening to a true crime podcast, but instead of being thrilled by what might happen next, Dylan was filled with dread because this was her real life.

"Aunt Lou wanted to go on a quick weekend away, so I suggested a . . . specific time of the month and that we go out of state somewhere, maybe visit old friends around L'Academie. Before we left, I set up an appointment at a fertility clinic there. And, well . . ." Her mom trailed off.

"You used a sperm donor without Dad's permission," Dylan finished for her. "Like, an IUI or whatever it's called."

"Love makes people do things that are way out of character. Wait—not love. More like the delusion of love. I was out-of-my-mind in love with Darren. Literally."

Dylan couldn't get past the logistics. "How was that even possible? Getting that done without Dad signing anything?"

Her mom shook her head. "All I had to do was check the boxes that said I was financially stable and single. I had to take a trip on my own beforehand, for my consultation, so I told your dad I was a guest speaker at L'Academie. But you have to understand, back then it wasn't hard to find a fertility doctor eager to experiment. There was no Google to connect my face and maiden name on my old Maryland ID to a Darren Turner multiple states away. Unlike other doctors, this guy was organized enough to have his donors labeled with basic physical features—things like height and hair color. He could call specific people to come in depending on the request."

It all checked out, including the part where Christopher T. Berk might be her biological father. Her mom could go on her first girls' trip with Aunt Lou and visit L'Academie in Gaithersburg, slipping away from Aunt Lou long enough to visit a fertility clinic near the University of Maryland, where her biological father, who happened to donate samples in college, attended. On that trip, Candis and Lou could snap a photo in front of their old school.

And now Dylan could look at that photo knowing she was there too. Aunt Lou had told her she wasn't an accident, but right now she felt like some second-choice child. The gift from one lovestruck woman to her unrequited love.

"People lie. Public records even lie. But DNA doesn't lie," she could hear Raj saying in his office.

Dylan looked down at her hands, the tears welling. She finally knew the truth, and for once, she'd heard it straight from her mom's mouth instead of through a friend or the internet.

Her mom fell back into her seat and looked straight ahead, her shoulders relaxing. "I think the other reason I left the Red Knot behind and followed Darren from city to city was because I felt so guilty for what I did."

Hearing her mom call her dad *Darren* made it sound like they were talking as friends, not mother and child. She wasn't used to it yet—didn't know if any of this would ever become second nature.

"What kills me is that Darren never felt guilty," her mom continued. "He didn't see his constant manipulation as being unfaithful to our wedding vows."

Her mom wiped at her face, then pulled out another tissue from her purse and blew her nose. Finally, she opened a small bottle of sanitizer and wiped it on her hands, making Dylan's nose tingle with the smell of alcohol. If only her story could be sanitized into something she could display on a cute family tree for an elementary class project.

Her mom turned and put her hand on Dylan's cheek, brushing it with her thumb. "I'm sorry I never told you the truth. But I'm not here to ask you to forgive me. Not yet."

## 41

# Riddle Me That

"What do you mean?" Dylan asked.

"I want to give you time to work through all this. I hope, though, that eventually there will be a way for me to still be in your life. Whatever that takes."

A growl worked through Dylan's stomach, playing a medley of tuba notes before finishing on a high-pitched gurgle. Not exactly how she wanted to honor the moment she was having with her mom.

She hugged her middle to soften the noise, but her mom raised an eyebrow. "Sounds like you need more than time. Can I buy you dinner before I drive you home?"

"It's okay, Mom—"

"I insist. What's that place you always get burgers from? Three Men and a Baby?"

She smirked. "I think you mean Five Guys, but I'm not sure it's exactly Chef Candis Turner's style."

Her mom picked up her car keys and started the car. "I can't believe I'm saying this, but some things aren't about the food."

Her stomach growled again, so she pulled out her phone. "According to this map, there's one just a few minutes from here."

Candis exited the parking garage and followed Dylan's directions to the restaurant. They ordered Dylan's usual, plus two chocolate shakes per Candis's suggestion, and found a table.

Dylan wondered what it would taste like to blend a piece of chocolate cake into her shake.

Her mom sat across from her and divvied up their tray of food. "Is it okay if I ask you some questions about Jacksonville? Starting with who, what, when, where, and why? Anything you're willing to share."

"I'll start with the why." She took a big bite, savoring every familiar texture and flavor, then dug around for the birthday card her dad had given her.

"Wait. Is that . . . with the blue flowers?" Her mom pointed at something else in her purse.

She held up her green journal. "The *Record of Rage* you gave me when I was eight? Yes, it is."

Candis slapped the table. "I can't believe you still have that."

"I hadn't looked at it in a while, but I took it with me to Jacksonville. Reading it helped me notice a few things about Dad I didn't before. I'm pretty sure writing in it over the years helped me commit less murder too—like you hoped."

Her mom rested her face on her hand. "How many pages am I featured on? Wait. Don't answer that."

"Too many, but I think I have a little rewriting to do as I process everything."

"I have one too, but it's all about your dad. Maybe we should have a burn party sometime."

"Maybe." Dylan pushed the journal down and picked out the birthday card. It looked like it had done hard time in her purse. "As you well know, we took that genealogy test together, but when I got home from the funeral, I realized Dad changed the name of our shared family tree to Jacksonville."

Candis winced as Dylan held out the birthday card.

"He also wrote this under his birthday riddle."

"The annual birthday riddle?" Her mom took the card and read it out loud. "*I hurt the most when lost yet also when not had at all. I'm sometimes the hardest to express but the easiest to ignore. I can be given to many or just one. What am I?"*

Dylan pointed to the bottom. "Look at the postscript too: *TH3 P3N 1S M16TIER thAN tce SWORD*. Those random numbers and mixed-case letters turned out to be an address to a property Rob Westmore is developing."

Her mom took a swig from her bottle of water, then wiped her face with a napkin. "I always thought your dad knew, or maybe I was always *paranoid* he knew. And now a test and an address led you to Rob, which leads him to sue me for whatever Dad has left."

As relieved as Dylan was to know her origin story, the mess was far from being tied up with a pretty bow. "What happened between them? Dad and Mr. Westmore?"

"The first time Dad got fired from VentureGold Group, he went to the board behind Rob's back and tried to blame him for his bad investments and millions of dollars lost. The second time we lived in Jacksonville, Dad spent all of MATRIC's money stealing Rob's clients away from him. MATRIC loved their client list growing, but Dad overspent their budget by tens of thousands of dollars and got fired from there too. It doesn't surprise me Rob is mad. I just wish he wouldn't take it out on me."

Dylan shook her head. "I ran into Brooke too. It was strange to see her after all these years. She said she wrote me letters too. Isn't that weird? Neither of us got them."

"About that." Her mom shifted in her seat and dug into her purse. "While cleaning a few boxes out from the attic, I came across these. They must've gotten stuck into one of the junk drawer boxes we never unpacked when we moved."

She pulled out four dusty, yellowed envelopes and placed them on the table. Two were written in her eight-year-old handwriting, addressed to Brooke Westmore. And two were addressed to her.

Her dad had hidden their letters. He'd let her think her friend had forgotten her. He'd let her think she didn't need friends. He wasn't just some morally gray guy. He'd done stuff that was straight-up evil to a kid's mind.

She wiped at her eyes, unsure of how to process the artifacts in her hands. More proof to put in her folder from Hendrix.

"Did you hire a lawyer? To fight Rob?"

"I haven't been out of the hospital long enough to get my affairs in order. Darren gave me a credit card, but he was adamant about keeping and recording the finances. I have no idea what's left or if I even have access to it. It's another way he's made me feel helpless."

Dylan took a sip of her chocolate shake. The brain freeze hit her for a second, but so did an idea. "I think I have something that might help."

"What do you mean?"

"I mean, we haven't gotten there yet, but I met one of my biological relatives while I was in Jacksonville. It's a long story, but she wants me to sign something saying I won't try to contact her or the rest of their family. She promised ten grand."

"Ten thousand dollars. What do they have to hide?"

"Apparently, an entire enterprise from their greedy half-blooded family members. I could sign it, and you could use the money to cover at least some of the legal nonsense."

"Don't sign it, Dylan." Her mom wasn't smiling.

"Why not? You could use the money. Or honestly, I could use it to buy a new car."

"Sign it, then, but don't do it for me. Use the money for a car or school or a down payment or to start a business—something that matters to you."

"How are you going to fix this? What if Dad left you nothing?"

"I don't know. People like Rob and Darren are greedy and smart, but that's not the point. The point is, you shouldn't have to spend your life paying for your parents' mistakes."

"I'm just trying to help." The arguing was familiar. Salty, like the greasy fry she'd just slathered in the glob of ketchup.

Candis reached across the table and squeezed Dylan's hand. "Try helping less. Besides, my hope is that someday my head will clear enough to work again."

"Like, opening your own restaurant?"

Her mom shrugged. "That might be a bit much, but I'm so excited I think I'd be up for anything."

"I'm excited to watch." Dylan studied her fries, caught in the discomfort of whatever this moment between them was.

"It's *love*, by the way," her mom said.

"What?"

"The answer to the riddle. It's *love*."

Dylan grabbed the card and read the lines again, filling in the blanks:

> *Love hurts the most when lost yet also when not had at all.*
> *Love is sometimes the hardest to express but the easiest to ignore.*
> *Love can be given to many or just one.*

Heat pulsed through her while she tried to make sense of it.

Her mom rolled her eyes. "It's ironic and perfectly fitting all at the same time."

"Because his love was a riddle."

"And now that he's gone, we can release the fantasy that his love is something we could solve."

Her dad had used her like a pawn, slowly discrediting her mom while making Dylan believe he loved her more. Making her forget which parent she was being uprooted by and which was taking care of her. Which *took* and which *sacrificed*.

"Do you want to hear about the who, what, when, and where of Jacksonville now? Or is your burger too good to focus?"

Her mom laughed. "My burger is good, *and* I want you to tell me all about it."

Dylan started with Rob and Brooke. She added Hendrix, Kathleen, Aunt Lou, and Demetrius. Her mom listened, her face reacting as if Dylan's week were dragging her on a roller-coaster ride, even without a few of the more tender details: Hendrix's kiss and betrayal. The timing of her mom's text. Aunt Lou's teacups. Anna Claire hanging on James's arm.

"I think I found my bio dad," she blurted last, picturing the screenshot of Christopher T. Berk saved to her phone. "I think he's Kathleen Schulz's nephew. Do you want to see a picture of him?"

She started reaching for her phone, but the look on her mom's face stopped her. She was squinting like she had a headache.

"Actually, Dylan, I'm not sure I'm ready. Is it okay if I wait? I want to see it soon. It's just . . ."

"*Be patient.*" She remembered Aunt Lou's words. Everything was going to take time. "It's okay. It's been a big day."

Her mom picked up her milkshake and took a long sip from her straw. "We've covered a lot of ground, though."

She grabbed her cup and tapped it against her mom's. "Like a couple of red knots."

## 42

# Solving Triangular Equations

She didn't care whether it was genuine happiness or nostalgia lying to her. She was thrilled to close the last thirty-five-minute gap between herself and the apartment that felt like *home*.

"Would it be okay to put something on the calendar to see each other again?" her mom asked when they parked outside the building.

Dylan pulled out her phone and opened the calendar app. "I'll look, but it might be a little bit because of all the days I took off for the funeral and Jacksonville." Her extended birthday celebrations, she'd let James believe. "It looks like my next day off is October 4."

Her mom leaned into the back and pulled something off the seat—a full-sized paper calendar.

"Mom," she groaned.

"Technology is fickle, but paper calendars are forever." She flipped through its giant pages to October. "The fourth is open for me, as is the first, second, third, fifth, and sixth. All I have are appointments and a lawsuit to fight. I can come back here, or we could meet halfway and catch a show at the Genesee Theatre."

Her mom had thought through all the details.

"That sounds great. I'll pencil it into my electronic calendar." Dylan got out of the car and headed for the trunk.

"Dylan?" her mom called through the open passenger side door.

"Yeah?"

Her mom unbuckled, got out too, and placed one gentle hand on Dylan's shoulder, then twiddled with a loose piece of her hair with the other. "While I was at the hospital, reading about DNA and genealogy and all that, I came across something interesting. This woman explained that if you would count a mere nine generations back, it took five hundred and twelve people's DNA to make one person. *Five hundred and twelve.* The generations before you made some awful mistakes, Dylan, but I'm grateful to God that all those people led to you."

*Who am I?*

*Why didn't my mom tell me?*

Her mom pulled her into her arms. "I love you," she whispered.

It was still so new to hear from her mom's mouth. Dylan hesitated, knowing both the memories and the lies were making it hard to trust. She hoped that would change, that moments like this, over time, might add up to them healing together.

"Thank you."

Her mom sniffled, then pulled back and reached into the trunk for Dylan's suitcase. "October 4?"

She smiled. "October 4."

---

Suitcase in hand, she turned and walked into her building, then dropped her bags inside her own apartment. She'd take care of them later and probably pick up more baggage, too, filled with worry over her mom and one greedy Mr. Rob Westmore.

But first, she'd go pick up her pigs. She'd already texted Tara she was on her way home. It was just a matter of how hard Tate would take it.

She knocked.

"Tate, get the door for Ms. Dylan." The voice came from behind the door.

"But I don't want to give them back," a muffled voice whined.

"Answer the door when I tell you."

The door creaked open at a snail's pace. Dylan tilted her head and smiled.

"Hey, Tate. And hey, Tara," she called into the apartment.

Tara walked up and put her arm around her son's sagging shoulders. "How was your trip?"

"It was . . . helpful." She didn't want to lie with *good* or *fine*. "I'm just glad Gale and Peeta were in good hands."

"I took the best care of them—I promise," Tate piped up.

She scrunched down until she was at his eye level. "I believe you. My question is, Were they nice to *you*?"

The boy crossed his arms and nodded. "Most of the time. Peeta sure is a shy guy, though."

She glanced at Tara, who was stifling her own smile. "I've noticed the same thing. I wonder how long it will take for him to let me hold him again."

Tate raised an eyebrow. "Give him an hour or so. That's my advice."

"You give great advice, and this is for helping me out this week." She handed him an envelope.

Tate threw himself forward and gave her a hug, almost knocking her over. "Thank you for the job of a lifetime, Ms. Dylan."

She patted his back. "I'm right down the hall, and you're welcome to come by and see them anytime."

Once she got the guinea pigs' cage back to their permanent home on her apartment floor, she opened the bag of leftover veggies Tate had given her and picked out two carrot sticks. She held them out for Gale and Peeta, who were each cowering in their own hideouts. After disappearing for a week, she'd have to start slow.

Gale was the first to crawl out. While nibbling the end of the carrot, he puffed up his fur.

She used her free hand to brush his side. "No need to be aggressive. You know your friend over there isn't going to steal from you."

She moved her hand from Gale nearer to Peeta.

"And what about you, buddy?"

He retreated farther into his hideout.

"Greedy people are tiring, aren't they?"

Next to her, her phone rang. It was a number she'd deleted from her phone almost as quickly as she'd gotten it, but she still recognized it. Speaking of greedy people.

She answered the phone. "Why are you calling me?"

"Not even a 'Hey, Hendrix. How are you, Hendrix?'" The voice came through the other end.

"I deleted your number. Please do me the courtesy of deleting mine."

"Wait, Turner."

She didn't correct him this time. "What?"

"I have some information that might be useful."

"I was the target for your last client. I think I have all the information I need."

"It's not about you. It's about Rob Westmore."

Now she couldn't ignore him or hang up on him. "What about Rob Westmore?"

"The guy rubbed me the wrong way, and then you mentioned he was going after your dad's estate, which is essentially going after your mom, so I've been looking more into him."

She hoped she wouldn't regret this. "Find anything worthwhile?"

"More like *everything* worthwhile. Let's just say, Rob Westmore is a bingo card of dirty money."

She stared at Peeta, who was starting to venture out of his hideout for a stray vegetable. "How did you even get this information? Wait. Don't answer that."

"It helps that the person who knows his record of wrongs divorced him years ago. Looks like you *and* Brooke have been kept in the dark about a lot of things. But his ex-wife has the receipts too, and I promise you there's enough paperwork to keep him off your mom's back."

"The pen is mightier than the sword after all."

"In my line of work, that's always been true."

She didn't know if she should thank him or run the other direction.

"Consider it my apology," he added. "Next time, I'll have to charge you."

"I wish you the best, but I genuinely hope there's no next time. I'm back in Illinois."

There was silence on the other end. "How's Captain Jim James?"

She pictured Anna Claire, the barnacle stuck to him. "Being awarded Captain of the Year right now, probably."

"Yeah, yeah. He's practically the eighth wonder of the world."

"I like to think of it as a green flag."

"All right, Turner."

"I'll send you the contact info for my mom's lawyer when I have it. Bye, Hendrix."

She hung up her phone and set it on the floor, then pulled out her laptop. Talking about Rob Westmore reminded her of the kind of people she didn't want to entangle herself with. She waited for the webpage to load, logged in, then typed a message far more polite than she wanted to compose.

Decision made.

## KindreDNA Messenger

Dylan Turner, K. Schulz
(Dylan Turner created this group)

Sat 9:43 P.M.

**Dylan Turner wrote:**

Ms. Schulz,

Thank you for the opportunity to earn $10,000 by signing your nondisclosure agreement. However, I have decided to move my life forward in a different direction and am turning it down. I will still leave you alone.

Regards.

<A note from KindreDNA before you press Send! Our advanced AI Messaging Assistant detects either sarcasm, discrimination, and/or ethical issues with your message. For only $13.99/month, you can upgrade your account to include our AI Messaging Assistant who can fix grammar, errors, and tone with just one click!>

# 43

## The Cashew Problem

Monday, September 29

If a single day can be as a thousand years, that would explain Dylan's aches and pains as she stood at the threshold of Trader Joe's on Monday morning. She'd lived too much life in the last seven.

Yesterday, in an effort to sweat out her rage instead of writing it down, she'd put on her running shoes and sprinted five miles through the forest preserve, then walked four more. By the end, she hadn't been able to tell the difference between her sweat and her tears—or whether she was crying over her dad dying or over the way he'd lived.

To top things off, she'd taken an Uber to the body shop this morning, where she got an unfortunate prognosis from a mechanic who didn't believe in mincing words.

"It's not worth saving." He'd wiped his greasy hands on a towel and walked away. "Use your money to buy a different car."

Now, after saying goodbye to Brenda and taking another Uber to work, she looked up at the Trader Joe's sign and exhaled, hoping to loosen the knot in her chest. Her body wanted more time—days, another year—not only to get back home but to heal.

In that same dream scenario, she wanted someone to hold a bullhorn to her face and say, *Attention, Dylan Turner. Please listen to the following instructions on how to move forward with your life. Details will include compatible career options, making friends as an adult without acting like a total moron, and precise words for how to tell Captain James to tell Anna Claire to please back off because you're very into him. Also, here's a legitimate $10K for a new car.*

There was no bullhorn. No message written in the clouds or on a billboard. There wasn't even a gut feeling like the one she'd had late Saturday night when she turned down Kathleen's offer. Aunt Lou was probably right. She'd have to get comfortable with the unknown.

There was, however, real life—bills needing to be paid and a pallet of cashews waiting to be stocked.

James was also in the back of the store, which sent her insides summersaulting, but his back was to her as he took inventory and gave instructions to Olivia and Avery.

Teresa was prepping her own pallet.

"Hey, Teresa." She waved in case Teresa couldn't hear through the large headphones she was wearing.

"Welcome back," Teresa replied, louder than necessary.

She didn't want to interrupt her co-worker's music, so she focused on cutting through layers of shrink-wrap and taking her pallet to the snack aisle. The first box she opened was full of Thai Lime & Chili Cashews, a customer favorite, though she couldn't remember why. It had been so long since management set out bags of them in the break room for employees to taste test, and since then, she'd chosen to never bring them home.

Why, though? Why had she spent the last twelve years worrying she'd choke on a cashew all alone in her apartment? That was the problem with choices. She had to live with the consequences, and she was starting to believe some of the choices she'd made were keeping her from actually enjoying the flavor life had to offer her.

Determined to change that, she'd start with a symbolic gesture. Using the same fingers that had typed her message to Kathleen, she grabbed a bag of Thai Lime & Chili Cashews and ripped it open—the smell of chilis and citrus pluming from the bag and kicking her in the nostrils. She grabbed a tiny handful and threw them into her mouth.

The cashews were spicy, far spicier than she'd expected or would have chosen for 7:00 A.M. on a Monday. She chewed and tossed them around her mouth, trying to cool down the heat. That didn't work, so she sucked in a deep breath. *That* didn't work, either, because it sent a single cashew down the back of her throat, where it lodged.

She tried swallowing and then coughing, but nothing budged.

She was choking.

On a cashew.

Alone in her aisle.

The irony was enraging.

She had it all wrong. Everything sounded good in theory—including living her life to the fullest—but doing it was risky. It would leave her choking on a cashew in the middle of Trader Joe's without ten grand, wondering who had her back while dealing with the consequences of her own dumb choices.

Hands on her throat, she ran to produce, where Teresa was working, large headphones still on.

Teresa nodded. "I agree. Monday mornings are the worst," she said, again too loudly.

Dylan pointed at her throat.

"Wait. Are you . . ." Teresa ripped off her headphones and ran behind Dylan. "Don't worry. I saw how to do this on a TikTok once."

Teresa jabbed her fists into Dylan's rib cage and heaved.

She felt like she was being thrown to the ground in self-defense class, not being given first aid.

Nothing budged.

Again, Teresa jammed and heaved.

Dylan's lungs were burning, and her brain was getting tired.

Her worst nightmare was coming true.

## 44

# Coming Up for Care

Somewhere between full consciousness, near fainting, and Teresa yelling, "Don't go dying on me now! I like you too much!" she pictured herself in the church again. The sight took her breath away. Of course, some of the breathlessness was because of the cashew lodged in her throat and from being repeatedly gut punched by Teresa's TikTok methods of emergency medicine. But this time, the church wasn't completely empty.

In the pews were Mom. Aunt Lou. Tara, Logan, and Tate.

Was that James?

And now Teresa.

It wasn't a packed house, but it was a dearly beloved few.

She coughed and then fell to the floor in an even more intense coughing fit. Coughing never felt so good. It meant the cashew had finally dislodged and air was filling her lungs.

"Dylan, you scared us to death!" Teresa was standing over her, while Olivia and Avery hovered nearby.

She put her hand on her ribs, which were sore from being saved. "Funny. You weren't the one choking on a cashew."

Olivia grabbed her hand and pulled her up. "Sheesh, Dylan. For a second you were sending me."

Avery was already typing into her phone. "According to the Gram, you're supposed to see a doctor."

Dylan smiled at their genuine concern, even if she needed a

translator. "Thank you. First, I have to pay for the bag of cashews I opened." She looked at Teresa. "Would you mind ringing me up?"

Teresa folded her arms. "Isn't that like taking your own assassin on a date?"

"Probably."

As they walked to the front of the store, Teresa pulled something out of her back pocket.

An envelope.

"This is probably the worst time to give you this, but we heard you turned thirty a few days back."

Dylan looked at Teresa and then at the envelope and opened it. It was a card with a guinea pig on the front: *It's guinea be a great day!*

"I thought you said you have guinea pigs," Teresa explained.

"I do. They're my favorite." She opened the card, and three ten-dollar bills fell out.

"Thirty bucks for turning thirty." Teresa patted Dylan's arm. "We thought you might be too boomer to do Cash App, now that you're thirty and all."

The inside of the card said, *Pig out. Have fun.*

Five of her co-workers had written notes in it.

"Pig out on anything but cashews," Teresa added.

Dylan couldn't stop the smile from spreading all over her face, even if it tugged at her sore throat. She hugged the card close to her chest.

"Teresa, thank you. This means . . . more than you realize." She opened the card again. "Even James signed it?"

Her co-worker whipped around. "Who's James?"

# 45

# Green Flags

She found James outside, picking litter off the sidewalk and putting it in a large garbage bag. He wasn't wearing his sharp suit, but red hibiscus and wholesome deeds were still a good look on him.

"Captain Jim," she called and then regretted it with her throat so sore.

He smirked, then took a step toward her. "I don't like you calling me that anymore. Happy Monday, though."

She took her own step closer. "Is it? I just choked on a Thai Lime & Chili cashew in the snack aisle. Teresa saved me. And TikTok."

He dropped the bag of trash and walked straight to her. "Are you serious?"

"According to Olivia and 'the Gram,' I should see a doctor, but I think I'll be okay."

"In that case, you're really messing with our streak of incident-free days at Trader Joe's Store 796."

She laughed. "I think there's a bright side, though. Going through something so terrifying is making me reconsider my life's choices."

He bit his lip. His beautiful lip. "I hope seeing me isn't one of the choices you're regretting."

"Working for Trader Joe's Captain of the Year? People would kill and steal treasure on the high seas for this job."

James shook his head, blushing. "I think I need to clarify something—"

"Anna Claire?"

He nodded. "She's just a friend. Though one who's a little touchier than I tend to be with people I'm just friends with. So, anyway, I thought maybe you'd be interested in having that information, because, well, I don't know. . . . I would *never* make you switch jobs or anything, but . . ."

She thought about letting him continue to fumble but decided to put him out of his misery. She hoped his company would be a bright spot in some of her own misery too.

"I'm glad you told me," she whispered, stepping close enough to leave no room for doubt.

He wasn't some second choice. He was kind and good. Good *for* her.

He put his hand on her face, leaned down, and brushed her lips with the gentlest kiss.

When he pulled back, she grabbed him again, relishing the feel of his hands on her waist, holding her. His lips on hers.

She had a lot to figure out, but one of the ways she was ready more than ever to spice up her life—even if Teresa considered it a beige sort of spice—was with James. It had been too easy to isolate herself, build walls, and trust no one, but the theory slowly chipping away at the layers of anger around her heart was this: He was worth the risk.

"Would you like to get together sometime? Over chocolate cake shakes?"

"I'm free tonight."

He smiled and leaned in for another kiss.

**Page 125**

## Four Questions Re-Reprised
### (age 33)

1. Who ~~is my biological father?~~ are the people that care about me?

2. Why ~~didn't my mom tell me?~~ does love have to be so risky?

3. Doesn't everyone ~~know but me?~~ want to be seen, heard, and known?

4. ~~Who am I?~~ am NOT an accident.

## Out of the Ashes: Chef Candis Turner Is Back, Pairing Fare with Finesse

*Milwaukee Journal Sentinel*

Guest Article by Demetrius Ross, retired journalist from
*The Jacksonville Times*

Published 6:07 A.M. CT June 12

---

After a thirty-three-year hiatus, Chef Candis Turner is marking her return by opening a new restaurant called Violet Robin. Nestled in the heart of the Walker's Point neighborhood in Milwaukee, Violet Robin will not only rock your taste buds with dishes like Wood Violet Wellington and Cheerily Chickpea Salad but will also add itself to a growing list of experiential dining establishments throughout the city. Violet Robin's experience? Getting to choose from one of its many single-group dining rooms or lush outdoor patios in and around the historic Queen Anne–style home.

"I wanted to give people a chance to enjoy my top-tier dishes in the atmosphere of their choice, each reflecting one of the many places I've lived over the years," Chef Turner explained. "Some rooms offer light and airy brunch vibes, while others are sultry candlelit spaces perfect for celebrating a romantic occasion, but each one is me welcoming you into my home."

While some are questioning her long absence from a professional kitchen, Chef Turner says society needs to stop elevating young stardom over later starts. "We're all living life and its trials at our own pace," she said, adding, "Age isn't the same commodity as skill, curiosity, and passion."

True to the unique hands holding its knives, Violet Robin's opening ceremony wasn't a ribbon cutting but a scattering of ashes in memory of Chef Turner's late husband, Darren, who died of a rare cancer three years ago. She and her daughter,

Dylan Jacobson, cast his ashes into the natural Wisconsin garden that envelops the front of Violet Robin and adds to its already-charming curb appeal. "Casting his ashes here reminds me of all the beauty and joy that can grow from long seasons of mourning and despair. But outward appearances aren't everything. We hope people will visit and taste for themselves that the food inside Violet Robin is even better than how she looks from the sidewalk."

When asked why she didn't return to her roots in sunny Florida, Chef Turner said she wanted to be closer to her daughter, who is currently studying hospitality leadership at DePaul University in Chicago. "Though I miss southern winters, I'm content living in the heat of my kitchen if it means getting to be closer to my favorite person."

[Pictured: Chef Candis Turner and her daughter, Dylan Jacobson, standing in front of Violet Robin's engaging entry garden, scattering Darren Turner's ashes.]

## INBOX (2)—DYLANTURNER918@GMAIL.COM

**From:** KindreDNA <testresults@KindreDNA.com>
**Date:** June 24
**To:** Turner, Dylan <dylanturner918@gmail.com>
**Subject:** You Have a New Genetic Match on KindreDNA!

### NEW GENETIC MATCH!

You and Nellie A. share DNA.

**Genetic Match:** Close Family, 25%

**Possible Relationships:** Half Sibling, Niece or Nephew, Aunt or Uncle, Grandparent or Grandchild, Great-Grandparent or Great-Grandchild

<Renew your Premium Membership
and receive a $0.50/month discount!>

**From:** KindreDNA <info@KindreDNA.com>
**Date:** June 24
**To:** Turner, Dylan <dylanturner918@gmail.com>
**Subject:** You Have a New Message on KindreDNA!

### NEW MESSAGE!

You have a new message from: **Nellie A.**
To view this message in the KindreDNA app, click here.

**From Nellie A.:**

Hey Dylan.

Just saw we are a scary close match and close in age and am wondering if you'd be willing to connect to figure out how we're related??

—Nellie

<Want to learn if the sun makes you sneeze, if you are good at remembering your dreams, or if you have a unibrow? For only $9.99/month, you can sign up for KindreDNA's KINfluencer Kit to find out how *your* DNA influences you!>

# READERS GUIDE

1. Describe the ways technology is portrayed throughout the book. Does technology enhance Dylan's life or distract from it?
2. Candis tells Dylan that the truth would be too painful, implying that there is often stability in a lie. What do you think about Candis's perspective? Is the stability of a lie ever more important than knowing the truth?
3. When Dylan finds out Darren isn't her biological father, one of her first questions is *Who am I?* Why do you think her family's spilled secret opens up a struggle over her own identity? What parts of a person make up their identity?
4. Candis and Darren's marriage offers a tumultuous look at mental health, narcissism, and abuse. How might their story have ended differently if their relationship started today versus thirty-five years ago? In what ways has society, then and now, valued charisma over character?
5. How does nostalgia play a part in Dylan's memories of her parents, in both positive and negative ways? How might Dylan figure out which memories are true and which were manipulated?
6. Candis tells Dylan she has a routine, not a life, while Dylan describes her life as quiet. Whose perspective do you agree with? What's the difference between the two?
7. With all the complicated dynamics involved, family members must be sensitive to one another's differing experiences in the

world. How can Dylan and Candis be more compassionate toward each other's experiences? In their case, is reconciliation possible or only forgiveness?

8. What specific steps should Dylan take to connect authentically with other people? How can she navigate the reality that not all people are trustworthy while learning that love requires the risk of vulnerability?

9. Dylan experiences passionate sparks with Hendrix but is eventually drawn to James's faithful character. How might the tension between sparks and faithfulness play out in a healthy romantic relationship?

10. How does Aunt Lou encourage Dylan as she searches for the truth about herself and her parents' past? What encouragement would you give to Dylan?

11. Discuss the title, *Nearly Beloved,* and how it relates to Dylan's struggles throughout her story.

# NOTES AND ACKNOWLEDGMENTS

I had a title: *Nearly Beloved*. And I had themes: *identity, family,* and *connection*. But it was my editor, Jamie Lapeyrolerie, who asked, *What if you put them in a story about a DNA mishap? Like, a woman who finds out her dad isn't her biological father?*

This is often referred to as a nonpaternity event (NPE), or when the person assumed to be someone's biological parent is not. I was shocked to learn that—according to Legacy Tree Genealogists— "approximately 13% of individuals in the general population will have at least one case of misattributed parentage in the first three generations of their family tree (for themselves, a parent, or a grandparent)."[1]

Not only are these circumstances weighty; they're also varied. Some may never find their biological parent(s), while others make an immediate match with them on sites like Ancestry.com. The reasons for an NPE range from adoption, to a medically assisted donor conception, to a one-night stand, affair, or sexual assault. No NPE—with its questions, answers, rejections, pain, and connected dots—is the exact same experience as another. And with at-home genetic test kits being available to the public since 2000, many family secrets have come to light over the past couple of decades. Dylan's story is simply one story, not the entire conversation that could be had on NPEs.

1. Paul Woodbury, "6 Signs of Misattributed Parentage in Your Genetic Family Tree," Legacy Tree Genealogists, accessed May 20, 2025, www.legacytree.com/blog/6-signs-of-misattributed-parentage-in-your-genetic-family-tree.

There were many things about NPEs, DNA, and genealogy I didn't know before doing my own test through Ancestry.com and setting out to write *Nearly Beloved*. I'm grateful for Dani Shapiro's memoir *Inheritance*, which sheds light on the NPE experience in an intimate and profound way. Diahan Southard, founder of Your DNA Guide, is a wealth of knowledge and insight. On a related note, the use and explanation of Neufeld's Traffic Circle came from the book *Adoption Unfiltered: Revelations from Adoptees, Birth Parents, Adoptive Parents, and Allies*, written by Sara Easterly, Kelsey Vander Vliet Ranyard, and Lori Holden. While nonpaternity events are not the same as adoption, I'm grateful for the way this metaphor helps those working through surprising and complex family dynamics. Any mistakes or extrapolations I made for the sake of Dylan's story are my responsibility.

If you or someone you know needs support through a nonpaternity event, the ministry DNAngels (www.dnangels.org) offers help finding biological family members, support, and resources. Not surprisingly, these kinds of discoveries can lead to increased rates of depression, anxiety, and suicidal ideation. Help is available:

- Suicide & Crisis Lifeline: Call or text 988

- National Alliance on Mental Illness: 1-800-950-6264 or text *NAMI* to 62640

- National Sexual Assault Hotline (RAINN): 1-800-656-4673

- Crisis Text Line: Within the United States, text *HOME* to 741741

The other heavy thread in this story is Darren's mental health and the narcissistic abuse both Candis and, by extension, Dylan experienced. Narcissism is not simply a person acting selfishly. Clinical psychologist Dr. Ramani Durvasula defines it as "lack of empathy, grandiosity, a chronic sense of entitlement and a chronic need to seek out admiration from other people and validation from other people"—all of which can lead to emotionally abusive relationships.[2]

At first, it seemed unlikely that a child could grow up with a narcissistic parent and not grasp it, until I learned more about the concept of triangulation—when a narcissist plays two people against each other in order to feed their own ego and maintain control. In an unhealthy home situation, this might look like a narcissist treating one member of the family like they are the all-good, golden person (Dylan) and another like they are the all-bad scapegoat (Candis).

As Candis experienced in this story, this kind of emotional manipulation can distort someone's reality, making them feel like they're going crazy. A relationship with a narcissist often cycles through an early stage of romance (praise, grand gestures, big plans), fades into a middle stage of dismissive communication (deprecating language and humiliation), and drops into withdrawal (infidelity, lies, isolation, and gaslighting). The abuse victim can be stuck in the cycle by believing if they can "fix" themselves or do enough to make their narcissistic partner happy, the version of the person they fell in love with will resurface. Even though that version never really existed.

Because this kind of abuse is not always physical, it can be hard for victims to identify or even know how to get help. If you or someone you know needs help because of an emotionally abusive relationship, call (1-800-799-7233) or text (*START* to 88788) the National Domestic Violence Hotline or connect with therapists and support groups at www.helpwithinreach.com and www.ibelieve yourabuse.com.

2. Ramani Durvasula, interview by Audrey Hamilton, host, *Speaking of Psychology*, podcast, episode 37, "Recognizing a Narcissist, with Ramani Durvasula, PhD," American Psychological Association, May 13, 2016, www.apa.org/news/podcasts/speaking-of-psychology/narcissism.

While writing is often a solitary act, I keep learning that writing can't be a solitary lifestyle. These are just a few of the many who've helped me live a better writing life, specifically during the year and a half I brainstormed, wrote, and edited *Nearly Beloved*.

First, I want to thank you, dear reader, for offering your precious time to read Dylan's story. You make my work possible.

Next, I want to thank my literary agent, Tamela Hancock Murray, for continuing to encourage me on the long game that is a writing career.

Also, I want to thank those who helped me have real, quiet minutes to write, and by that, I mean they cared for one to four of my children at a time. Rachel Patton, Mackenna Korpela, Karen Broekhuis, Kelli Dunn, and my husband, Collin—you were key this time around.

Speaking of my husband, he's my favorite person to write with. I never thought I'd add brainstorming and troubleshooting plot points to the list of the marital bonding activities I enjoy, but here we are. This was way better than updating a bathroom together.

And then there's DesAnne Hippe, who I often vent to about the tender aspects of writing. DesAnne, thank you for your listening ear, encouragement, and friendship.

For her careful eye and thoughtful feedback, a million thanks go to Rachel Carlberg. Thank you, you smart, thoughtful, precious bookworm, you.

Jen Mueller helped me process the topic of identity through her lens of being a third-culture kid. I'm grateful for your sensitive insight, Jen.

Jeanetta Nieuwsma helped clarify the processes and boundaries of social work—thank you.

To WaterBrook, thank you for another opportunity to work with you. That includes many thanks to Jamie Lapeyrolerie for editing *Nearly Beloved*. Once again, she listened to my ideas and helped me craft them into a story (and genre) that actually made sense. You get all the credit for this story idea, Jamie. Thank you, and I love working with you.

For their eyes on the tiny details that tightened this story, I'm grateful to Laura Wright, Rose Decaen, and Kayla Fenstermaker. And for those bookmaking people who work behind the scenes, including Julia Wallace and Sarah Feightner.

I want to thank Ming Loong Teo for her thoughtful review as an authenticity reader on the narcissism and mental-health thread of Dylan's story.

Redbud Writers Guild and American Christian Fiction Writers have been encouraging spaces for me as an author. Thank you for your support in the writing life, friends.

There is nothing new under the sun, including the ways I incorporated internet searches, articles, emails, texts, and interviews to move this story forward. As an author, I've been inspired by the creative work and formatting in novels such as Nicola Yoon's *Everything Everything,* Taylor Jenkins Reid's *Daisy Jones and the Six,* Jessica George's *Maame,* and Nicole Baart's *The Long Way Back*—to name a few.

This is weird, but I owe one to my brother-in-law James for letting me use his name without charging royalties. Thank you, James Fraser. (Not the *Outlander* one.)

Finally and foremost, I'm thankful to God for being my Father, Savior, and Comforter. Thank you for this opportunity to write—and what an opportunity it is. The work is the reward.

# ABOUT THE AUTHOR

**KENDRA BROEKHUIS** writes stories that touch on heavy topics with a dose of humor and a lot of love. She is the author of the novels *Nearly Beloved* and *Between You and Us,* as well as the nonfiction book *Here Goes Nothing: An Introvert's Reckless Attempt to Love Her Neighbor.* For her day job, she stays home with her four kids and drives them from one place to another in her minivan. She and her family live in Milwaukee. You can find her on social media and online at www.kendrabroekhuis.com.

# Also from author
# Kendra Broekhuis

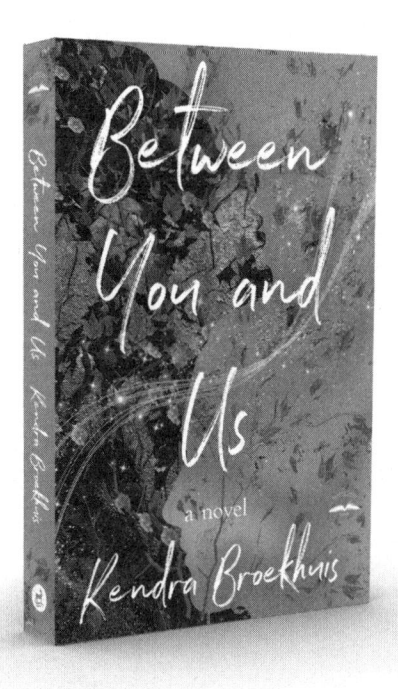

When a grieving woman unexpectedly steps into a different version of her life, she must choose between the husband she loves and the daughter she lost in this brave, gripping novel.

**WATERBROOK**

Learn more about Kendra's books at
waterbrookmultnomah.com.